ANNIE GROVES

Christmas on the Mersey

HARPER

Harper
An imprint of HarperCollins*Publishers*
77–85 Fulham Palace Road,
Hammersmith, London W6 8JB

www.harpercollins.co.uk

This paperback edition 2014
1

A catalogue record for this book is
available from the British Library

ISBN: 978-0-00-755082-1

Set in Sabon LT Std by Palimpsest Book Production Limited,
Falkirk, Stirlingshire

Printed and bound in Great Britain by Clays Ltd, St Ives plc

MIX
Paper from
responsible sources
FSC™ C007454

ACKNOWLEDGEMENTS

I would like to acknowledge the tireless dedication of author and local historian Neil Holmes, whose specialist field is the Blitz on Merseyside and whose books, *Liverpool Blitzed* and *Merseyside Blitzed*, have been an inspiration.

Also, *How We Lived Then* by Norman Longmate is, I feel, the ultimate World War Two bible for writers of that era.

I also gladly acknowledge the dedication of Teresa Chris my agent, Kate Bradley my editor and the whole team at HarperCollins who give unsparingly of their time and expertise.

To the memory of my wonderful Mum and Dad
(You always believed in me xxx)

CHAPTER ONE

October 1940

'The patients who are too ill to be moved will have to go under the beds!' Sister Rita Kennedy said as she hurried down the long ward, clearing it of patients who could be moved to the basement. The Germans had been dropping bombs almost every night since August. Now they were targeting the docks, so close to the hospital that Sister Kennedy imagined the pilot could probably smell the antiseptic they cleaned the floors with.

Many of the patients had been moved to hospitals in safer locations months ago. This hospital, close to the vital supply line, was a prime target. Everybody around here knew that to put the docks out of operation would be seen as a major coup for Germany. These remaining patients were emergency cases, brought in for assessment or emergency surgery before being sent elsewhere. The ward was busy every day, but since the raid started, only moments ago, it was like Lime Street Station at rush hour.

'Johnny the porter said an enemy plane has been shot down over Gladstone Dock!' Sister Kennedy did not have to listen too carefully to hear the probationer nurse's excited words. 'He said the pilot has landed in the Mersey.' Sister Kennedy, like everybody else in this hospital, had friends and family who were serving, but this was neither the time nor the place to gloat.

'They say he's still alive and they've sent a crew to seize him!'

'Do you think they'll bring him here?' another nurse enquired as they helped an old woman from her bed. The sound of anti-aircraft fire almost drowned out her question.

'There's no time for idle gossip, just get on with making the patients as safe as you can, please.' Twenty-five-year-old Rita's nerves were raw; her own children, just a few minutes' walk away from the dockside hospital, had been brought back from the farm to which they were once evacuated. They were so happy there, Rita knew, but now they were in as much danger as everybody else.

'Let's not frighten the patients with supposition, Nurse,' Rita whispered, and the young nurse nodded.

Promoted to ward sister just last week, Rita had no intention of voicing or showing her fears to the junior nurses. Panic could spread, she knew, and keeping a cool head was vital. Hitler's Luftwaffe had so far failed to invade Britain by defeating the RAF in the skies over the South-East, but there was no let-up in their attempts, and they were now attacking the industrial cities and ports across the country. Rita pushed down on her growing anxiety. Why had she insisted on bringing the children home from the safety of their countryside billet near Southport?

There were so many of her family to worry about, too. Rita said a quick, silent prayer for her brother Eddy. He was sailing with the convoys in the North Atlantic, bringing back vital food and supplies. He told her, when he was home last time, that the wild, impetuous ocean could be a terrifying place for the most experienced sailor, and that was without torpedoes firing at them. Now Rita thought she knew a little of what he was going through.

'That's enough chattering.' Rita, impatient now, worried that the two young nurses, still speculating about the shot-down German bomber, were not moving fast enough. 'You know what they say about loose lips!' This hospital would be the first place to bring the injured aviator – even if he was an enemy pilot. However, they were not here to judge but to ease the suffering of every patient brought through the double doors of the hospital, no matter what his nationality. 'Go to it!'

'Yes, Sister,' the junior nurses chorused and resumed their duties. Rita kept half an ear on the drone of enemy aircraft as she made her patients safe, her practised demeanour professional and efficient. Internally, however, her terrified thoughts were with her children, Michael and Megan.

Please, Lord, make them safe, she prayed silently. Don't let anything happen to my babies.

Michael and Megan would now be huddled in the

corner of the cellar beneath the shop where Rita lived with her husband, Charlie, and his poisonous mother, Winnie Kennedy, who owned and ran the corner store. The cellar was where she stored her stock and they should be safe down there. Rita wished that she were there with them, but when the country was crying out for nurses, how could she duck her duty, especially after the fall of France last June? The enemy was only just across the Channel.

'Jesus, Mary and Joseph!' Nurse Maeve Kerrigan said. 'Sounds like all hell is breaking loose out there.' Rita and Maeve had been firm friends since they started work at Bootle Infirmary on the same day. Maeve had been a cheeky upstart but her sense of humour and ability to keep everyone's spirits up had built bridges with Matron, and the patients all adored her. Maeve quickly took in Rita's furrowed brow.

'I can imagine what's going through your head. But the ould battle-axe will manage your two young snappers,' she said quietly, so as no one would overhear. 'She might be a witch, but she's still their granny.'

'But she's not their mother.' Rita knew her friend was trying to calm her as they eased a post-operative patient into a wheelchair. 'I'll never forgive myself if anything—'

'Enough of that,' Maeve whispered. 'You'll drive yourself demented if you carry on thinking that way.'

Rita nodded, turning to help another patient into his dressing gown. It was impossible not to be burdened with maternal guilt. If one hair on either of their heads was hurt . . .

'Anyway, if the Germans did land, you could hand her over first. They'd swim back over the Channel faster than you can say "Jack Robinson" once they got an earful of her bile. She'd make up a whole new front!' Maeve added in that crisp Irish tone that could change from angelic to raucous in the blink of an eye.

'Come on, let's get the patients out of here.' Rita pulled herself together and took a deep breath to calm her racing heart; there were thousands of mothers going through the same thing all over England. She had her patients to think about now.

The almost deafening sound of an explosion close by made the medical staff move even faster.

Michael and Megan would be terrified. The thought made Rita blanch. Her skin was now clammy. It would be her fault if anything happened to her children. She was the one who had persuaded Charlie to let her bring them home from the farm when there were no signs of air raids or invasion, something the newspapers called 'the phoney war'. Charlie had said Michael and Megan were safer in the countryside, but after Rita's repeated begging, he had reluctantly agreed to let them come home. However, now Rita was certain she had done the wrong thing – Empire Street, right by the docks, was one of the most dangerous places in the world.

Please Lord, Rita sent another silent prayer to heaven as she moved the patients, *please keep my children safe.*

Rita could recall with clarity the look on Charlie's face seven and a half years ago when he held Michael for the first time. Sometimes, Rita could still feel the crippling remorse that she experienced then, but now it was for a different reason. Now her remorse was for the choices she had made and for the life she would never have. Any guilt she had left was for her children and her inability to give them a happy home life and an adoring father. Her husband had proved himself to be a liar, a cheat and a brute.

However, this was not the time for thinking such things, she acknowledged as another barrage of anti-aircraft fire stalled further thoughts. Right now her priority was the safety of her patients.

The blast from nearby incendiaries shuddered through the building and Rita fought the urge to duck under the nearest bed, instead calling for the nurses to remain calm and go about their work as quickly as they could. She thought she had moved all the patients from along the far wall where splintered glass from a whole row of shattered windows jettisoned onto the ward, causing the blinds to flap like startled blackbirds in the chilly, damp night air. To her horror, however, Rita could now see that Albert Scott, a kindly old man who had taken a nasty fall during one of the recent raids and had broken his hip, was still in his bed near the window and urgently needed moving into the middle of the ward.

'Don't worry, Bert, I'm on my way,' she called as she ran across, careful to sidestep the broken glass that littered the whole floor. The deafening roar of exploding bombs and anti-aircraft fire coming through the windows was disconcerting, but Rita could see that the ward was a sitting duck for the bombers with the blown-out windows and blackout curtains torn to shreds.

'Turn those lights off!' she yelled, and the room switched to sudden blackness, lit only by the fires that blazed outside and the searchlights directing the ack-ack gunfire.

'Are you all right, Bert?' she asked, taking the old man's hand.

He gripped hers tightly, but his voice, though weak, was determined. 'Don't you be worrying about me, love. I saw worse than this in the trenches. Jerry didn't get me then, and he won't get me now.'

'You tell 'em, Bert.' She squeezed his hand. 'Now bear with me while I just try and get you a bit more comfortable. Maeve, come here and give me a hand with this.'

Rita shook broken glass from the blankets, then asked Maeve to help her manoeuvre a heavy mattress from one of the empty beds over Bert, who could not move from his own. But the mattress was covered with shards of broken glass and Rita had underestimated the weight of it. It took the combined strength of both women to lift it off. As they did, there was another ear-splitting scream overhead and then another blast shook the building, loosening more glass from the damaged windows.

'For God's sake, get down!' Rita screamed, and Maeve fell to the floor and crawled beneath one of the beds, while Rita desperately tried to cushion herself and Bert with the mattress. The bombardment continued for several more minutes though it seemed to Rita to last for hours.

Once the planes had dropped their deadly load and passed over, Rita lifted her head and saw to her horror that it was too late. She had managed to shield Bert from the worst of the falling glass and masonry, but it had all been too much for him and she thought that his heart had given out. He lay still, his eyes glassy and empty. 'He's dead. The bastards!' Maeve swore to the sky. Rita did not admonish Maeve – she felt exactly the same way – but she urged Maeve to keep her voice down so as not to scare the other patients.

'Oh, Bert,' Rita whispered, looking sadly down at the dead man. Gently she touched his pale and wrinkled hand. 'He'd already been through so much.'

Rita felt the sting of tears behind her eyes but she knew there was no time for indulging her emotions. The all clear was sounding and she had to organise the clear-up.

'Right, everyone, we need to get the ARP to help us board up these windows and get all of this glass up. Don't be tempted to clean it up yourselves; you're likely to be cut to shreds.'

Over the next few hours, Rita even had the staff singing to keep up morale as they moved the patients back to bed and continued the clean-up. Eventually, the glass was cleared and they were busy boarding up the windows.

After welcome cups of cocoa and slices of freshly made toast were given to the shaken-up patients, the nurses themselves were able to take a breather and headed for their own cups of cocoa in the small kitchen at the end of the ward. It is a wonder no other patients were harmed tonight, Rita thought. The dead man was taken to the morgue while she said a silent prayer of thanks that everybody else had come through the awful barrage unscathed.

Tired but keen to get home at the end of her shift, she hurried down the long corridor. The cabbage-green tiled walls felt as if they were closing in on her now. She was desperate to get home to see her children.

Picking up a daily newspaper on her way home, Rita was eager for any news of the war at sea. She was the eldest of Pop and Dolly Kennedy's five children. Frank, a petty officer in the Royal Navy, had frightened the living daylights out of everyone when he had lost a leg after his ship was torpedoed. He was making a good recovery but Rita knew that the scars ran deep. Her younger brother, Eddy, the merchant seaman, was in great danger of falling victim to German U-boats in the North Atlantic convoys. Front-line warriors, Pop called them, although it was the air battles that still seemed to dominate the news. Not surprising after the Royal Air Force had success-fully defended the skies of the South-East in the conflict Mr Churchill called the Battle of Britain. Rita's younger sister, Sarah, was also doing her bit by training to be a Red Cross nurse.

Reading between the lines of the news reports, it was hard to get a handle on the real story. The paper was full of the victories of Fighter Command, but

Pop said that the papers weren't allowed to be honest about the real losses as it would be bad for morale. But there was no doubt that the RAF had carried out a heroic defence of the country and that ordinary people had so much to be thankful for. It was far from over, however. Day after day, the Luftwaffe continued their deadly assaults on the larger cities all over the country. There was no hiding the reality of the destructive power of the German air raids. Fighter Command were under extreme pressure, the news-paper said.

'Don't we know it,' Rita said aloud, aware that people in this part of the country were as much in the front line as the soldiers and the fighter pilots. It was not just the men like Eddy that risked their lives, but also those who loaded and unloaded the ships that ferried the necessities of war and civilian life. They too were the target of the Luftwaffe.

Rita now knew the truth of the rumour that a young German pilot had been brought in injured. She pushed down the hope that he was suffering as much as Frank, whose leg had had to be amputated below the knee after infection had set in. She also tried to rid her mind of the fact that the German may know others who would try to blow up the supply ship on which Eddy served, and which had to run the gauntlet of torpedoes and mines every single day. Yes, she was ashamed of feeling that way; it was unchristian as well as cruel. But when she thought again of Bert's lifeless body, she couldn't help herself.

*   *   *

'Mammy!' Michael and Megan shot up from the breakfast table to greet their mother, and Rita's heart sang with joy and relief.

'Oh, thank God you are safe!' She scooped her children into her arms, thankful beyond words that they were unharmed.

'Mammy, we could hear the German planes dropping their bombs. It was so exciting – can I go out and look at the flattened houses?' Rita looked in amazement at Michael. His eyes were shining with excitement and for a moment she could almost feel what it must be like to be a seven-year-old boy living through these interesting times. But then her anxiety kicked in again and she prayed that she would not have to go through another night of worry as she had last night, knowing there was little she could do about it now the hospital needed her. But her children needed her too. How many other women were feeling like she did this morning, she wondered, torn between her nursing duty and a mother's fear? Rita felt absolutely wretched at the thought of another night away from them.

'You'll do no such thing,' she admonished gently, ruffling her son's hair as he chattered away nineteen to the dozen. Rita felt a little hand squeeze her own and looked down to see the pale face of Megan. Unlike Michael, she was quiet and clingy. Rita hugged Megan to her and felt her heart wrench at how frightened the little girl must have been without her.

'Small thanks to you, they are fine.'

Charlie's barbed words caused that familiar feeling

11

of guilt to rise up in Rita's heart as he entered the small breakfast room, his mother – making a great play of her bad leg – following behind. Rita looked at him. He was lean and once upon a time she had thought him handsome, but now his hair was thinning and his face always bore a sneer, or his words a put-down. Sometimes she could barely bring herself to look at him. Now his icy glare seized her and held her in its grasp. Rita knew that trouble had been brewing and she steeled herself for his onslaught.

'What kind of a mother leaves her children during an air raid?' Charlie's voice was laced with malice as he addressed his mother, who nodded in agreement.

Ma Kennedy had assumed her usual seat by the window. She was wearing her housecoat and had her hair in curlers, covered by a headscarf. Her face wore the sour look of disapproval that Rita had come to know so well.

'I know Charles, it is unforgivable! You have an obligation to your family, Rita!' Mrs Kennedy's mouth puckered and her condescending expression told Rita she thought she wasn't much of a mother if she could not be here for her own children during an air raid.

Rita felt that she had little room for manoeuvre when they ganged up on her like this. These days she usually put up a strong resistance, but her own guilt and anxiety were threatening to gang up on her too. She felt weak, tired and unable to defend herself. She should have been here. Of course, she should.

'You both know that hospitals all over the land

are in dire need of trained staff. People like me are in short supply,' she countered weakly.

'People like you?' Charlie sneered. 'Listen to Rita, Mother! Looks like she's going to save the country single-handed. Shame she doesn't feel as strongly about her own kids.'

Rita felt her stomach dip.

'You'll have to tell her, Charles.' His mother was standing now, poker stiff at the side of the table while Rita, feeling as bad as it was possible for a mother to feel, none the less did not fail to notice the sidelong, warning glance Charlie gave his mother.

'Mind your own business, can't you?' His tone now turned to impatience as he barked at the children, 'Michael, take Megan through next door to the lounge and put the wireless on.'

The children both looked at Rita uncertainly, but she nodded for them to go. It wouldn't do for them to get caught up in a row.

'Tell me what?' Rita's throat tightened and she found it difficult to swallow, her mouth now paper dry with trepidation.

'The children are being evacuated today – this morning,' Charlie said without preamble. 'It's all arranged – and don't even think about trying to stop it.' He did not hang around long enough for Rita to answer but stalked from the room. She could hear him taking the stairs two at a time.

Rita was confused. What did he mean, they were going to be evacuated today? Where to? They'd been back home for only a few months. She scraped back the chair and stood up, but before she left the room she laid her hands flat upon the table and leaned towards Mrs Kennedy.

'Did you know about this?' She knew her husband couldn't organise the children's evacuation on his own. He would not have the foggiest idea where to start.

Ma Kennedy folded her arms and looked away. 'I'm saying nothing,' was all she offered.

Rita pushed down her anger at her mother-in-law and headed for the stairs at a run. She opened Megan's bedroom door to find Charlie there, and her heart lurched. There were two suitcases on the bed, one for each of her children, and he was folding Megan's clothes into hers.

'Are you sending them back to Freshfield Farm?' It had been so harrowing when they were evacuated last time, billeted on a farm way outside the city. The people that had looked after the children were decent folk and the children were happy. Rita knew that they had been well looked after. If they had to go away again, it would break her heart, but she also knew that the children were no longer safe. Charlie was right.

'No. I've made other arrangements.'

Cold fear ran through Rita's veins as she heard these words and her voice shook. 'What other arrangements? What do you mean? Tell me!'

'Get a grip of yourself, woman.' Charlie's voice was full of scorn. 'I've got a place lined up . . .'

'Where?' Rita asked.

At first he said nothing, ignoring her as he put a few

more items into Megan's suitcase, which had been neatly packed. Charlie never lifted a finger around the house and would have as much idea about packing a suitcase as flying a Spitfire. His mother must have helped him. He stopped what he was doing and straightened up, his expression full of contempt for her.

'I know of a little boarding house in Southport.'

'How?' Rita asked. 'We don't have any family there.'

'It's run by an old lady Mother knows, Elsie Lowe . . .' Charlie looked away again and shut the lid of Michael's suitcase.

'Is this your mother's doing? She's never liked the children being here. This would be her way of getting them out from under her feet . . .'

'You were the one who said they should come back here to the Luftwaffe's playground,' Charlie said, his unwavering stare boring into her. 'It was you who put them in danger, remember that.'

'There were no raids when they came home!' Rita tried to remain calm, but was finding it difficult. What was Charlie up to? She knew Michael and Megan should be somewhere safer but why wasn't he taking them back to the farm?

'If anything had happened to them last night, it would have been your fault, Rita. Yours! Nobody else's.' He was quiet for a moment. 'What kind of mother puts strangers before her own kids?'

'It is my duty as a trained nurse to serve,' Rita answered, knowing he had made no great shakes to oblige his country in any capacity yet, and by the look of it he had no intention of doing so now.

'It's also your duty to look after your children. But you can't do that with your precious work so I will be going with them.'

Rita tried a different tactic; if she fought him he would become even more determined. 'Of course you are right, as always.' His shoulders relaxed just a little. 'But, as you know, when people started calling it "the phoney war" it seemed ridiculous to keep the kids away from home.'

'Well, it's not so phoney now, is it, Rita?' His shoulders stiffened again, indicating his mind was made up.

Rita told herself any mother would have brought her children home when there was no threat – and a lot of children had come home, like Tommy, Kitty Callaghan's little brother just up the street. Rita had begged and begged for her children to be allowed to come back, but Charlie refused her pleas until it suited him. Until then, Rita had had to make do with monthly visits; it was all her shifts at the hospital could accommodate.

Rita was starting to lose control of her emotions. The words came out like gunfire.

'You've never cared about the children. The only reason you brought them back was because you wanted to get me back into the marital bed again. You don't give a damn for their wellbeing – all you care about is yourself!'

Rita tried not to think about the terrible events following Sonny Callaghan's funeral. Charlie had found her with Jack Callaghan and, though they had done nothing wrong, he had viciously attacked and forced himself on her, though Rita knew her marriage was in tatters before then. Charlie's squandering of their life savings had seen to that, but this had been an unspeakable act. Rita had sworn that she would never let him near her again, but the high price for getting her children home was moving back into the marital bed. After he and Rita had married, Charlie had ceased to show any interest in her sexually and Rita knew this wasn't normal. But since Charlie had attacked her that time, he got a perverse pleasure from his cruelty and bedtimes were something that she now dreaded.

'On the contrary, Rita, everyone thinks that it's you that doesn't give a damn for your children, so maybe you should have thought harder before you went off to play Florence Nightingale!'

Rita had lost the battle to stop the panic rising in her voice. 'There's no way I'm letting you take my kids away to God knows where with God knows who. I'll give my notice at the hospital and I'll go with them.' Rita knew she was clutching at straws.

'You have work to do here. Remember?'

'I can get a transfer; they need nurses in other hospitals too.'

'We are moving somewhere safer; to a better-class neighbourhood.' Charlie's voice dripped scorn and Rita knew that he'd made his mind up. There was something dangerous about his mood, too – she'd seen him like this before. When he behaved this way he could turn and either lose all control or terrorise her in that low, underhand way. His cold eyes were a familiar indication of the depraved depths to which Rita knew her husband could sink.

Charlie, menacing now, edged forward. 'Poor Rita. Going to miss your children, are you? Or is it really me that you're going to miss?' Rita felt her parched tongue slide over the roof of her mouth, now paper dry with fear. He was between her and the door. She would not get out this time without a struggle.

'I don't know what you mean.' Her voice was low now, sticking in her throat. *Don't show him you're scared, Rita, that's what he wants.*

'I know how you really like it, Rita, just like at the beginning, flaunting yourself like the slut you are.' He gave a small contemptible laugh. 'You never thought I'd cotton on, did you . . . you tricked me into marrying you and caught me good and proper . . .' His face twisted into something ugly now. *'Take me, Charlie . . . I need you, Charlie . . . we are good together, Charlie!'* he jeered.

'I did not say those things!' Outrage replaced Rita's fear.

'You threw yourself at me,' Charlie spat accusingly, 'just to get a husband . . .'

Rita remembered only too well what had happened between her and Charlie. It was seared indelibly on her mind. Even when his hands were all over her she knew it was wrong . . . The eau-de-Cologne scent of gin still made her retch even now. Charlie was right, she had tricked him. But not for the reasons he thought. Charlie never allowed her to forget she let him 'have her' before marriage. Once – just once – but it was enough and she had paid for it every day since. If Charlie ever found out why she'd allowed it . . . the thought of it alone made her feel sick.

'I could have been out of this lousy street long before now.' Charlie made a sudden movement with his hand, making her flinch. She could see her nervousness amused him by the way his lazy grin made his thin yard-brush moustache bristle. Any fond feelings she had had for him at the beginning of their marriage were now dead. He'd seen to that. Rita thought she could change him into a more caring person when they were married. She had been a fool.

'I didn't marry you because I loved you . . . I married you to stop you marrying Jack Callaghan.' His callous words were snarled low, for her hearing alone. 'The great Jack Callaghan, the pride of Merseyside. The love of your life.' Charlie looked at her with something akin to hate now when he said, 'Don't think I didn't see the way he looked at you, or the way you looked at him when you thought nobody could see. Well, I saw! I saw plenty. But I'll tell you this for nowt – you're mine now . . . remember that!'

With mention of Jack Callaghan, Rita had a sudden vision of him, his kind eyes and strong face looking into her own. *I've always loved you, Rita. You know that, don't you?* If only Jack were here now. He'd never let Charlie treat her this way. But she had married Charlie instead of Jack. She had been a deceiver and this was the price she was paying. All the same, the thought of Jack and his words gave her strength.

'I know you, Charlie Kennedy, you're up to

something.' Even in her anxious state, something was niggling away at her.

Charlie was still managing to evade conscription but that wouldn't last for ever. Men were being called up all over Liverpool and Charlie's turn would come. Was leaving with the kids some way of avoiding his duty? He couldn't look at the children most days, let alone show them affection. Were the children to be solely in his hands, she feared for their welfare. And what about his job? How could he look after Michael and Megan when he was working all day? Questions tumbled inside her head.

'The appeal of marriage soon wore off when you got the gold ring on your finger . . . Prim and proper on the outside, but I know different,' Charlie continued.

Rita bit back a retort, knowing it was wise not to antagonise him. What choice did she have? Her husband's put-downs, while making her feel stupid, were a small reminder of the wrong she had done. To add to the misery, his mother expected her to carry the burden of running the corner shop and raising two children virtually alone. Was it any wonder she went back to nursing with her arms wide open as soon as the children were evacuated?

While accepting this was her lot in life, Rita adored her beloved children above all else.

You play with the hand you're dealt, Rita. Her mind echoed Charlie's sentiments now and Rita felt she was getting no more than she deserved. Like most women round here, she had made her bed and now she must lie in it. Being Catholic, she would never contemplate divorce – the idea was ludicrous in a place like Empire Street, where women married for life but not always for love. For women like her, happiness was a bonus, not an expectation.

'I don't understand why they can't just go back to Freshfield,' she said again.

'Those people tried turning my children against me.' Charlie went back to the suitcase and Rita wondered what excuse he would make next. 'They hid behind the old woman's skirts like I was the bogeyman.'

'You hadn't been to see them for months,' Rita explained. 'They thought they had done something wrong when you attacked the farmer!'

'He tried to stop me taking them home.'

'He'd never seen you before.' Rita knew that Charlie was lucky he had not been threatened with a shotgun – 'Uncle Seth', as the children called the farmer, was very protective of Michael and Megan and a very good shot.

'Michael took his time confirming I was, in fact, his father,' Charlie straightened himself to his full six foot, 'which just goes to show they were in need of a firm hand!'

Rita gasped at his delusions of civil paternity . . . Charlie had no patience with his children or, indeed, anyone else.

'I can take them to the farm myself,' Rita said. 'Joan would be thrilled to have them back. I got a letter from her yesterday. She asked if . . .'

Charlie's head was still bent as he raised his eyes. They cut her with a warning glare that told her to be quiet or else; to say no more. It told her that she was making things worse for herself.

'Go down. You're wasting precious time with your beloved children,' he said. 'You've shown where your priorities lie, even when it is obvious your own flesh and blood need you more.'

'Charlie, there is a war on. People are dying and the hospitals need all the nurses they can get.'

'Of course.' His eyes were full of scorn. 'That is why I am releasing you of the burden of your own children.'

'They have never been a burden! You must tell me where you are taking them!' Rita's voice was rising, becoming shrill with anxiety. She must remain calm. Think straight. He would want her to dissolve into hysterics. That way he was in control. His lips parted into a disparaging grin as he mimicked her words in better times.

'*I love my children more than life itself!*' He threw his head back and gave a laugh that was far from humorous. 'You should be on the stage at the Metropole, Rita.'

There was a cold gleam in his eyes and Charlie's words were low when he said, 'All in good time, Rita. You know, you can be very entertaining when you're riled.'

Horrified, she watched Charlie stop packing the little suitcase. His eyes were now taking in every inch of her body, pausing on the parts he would claim without consent, given the chance. Rita froze, aware now what he had in mind. He was going to put her in her place. This was the real reason he had agreed to bringing the children back from evacuation. His violent attentions – she could never call it lovemaking – were so painful they reduced her to tears. She prayed for him to stop, unable to cry out for fear the children would hear. It was her duty to preserve her children's innocence.

Her eyes never left him as he edged towards her. Bitter bile was searing her throat. How far was she from the closed bedroom door? She would never get past him from this distance.

Rita felt the blood run like cold water through her veins. It was broad daylight. Her children were downstairs having breakfast. She could hear them chatting away. He wouldn't . . . Not now . . .

Charlie moved inch . . . by inch . . . enjoying her torment.

Please Lord, don't let him do this to me again . . .

CHAPTER TWO

'Mrs Kerrigan, have you seen the rest of my Lady Jane's?' Nancy Kerrigan, twenty-year-old wife of Corporal Sid Kerrigan, POW, of the Cheshire Regiment, had wound half of her shoulder-length, Titian-coloured hair into little Catherine-wheel twists before securing them with silver clips. If she's given them to the salvage men, Nancy thought, she'll get the sharp edge of my tongue!

'You left them in the parlour,' Mrs Kerrigan said, bringing a paper bag into the back kitchen, where Nancy was standing on the tips of her toes looking into the oval mirror hanging from the nail above the deep stone sink. Nancy let out an impatient sigh; her mother-in-law was always snooping in her private things. She didn't know what the old woman expected to find but she was going to be disappointed.

'What did you want in the parlour?' Nancy asked, her suspicions aroused when Mrs Kerrigan put the paper bag containing the rest of her clips onto the wet draining board, so that the paper became all soggy.

24

'You had no right going into my private sitting room.' She paid Sid's mother good rent out of Sid's army allowance money every week. 'There's no privacy in this house.'

Through the looking-glass, she could see the older woman's glare of disapproval, looking down her pointed nose and flaring her thin nostrils, though she did not answer.

'Off out again, are we?' Mrs Kerrigan asked instead, in that pained voice that grated on Nancy's nerves. Nancy knew if her husband were here the old bag would not speak to her like that. She would make sure she told him next time she wrote. He would soon put his mother straight on a few things, including how to treat his wife and mother of his son.

'Yes, with my friend Gloria – you know Gloria, don't you?' Nancy said innocently, winding a section of hair around her index finger, placing it in a way she had done hundreds of times before against her scalp and pinning it in place with another clip. Nancy was pleased with the way she looked. Eyeing herself in the glass she wondered if she was a bit thinner these last few months. Everyone was going without and there was seemingly nothing that wasn't either rationed or in short supply. Her Sid preferred her with a few curves, but Nancy quite liked the new sharpness to her cheekbones.

'Oh, yes, I know Gloria, a good-time girl if ever there was one.' There was no mistaking the contempt in Mrs Kerrigan's voice. 'Half the foreign fleet know Gloria.'

Nancy could feel the hairs on the back of her neck stand to attention. She yearned to tell the po-faced woman what she thought of her pious ways; spending as much time polishing the altar rails with her prayers as she did calling her neighbours fit to burn in hell. How could Sid's mam be so religious when she was so nasty?

'Only half of them?' Nancy could not contain herself. 'My word, she is slipping!' She took a sideways glance at the older woman, who banged a cast-iron pan on the stove to show how angry she was. Nancy returned to the mirror, now applying her new bright red lipstick. When she and Gloria had last been to the Adelphi, one of the RAF servicemen had complimented her, telling her that she looked a bit like Rita Hayworth, which she'd always secretly thought herself. Nancy almost smiled at the recollection but the presence of her harping mother-in-law was enough to sour the memory. She'd had enough of her sniping, but she'd been brought up not to cheek her elders, no matter how much she was provoked. Also, she had Sid to think about.

'It's not like this is a regular thing.' She had to be careful now, knowing Mrs Kerrigan kept nothing from Sid. 'I went out twice last week. I treated Mam to a George Formby film, because she looked after little Georgie while I went to Mass.' *Because you would never dream of offering.*

'Which film was it?' Mrs Kerrigan was also very suspicious. 'I've seen all of George Formby's.'

'*Let George Do It.* Mam loves him playing his

ukulele.' She breathed a sigh of relief when Mrs Kerrigan seemed satisfied. Nancy had overheard two women in the corner shop regaling the merits of the film yesterday, and if Mrs Kerrigan found out Nancy had been drinking in the parlour of the Sailor's Rest with Gloria, she knew she would never hear the end of it.

'What about Sunday?'

'Me and Gloria went to see that Margaret Lockwood film about a girl who went to a concentration camp and befriended a man who turns out to be a Nazi spy. We don't go out as often as we used to, you know.'

'I should think not! My Sid would be ever so upset. What woman wants to see her brave son's wife behaving like a tuppenny trollop? I can't turn a blind eye. People will talk.'

'I beg your pardon!' Nancy could not believe her ears. 'Are you saying I'm up to no good?' She put her hands on her hips. Mrs Kerrigan was the limit! Nancy certainly got lots of attention from men when they were out. Gloria was something of a local celebrity and they were never short of company, but Nancy was well aware that she was a married woman and didn't need reminding by busybodies like Mrs Kerrigan.

'Well, you must admit, there aren't many other girls gallivanting around like you are while their husbands are off fighting.'

This said much for Mrs Kerrigan's sheltered life because Nancy knew that there were other girls who were far from squeaky clean. You would have to have your head in the sand not to be aware of some of the things that were going on. The city was now flooded with servicemen, not just from other parts of the country but from all around the world. Many women who were without their husbands and fiancés were taking up offers of a night out from the Canadian and Polish servicemen, and didn't they all know that while the cat's away the mice will have their little bit of fun? Why shouldn't they? thought Nancy. Who knew what tomorrow might bring? Her Sid might be killed and where would she and little Georgie be left then? She looked over at her son, sitting happily in his playpen playing with his pull-along dog. He looked just like his dad. For a moment, Nancy had an uncomfortable vision of Sid, somewhere in Europe, held prisoner God only knew where. Was he thinking of them now? She pushed the thought away. No, it wouldn't do to dwell.

'I'm thinking of getting a job in one of those munitions factories, if you must know!' Nancy did not know where the idea came from but thinking on it now, it was clear that all the women she knew who had gone back to work were having a ball. Nancy missed her job at the George Henry Lee department store. She loved the gossip and the camaraderie as well as all that extra money in her purse. Not that there would be much to buy soon if this rationing lark continued.

'And who's going to look after little Georgie, might I ask?' Mrs Kerrigan said with a look that suggested there was a bad smell under her pointed nose.

'Mam said she'd do it.' Nancy's fingers were crossed behind her back. She would have to ask her mother, but she was confident Mam would not let her down.

The look on Mrs Kerrigan's face was priceless. 'In my day it was unheard of for a married woman to go out to work – unless she was very *poor* or widowed.'

'Well, now they're in uniform and doing jobs deemed fit only for men just a couple of years ago!' Nancy answered, knowing she would have enjoyed going into the Forces. All those strong, virile men . . . However, her mother-in-law's stern expression did not encourage frivolity, so she said with every ounce of patriotic fervour she could muster, 'While our men are in the Armed Forces, us women have got to keep the country going.'

'Heaven help us if they're all like you!' Mrs Kerrigan muttered under her breath, though loud enough for Nancy to hear, and made the sign of the cross on her chest. Nancy decided to ignore the slight and taking a deep breath she tried to remain dignified like Mam said she should – turn the other cheek and all that.

'Mr Churchill said everyone's home is on the "front line", so we have to be vigilant.'

'Did he now?' Mrs Kerrigan's ever-flaring nostrils were dancing now, while Nancy, with a lot of effort, remained serene on the outside.

'If women work like men, then I believe they have the right to relax any way they choose,' Nancy said. 'Women are coping very well without the help of their husbands.'

'Oh, I know you are,' Mrs Kerrigan pointed out.

'But you and your kind would never have behaved in such a carefree way in my day. It wouldn't have been allowed.'

'Just as well I wasn't around in your day then,' Nancy smiled, but inside she was fuming. Who died and left you a day? Her own mother would not have said such things. She'd had enough. Why the hell shouldn't she have the odd night out? She didn't care if Mrs Kerrigan told Sid or not!

'Just so you know,' Nancy said in a tone sweet enough to encourage diabetes, 'I'm going to see Gloria, who's singing in the Adelphi again tonight. I don't know how she manages to entertain such big audiences after working all day in munitions – twice since last Friday, in fact – while some people just sit at home criticising and leaving others to do all the hard work!'

Mrs Kerrigan's voice was now a pathetic whine. 'Last night's raid frightened the life out of me. I thought my end had come! While you're out the Nazis could make their way over here and carry me off.'

'They might take you, but they'd soon bring you back,' Nancy muttered under her breath, then said out loud, the clips still between her teeth, 'I was only next door in the parlour last night, Mrs Kerrigan, and I won't be long tonight.' The Allies could use her as an early warning signal, she thought: she screams before the enemy planes have turned on their engines.

There was a moment's silence and Nancy imagined Mrs Kerrigan was looking for something else to carp about. It didn't take her long to find it.

'My poor Sid – how can you bear to go out and enjoy yourself, knowing that poor Sidney is suffering? He could be ill or injured and you don't seem to care.'

'Of course I care about Sid too! Just because you're crying into the bottom of your teacup all of the time, doesn't give you the moral high ground, you know,' Nancy answered, knowing if Mrs Kerrigan couldn't get her one way she would get her another. If Sid was ill the Red Cross would tell them, wouldn't they? Nancy put the hot prickle at the back of her neck down to annoyance rather than the guilt she knew she should be feeling for not missing Sid like she should. It was Mrs Kerrigan's fault she felt that way – emotional blackmail was her mother-in-law's speciality. It's what kept Sid tied to her apron strings for so long. No wonder Mr Kerrigan, her husband, worked nights on *The Liverpool Post* and no one ever saw him. He was probably desperate to get away from her.

'He could have had anybody he wanted.' Sid's mother brought the brown earthenware teapot from the range in the kitchen and poured herself a cup of stewed black tea, not offering any to Nancy. Not that Nancy was in the least bit bothered; her mother-in-law's tea, left to steep, would strip the taste buds from your tongue, it was that strong.

'When he gets home he will have eyes for nobody except me!' Nancy's honeyed words had the desired effect and Sid's mother flounced out of the back kitchen.

'Well, just you think on, lady – I tell him everything in my letters,' Mrs Kerrigan shouted from the kitchen.

I bet you do, you nosy old bag. And what you don't know you'll make up.

Nancy secured the last clip and looked at herself in the mirror. She was pleased with the reflection that stared back at her. How could Mrs Kerrigan expect her to stay in night after night, keeping her company? Nancy might be married but she wasn't dead!

'Tell him I'm keeping my pecker up – for little Georgie's sake! We've all got to do our bit for the war effort. Mr Churchill said so.'

'I don't think he meant entertaining the foreign troops,' Mrs Kerrigan reminded her.

Looking around at the drab distempered walls and heavy black furniture Nancy felt that living here was like being in a mausoleum. It was bigger than Mam's house in Empire Street, with six empty bedrooms and dark stairs that led to echoing shadowy attics. The cellar had been reinforced to use as an air raid shelter, but it was cold and damp and full of cockroaches and mice. The place gave her the creeps – a far cry from Mam's cheery kitchen.

Nancy sighed as dying flies buzzed nonstop about the kitchen. No matter how much she cleaned it with bleach and disinfectant, the place still smelled damp and inhospitable. Not like Mam's happy kitchen, which always had somebody chattering away. Nancy's heart lurched. What was it Mrs Kerrigan said about marrying in haste? *Well, you're repenting now all right, Nance.*

Picking up her bag of remaining clips, Nancy put baby George into his pram, pulled a headscarf around her pin-curled hair and tied a knot under her chin. Then, sneaking her glad rags under the canopy of the pram for later, Nancy closed the front door behind her without another word.

Through the narrow entries, she pushed the pram, saying a little prayer that Mam did not repeat her stoic phrase that she had made her bed and now she must lie in it! Well, if Mam didn't let her stay in Empire Street she was going to have to look for a room somewhere. 'Because I just can't take no more of that woman, little Georgie,' Nancy said in the foggy miasma of a damp afternoon. 'I can't take no more.'

'You'll be lucky to find anything these days,' said Sarah, who had just come into the kitchen after changing into her Red Cross uniform. 'There are no spare places after the raids.' She leaned over Nancy's shoulder and picked up a couple of clips Nancy had taken from her hair.

'Can I borrow a couple of these to keep my cap in place?' she asked.

'And keep those unruly curls in check,' Nancy offered. It was a wonder their Sarah's halo didn't fall down and choke her. Her sixteen-year-old sister got away with everything just because she was the youngest. Rita got away with everything because she was the eldest. And I get away with bugger-all! Nancy moaned.

'Where did you say you were going tonight?' Dolly worried her headstrong daughter was not behaving as a young wife should.

Not long after the telegram came telling Nancy her husband had been taken prisoner, she was off dancing with Gloria or popping over to the Sailor's Rest at the bottom of Empire Street where Gloria's father ran the pub. Dolly liked Gloria, but she knew the young woman was a law unto herself and no one could tell her what to do. Her parents had certainly given her plenty of rope, but Dolly worried that she'd hang herself with it if she wasn't careful. Besides, Gloria wasn't married but Nancy was and she needed to behave herself. Not that she'd had much truck with behaving herself in the past, as Nancy was already pregnant with little Georgie when she walked down the aisle. Despite being a strong Catholic, Dolly was also pragmatic and had seen it all. At least Nancy had wanted to marry Sid. She was less sure about Rita, her eldest daughter, who had found herself in the same situation before marrying Charlie Kennedy. Dolly hated the thought that Rita was stuck with that charmless man. She knew that he and his mother looked down on the Feeny family, but they were too cowardly to say it out loud. Dolly swore she would take a brickbat to him if he ever so much as hinted at it. She and her brood were worth a hundred of the Kennedys.

Looking at Nancy, Dolly knew the old miseries said it could all end in tears, but what was a young, healthy woman to do? Just the other day she'd heard Vera Delaney saying that kind of behaviour wouldn't be allowed in her day.

'I don't blame the young living life to the full – why

not?' she had replied, then reminded Vera of Mr Churchill's speech at the end of August: '". . . Never in the field of human conflict was so much owed by so many to so few."'

'I don't think he meant your Nancy!' Vera had sniffed as she approached her front door.

'You could have knocked me over with a fender!' Dolly told her daughters, accepting their sudden tight-lipped smiles. 'I resemble that remark! It's a good thing women are going out and enjoying themselves . . . What's up with you two? Did I say something funny?'

'It's all right, Mam.' Tears of laughter ran down Nancy and Sarah's faces at their mother's mangling of the English language. 'It wouldn't do for Georgie to have a miserable family.'

Dolly agreed. 'Things are bad enough without adding long faces to the situation. There's nothing wrong in a bit of good clean fun, I say.'

'Did I tell you Gloria's singing at the Adelphi tonight?' Nancy was hopeful as she eyed her mother through the looking-glass over the mantelpiece. 'She got me a ticket and it's been ages since I've had a night out to anywhere smart.' She put her head to one side and smiled, encouraging her mother to agree.

'That's nice,' Dolly said; she knew what Nancy was up to, it was as plain as the nose on her face, but she'd let her carry on for a bit longer . . . She might like her daughter to keep her chin up but that didn't mean she could take advantage.

'Somewhere classy,' Nancy said, 'where I can get

dressed up and have a dance . . . Gloria's hoping for a regular spot,' she said while Mam was still listening. 'I should support her, don't you think, Mam? After all, she's been so good since Sid . . .'

Dolly had a sneaking suspicion that Nancy had come here to get ready because she didn't want Sid's mother to see her all dolled up in her glad rags. She wondered if her daughter intended to stay here tonight as she did sometimes when she was too late to take Georgie home after a night out. If she could, Dolly knew her daughter would stay until Sid was released. However, she also knew she would be the one left holding the baby.

'You don't mind if I stay the night, do you, Mam, what with that fog?'

'It'll be a bit cramped with you and the baby sharing with Sarah in the small back room.'

'I could always go in Eddy's room.' Nancy was persuasive, that was for sure.

'Eddy or Frank will need the room when they come home.' Dolly knew Nancy's game: she wanted to come back home and if she put herself in the boys' room Dolly would never get her out again. 'There's no way they're sleeping on the sofa in the parlour after giving their all for King and country!'

'It's just a night out, Mam.'

'Hmm, I suppose so.' Dolly was not sure. 'Sarah's on night duty.'

Sarah sighed. She would be that tired when she got in tomorrow morning she didn't care who was in her bed – but Nancy would not be there for long, if she had anything to do with it, that's for sure.

36

'So, now that's agreed will you mind Georgie for me? It's been so long since I went dancing and . . .'

'Yeah, since all of last week. Aye, go on then, I will,' Dolly said, putting the flat iron back on the stove. Folding the baby's rompers, she lovingly placed them on the pile of ironed laundry. Nancy was young, she had her whole life ahead of her to be housebound, looking after kids and doing her duty. 'I know how much you loved to dance before . . .' Life is short enough, thought Dolly, there was no point in sitting on the hob, moping.

'Thanks, Mam.' Nancy gave her mother a loving squeeze. 'I managed to get a new lippy in Boots – d'you want to try it? Some woman in a feathered hat tried to snatch it out of my hands, but I clung on,' Nancy's blue eyes were wide with indignation. 'I said to her, "My husband died for this country – the least you can do is let me have a lipstick!" She soon let go.'

'You never said such a wicked thing – you'll be tempting fate if you're not careful!' Dolly could not believe her own ears.

'Don't be silly and superstitious. It got me the lippy, didn't it?' Nancy said through stretched lips as she applied a generous coat of crimson lipstick, pouting in the mirror. Then she noticed that Dolly had disappeared into the back kitchen. 'I managed to get some Amami shampoo as well!' Nancy called after her excitedly. 'Shall I wash your hair later?'

'And what did you have to say to get that, I wonder.' Dolly sounded a bit put out.

Nancy followed her into the back kitchen. 'I wouldn't mind, but she was on her last knockings! She must have been at least forty,' she said with a nod of her pin-curled head.

'That doesn't say much for your ancient babysitter, Nance,' Dolly answered, putting some thinly peeled potatoes into just enough water to cover them. On top of them, in place of a steamer, she put her colander containing diced carrots and peas and covered the whole lot with a tin lid. 'I just hope that you know what you're doing, that's all.' She would not want to see Nancy getting herself into any kind of trouble.

'Did you know that the dull surface of a pan absorbs heat more rapidly than a shiny one?' Dolly asked, changing the subject.

Nancy did not look interested one way or the other. 'Have you been reading those leaflets you deliver again, Mam?' she laughed, knowing women of the Home Front, as it was now being called, were being advised on all things domesticated to eke out the rations and save waste.

'Gert and Daisy mentioned it on the wireless this morning.'

'I learned everything I know from you, Mam; you could teach the Ministry of Food a thing or two.'

'We mustn't waste fuel that is needed for the war industry.'

Dolly knew when she was being soft-soaped. Nancy was always free with the charm and the compliments when she wanted her own way and Dolly knew Nancy could wind her old mother round her little finger. 'I'm going to start a make-do-and-mend club with Mrs Ashby. Come on now, get out from under my feet. If you're going out then get going, before I change my mind.'

CHAPTER THREE

A dry, strangled sound escaped Rita's lips when Charlie's narrowed eyes signalled her to be quiet. He stepped forward, his manner threatening. She knew that this time she had nothing to lose.

Rita was determined she would not let him intimidate her. If he dared to come anywhere near, so help her she would not be responsible for her actions. You can whip a dog only so much before it turns, she thought.

He edged closer.

Her blue-green eyes blazed and her fingernails dug deep into the palm of her hands. She was no longer that meek young girl who had married him back then. So young and terrified of bringing disgrace to Mam and Pop that she had panicked. However, Rita had plenty of time to regret her decision; for over three thousand days she had woken up and regretted her choice. Why couldn't she have been more like Nancy, who lived each day as if it were her last?

Rita matched his cold stare now, daring him to

cross her. The thought of her family gave her courage and she knew if he laid one finger on her this time, she would fight him all the way! Lifting a defiant chin, she could feel cold perspiration break out on the back of her neck as he drew closer.

Charlie's tread was slow, ominous, his eyes never leaving hers. They were wary of each other now, like two cats after the same mouse. In a trice, he was standing in front of her and, as if in slow motion, she watched him lift his hand. His eyes softened.

For one fleeting moment, her guard was down and Rita thought he was going to caress her cheek. His hand shot to the nape of her thick auburn curls and he gripped them so tight her head was forced back.

'You will do as you are told.' He stressed every word. His face was so close to hers she could see white foamy saliva gather in the corner of his mouth. The smell of stale whisky and tobacco fumes on his breath made her stomach heave. 'And you will like it.' Awful memories flashed through her mind making her feel soiled. The last time he was like this . . . The last time . . .

Rita prayed for the strength to extinguish the sickening gleam of control in his eyes. What did she have to lose? Charlie was taking the children. But in the eyes of the law, he had every right. The realisation hit her with such force she did not care what she did next.

She lifted her hand to strike him but he was faster and his grip was a damn sight stronger. But Rita Kennedy was brought up in the rough, tough streets of Bootle, where a girl had to be able to look after herself. She brought her knee up sharply to his groin and her action was quick and it was effective. He doubled up in pain, clutching at his injured parts.

Shaking her fiery mane free, Rita summoned all her strength, using the full force of her slight frame to push him away. Where she got the strength from she would never know, but the element of surprise was hers now and the shocked and pained expression on Charlie's face sustained her. She felt triumphant, but her sense of achievement was short-lived when Charlie, gathering himself with a quickness that surprised her – and apparently no longer worried if his mother heard or not – scorned her little triumph.

'You can take the girl out of the dirt,' he sneered, 'but you can't take the dirt out of the girl.'

'At least my dirt washes off, Charlie,' Rita was breathless now with the exertion of her achievement, 'but yours never will!' Not for the first time, she wished she had had the courage to walk out on him years ago. But she could never abandon her children and he would never let her take them.

Better now they had somewhere safe to go while she regrouped and decided what to do next. No matter what she thought of Charlie, she believed that deep down he loved his children and she didn't think he would put them in harm's way. She had to trust in that – for now at least. She would bide her time. This place where there were people his mother knew should be easy enough to find. Charlie couldn't hide her children for ever and she would find them, that was for sure. He would never tell her, but she had friends and she had family. They would find a way.

'Charles! Charles . . . Look at the time!' His mother's screech echoed up the stairs and Rita and Charlie looked at each other, no longer husband and wife, but sworn adversaries.

'You will pay for your little victory,' Charlie said, his voice dripping menace as he turned from her with a small suitcase dangling from each hand. In a flash, she was between him and the bedroom door. She rested her back against it.

'I swear, Charlie, as God is my witness that if any harm comes to those children, you'll not only have me to reckon with but the whole of the Feeny family. I'll find my children whether you want me to or not and I'll make sure that every single person in Empire Street knows what a guttersnipe you are. Everyone will know, from the bakers round the corner to the Sailor's Rest, that you are a dirty, perverted, lying, cheating bastard. They'll whisper it as you walk past and soon neither you nor your mother will be able to show your faces in Empire Street again, Charlie. And that's a promise.'

Rita watched as Charlie's smug expression turned from one of triumph to something much darker. Her words had hit home, she could see, but she was too slow to anticipate his hand as he struck out at her and she barely felt the sharp corner of the chest of drawers as it sliced into her scalp.

Rita put her hand to her head and felt the warm damp spot where the gash had broken the skin. Blood trickled down her cheek from the wound. Charlie looked over his shoulder as he opened the bedroom door.

'Dear dear, Rita, what a clumsy woman you are. You should get a plaster on that cut, it looks nasty.' He shut the door behind him.

Rita was damned if she was going to give Charlie the satisfaction of taking her children away from her without even a goodbye. Despite feeling slightly woozy, she rushed over to the chest of drawers and poured some water from the jug onto her hankie. Dabbing at the cut, she fished out a headscarf from the top drawer and hastily tied it in a turban, the way that women doing their housework often did. Then she hurried to the front bedroom from where she could see Charlie loading up the car. Charlie's job as an insurance salesman meant that he had one of the few cars in the area – a recent acquisition of which he was tremendously proud – and today it was the only one on Empire Street. She raced out of the bedroom and down the stairs to find Mrs Kennedy bundling the children into their coats and ushering them out of the door.

'I'll do that,' Rita snapped, stepping between her mother-in-law and her children. 'Perhaps you should go and make yourself a cup of tea while I see to them.'

She could see that Ma Kennedy was ready to make a challenge but Rita was having none of it and the mutinous look in her own eye quelled any response so Ma Kennedy retreated into the back room.

'Where are we going, Mummy?' asked Megan, quietly. Rita looked at her little girl. She was barely six years old and she still desperately needed her mother. But whatever Charlie was wrong about, he was right that the children needed to be got out of the city. Rita would have to bear the pain, the same as all the other mothers in London, Birmingham, Liverpool and beyond were having to.

'Daddy's taking you on an adventure.'

Michael jumped up and down excitedly. 'Are we going back to the farm again? I miss Bessie the goat; she used to eat Uncle Seth's hat!'

Rita forced a laugh. 'Not this time. Daddy's taking you to a place called Southport. It's safer there and there's a beach and a pier.'

Michael's eyes lit up. 'Can I have a bucket and a net, Dad? Tommy Callaghan told me that you can catch all sorts of strange creatures in rock pools . . .' Michael's excited babble continued as Rita gave him a quick kiss and his father bundled him into the car.

Rita turned back to her younger child.

'Are you coming too, Mummy?' Megan's eyes looked imploringly at her.

'Not today, darling. But I'll be down very soon and I'll take you both to the beach myself. We can walk along the pier and I can buy you an ice cream.'

Megan gave her a weak smile, but Rita could see that she was close to tears. It was better to be quick. Rita held her hand and placed her in the back seat of the car where Michael was making rat-a-tat sounds while he swooped a paper plane through the air.

'Promise me, you'll look after your little sister, Michael.'

'I will, Mum, don't worry.' Michael took his sister's hand and gave his mother a brave smile.

'That's my boy.'

Rita bent down to give Megan a kiss on her cheek, but the moment was too much for the child and she threw her arms around her mother's neck and let out an anguished sob.

'Please come, Mummy.'

Rita tried hard to mask her own emotions, but her heart was breaking and she couldn't disguise the catch in her voice as she said, 'I'll be thinking of you both every moment of every day and as soon as Daddy has settled you in, I'll be there. It won't be long, I promise.'

Rita removed her daughter's arms from around her and picked up the little bear that Megan was holding.

'Bobby Bear is going to give you a cuddle every night and sing you to sleep, aren't you, Bobby?' Rita made the bear nod his head and give a little dance. Megan giggled, Rita was pleased to see. She handed Megan the bear to hold again and as she shut the back car door, Charlie cut in.

'Sorry to interrupt this touching scene, but it's time to go.' He barely glanced over his shoulder at her as he started the car and made to shut his door, but before he did, Rita said, 'Remember what I said, Charlie. I meant every word.'

Charlie gave her a cold look and started the engine. 'Goodbye, Rita.'

'Goodbye, Charlie. I'll be seeing you, you can be sure of that.'

As the car drove away, Rita saw the two faces of her children, smiling and waving as they retreated into the distance, followed noisily by a gang of children who still hadn't got over the novelty of having a motor car on their doorstep. Rita watched until the car reached the end of Empire Street then turned the corner, her children disappearing with it.

She returned slowly to the house, where Mrs Kennedy had taken up her usual place by the window, all the better to see what the rest of the street was up to.

'Are you happy now?' Rita asked her mother-in-law.

Ma Kennedy pursed her lips. 'You should be proud of Charlie, taking it into his own hands to make the children safe.' She paused and stared at Rita, who put her hand to her forehead and felt a trickle of blood seep through the headscarf. Her head was now starting to throb painfully. *Damn Charlie Kennedy.*

'What happened to you?' For the first time, Rita thought she saw an element of doubt flicker across the older woman's face.

'That's right, Ma. You've got a son to be proud of all right. Anyone can see that.'

And with that, she left her mother-in-law to her own thoughts and headed out to Empire Street, where the children were now playing a game of coins up against the corner shop wall.

CHAPTER FOUR

The light drizzle was turning heavier as Kitty turned into Empire Street. It had been a long day at the NAAFI canteen where she worked and she would be glad to get home this evening. She hoped that her brothers, Danny and Tommy, weren't in before her. Danny, who was twenty, had got a new job on the docks and Kitty hoped that working alongside older men with families and responsibilities would knock some of the rough edges off him. Danny had a habit of sailing a bit close to the wind in the law-abiding department and Kitty worried that he would get his collar felt one of these days. Tommy, meanwhile, was still a little weak after contracting a nasty bout of diphtheria while an evacuee, and his health was a constant nagging anxiety for her. Despite the bombing Kitty was loath to send him away again and in the face of all of the warning voices around her, she wouldn't ever trust anyone outside of the family with his wellbeing again.

Kitty had looked after her brother and her father,

Sonny, since her mother died when she was just a young girl. Her father had hardly done his best by his children and they had often had to go without while he drank away his meagre earnings at the Sailor's Rest. They'd frequently had to rely solely on their older brother, Jack's, wages from the foundry, but they had all been floored when Sonny had died just before last Christmas, even Jack, who'd had a difficult relationship with their father. Kitty found comfort in believing that her mother and father were united again, and never questioned the burden of running a family from such a young age.

She sidestepped the puddles in the gutter as she made her way across the street. There was a big hole in her shoe but money was tight and she hadn't scraped enough together to get a new pair. She'd been trying to put a bit aside each week, but her savings weren't growing very fast. She hoped she'd have a new pair before the bad weather set in. There were now short-ages and rationing for most of the essentials. Kitty had heard a rumour that clothes rationing was going to be introduced and she half thought that she was more likely to get a new pair of shoes with rationing than without.

She was keen to get the dinner on. She'd managed to pick up a few sausages extra to the ration from the butcher and Pop had given her some potatoes from his allotment, so she was looking forward to making some hearty sausage and mash for the three of them. When Pop had brought the potatoes round this morning before she left for work he had also told her that their Frank was coming home. Kitty's heart was almost in her mouth at this news. The last she'd seen of Frank was before he'd gone off for rehabilitation after losing his leg. Things had been awkward between them and Kitty had been forced to remind herself that there was no reason that Frank should give her any special treatment. He'd been through a lot and any idea she'd had that there was something between them was just a lot of silly girlish nonsense. Frank just saw her as one of the family; the girl across the road. That was that.

Still, Kitty couldn't help a pang of emotion when she thought about the dance and the kiss that they had shared the night before he'd returned to his ship. She didn't think she'd ever forget it. She sighed now as she pushed open the door to their little terrace – it was never locked. She still hoped she'd see Frank, though. Perhaps she'd pop round with something later on or tomorrow . . . perhaps an apple pie? The butter ration didn't go far but she'd managed to eke it out. Frank would like that. He had a sweet tooth.

Frank watched from the shadows as Kitty closed the street door behind her. Even though he couldn't see her closely, his heart had ached as he took in her dark hair and fine features. Kitty was beautiful and she didn't even know it. Frank cursed himself for being a romantic twit. He'd walked past Kitty's house at least a dozen times earlier on his stiff false leg. However, he couldn't bring himself to 'just call in' like he always had in the past. Too much had happened since this bloody war had started. What could she possibly see in a man like him – one who was damaged beyond repair? Nothing, he imagined. He and Kitty had grown up together, and since her mother had died he'd been like a brother to her, but now what he felt for her was more than brotherly love. Something had changed between them but since he'd lost his leg he knew that he would never be good enough for her.

Dressed in his uniform of a petty officer of the Royal Navy, Frank acknowledged cheery greetings from passers-by he had known all his life. He smiled to hide his shame, but that was all that he could feel now: shame for being half the man he had been. He hated the two sticks that enabled him to manoeuvre on his new tin leg. He'd had it only a couple of months and it still didn't feel comfortable. It rubbed like hell, and each day he had to massage the tender stump before re-dressing it ready for the false leg. Kitty would be sickened, he was sure.

However, he was glad of one thing: he had been allowed to stay in the navy – in the recently established Weapon and Radio branch at HMS *Collingwood* naval base – which spared him the humiliation of being invalided home.

Gulls and pigeons bullied the sparrows that swooped for scraps from the hessian sacks being carted along the busy dock road. Frank had arrived home only that morning and it was wonderful to see his family, but the constant questions and chatter were wearing him down already.

He toyed with the idea of knocking on Kitty's door

again. Seeing her up close and in the flesh would be a sight for sore eyes. He imagined her face, lit up like a Christmas tree when she was happy – God, imagining it was unbearable. But then he imagined her face as she took in his new leg. He did not want to see the pitying look in her eyes nor the exaggerated look of pleasure when she saw he was actually walking again. No, Kitty had her own life – she didn't need to be hindered by a cripple. Frank was scared of neither man nor beast but the thought of being rejected by Kitty put the fear of God into him. Better leave things alone, he thought as he ambled along, knowing he could fight most things but he could not battle his feelings for Kitty Callaghan . . .

Frank's thoughts were interrupted by a swaying woman who might well have been pretty at one time, but was now hard-looking and weary. She came towards him, scraping her heels against the stone pavement as if the effort to hold herself upright was too much to bear; she greeted him with a practised smile.

'Hello 'andsome, fancy a jar?' By the sound of her tired voice she couldn't care less if he wanted one or not.

'Not tonight, girl,' Frank smiled politely, 'but here, have one on me.' He gave her half a crown and hoped she would go home to her kids, or whoever it was who was waiting there for her. She kissed him on the cheek.

'God bless yer, lad, you don't know what that means ter me.'

Frank could only imagine as she wended her way along the dock road. He gave a gentle laugh and shook his head. He'd called her 'girl'. He was sure she hadn't been a girl since Adam was a lad!

'How did that happen?' Dolly's eyes were wide when she saw the gash on the side of her daughter's forehead the day after Frank's return.

Rita called in most days but had tried to keep out of the way yesterday. However, she wanted to hear all about Frank.

'It happened during the raid,' Rita lied, knowing Pop would be out on horseback looking for Charlie Kennedy if he suspected Rita had been mistreated. 'The windows on the ward were blown in. Luckily we were over the other side but when I dived under the bed I caught it on the steel frame.' Rita was amazed at the ease with which the lies tripped off her tongue.

'I hope you got one of the doctors to look at it,' Dolly said, her brows pleating. 'Is it sore?'

'It's fine, Mam!' Rita said a little impatiently, then she relented. It was normal for her mother to be concerned and so she said in a more tender tone, 'At least I came through it.'

'Glory be to God!' Dolly said in her quick Celtic way, but she couldn't help but feeling uneasy all the same. There had been no suggestion before this that Charlie was violent with her daughter, but Dolly heard the rumours, the same as everyone else, and she knew that of late he had taken increasingly to gambling and to drink. He'd been ruined by his own mother, Dolly knew, and if he ever harmed her daughter . . .

'So help me, I'll swing for him!' she muttered out of Rita's hearing.

'Oh, Mam, I will miss Michael and Megan even more after having them home for the past months.' Rita sat at the table in the kitchen of her mother's three-bedroomed, gas-lit terraced house, situated on the other side of the alleyway from Winnie Kennedy's corner shop.

'Who did he say they were staying with?' Dolly, a loving, sensible mother who was everybody's main-stay, was pouring tea into a cup with a hairline crack, something that would never have happened before the war. The cup rattled a little on the saucer as Rita took the hot tea. It would never occur to Dolly to offer a cup of tea without a saucer. She still had her impeccable standards, even though the shortages had forced her and the rest of the country to lower them a little.

'A woman called Elsie Lowe, someone Charlie's mother knows . . . She runs a boarding house for businessmen, in Southport.' Rita sipped at the hot tea, used to not having sugar since it became rationed last January.

'Is she old, then?' Dolly asked. 'I mean, won't the kids be a bit of a handful for a woman who has a boarding house to run?'

'Apparently not,' Rita answered, nodding to Nancy, who was just bringing baby George in from his nap in his pram, which was parked on the small terracotta-tiled pathway under the parlour window.

'Did you use the cat net?' Dolly asked Nancy, who

scowled. 'Only, you forgot it yesterday and next door's tabby was sniffing around the pram for milk.'

'I won't forget again in a hurry, not after it lay on his face and almost suffocated him!' Nancy said with venom. 'I'll get Pop's gun and shoot that bloody cat!' Pop was the local ARP warden and allowed to have a gun in the house. Not that there had been any reason to use it. They even had a white diamond painted at the side of the front door to identify this as the warden's house.

'Everybody in the hospital was talking about the raids,' said Rita, trying to take her mind off her own troubles. She did not mention the fact that they had a German airman in a single secure ward with armed soldiers standing guard outside. 'The wards have been cleared of patients who were almost ready for discharge and allowed an early release.'

The raids had people's nerves rattling, their tetchiness showing in all sorts of different ways. In Nancy's case she thought she had the given right to go around with a scowl on her face just because Gloria had come over the other night after Nancy had got all dolled up and told her that the dances were off for the foreseeable due to the raids.

'I'll go mad if they close down all the dance halls and theatres the way they did at the beginning of the war,' Nancy said, passing her son to Rita, who wrinkled her nose before proceeding to remove his blue cotton helmet. Giving George a loving kiss on his plump little cheek brought a gurgle of baby bubbles from his smiling pink lips.

'I love them at this age,' Rita said, missing her own two desperately already. 'Are you going to have him evacuated, Nancy?'

'He's only six months old. Children under five years old are being evacuated with their mothers.' The question needed to be asked, especially after the latest raids, and Rita knew her mother was on pins worrying about little Georgie's welfare; they all were.

'It's at their mothers' discretion,' Nancy added tartly.

'You can't be serious, Nancy!' Rita exclaimed. She knew the port of London had ceased to be an operative channel for worldwide trade since Germany took control of the French coast. Mines had been laid by both the Allies and Axis powers, making the English Channel far too dangerous for large-scale cargo, so the Mersey docks were now handling all vital cargoes. They were an ideal target for the enemy.

'I am not having him evacuated!' Nancy was adamant. 'Where I go he goes and I'm going nowhere!' Not even back to Mrs Kerrigan's house if she could help it. She had already wangled a few nights' stay here, but now their Frank was home there wasn't going to be much room for her and little Georgie so she would have to be canny.

Nancy had lost her naïve charm since the war started, Rita noticed. Since Sid had been reported missing, then found and reported as a POW, Nancy had developed a fatalistic attitude of almost selfish what-will-be-will-be.

'We're not going to the countryside. We're staying here in the bosom of our family,' Nancy said, opening the sideboard door and taking out a clean towelling napkin.

'I should imagine they won't have much in the way of dance halls in the countryside, either,' Dolly remarked with her unmistakable Irish humour. Rita suspected her light-hearted banter disguised her worry about their Eddy. He had not been home for months.

After their Frank was brought home injured, Mam almost closed her mind off from the serious aspects of life, and concentrated on safer things instead. Like minding the nation's business instead of just her family. Her WVS work kept her going, and so too did salvage collection and setting up cookery classes for young women who were going through a war for the first time – after all, Mam had already gone through one war. She was a fountain of information, even if she did get her words wrong explaining things.

'I can see now that it was a mistake for me to bring mine home when I did. They were safer on the farm,' Rita said, causing the women in the room to focus their attention on her now. 'I know Michael and Megan will be safer away from the air raids, but there's no substitute for a mother's love.'

'It was a bit sudden, the kids going like that,' Nancy said, and Rita nodded, making no comment, still bristling and feeling anxious about Charlie's motives for taking the children. As she unbuttoned little George's romper suit her mind was in turmoil.

It must be difficult for Nancy, having no man to talk things over with. Nevertheless Rita would prefer that to having Charlie Kennedy hanging around tormenting her and ignoring her all at the same time. It was mental cruelty – that's what it was. However, although she suspected Nancy missed Sid, Rita noticed that her sister was talking a little less of him each day.

'*Georgie Porgie, pudding and pie, kissed the girls and made them cry.*' Rita's dum-de-dum nursery rhyme made the young baby chuckle as she rubbed her nose in time to the rhythm. '*When the boys came out to play, Georgie Porgie ran away.*'

'My little man would never run away!' Kitty Callaghan popped her head around the door. She was carrying a plate covered with a clean tea towel and said, 'I'm just on my way to the NAAFI and I thought I'd bring this apple pie over, Aunty Doll.'

'Oh, you are a little darlin', Kit,' Dolly said. 'That won't be wasted, for sure.' She was not Kitty's aunty by blood but, having been a great friend of her mother who died when Kitty was just eleven years old, she was the closest woman to a mother Kitty, Danny and young Tommy had known.

Kitty was always working. Making delicious pies and cakes for the NAAFI, which were the talk of the neighbourhood, was her biggest pleasure in life. When there was a glut of apples, like now, Dolly was the lucky recipient of a plate apple pie or two. Sometimes it seemed as though rationing had not reached number two Empire Street, but nobody asked questions, realising it was better not to know. The area was poor and if people got a little extra they did not shout about it. Even if information was available there would be a rush for ears to be covered. What you didn't know you couldn't tell lies about – that was Dolly's philosophy.

'Have you seen our Tommy, Aunty Doll?' Kitty asked after greeting the other women present.

'I saw him this morning, but he's not been in here since then.'

Kitty had hoped to catch Frank, whom she knew was home for only a short while. However, noting his chair was empty and feeling a little disappointed dip inside, she knew she must pull herself together. On such a short visit home, he would have people to see, places to be.

'I'll give Tommy his tea, don't worry,' Dolly said, noting the white turban covering Kitty's ebony curls and the dark blue overall that covered her slim frame were spotless and ironed.

'Is Frank not in then?' Kitty asked, disappointed despite her resolve.

'You just missed him,' Dolly said. She was delighted to have him home again, even for a short while, and unable to fathom why he wanted to go back on duty. Anybody in their right mind would have got right out of the navy and away from those U-boats if they had a chance, and no one would blame him in the circumstances. Although, Dolly thought proudly, even with half a leg missing her elder son was still a catch; everybody said so.

'I'm bringing fresh tea in now, Kit,' Dolly called as she got up and went to the back kitchen, where she put the pie on the cold shelf and covered it with a clean tea towel of her own. Bringing Kitty's cloth back, along with the fresh pot of tea, she asked lightly, 'Have you got time for a cuppa before work?'

Kitty nodded. 'Aunty Dolly, I want to ask your advice. Our Tommy's turning into a right little tearaway lately.' Her dark blue eyes darkened further. 'I don't know what I'm going to do with him.'

'Oh, he's not bad, Kitty. He's just restless,' Dolly said, knowing that up until recently Tommy was in here more than he was in his own house. Now he was in with some bigger boys who lived near Marsh Lane and had been seen hanging around the emergency water tank in Strand Road. 'He'll call in when his belly's empty, you wait and see. I'll save him a bit of that apple pie.'

Nancy wrinkled her nose as she picked up George's dirty nappy and, holding it away from her, she handed her sister the tin of talcum powder with her free hand. 'Go easy with the talc, Rita. I can't get me hands on any more and you're shaking it on him like you're salting a bag of fish and chips,' she said as her older sister expertly lifted her nephew by his ankles and liberally doused his nooks and crannies with a snowy covering of scented powder.

'He loves it.' Rita was holding him like a prized chicken in the butcher's window, before expertly slipping the clean towelling nappy under him and, joining both sides together, secured it to his vest with a large pin either side.

'How did you manage to hide these nappy pins from our Sarah?' Rita asked, knowing their younger sister was an avid salvage collector these days.

'She's not getting her hands on those, even if it will help the war effort. I need them to cover my son's modesty,' Nancy quipped.

'Our flying boys need all the nappy pins they can get now,' Rita admonished. 'Isn't that right, Kit?'

Kitty nodded. Her brother Jack was now a pilot in the Fleet Air Arm, having transferred from the RAF as his skills as a shipwright were in great demand after serving an apprenticeship at Harland and Wolff, the ship-builders in Belfast, returning as a skilled man to their foundry in Strand Road.

'Mrs Ashby's grandson's joined the army,' Dolly said when there was a lull in conversation. 'She says he's being shipped to the desert.'

'I saw your Jack the other day,' Rita couldn't resist saying, knowing Kitty's elder brother could not get away from the Borough quick enough. And even though he came back to Bootle, he never stayed in the house he grew up in across the street. Rita often wondered what it was that drew him back home even now; given the chance, Jack could be anything he wanted to be.

'He had a day's leave. He said he'll try and get home for Christmas.'

Rita took a deep breath, staying silent. She and Jack had been in love – childhood sweethearts, some called them – but they'd been too young, and then he had gone away to Belfast for his apprenticeship. It was after he had left that things all went wrong, and she had got together with Charlie for all of the wrong reasons . . . But she and Jack would always remember their feelings. They may not be together

61

now, and there was no way that they ever could be, but he was still a good friend to her and that would have to be enough, for both of them.

Fastening Georgie's romper suit, she tried to push down the painful lump of melancholy that thoughts of Jack always brought. He wanted a life away from Empire Street. He wanted to see the world, conquer mountains. Lifting her nephew into the air she pushed the low point of her life from her thoughts, concentrating instead on baby George and making daft duck noises. This made George laugh, and the sight of his smiling little face raised her own spirits. 'Just be thankful he's not old enough to go and fight.'

'Perish the thought,' Dolly shuddered, refilling the tea cups.

'My Sid always used to be up to something, his mother told me.' All the women in the room knew that Nancy had elevated her Sid almost to the point of sainthood since he became a prisoner of war, which was strange because the two of them did nothing but bicker before his Territorial unit was called up and shipped out to France with the British Expeditionary Force. 'Boys will be boys.'

No matter how much she tried to behave herself Nancy could not. Playing the dutiful wife did not suit her. She wanted to go out dancing with Gloria. She felt she deserved a little fun after nine months of pregnancy, much of it spent living alone at Sid's mother's. There was no use moping about the war, she decided. She absolutely refused to be miserable for long and drag everybody else down.

Rita was happy bouncing baby Georgie on her knee. His little gurgles of delight took her mind off her own children momentarily, especially when the infant chuckled, *really* chuckled, for the first time. Then he dribbled all over her, making everybody laugh. Who would think that talk of a nappy pin could bring forth such powerful emotions, she thought.

'Drink your tea while it's still hot, love,' Dolly said in that gentle sensitive way that told Rita she knew exactly what she was going through. She gave her a tight, encouraging smile. 'It doesn't matter how old your kids are, you still miss them.'

Suddenly tearful, Rita turned her eyes away from her mother now. She did not want to share her fears with her mam about Charlie taking the kids away. Mam had enough on her plate with Frank being home.

CHAPTER FIVE

'D'you know where I found this fella?' Kitty, holding on to her ten-year-old brother by the collar, marched Tommy into the kitchen the following day. His grubby shirt looked especially dirty against his shiny clean face. 'Swimming in the emergency water tank in Strand Road, that's where he was! In this weather.' Kitty gave Tommy a little shove to emphasise her words. 'It's a wonder he didn't catch pneumonia, or drown!'

'Getaway?' Danny was sitting on a rickety chair near the sash window, his elbows resting on the table scrubbed clean of any varnish with age and use. He hardly lifted his eyes from the newspaper, spread out on the kitchen table so he could study the weekly football results.

'Did you wallop him?' Danny's words bounced off the sports page, reduced because of paper shortages. He knew there was not much football to study either these days. Most fixtures were cancelled as attention turned to the war effort, although local league competitions were set up and a few, such as the Northern League, did manage to complete the last season. It cut Danny to think more than half of the footballers were unable to fulfil all their fixtures because they had been called up. Teams were dwindling, although when possible guest players would be fielded instead. He sighed; even the footy players were doing their bit.

So far he had been able to dodge Kitty's questions. At first, before he got this new job, it was natural she should be curious as to why he had not been called up like the other blokes from around here. When he first found out he could not serve his country because of an enlarged heart he had thought of telling his sister he was a conscientious objector, but he knew she would never believe that. The only thing Danny had ever wanted to do was to join the Forces and Kitty knew it.

'You haven't listened to a word I said, Danny Callaghan!' Kitty wondered why she bothered even trying to keep Tommy out of trouble. Danger was like a magnet to the curious boy. 'He can't just roam the streets and I've got to go back to work again. There's a Forces dance tonight and I've got to do an added shift! I won't be home until eleven.'

'I can only mind him until nine,' Danny said, raising his head now. 'I've got to make a delivery.' Danny, having been exempted from military duty, was now in a reserved occupation on the docks and earning a regular wage. The reserved occupation conveniently answered the question as to why he hadn't been called up. Not that Kitty would ever judge him – or anybody else for that matter. She had a heart of gold.

However, Danny had no intention of telling her he had a dicky ticker. He didn't want to worry her any more than he had to when she was constantly anxious about Tommy's fragile health and about Jack.

It seemed to Danny that one worry replaced another for everybody. Their fortunes might have taken a turn for the better with regular work for both Danny and Kitty, but there was little to spend the money on. The Government was requisitioning even the most basic things for the war effort, and there was a lack of everything – unless you knew the right people.

'I don't like to ask Aunty Doll.' Kitty looked thoughtful, not always a good sign, thought Danny. 'She goes to bed around ten if there's no sign of a raid.'

'I'm sure she won't mind this once – shall I go over and ask?' Danny hardly took his eyes off the paper.

'I'll go for a tanner, if you like?' Tommy said, hoping to get out of his sister's iron grip. 'It's no bother.'

'I bet it's not, you little twerp,' Danny said, getting up from the chair and folding his paper. Tucking it under his arm, he took his cap from the shelf in the alcove near the window and, placing it on his head, he sauntered down the long narrow lobby whistling 'Underneath the Arches', his favourite Flanagan and Allen tune.

He had already reached the ever-open front door when Tommy called mischievously, 'By the way, Sarah's not in. I saw her going out earlier.' He grinned when he heard Danny's footsteps returning up the clean but faded linoleum.

'And what makes you think that bothers me?' Danny asked, pushing his flat cap to the back of his thick, black wavy hair, his easy smile showing white straight teeth.

'I know you've got your eye on her. I've seen you looking every time she walks up the street.' Tommy's mischievous grin lit up his blue eyes. 'That's why you call into Aunty Doll's every chance you get.'

'You might just land yourself in trouble, spreading tales like that.' Danny was hoping to catch sight of Sarah before she started her Voluntary Aid Detachment work at the Royal Infirmary. She wasn't around so much as he would have liked. And, even though he threatened Tommy on a daily basis, his younger brother knew Danny would never lay a finger on him.

'What's it worth to keep me trap shut?' Tommy asked. Like his older brother, he was always on the lookout to earn a few coppers and had no intention of letting this prized opportunity go. 'If you give me a tanner I won't tell.'

'A tanner!' Danny's eyes widened. 'Do you know how long I've got to work to earn sixpence?' He was proud of the fact he had spare coppers to give Tommy in the middle of the week. It hadn't always been this way, especially when Dad was alive. Memories of the hungry thirties were still fresh in his mind. Danny rattled the change in his pockets, tormenting his younger brother. The war did have some good points. An eternal optimist, Danny always tried to see some good, no matter how bad the situation. He had taken a knock to his confidence when he had been refused for the Forces, but he had bounced back. Worse things happened at sea, he reasoned.

'Ahh, go on, Dan, mug me to a tanner.' Tommy's wheedling nearly always got him what he wanted. Their Danny, even though he would never admit it, was a soft touch, although Tommy was wise enough not to play on it.

'A thrupenny bit is all I've got – you won't get a penny more.' Danny brought a handful of loose coppers from the pocket of his heavy corduroy trousers and handed the little coin to his brother.

'I suppose that'll have to do.' Tommy, though careful not to sound eager, was satisfied. He only wanted three pence in the first place. And even though their Danny was generous to a fault, Tommy was surprised at the ease with which he got it.

'Here, you little Shylock.' Danny handed Tommy a twelve-sided copper coin. 'Here's your pound of flesh.' After Tommy's hospital scare last Christmas, Danny and Kitty didn't want him evacuated again. Not since he had walked all the way home from Southport and arrived half dead, then collapsed in the yard from diphtheria. Only the Good Lord knew how Tommy had managed the journey.

'I've got enough for a *Comic Cuts* and a *Dandy* – if they've got any in the shop.' Tommy laughed and ducked as Danny flicked the back of his hand towards his ear, deliberately missing; nobody ever laid a hand on Tommy in this house.

'Who's this Shylock, then?' Tommy asked, leaning on the doorframe while shoving the coin down one of his grey, concertinaed socks, knowing he had holes in the pocket of his knee-length woollen trousers due to carrying all the treasures their Kitty called rubbish, like his peashooter and his catapult, and odd bits of shrapnel, which were a bit of a curse because the sharp bits ripped your pockets.

'Shylock's a character in some posh play called *The Merchant of Venice* and was written by a bloke called William Shakespeare.' Danny spoke with some authority and Tommy was transfixed. He looked up to his older brother, who was dead clever. If Danny said something was right then Tommy believed him.

'If you ever go back to school – when the teachers come back from evacuation – you can tell them your big brother taught you that. Oh, and by the way, Shylock was a moneylender.' Danny looked very pleased with himself.

'Like you, Dan?' Tommy said innocently, knowing his brother loaned money to people in need – and he charged less interest than Mrs Kennedy. He was great, their Danny.

Kitty gave an exaggerated look of surprise that Tommy should know such things. Danny shook his head, laughing now and eager to change the subject. 'I read that in a magazine when I went to the doctor's about me chest.' He did not tell them he had been for one of his regular check-ups to see the heart doctor at the Royal Infirmary in town. Kitty had enough on her plate worrying about Tommy. However, Danny did have a few worries, too. Alfie Delaney was still poking around trying to get him to take the medical examinations for 'businessmen' who had the wherewithal but wanted to duck out of military service. Danny did not want to go anywhere near that caper. That was fraud and it was immoral. Danny believed in fighting for your country and not trying to dodge your duty when other men were dying for what they believed in.

Tommy knew school was never high on the list of family priorities when times were hard, their Kitty had told him often enough, not when a few earned coppers here and there were more important to their survival. Danny's ability to make money and the money that Jack gave them had seen them all through many hard times.

'Listen, Tom,' Danny said, pointing his finger in the little fella's direction, hardly able to suppress his amused grin, 'I know a lot of stuff, and I'll tell you this for nothing: I won't always be poor either. People will look up to me one day.'

'Just as long as it's not the bottom of your feet,' Kitty said, knowing their Danny was not averse to the odd not-strictly-legal skirmish.

'O ye of little faith . . .' Danny scoffed as he headed back towards the lobby.

'Does she have to stare at me like I've grown another head?' Charlie Kennedy sat in his usual seat at the table facing the bay window of number thirteen Sandy Avenue, so he could keep his eye on the long tree-lined thoroughfare. He didn't trust his mother to keep his address secret. If Rita turned up here it would not be good news.

He was addressing Elsie Lowe, landlady of the boarding house his mother owned, though this was something Winnie chose to keep to herself.

The younger woman, Elsie's constant companion, stared at him, her gaze steady and impenetrable. He wriggled under the doll-like stare. Charlie never used Ruby's name and acknowledged her even less. She was nothing to him. Elsie, on the other hand, was a good sport and far more accommodating in every way than Rita had ever been.

Charlie found it hard to decide how old Ruby was. She could be anywhere between fifteen and forty years old. She said little – answering any questions with just a nod or the shake of her head – unless the children spoke to her and then she was quite chatty.

'Ruby's not used to you, that's all.' Elsie, a well-preserved and attractive woman who was cagey about her own age, gave the young woman a wide, reassuring smile. 'She takes a while to get used to strangers. She'll come around, you'll see.' Ruby was not Elsie's daughter but the older woman had reared her from a baby.

No matter. Charlie's only concern was Rita; he didn't want her ever to find out this address or his whereabouts. He was doing everything he possibly could to dodge being called up for duty. He was thinking of writing to the authorities saying he was a conscientious objector and he expected to attend a tribunal or somesuch. He did not intend to be killed fighting.

If Rita knew where he was staying she would shop him as soon as possible. However, he had heard that if a woman had children under fourteen she was exempt from war work. Maybe the law was the same for the fathers. He was not going to go to the trouble of finding out. No point in stirring up questions for himself. To the neighbours he was in a reserved occupation, which could not be talked about – job done.

He had taken a transfer to the insurance office in Southport. They hadn't asked any questions; with the war, staff were thin on the ground and the insurance business was booming.

He didn't want Rita mooching around sticking her neb in and causing net curtains to flutter. That nosy old bat next door was always on the lookout for a bit of gossip, too. People like her looked innocent enough but who knew what they did with the information?

He did not miss Rita one bit – why should he when he had Elsie to keep his cockles warm?

The first couple of years with Rita had been good. Well, he hadn't known her sneaky ways then, had he? But Ma saw them straight away. *Watch her, she'll take you for every penny.*

He did watch her from then on and he did not like what he saw. Rita was too fond of nipping into her mother's next door. He'd hear them laughing over the wall and his blood would boil – sure they were laughing at him. His mother had been right all along when she said Rita was no good.

The children were settling in well. Well, Michael was. Megan would take a little longer. She still cried for her mother at night but taking a tough hand was the way to go. No sense in mollycoddling the children.

Rita had done too much of that already and spoiled them. He'd written to his mother and told her that he had enrolled them at the local school where there were other evacuated children and they were making friends. Perhaps he would – but not now, he didn't want any nosey parkers prying into his private affairs.

Yes, Charlie thought. This was going to work out just fine. He went back to watching the street and tried to ignore Ruby, still directing her inscrutable gaze in his direction.

'Roast beef?' Winnie Kennedy gave a false laugh, her voice overloud as Sarah Feeny walked into the corner shop. 'You'll be lucky, Vera! Don't you know there's a war on? We've not had roast beef in here for weeks . . .'

Sarah did not fail to notice Mrs Kennedy thrust something that looked suspiciously like a large joint of roast beef under the counter, and it was obvious by Vera Delaney's shifty appearance that they had been discussing something they did not want made public.

'Oh, hello, Sarah love, how's your mother?'

Nor did Sarah miss the warning sidelong glance Ma Kennedy gave Vera Delaney. It would be easy for Mrs Kennedy to store some choice cuts; she had a refrigerated cabinet out the back for ice cream and such – when you could buy ice cream, that was.

'Mam's fine, Mrs Kennedy. She's getting stuck into her salvage work as usual, helping those less fortunate, as you do.' Sarah gave Mrs Delaney a smile that did not quite reach her eyes. Nothing got past Vera in this street. She had her nostrils permanently flared, which gave her the disapproving appearance of a cartoon butler, and was into everybody's business yet nobody seemed to know what was going on behind her closed front door.

'How's poor Frank doing?' Mrs Kennedy's honeyed tones did nothing to assuage Sarah's suspicions. 'Has he got his new leg yet?'

Sarah could feel the hairs on the back of her neck rise. Her older brother would go mad if he heard anybody, especially Mrs Kennedy, referring to him as 'poor Frank'! Mrs Kennedy was one of the few people Sarah genuinely did not like, not because she had more faces than the town hall clock, but because she gave her older sister Rita a dog's life, and would no longer let her take advantage since Charlie took the kids to live in Southport.

'Any news of the kids?' Sarah asked boldly. 'Only, Mam was asking.' After all, they were Dolly's grand-children too.

'Charlie wrote saying that the kids are doing just fine, thank you very much.' Winnie Kennedy thought that Sarah Feeny was too cheeky for her own good. She had a defiant streak in her and the two of them had locked horns more than once. That Dolly Feeny would do well to keep more of an eye on her children, she thought. They were all a bit wild.

'So, Frank's home again, is he? Have they managed to find him a desk job somewhere, then?' Vera asked. Sarah knew she was not one for small talk – if Vera wanted to know something she just came right out and asked. However, Sarah was doing as the posters said and keeping her opinions to herself. Careless talk cost lives, and all that. She did not intend to put either of her brothers' lives in jeopardy for the sake of corner shop tittle-tattle.

'Frank wants to know if you've got any cigarettes in yet,' Sarah said, ignoring Vera's nosy questions, 'but I'll wait my turn. Mrs Delaney had not been served yet.' Sarah watched Vera's face flush with guilty colour, which undoubtedly confirmed her suspicions that she had walked in on an under-the-counter transaction. She wouldn't put anything past these two.

'Oh, I don't mind waiting.' Vera moved out of the way, allowing Sarah to get closer to the counter. 'You go ahead, love; anything for our brave fighters.' Then, lowering her voice, she said, 'Not like that Danny Callaghan over there.' She screwed her face in disgust as her eyes locked onto the chipped paint of the Callaghans' front door. 'You won't find him fighting for his country in a hurry.'

'And how's your Alfie, Mrs Delaney? Still doing his bit on the dock?' Sarah asked sarcastically, knowing that Alfie was as likely to sign up for duty as Hitler was to decide to give all this war lark in and keep pigeons instead. She wasn't having this old bat slagging off Danny Callaghan.

'He is doing a job as valuable as any in the Forces,' said Vera with a dismissive shrug of her shoulders.

'Danny works alongside, doesn't he?' Sarah said pointedly. 'So he's also doing a valuable job too, I would say. Didn't your husband get out of going to France in the last war?' Sarah knew Mam would skin her alive for talking to a neighbour like this, but she couldn't resist. Mrs Delaney was far too free with her opinions of others when she ignored her own family's shortcomings altogether.

'Mr Delaney died during the last war!'

Kicked by a dray horse when he was coming home drunk, I heard. Sarah did not voice her thoughts, knowing her mother would not stand for any of her offspring giving cheek to anyone.

'I'm sure he did his best,' she said. She did not know much about the Great War as Pop hardly mentioned it. However, she did know Danny had done everything in his power to enlist, but his enlarged heart meant he failed every time. He had exemption slips from every military office in Great Britain. Nobody would take him. He had no choice but to take a reserved occupation on the docks.

Sometimes she worried that the work was too strenuous for him, but she would never dare voice her concerns, knowing how proud Danny was. Like most men around here, being tough was a way of life, and to show weakness of any kind was unheard of.

Danny had sworn Sarah to secrecy so she kept quiet, no matter how much she wanted to tell the po-faced woman that Danny was worth ten of her son, a charge hand on the same dock. Sarah recalled the time Alfie Delaney told her he would turn conchie rather than fight. He would rather serve a prison sentence than risk his life for King and country. How

Sarah despised Mrs Delaney's cowardly upstart of a son.

'Tell Frank,' Mrs Kennedy's voice was low as she beckoned Sarah to come closer and, leaning across the counter, she winked her eye conspiratorially, 'I am taking delivery of Craven "A" cigarettes after the shop has shut. I'll pass a packet into him – personally.'

'That's good of you, Mrs Kennedy.' Fancy walking all that way, Sarah thought. It must be all of five yards from here to our front door.

'Don't give it another thought. It's my pleasure for a local hero.'

You don't say. The words floated through Sarah's head but the lack of expression on her face did not give her thoughts away. 'I'll tell him.'

With that, she left the two women to their jangling. No doubt calling poor Danny fit to burn. As she walked out of the shop, the sun in her eyes, she bumped right into him!

'Hello, Sar, where've you been then?' Danny's cheerful banter gave Sarah a little *frisson* of delight. She liked him. A lot. He was genuine. No matter what some people said. However, at twenty he was far too worldly wise to look at somebody like her. Danny had no shortage of female appreciation, especially Betty Parker, who was supposed to be Sarah's best friend and hung around their house every chance she got just so she could look out of their parlour window in case Danny should walk down the street. She was a right one, that Betty. She had no shame.

'I went to see if there were any cigs in the shop for

our Frank,' Sarah said as they headed to the Feenys' front door, which like most of the others in Empire Street, was usually open until late every night, even though there was a threat of a German invasion. People looked out for each other in this street, and there was always someone sitting on their step, like old Mrs Ashby, who was always ready for a natter, no matter what time of the day. She kept her eye to business, all right, although a proud and discreet woman, which was why Mam liked her and always made her a small pie or some potato cakes. Sarah and Danny waved and Mrs Ashby waved back and gave them a toothless smile.

'When did your Frank get home? I'll have to come across and see him later.'

'It's just a flying visit, to show the family his new leg . . . It's tin, you know.' Then, whispered: 'He's going back tomorrow night.'

'Has he got no cigs, then?' Danny asked. 'The navy are slipping if they're leaving their men without a smoke.' Before Sarah could tell him Frank had left his back at base, Danny took a squashed packet of five Woodbines out of his pocket. 'Here, give him these. They're a bit crumpled but they're fine. I can always get more later.'

'Are you sure?' Sarah asked, glad their Frank could have a smoke while he was listening to the wireless. The whole family liked to settle down for *ITMA* and listen to Tommy Handley's comic capers.

Then, but only ever after Mam had gone to bed, Pop would twiddle the wireless knob and he and

Frank would secretly tune in to Lord Haw-Haw. Mam said it was unpatriotic to listen to the Nazi propaganda, which frequently offered spurious details of raids. Nevertheless, among the ranting, sometimes the only details available from behind enemy lines were the ones given by the traitor, as everything was kept very hush-hush to protect British and Allied sailors. Pop liked to keep his ears open for news of any ships in the hostile North Atlantic where Eddy, serving in the Merchant Navy, was helping to bring much-needed food to England. Frank was interested to know what lies the enemy were spouting this time.

'Between you and me,' Danny said in a low whisper, looking around to make sure nobody could hear him, 'a consignment of Craven "A" came in from Canada this afternoon. They're like gold dust, but the shop will have some in tomorrow.'

'Mrs Snooty said she'll pass a packet in for our Frank after the shop is shut.'

'Did she now?' Danny said and, knowing he could trust Sarah to be discreet, he added, 'They're not going off the dock until tomorrow morning.' He knew that if Mrs Kennedy was getting her order tonight she was not going to get them by legal means. He shook his head. The crafty old cow . . . 'Looking down her nose at everybody else while she is creaming off the top.' Well, that was handy to know.

'Are you coming in for a cup of tea?' Sarah asked. She liked being around Danny. He made her feel . . . safe.

'I'll have to get going,' Danny answered. 'I'm on

the twilight shift on the dock tonight but tell Frank I'll see him before he goes.'

He had turned to walk away when Sarah said, 'Were you going to our house for anything in particular?' She smiled when Danny smacked his forehead with the palm of his hand.

'I'd forget my head if it wasn't stuck on,' he laughed. 'Our Kitty wanted to know if your mam would look out for Tommy until she gets home from the NAAFI? There's a dance on and she's got to work an evening shift.'

'Send him over,' Sarah said. 'He can help me sort the bag of woollens I collected this morning with Mam, and I've got some pullovers that need unravelling.'

'He'll love that, I'm sure,' Danny laughed, 'but only if it means he can listen to your wireless.' With that, he turned and crossed back over the cobbled road, wondering if he could get his hands on a wireless set, now they were a bit flush, like. It would be Kitty's twenty-second birthday in a few weeks; Danny would love to surprise her, and to surprise her with a wireless would be the gear . . .

Sarah was a lovely girl. The thought popped into his head without invitation, as it did a lot of late.

'Was there any word from Charlie this morning?' Rita asked her mother-in-law as she saw her place a small pile of post, retrieved from the doormat, on the counter. Rita had just returned from night duty at the hospital.

'Not this morning,' Ma Kennedy replied airily. 'I'm sure he has got more on his mind than writing to us every five minutes. He has got a job and two children to look after, you know.'

Rita eyed the woman coldly. 'He should have given us his address by now. He can't just up and disappear with two kids in tow!'

'Of course he hasn't just upped and disappeared,' Mrs Kennedy said. 'I've never heard anything so ridiculous in my life.' Her protestations were determined. 'He has written already and said that they are all fine. He must have forgotten to put his address on, that's all. He said that he wants the children to settle in for now and not have any upsetting emotional visits.' She seemed overly bright to Rita this morning, even a bit giddy. 'You listen to far too many of those daft dramas on the wireless. Then you get all worked up over nothing.'

Rita gave her mother-in-law a sideways glance but kept quiet. Ma Kennedy claimed she had given Charlie the only copy of this friend Elsie Lowe's address that she had, and as she wasn't in touch regularly she couldn't remember it at all. Surely if Mrs Kennedy really did not know the address where her son had gone with the children she would move heaven and earth to find out . . . It had been nearly two weeks and that was all they had heard. Every morning Rita hovered around the door waiting for some news, or hurried home from the hospital after her shift in a state of high anticipation, only to be bitterly disappointed when she got the news from Mrs Kennedy that there was no news today.

Watching the older woman fiddle with the morning

newspapers stacked on the counter, unfolding the top one, smoothing it down and then carefully joining the edges together, Rita knew it was a nervous gesture, a sure sign that Winnie had something to hide.

What a fool she had been to think Mrs Kennedy, as a mother, would sympathise with her plight. However, looking at her now, and reading the tell-tail signs that the Kennedys unconsciously displayed when they were trying to hide something, Rita suspected the crafty old woman did know something; Charlie would not go one day without talking to his mother, let alone two weeks. They were in cahoots, obviously.

Rita was trying not to panic. Charlie had been in touch at least and there was no reason to think that the children were in any danger.

'Put those out for the paper man, would you?' Ma Kennedy pointed at the pile of newsprint and then headed for the back room and her usual spot by the window.

'What did your last slave die of?' Rita muttered, but she was tired and in no mood for an argument this morning. She went to pick up the bundle of papers and before she did so, she idly looked at the pile of letters that the postman had brought. There were the usual bills and these days there was often some official pronouncement about saving water or paper, or important information about more essentials that were being rationed. Today there was also something different. It was an official-looking letter addressed to Charlie. Rita turned the brown paper envelope over to see if she could see where it had come from and gasped when she saw the name of the sender was the War Office.

So, she thought, Charlie's papers had finally come. There could be no escape for him now.

CHAPTER SIX

'Rita! Cooee!'

Rita, deep in thought as she entered Empire Street, turned to see Kitty Callaghan beckoning her across the road. Rita smiled; she had not spoken to Kitty for ages as their shifts were often at different times, and even though they lived almost opposite each other they never seemed to have time for a catch-up these days.

Kitty looked a little perturbed. 'There's something I've got to show you. Have you got a minute?' She led Rita up the narrow passageway to her kitchen.

It all seemed very cloak-and-dagger, Rita thought, intrigued. Entering the warm, cosy kitchen where the clean smell of Mansion polish mixed with the delicious aroma of a stew bubbling away on the stove, Rita felt suddenly hungry.

'Stay and have a bite to eat,' Kitty said, and she invited Rita to sit at the table before opening the sideboard drawer and taking out an air-mail envelope.

'This came for you yesterday.' Kitty's face was

suddenly infused with a pink blush. 'I didn't want to take it over the road in case Ma Long-nose saw it and started asking awkward questions. You can do without that kind of thing when you're busy.'

'A letter? For me?' Rita asked, then recognised the careful, copperplate handwriting on the envelope. Jack had sent it. He had sent a few letters to the hospital and she had answered them. They were just friendly and informative, but reading between the lines Rita could tell that Jack still thought a lot of her and she also thought much of him.

A thrill ran right through her. She always looked forward to hearing from Jack. He told her of the long periods of boredom punctuated with bursts of frightening activity. To curb the tedium, he read. Rita knew now that Jack had learned to read and write only while serving his apprenticeship in Belfast. He had told her that he could never have read the letter that she sent to him. The one asking him to come home . . . the one before she made a decision that would break both of their hearts.

He was now an avid reader and he devoured books of every kind. The last he had read was an Agatha Christie murder mystery, and Rita had hurried to Bootle library to get herself a copy so they could discuss it the next time they saw each other. Rita crushed down the unspoken fear that they all had. The fear about the men they cared for and the danger that they faced in this blasted war. If anything should happen to Jack . . . He also told her what films he had managed to see when he was not on duty and when Rita saw the Marx Brothers in *Duck Soup* she knew she was laughing at the same things Jack had laughed along with. She tried to push away the thought that all of this was a fantasy; that the closeness she was trying to create was one that could never happen between them in real life – all it could ever be was a dream . . .

Kitty hoped her expression gave nothing away, unaware that the way she was twisting the dishcloth in her hands showed her concern.

'It's not what it seems,' Rita spluttered, putting her hand on Kitty's arm.

'I don't think anything, Rita. We've know each other for ever,' Kitty said quietly. 'We've been friends since we were kids. You're the closest person I've had to a sister, my best friend; I could tell you anything and you'd keep it secret until your dying day.'

Kitty was quiet for a moment; Rita didn't need to question her loyalty. Rita would take it for granted the letter would remain a secret.

She knew their Jack had eyes for no woman but Rita. He never had. She hoped he would meet a nice girl and settle down but he never had done. Kitty hoped they knew what they were doing. People around these parts could be brutal when it suited them, even though she knew that Jack and Rita were both the souls of propriety.

'They are just letters, Kitty,' Rita said, wanting to reassure her friend, though Jack's being far away and in danger was tearing her apart. He could be killed at any time and she had never even told him how she felt. Not since they were young. Now she knew she loved him with every beat of her heart and she always would. 'We keep each other's spirits up. I know that you worry for us, but we're just being good friends to each other.'

'He's never got over you,' Kitty said, 'and it took a long time for him to stop talking about you. Little things like, "Rita likes those" or "Rita used to say that too" told me that he still thought about you every day.'

'Did he?' Rita had tears in her eyes now. Cruel fate had conspired to keep her and Jack apart. When he went to Belfast and she thought he wasn't coming back, she was scared and confused. She had made a rash decision and a life with Charlie Kennedy was the price she must pay. How could she have been so immature, so stupid to think she could make a life with someone she didn't really love, and who had never, ever loved her?

'It's none of my business, Reet, but . . . I know that you and Jack will always do what is right.' Kitty used the name that only Jack ever called her by and Rita's relief washed over her when she realised Kitty was saying this with the best of intentions. This conversation must be embarrassing Kitty. She had never stepped out of line in her life. Her social standing was impeccable. To agree to say nothing about the letter was tantamount to agreeing with what they were doing. After all, Jack was a single man.

'I'm a married woman with two children,' Rita whispered. 'Nothing can come of a relationship like ours – except heartache, is that what you're thinking, Kit?'

'No, I'm not thinking anything of the sort,' Kitty answered, pulling tiny pieces of dry bread from the piece she had sliced earlier and dropping it into her stew while Rita's remained untouched. 'I'm glad you and Jack write to each other, there's no law against it . . .'

'Say what you need to say, Kitty. I'm a grown up.'

'I just don't want you or Jack to be hurt any more. Especially Jack, Rita. He needs to make a life for himself. He's already made so many sacrifices for me and Danny and Tommy.' Kitty shook her head. 'But, I won't say a word to anybody, you know that.'

Rita nodded. Kitty was right. Jack deserved to find someone and have a wife and family of his own. She was selfish to harbour any feelings for him. Rita vowed then that she would write to Jack once more, but this time she'd tell him they must stop. It wouldn't be right to continue. While she was Charlie's wife, she must be above criticism. For the sake of the family and for her children.

Kitty gave Rita a gentle smile and then nodded to Rita's bowl. 'It's getting cold . . .'

Rita had a job to stop tears welling up as she rose from the table and hugged her friend as she would hug her own sisters. Kitty was such a good and loyal friend.

Kitty saw the emotion in her friend's face. 'You soppy ha'p'orth,' she smiled as tears formed in her own eyes. Life was so rotten now that it could not be wrong to find consolation anywhere you could get it.

'Why don't you stay and put your feet up for a cuppa before you go back? I'll put the kettle on and you can share Jack's news,' Kitty said, lifting the teapot and making her way out of the kitchen. Rita turned the regulation envelope over in her hands, her fingers itching to tear it open. Yet the bittersweet anticipation stilled her hands.

She was too overwhelmed to reply.

She skimmed the letter quickly, absorbing it only lightly, then went back to the beginning and started again, to savour his words. She imagined his voice in her head as she read. The words were pure Jack: funny, insubordinate when he talked about his superiors, jokey when talking of the mess pranks. They sounded more like naughty twelve-year-olds than Britain's proud fighting men. However, his true nature came to the fore when he told her that while on shore leave, he and his 'oppo' (his opposite number) had found a kitten nestling next to its dead mother:

He is as black as the hobs of hell, Reet, I couldn't just leave him there, and the poor thing would have died before the night was out. So I gently picked him up and snook him into my duffel coat and took him on board the ship. I put him in a cardboard box under my bunk – he was comfy as anything, but the lads said he cried so much when I was out with the squad that I had to take him up with me inside my flying jacket – he loved it – so I've called him Winco – he's my good luck cat.

Rita smiled as she read the letter; trust Jack to be so sensitive and so thoughtful. The war had not changed him – thank goodness.

'Do you want me to mind the letter for you?' Kitty asked.

Rita knew that when Kitty said 'mind' the letter she meant 'hide'.

'No, thanks, Kit; I don't want you to get into bother for me. But thank you for being so understanding.'

'If there are any more I'll keep them here for you and I'll let you know as soon as they arrive.'

'You're a pal, Kit.'

Rita hugged her friend again and her throat tightened when Kitty said, 'I wish our Jack had seen sense all those years ago and married you instead of going to Belfast.'

So do I, Kit, thought Rita, so do I.

Petty Officer Jack Callaghan took Rita's letter out of the envelope and carefully unfolded it against the stiff breeze blowing onto the flight deck of HMS *Distinguished*.

An aviator in the Fleet Air Arm, after intensive shore-based training and successfully qualifying, he piloted a Swordfish biplane.

The aircraft carrier had been reprieved from the ships' graveyard at the eleventh hour, and was now heading for home from European waters to replenish essentials.

Jack adored his job and loved nothing better than flying his steadfast, if somewhat uncomfortable aircraft, commonly known as the 'string bag' by the flight crew, to carry out night attacks. The excitement of the chase whilst serving in almost every theatre of war gave Jack little time to worry about what was going on at home, although word was coming through that Merseyside was taking a right hammering.

The reply from Rita was dated almost a month ago! However, airmail was not a priority right now, even if it did boost morale. Jack's eyes flew over Rita's carefully penned words, knowing it would have taken a lot of courage to reply.

Rita was a good letter writer and Jack was looking forward to what she had to say. Smiling, he noted that she did not miss anything out, giving him all the local gossip, even telling him things that would not usually interest him – however, even the most trivial news was now of the utmost importance. He needed something to focus on, something to keep his mind occupied when he was off duty. Winco the cat was quite big now and had proved himself adept at keeping the ship's rat population in check as well as boosting morale. Jack knew that the officers were turning a blind eye, but he thought that he would probably have to find a new home for the cat when he finally reached land – if he ever reached land. The cat was a good distraction, and instead of the never-ending seascape of grey, Jack would dream of Rita, beautiful, unreachable, untouchable Rita. However, if every day were like today, it would all be worth the long agonising wait to go home.

Having been stuck right in the thick of a lightning raid over Italy, he hadn't had time to sit and read Rita's letter in its entirety – he knew all of the others off by heart now. Thankfully, every plane had made it back, including his own and there was now time to catch up with Rita's news.

The post had arrived on board this afternoon and everybody was eager to lose themselves in somebody else's life. The place was silent save for the sound of the sea and a few eager matelots who had come on deck wanting to know where their post was. The best days were those when the mail drop came. The whole of the ship's company got excited as the crew scrambled around the 'postie'.

'No post for you today, Atkins.'

Jack looked up to see Able Seaman Atkins' face cloud over. It was the worst bit of news they could get after being starved of familiar news, not knowing when the next mail drop would arrive. Atkins' nonchalant shrug belied the disappointment he must have felt.

'Got no mates, son?' the straight-faced postie asked. 'Never mind, yours might be in with the next drop,' he quipped, 'although someone more popular is bound to let you read one of theirs.' He continued giving out the mail and pretended he did not see the matelot offer a surreptitious two-fingered salute. However, Jack knew nobody liked to see one of the men missing their letters from home.

'Here, have a read of this.' He leaned over and passed Atkins one of his younger brother Danny's letters. It did not have news about personal stuff or family stuff – Danny's never did – but it did keep him up to date about any football matches played back home or other trivialities that were just the thing to keep you sane in this vast wilderness of water.

'Cheers, mate,' said Atkins with a grin. It did not matter that the letter was not for him as long as he had something from home, no matter how small. Jack knew it would get him through today, and smiled as his mate settled down to read the letter.

'You would do the same for me,' Jack said as the evening sun, still warm on his already tanned, taut body, began to dip a little. He shifted, relaxed now albeit alert, in second-degree readiness and available for call to action stations if there were signals of enemy ships, or aircraft sighted . . .

Jack started Rita's letter again from the beginning and smiled as she recounted stories about people and places who were so familiar to him but who now seemed like a world away. Rita tried hard not to mention Charlie, he knew, but in her letter she told him that Charlie had taken the children away to the seaside to keep them safe. Reading between the lines, Jack sensed an unspoken anxiety in Rita's tone. What could Charlie be up to now? Charlie Kennedy was a coward in Jack's eyes, a jumped-up prig who had used his mother's money to get all he ever wanted. Jack thrilled to the fact that Kennedy no longer lived with Rita. That was, at least, something to be thankful for in this damned war, he thought.

He reached the last page of Rita's letter and read her words.

This will be the last letter from me for a while, Jack. I think we both know this is for the best. We're not our own people and don't have the freedom to do as we wish. Once you asked me to tell you what was really in that letter that I wrote to you in Belfast. I hope one day we'll be able to sit down as friends and tell each other all the things that are in our hearts, but that time isn't now. Take good care, Jack. I think of you always and may God go with you.
Rita

A short time later as the sun dipped behind the clouds and the crew of *Distinguished* retired to the bar on the mess deck, Jack continued in his solitude. With only his thoughts for company, he gazed up to the stone-coloured streaks that whipped across the vast cerulean sky, recalling the familiar landscapes Rita's letter had evoked.

To the right alehouses on every corner of the back-to-back, soot-covered terraced streets that ribbed the backbone of the dock road. To the left the docks, Canada, Brocklebank, Langton, Alexandra, Gladstone . . . Then on to Seaforth Sands, which contrasted with the bleak, titanic warehouses and timber yards; forbidden playgrounds for him and his brothers . . . His brothers . . . What was to become of his brothers? Jack shivered now, recalling the smoke-filled consumptive air from many chimneys, heavy with the tang of lumber from lands across the sea.

But his thoughts, as usual, turned back to Rita. The girl he adored with every beat of his heart. Jack bitterly regretted going to Belfast to finish his training when he was young and even more headstrong than he was today. If it had not been for the argument with his father, he would have . . . Or would he – have stayed put? Nevertheless, he wished he could have written to Rita to explain. But he couldn't, for the simple fact he had never learned how to write and the shame he had felt then was still powerful now.

Every time he laid eyes on her, Jack knew he had made the biggest mistake of his life; to see her and not be able to share the things they once shared was torture. He had nobody to blame but himself, he realised. Although Jack knew that after his hasty departure, Kennedy made it his business to jump in and steal Rita from him . . .

Jack, lying on the flight deck, shifted onto his back, unable to get comfortable. There was no point in going over it all again for the umpteenth time. Nothing was going to change the facts.

The desperate need to go out and earn money to keep body and soul together when his father could not or would not work meant Jack had to start earning from an early age. He was not much of a scholar back then and if schooling was a luxury his family could not afford, it had suited him then to be earning rather than learning.

His enquiring mind enabled him to better himself

at an age when he was ready to learn. His determination to complete an apprenticeship, with the help of Bob, a patient foreman, who had taught Jack to read and write properly, allowed him to be what he was today. A quick learner through necessity, he had cruised through his examinations.

If only bearing his soul to Rita had been as easy, he thought, things could have been so different. What a fool he had been to think she would always be there waiting for him.

If only he had persuaded her that he was doing it all for her. Jack did not want her to work her fingers to the bone and die of exhaustion in childbirth like his poor beloved mam.

Fifteen when his mam died, Jack was a lad forced to work to keep a family from the poor house. His father wallowed in self-pity until the day he died last year. And although Jack did not begrudge one minute of taking evening jobs to keep his siblings fed and clothed, he hated the idea his old man spent much of his hard-earned money down the alehouse.

That last night in Empire Street, he had told Rita he had to go away. He did not tell her he was squirrelling away a few coppers here and there so he could buy her a ring. Maybe he should. It was meant to be a surprise . . . He never could abide surprises now.

Always an important part of his life, he was thrilled when Rita became a probationary nurse at the local hospital. Although earning a pittance while they were training, they could not resist the lure of their emotions; both wanting more than just a kiss and

cuddle. Jack's dream was making Rita his wife –
alongside him for the rest of his life.

We are too young, she said, and he agreed. Get
some training, Jack, she said, and he agreed. We have
our whole lives ahead of us, she said.

But he would never let Rita down, he would always
be there for her and he'd never give up. If there was
a God, and Jack truly believed there was, then Charlie
Kennedy would get what he deserved one day. In the
meantime, Jack resolved to continue writing to Rita.
He would not lose what little he had of her.

His eyelids grew heavy now in the shade of the
dipping sun, casting rays of gold and blushing pink
and palest lavender over the water. Jack could feel
the cares of the day seep from him . . . The afternoon
had been particularly busy.

Having been at sea for so long, Jack was counting
the days until he was home. Some of the others were
off duty and, relaxing as they called it, were doing
laps of the 850-foot flight deck. However, Jack knew
he did not need strenuous drill, not after completing
so many missions. All he needed was a bit of shut-eye
and oblivion. Being a light sleeper, he knew that was
impossible as the ship's Tannoy system would keep
him informed especially if anything exciting should
happen . . .

The gentle call of a woman's voice stirred him from
his slumber: 'Jack! Come on, son, you will be late.'
His mother's gentle Irish lilt, so clear, was surely not
a trick of his imagination. He was not dreaming, he
could not be, he felt fully conscious now.

'I'm awake, Ma,' he murmured, opening bleary eyes.

He was not surprised, or even startled, when he saw his mother standing there in front of him on the flight deck. Her beautiful dark hair, tied in the usual knot at the nape of her neck. Her hands on her hips. However, the beautiful almost iridescent blue of her eyes softened when she gazed at him. Giving a half-laugh, he raised a submissive hand.

'All right, Ma, you caught me.' Yawning now, he stretched and shivered, surprised to see the sun had gone down. He had no idea what time it was. A stiff breeze sailed over the flight deck rail.

'I'll just go and get a gansy, Ma.' Jack turned towards his quarters. 'A chap needs a woolly pullover when the sun goes down.' Turning back now to return her loving smile . . . he was sorely disap-pointed when his mother was no longer there. The silver moon dipped behind a thick cloud, and Jack suddenly felt so very much alone.

A shudder rippled through him now and every hair on his body stood on end when he realised the Swordfish biplanes were going through their final check before the night flights. He had heard many tales of servicemen seeing a departed loved one before something huge and exciting was about to take place, but he had never believed it until now.

Jack was not afraid. In fact, after 'seeing' his mother he was filled with renewed courage. The feeling he had now was different from anything he had known for many a long year. It was something akin to satis-faction; contentment he had not known since he was a young child at his mother's knee. His wish had finally come true. His mam had come to see him. He had known, absolutely and without a doubt, that she would one day. Rubbing his eyes now, Jack berated himself for falling asleep. Had he stayed awake he would have seen her sooner.

The moon had disappeared completely now and the ship was plunged into inky blackness so dense he could reach out and touch it. Jack did not know how long his mother had been calling him. However, one thing he did know . . . There was the unmistakable drone of a squadron of Stuka dive-bombers heading this way.

'What do they expect?' The twenty-two-year-old German officer struggled to sit up in the hospital bed and, meticulously straightening his striped pyjama top, managed, with much difficulty, to raise himself against his pillows to await his evening meal. 'Liverpool and Birkenhead is a prize,' he shrugged. 'Being the biggest west coast port it is not an easy target to miss.'

'I beg your pardon!' Rita could feel her temper rising. 'How dare you say that when we have given you every courtesy – and saved your life?' She was one of only two nurses allowed to minister care to Luftwaffe bomber pilot Kurt Eichmann.

'But not my leg,' he said drily, gazing at the space where his leg, amputated from the thigh, should have been. His leg had been badly injured in the crash of his Heinkel.

'I do not wish to be rude.' He spoke in such a

...ract way that Rita could not help but stop ...t she was doing to listen. 'Actually, the defences around Liverpool are very strong – but Merseyside is a big objective – it is very easy to locate.'

He was young and far from home, and in a rare moment of weakness, Rita remembered, Jack had trained to do exactly the same thing.

He leaned forward and began speaking in a low, barely audible voice, as if he was talking to somebody else, and she wondered if he was hallucinating – he had gone through a very big operation and the doctors had struggled to keep him alive.

'I put my plane into a dive at 12,000 feet and was hurtling towards the docks at 550 miles per hour . . . I knew the G-force would cause me to black out just as I released the bombs . . . When I regained consciousness I turned the bomber inland away from the illuminating fires of the city, to the sanctuary of darkness and home . . .' The young flight lieutenant had tears in his eyes now and he slumped back against the pillows as if the effort was too much. 'I felt so ashamed . . . It was not what I wanted when I trained to be a pilot . . . What good will these wars do?'

He turned his fevered head and looked towards the narrow window and out above the river, to the blue cloudless sky. Rita suspected he was not even aware she was in the room now. Taking the thermometer, she shook it before popping it into his mouth. As she anticipated, he had a temperature of one hundred and three. His forehead felt clammy to her touch.

'I'll get the doctor to come and have a look at

you,' Rita said, suspecting the infection from his amputated leg was beginning to take hold. Doctors had fought a long battle to try to get the infection under control but it appeared to be returning. She looked at him differently now. He was right. The detention of this young German brought home to her the hostility and the futility of war in the last few weeks. She put her hand under his head and raised him up, and then lifting a glass to his lips, she offered him sips of water.

'Is that better?' Rita asked, knowing the water would wet his parched lips, at least, but she doubted it would come anywhere near lowering his extremely high fever.

'*Danke sehr,*' he gratefully thanked Rita before flopping back on his pillow, exhausted now. His hand folded around a piece of card and Rita was obliged to ask what it was.

'Would you like to see it?' he said in a weak, almost whispery voice before holding out a small, sepia photograph of a smiling, pretty girl who looked not much older than Rita's sister Sarah.

'Is she your girl?' Rita asked. For the first six weeks after his arrival the junior hospital staff had been warned by Matron not to speak to him, but Rita had exchanged the odd word or two at first. She would hate to think her own brothers would be mistreated if they were captured. She was here to make people feel better.

'She is my wife,' said Hauptmann Eichmann as the ghost of a smile played about his lips. He looked so

...ugh he had never mentioned his wife before. ...s expecting our child – in time for Christmas!'

'That's something to look forward to.' Rita kept the conversation as normal as possible, knowing he was gravely ill now. She handed back the small photograph. 'What are you hoping for?'

'I am supposed to say a blond-haired, blue-eyed boy, am I not?' Eichmann gave a weak, cynical half-laugh. 'To perpetuate the Führer's vision of an Aryan race.' He slowly moved his head from side to side, too weak to shake it. 'In truth, I want a dark-haired daughter . . . as sweet and beautiful as her mother.'

'I hope you get your wish,' Rita said, knowing it would be a long time before he saw either his wife or his child. From here, he would be taken to the prisoner of war camp up at Ormskirk, or maybe out Cheshire way.

The doctor came to give him something stronger for the pain, and Rita could see that all he wanted to do now was sleep.

'I'm off duty in five minutes so I'll leave you with Nurse Kerrigan.'

Turning to Maeve, her fiery-haired friend who, as it turned out, was a cousin of Sid, Nancy's prisoner-of-war husband, Rita said in a low voice, 'Be gentle with him. He's just a kid.'

'Aye,' said Maeve in her down-to-earth Irish lilt, so like Dolly's, 'a kid who could knock the stuffing out of all of us! Let's hope Sid is being as well looked after,' she added and Rita nodded.

*　　*　　*

When Rita returned to work the following morning, she was surprised to see the young German's bed was empty.

'Have they moved him to the POW camp already?' she asked Maeve.

'There was nothing anybody could do,' said Maeve in a low voice. 'He was doing all right when I first checked on him – he even said good night – but when I went to check on him an hour or so later, he had died in his sleep.'

'Oh, no!' Rita's hands flew to her lips. 'He was only a lad!' She gazed at the bare mattress where an inexperienced young man had spent his last weeks, alone. Silently, she railed against the war that meant another generation of young men would lose their lives. Had they learned nothing from the last war, when a whole generation of slaughtered young men were now just a cherished memory?

As she turned to leave the small, austere room, Rita spotted something under the slim iron bed. She bent to pick it up. It was the photograph of Hauptmann Eichmann's young wife, who soon was to be given the most devastating news of her life.

For just a moment, Jack heard nothing, and then the call came over the Tannoy. The fleet was under attack! All the guns of the convoy had now opened fire and were giving the Stuka bombers everything they could. Immediately the ship was locked down. They were at action stations.

As Jack ran to grab his parachute and scramble for

action, something hit the ship aft. In moments the hangar was on fire, the noise was deafening. Standing in the centre of the burning hangar Jack noticed Atkins coming down from the flight deck; his rubber suit was full of holes and there was blood leaking from every one of them.

'Let's get him down to the casualty station!' Jack roared over the sound of gunfire and crackling flames, as he headed straight for Atkins and threw him over his shoulder. In no time, he had his pal below deck and on the operating table, although he did not hang around long enough to see what the surgeons were busy doing as the ship rolled and swayed. With adrenalin pumping through his veins, Jack raced towards the flight deck and his beloved biplane; he thought he was ready for anything now! What he wasn't ready for was a sudden almighty flash as a bomb pierced the deck and exploded.

CHAPTER SEVEN

'Hello, Kit.' Frank Feeny gave Kitty a tight smile when he entered the warm, smoke-filled NAAFI canteen with his father. Looking around, he noticed there was a pair of seats on the far wall by the steamed-up window. Pop hurried over to claim them before somebody else did. Frank sighed; all he wanted was a pack of cigs and a box of matches.

His heart lurched when Kitty looked up from pouring tea at the counter, a surprised expression on her beautiful face. She hadn't expected him to walk in here today. He was passing through Liverpool to pick up top secret files from Derby House, knowing the next important phase of the war was to be directed from the Combined Operations bunker, focusing on the area of the North Atlantic known as the Western Approaches.

'It's great to see you, Frank.' Kitty, feeling a bit awkward, didn't mention the walking sticks he used to help him manoeuvre on his new leg. She wasn't sure she ought to.

'On your birthday too!' Rene, Kitty's high-spirited deputy manager, gave an indiscreet wink of her eye as Frank watched Kitty's beautiful face flush bright pink.

'Happy birthday, Kit.' His voice was just perceptible now, embarrassed that he didn't even have a card to give her. If he'd had two good legs, he would have kicked himself.

Kitty felt her elated heart swell so much it almost took her breath away to see Frank so mobile. He might still need the help of two sticks, but he was standing and that was marvellous. Better still, he had come here to show her! This was the best birthday present she could wish for.

'You look fantastic!' Kitty laughed and, throwing caution to the wind, nodded to his new leg. 'You haven't lost that cocky swagger either!' There was no mistaking the fact that Frank had had a rough time of it, but she was sure he did not want to dwell on that. How she longed to run out to him and throw her arms around him. When they were younger, she would have done just that, not giving the friendly gesture a second thought, but it wasn't proper now she was older, somehow, and Frank was more distant since he'd been injured.

'It's just a flying – or should I say hopping – visit, Kit,' Frank said, leaning on one of his two sticks. He laughed, but Kitty noticed this wasn't his former care-free laughter; it seemed forced. Nevertheless she joined in, glad to see him no matter what.

There was a moment's silence and Frank felt

awkward, wishing Pop had not persuaded him to come into the NAAFI canteen and then disappeared to the table near the window. Frank had said he needed a pack of cigarettes at the little kiosk on the corner. However, Pop wouldn't hear of it; 'No, lad,' he'd said. 'Might as well go and see Kitty. She'll be made up to see you, and we can get ourselves a cup of tea and summat to eat while we're at it.'

Frank did not want Kitty to be 'made up'. Her feelings were likely to be misplaced pity, not the easy-going friendship they had once shared. What else could she possibly feel for a man who had half a leg? Not even her usual welcoming demeanour could force him to be as natural with her as he used to be.

'There's a dance on tonight, Frank,' Kitty said as she spooned another helping of tea into the huge teapot and gave it a quick stir with a tablespoon. 'You remember when you danced me around the street that time . . . ?' She bit her lip. How could she say such a stupid thing? Frank must think her an idiot with pease pudding for brains. How could he think about dancing now with only one leg? She blushed and fell silent.

Frank shuffled awkwardly. He didn't want to think back to those days now. That part of his life was over. Gone. Never to be revisited. Kitty had a new life now; she was running this place and making a great job of it, he'd heard.

Even though Kitty was mortified she was still over-awed by the sight of Frank. He was so handsome and his presence brightened the grey, murky afternoon no end. It was as if the sun itself had walked into the dingy canteen and shone its light for everyone to see. He was smartly dressed in his naval uniform, and Kitty was proud that she knew him. She had wished they could be more than friends, but Frank had other ideas, seeing her first as a neighbour and a friend of the family.

'I'll bring your tea over to your table,' Kitty said. She'd been hoping he would like to stay and talk but there was a queue forming behind him.

Frank's expression changed.

'I can manage,' he said. 'After all, it's only a tray.'

'Of course it is.' Straight away Kitty remembered the strong determination that prevented Frank being treated like an invalid.

Rita had told her that in the days before he was transferred to his rehabilitation centre down south he would visit the other patients in the wards, especially the little 'uns and try to keep their spirits up. It was in his nature to help others and Kitty knew without being told that Frank would hate to be pitied. She didn't pity him; she just wanted to tell him how much she admired him and, as he walked on that tin leg, how much she longed to walk by his side. She wasn't really surprised to see him out and about – the fussing around that he would get from Dolly and his sisters at home wouldn't suit him: all that fetching, carrying and trying to turn him into something useless.

'It looks like it's going to rain.' Frank knew his voice had been sharper than he intended and tried to make amends. What was he thinking? This was his beautiful Kitty, the girl he had known his entire life, whom he had hoped . . . Stop it, Frank, he checked himself.

'Anyway,' he said, trying to lighten the mood, 'if we get a bit of fog tonight I'd better watch out for Pop. He could take a wrong turn outside the Sailor's Rest and end up in the Mersey!'

The two of them laughed conspiratorially as they looked over at Pop, chatting away to the servicemen at the neighbouring table. For a moment it was as if the last year had never happened and the two of them were at ease again. Frank's eyes twinkled. This was the man Kitty remembered, the one she knew so well. Those smiling eyes – such a huge indicator of his personality – convinced Kitty that there was no man alive as brave as Frank Feeny. He was one of life's survivors, the man you would look for in a crisis. Before he came home injured he was the one who would always be her mainstay, her shoulder to cry on. And Kitty believed that wonderful man was still in there somewhere.

'If it's foggy,' Kitty said, 'Jerry won't come over and try to wipe us off the face of the earth like he tried the other week.'

'I'll have a word.' Frank looked up in the direction of heaven, past the cracked ceiling.

'Oh, go on now, Big Licks!' Kitty joked. 'You got friends in high places when they fitted a new leg, is that it?' She realised pity did not work with Frank; he was much more comfortable with cheeky banter.

'Don't knock me new leg, Kit,' Frank warned, relaxing now. 'It makes a hollow noise.'

She was amazed when Frank bent over and rapped his knuckles against his leg. Then, cool as you like he said, 'I might even show you it one day.'

A year ago Kitty might have blushed and be stuck for words, but working in the NAAFI canteen had given her the confidence to hold her own with the cheekiest of sailors. 'Don't be coming in here making promises you won't keep,' she laughed.

Frank returned her impish grin. He liked this new side to Kitty; it suited her.

Kitty put a pot of tea and two tea cups and saucers on a tray. 'Here, I can manage the tea,' Frank said, but there was an awkward pause as he eyed the tray and realised that it could be a step too far to manage both of his sticks as well.

Kitty quickly took in the situation and came to the rescue. 'I always take the tray to the table of my favourite customers – it's the only exercise I get. I'll bring the food over when it's ready.' She nodded towards the table where Pop was sitting.

But this time it was Frank's turn to blush. This was just the sort of thing that he dreaded and he was damned if he was going to be treated like a cripple, no matter how good Kitty's intentions.

'Like I said,' he insisted through gritted teeth, 'I can manage.'

Straightening his back Frank took one of his sticks and hung it on his left arm while propping his other stick up on the counter. He was usually quite able to stand unaided for a short time. Then he lifted the tea tray with his right hand and retrieved his stick with the other. Then slowly and painfully – his knee was throbbing now where his tin leg rubbed against the thin flesh – he wound his way through the throng as people pulled their chairs closer to their tables to allow him through. A hush almost descended across the room as his fellow servicemen watched him progress towards the table where his father sat, each with his heart in his mouth lest this crippled man should fall or miss his step. In each man's head was the thought: *there but for the grace of God go I* . . . Frank thought that running a marathon couldn't have been so difficult as covering the short distance between the counter and the table. *For God's sake, Frank,* he told himself, *don't drop this bloody tray.*

For Kitty, watching Frank was like a special kind of torture. She was torn between the urge to dash over and help him, or to leave him be and accept that this was his own way of preserving his dignity. Kitty understood now, in spite of his harsh words, that this was what he needed to do to help keep him sane. He'd rather fall flat on his face than be treated with kid gloves. *Please God, don't let him fall flat on his face,* she prayed.

The room breathed an almost audible sigh of relief as Frank reached the table, his father rising as Frank carefully placed the tea tray on the table. It seemed for a moment as if the exertion was too much – Pop gripped his son's elbow as he helped him into his seat and pain was etched into Frank's face as the perspiration made rivulets down his cheeks.

Then he called, for all to hear, 'And don't put so many sugars in my tea next time, Kitty!'

The tables around him laughed and the tension was broken, and it was only Pop who got a sense of how much the effort had cost his son. Kitty made a supreme effort to keep the tears that were threatening to fall from doing so. If Frank could be so brave, then so could she.

After a few minutes, when Frank had got his breath back, Pop said, 'I'll go and get the dinners. It's getting busy in here.' Frank knew his father, at six foot tall and worldly-wise, would not want Kitty carrying a full tray while passing the singing squaddies who were now letting off steam. 'They've been in here all afternoon, Pop.' Kitty had put extra on their plates, especially Frank's.

'What brings you in here then, Pop?' asked Rene, wiping the slops from the tea tray. 'Not that I'm not grateful, mind. It's nice to see a true gent for once,' she raised her voice and aimed it towards the high-spirited soldiers, 'instead of hairy-arsed squaddies with nothing better to do than come in here and mither me.' Rene lashed the wet dishcloth across the room and it caught one of the soldiers around the ear.

Kitty smiled. Pop was a fine-looking man in his fifties, and knew he was always sure of a warm welcome from Rene, although not in front of Dolly, the love of his life.

'Our Doll's out collecting salvage,' Pop said, 'putting her country before her beloved husband – again.' His weathered face held an almost comical, bemused expression. Kitty laughed, knowing Dolly would fight like a lioness to protect her husband from Rene's clutches. Everybody liked Pop, always cheerful even when there wasn't much to be cheerful about.

'You can't take your eyes off her, can you, son?' Pop asked, putting the tray of food on the table as the crowd of rowdy soldiers grew louder when Kitty passed by to collect empty cups. Frank watched with interest.

'You should have asked her out – it being her birthday,' Pop said conversationally.

'I'm sure she's already got plans, Pop,' he said. 'She's probably already going to a dance.'

Watching a couple of young ratings who had joined the squaddies and were larking about, Frank knew this was probably their first trip away from home. They were just having a bit of relief. Nevertheless, he would keep an eye on them. He did not want Kitty upset.

'You could always ask her,' Pop suggested, looking at Kitty, who was working hard behind the counter. 'You never know.'

'Pack it in, Pop.' Frank did his best to sound amused but he didn't quite pull it off. 'Kitty's twenty-two today. She won't want to be stuck in the pictures with a tin-legged man like she's in her dotage, will she?' Frank wondered where Pop left his brains sometimes.

'Although she might like a nice quiet night at the pictures after being on her feet all day,' Pop persisted.

'She's not some old dodderer yet, if you hadn't noticed!' Frank tapped his foot impatiently. What did

Pop know about anything? He had been married to Mam forever – he didn't have a clue how a young man felt these days!

'Aye, I suppose you're right, lad.' Pop finished his meal, sat back and puffed on his pipe.

Frank sighed. 'I didn't mean to sound so impatient, Pop, not with you.'

'I know that, lad.' Pop knew that Frank was soft on Kitty and he thought that Kitty returned his feelings. But there was no point in pushing these things. As his Dolly would say, love finds a way.

Suddenly their attention was caught by a bit of a rumpus over at the counter.

'He doesn't look old enough to be in the army,' Pop said, watching a young squaddie weaving about the canteen. 'It looks like he's paid the Sailor's Rest a visit before he came here.'

'Cyril doesn't mind if they're under twenty-one, he'll still serve them,' Frank said, also seeing that the lad was swaying. The squaddie was leaning over the counter now, laughing at something Kitty said, watching her shoo him away with her dishcloth. Smiling, she urged him to go and sit down. However, Frank did not like it when the young khaki-clad private reached over and tried to grab Kitty's hand. Neither did a few of the others who were enjoying an afternoon cup of tea.

'There could be trouble if the young 'un isn't careful,' said Frank, familiar with the antics of young men away from home maybe for the first time, and who now had more money than sense.

'He's talking broken biscuits, lad; she'll never

114

understand a word he says.' Pop patiently eyed the young upstart trying to give Kitty a hard time.

As she was about to give him his change the soldier grabbed her wrist tightly. Frank's body stiffened. He sat bolt upright. 'I don't like her working in here, having to put up with the likes of him!'

'Kitty will be all right, lad. There's plenty here to keep an eye on her,' Pop said with a knowing smile, 'and she's got to come in contact with men sometime.'

Frank was still watching the fracas by the counter. 'Aye, well if that young pup starts anything, I'll be sure to finish it!'

'Wrong change!' the young buck brayed, playing to his pals, who were sniggering at their table. Frank edged towards the front of his seat while Pop raised a casual hand and placed it on his son's sleeve.

'You only gave me a ten-bob note,' Kitty answered calmly. The canteen was packed with servicemen and their attention was beginning to turn to the counter.

'I gave you a pound, you robbing trollop!' the young soldier yelled for all to hear, and a hush descended upon the room as the customers all stopped to see who was causing the commotion. Frank bristled with fury but Pop's hand remained on the sleeve of his navy-blue greatcoat.

'I've heard all about you NAAFI girls,' the squaddie sneered, enjoying the attention, not realising he was attracting the wrong kind.

'No, sonny, not me, you've got the wrong girl.' Kitty kept her voice at a dignified level. Frank admired her cool.

'You won't say no to a night out with me, though, will you?' the young buck said, grabbing Kitty's arm. By now the audience was hanging on every word. Through a blurred window of alcohol, the squaddie might think he had the upper hand, Frank thought, but he didn't know Kitty.

'Now then, leave the girl alone,' a merchant seaman in oilskins called.

Kitty dragged her hand from the drunk's grip. Frank, about to stand up, stopped when Pop shook his head. They both watched as Kitty leaned across the counter. Her scornful expression turned to a warning smile, her voice almost inaudible. Frank and Pop strained to listen.

'For your information . . . sonny,' Kitty held up the ten-bob note that she had put behind the keys of the till and raised her voice, 'this is what you gave me.'

'She's right, lad,' said another soldier, standing next to the cocky young upstart trying it on. 'I've been watching the floor show from the start and you're on a hiding to nothing.'

'And,' said Kitty, as dignified as she was before, 'I suggest you change your whisky for something a bit less potent. It's a grown-up's drink, is that.' She did not like to belittle anybody, least of all a young lad who would feel very ashamed of himself after a good night's sleep.

Frank moved to get up again.

'She's doing quite well on her own, son,' Pop insisted.

'I've had enough, Pop,' said Frank. 'For two pins

I'd go over there and take her out of here.' He could not bear to watch her dealing with this lot.

'She won't thank you for butting in, lad,' said Pop with an admiring smile. 'She's got an independent spirit. There are worse places than the NAAFI.'

'Fancy a dance, Kit?' another Jack-the-lad asked as he waltzed an imaginary partner around the floor, letting off harmless steam before pushing on to who-knew-where. Frank involuntarily clenched his fist, remembering a time when he waltzed Kitty around Empire Street, the day Nancy had married Sid. He loved the innocent, malleable grace of her body, the sweet scent of her and the warm softness of her skin against his.

'Not tonight, sunshine!' Kitty smiled. 'My feet are on fire.' All she wanted was to go home and soak them in some Epsom salts.

'Told you she wouldn't fancy going dancing,' Pop said, but Frank wasn't listening, he was too engrossed in the way these young men thought they had a right to flirt with her. They'd soon know about it if he didn't have these bloody sticks to contend with.

Rene went to turn the sign on the door to 'Closed' and began emptying the tea urn while Kitty went round to remove used plates.

'Tara, lads, see you all tomorrow.' She expertly edged the stragglers towards the door as she spoke. 'Come on now, I've still got a floor to wash.' She opened the door, making a sweeping gesture with her hand, showing the young men the exit. One cheeky chap kissed her cheek.

'Happy birthday, Kit, you ravishing beauty.'

'Oi – cheeky,' Kitty laughed. 'You're only after a free breakfast.'

Frank was always happiest when he was engaging in banter, but watching Kitty now, he felt like he was on the outside looking in and that Kitty was as far away from him as she could possibly be. He could never be a part of her life now, and he was glad he had come here today. Seeing her here, confident and beautiful, only reinforced his feelings that she deserved someone without all the baggage that he would bring. There was no way that he would ever ask her out unless he could dance her around Orrell Park Ballroom. And that would never, ever happen.

'Come on, Pop, it's time we headed back, or Mam will have our guts for garters.' Frank gave a brief and cheery wave and Pop turned to give Kitty a sympathetic smile as they turned in the direction of Empire Street.

Kitty's heart ached with frustration. She had hoped Frank would ask her out on her birthday, but he hadn't, and the disappointment made her feel a little drained. She looked at the clock. 'Another hour,' she said. The clearing up seemed such an effort all of a sudden.

'Oh, leave all that for now,' Rene said half an hour later. 'It's your birthday; you get off and I'll lock up.'

'If you don't mind, Rene? That would be lovely,' Kitty said. It had been a long day.

She pulled the blackout blind on the door before

wearily leaning against it as Rene washed the dishes ready for the next day.

'You go and get your glad rags on, girl. It's not every day you're twenty-two.'

'It's not every day you're twenty-three or -four, for that matter,' Kitty laughed, 'and I've been running our home since I was eleven!'

'Well, no matter,' Rene laughed. 'You're a woman of the world and the world is your oyster – if you know what I mean. Why don't you pop into the Sailor's Rest on the way past and get yourself a drink?'

Kitty tapped her forefinger. 'For one, I would never go into a pub and buy myself a drink,' then her middle finger, 'and for two, I feel as if I've been married since I was that high, without the compensation of a loving husband to go with it. I've two fellas at home who'll be waiting for their teas.'

Rene laughed and nodded.

Kitty slipped her hand inside the second-hand herringbone coat she had bought from Cazneau Street market the week before. 'I wouldn't mind joining one of the Forces, though,' she said dreamily. 'The Waafs and the Wrens have got so much confidence; they are always laughing . . .'

'Aye, well, don't dwell on it now. You go home and treat yourself to something fancy for your birthday. Here, have a steak and kidney pie!' Rene pushed the warm dish into her hands and the two of them looked at each other for a moment, before they exploded with laughter. 'An American ship was in dock yesterday.' Rene looked a little sheepish. 'Let's just say the cook was a very generous man who liked his home cooking – no questions asked.'

'Pull the other one.' Kitty was already drooling at the thought of a nice bit of steak and kidney pie. Danny and Tommy would do cartwheels when they saw this. 'I can't think of a better birthday present.'

'If you were expecting diamonds or pearls from me you were going to be disappointed, Kit.' Rene wiped the clean plate that topped the pie with the cuff of her cardigan before taking it back from Kitty and wrapping the lot in a newspaper.

'The pie is just as precious, Rene. I'll be off then. See you tomorrow, Rene, and thanks for locking up.'

'Be off with you!' Rene gave her a hug before lifting the galvanised bucket of boiled water laced with thick 'Aunt Sally' disinfectant, ready to mop the floor.

For the last few weeks, on her day off, Rita had caught the train to Southport and walked the avenues and boulevards of the elegant seaside town in her quest to find Michael and Megan. She called out when she thought that perfect strangers were her own offspring and the sense of desperate frustration when she realised the little ones were not her own made her weep. Only last week, she had seen a little girl in a coat just like Megan's and, rushing forward to take the child's hand, she turned the auburn-haired infant to face her.

The child's face blanched with fright and her mother asked Rita what she was doing, whilst cradling the frightened child in her arms.

No amount of apologies could make up for the terrible fright she had caused both of them and Rita could not get off the tree-lined boulevard of Lord Street quick enough!

This morning, after a fruitless search of the streets at an hour the children would be going to school, Rita slipped into one of the seaside resort's quaint teashops where the small tables were adorned with lace tablecloths. She sat at a window where she could watch the world go by. The war might have been in another country. It certainly seemed not to have reached here.

However, the high-class shops, fountains, municipal gardens and elegant buildings of Lord Street held no fascination for Rita right now. Exhausted by her quest, wondering where else she could look that she had not searched before, she was too distraught to take in the surroundings.

She feigned interest when the waitress, dressed in black with a white frilled apron, her stiff white cap perched neatly at the back of her Victory Roll, took her order and then brought a tea tray. The delicate china teapot matching the cup, saucer and tiny milk jug, and the pristine linen napkin, the likes of which Rita had not seen since before the war, completed the air of genteel respectability.

'Sorry, we're all out of sugar.' The waitress put the tea things on the table. 'There is saccharine, if you prefer your tea sweet, although we do advise our regulars to bring their own, what with there being a war on,' she said in a friendly manner. Rita smiled and shook her head – she had not taken sugar in her tea for years.

This genteel tearoom was a world away from the dock road, the cranes, the warships in port, the soot-blackened buildings . . . the barrage balloons, the constant noise . . . Day and night, Bootle was busy, ships bringing supplies always coming in, trains taking supplies always going out.

Rita knew she was not at her most approachable. However, it did not stop the waitress informing her that Napoleon the Third was rumoured to frequent this tearoom, as he had lived in lodgings on this very street before becoming Emperor of France in 1852. Rita wondered, hypothetically, if Hitler's troops would have marched in and taken over the country if Napoleon had still been alive.

'Oh, yes,' the waitress said, hugging her little pad and pencil close to her bosom, 'the idea for those wide, tree-lined boulevards of Paris was fashioned from Napoleon's love of Lord Street. Pity the Germans have gone in and messed it all up.'

'It won't always be like this,' Rita said, almost trying to convince herself.

'I do hope you're right, dearie,' the waitress said as she excused herself and went to answer the telephone.

Rita had no intentions of eavesdropping but her attention was piqued when she heard the waitress say, 'Tell Mrs Lowe her bread will be delivered as usual tomorrow morning . . . Yes, I will add another brown loaf to the order . . . Goodbye.' She scribbled something and, ripping it from her pad, she hung the order on a nail behind the counter.

Mrs Lowe. Rita had heard that name before. She was sure it was the name of Charlie's elderly landlady! Finishing her tea, she went up to the counter and took out her purse.

'Oh, you should have called me, dearie; I would have come over to the table with your bill.'

'It's no bother,' Rita said, squinting at the order hung behind the counter while the waitress was getting her change from the till.

'I'll just go and get some change, dearie,' the waitress said, heading to the back of the shop. This gave Rita a chance to take a closer look at the order. It was a long shot – something you read about in a novel. She had seen something similar in *The Thirty-Nine Steps* at the pictures. However, she never thought she would see the day when she would steal behind the counter of a quaint tearoom, and try to find out where her husband had taken her children. Sandy Avenue. There was no number written down but at least Rita might now have the right street. She'd be bound to find someone to ask when she got there.

But Rita's quest to find the house was fruitless. The children were in school at this time of day. Birds tweeted in the trees and she could smell the tang of the sea on the stiff westerly breeze, but there was not a soul she could ask. It was as if the whole place was deserted. A shiver ran down Rita's back and even though a weak autumnal sun was shining, she felt a sudden chill.

At least she had somewhere she could return to another time, in the evening, maybe – when people were at home. Slowly, reluctantly, she made her way back to the train station. She would try again on her day off next week but she prayed that Charlie would write or even telephone the shop in the meantime, anything to let her know where they all were.

Frank waited in the snug of the Tram Tavern. Even though he had vowed that he would stay out of Kitty's life, he was drawn to her like a moth to a flame. He'd been unable to settle at home and had told Mam and Pop that he needed a little tipple down at the pub but he'd been unable to settle there either. He tipped his cap to the barman and, picking up his crutches, he made his way to the dock road, quieter now after a busy day, but still packed with men loading and unloading the waiting ships, knowing the turnaround had to be fast. Looking at his watch he saw that Kitty would be out from work in no time. He had no thought in his head of what he was going to do or say when he saw her, but he would be returning to his desk duties tomorrow and the thought that he wouldn't see her again was too much to bear.

He leaned against the unlit lamppost, opposite the NAAFI. Even though he could not see the dark forbidding alleyways between the warehouses, he had lived around here long enough to know every inch of the dock road. His eyes adjusted to the blackout as a tug sounded a plaintive moan on the river.

From his vantage point, Frank could hear, rather

than see, Rene unlocking the door to let Kitty out and he let her walk a bit further up the road. He didn't want her to think he was following her or keeping an eye out for her. However, he did not like the idea of her walking home alone in the dark either. Having been away for a while, he now realised how much he truly missed Kitty.

Kitty knew she would never have managed to tackle the canteen floor, so tired did she feel. They didn't even have time to have a bite to eat today, the canteen was so busy. All she wanted now was to have her tea and put her feet up. She did not hear the footsteps behind her as she headed towards Empire Street deep in thought.

Suddenly she felt a leather-gloved hand clasp her mouth while another dragged her into a deserted alleyway beside some bombed-out buildings. Kitty tried to scream but the force of the leather against her crushed lips blocked any sound. She began to kick but it was no use. Whoever had hold of her was far stronger than she was.

'Think you're someone now, don't yer!' growled the angry male voice. 'Manageress of the NAAFI now, is it?'

Kitty felt light-headed, her airway blocked by the huge hand. The wedge-heeled shoes that she had bought second-hand from the market were scraping along the icy ground and she could feel the dirty, freezing water splashing up the back of her legs. She was powerless to stop whoever it was from dragging her halfway down the pitch-black alley.

Oh my God, please help me! a voice inside her head

begged. The scream lodged in the back of her throat and her eyes were wide with terror. Kitty tore at the hand clamping her mouth shut but it was no good. He dropped his grip for only a moment to push her face and body up against the wet alley wall, scraping it against the soot-blackened brick. She could feel the water seeping through the front of her coat. He clamped her mouth again when she took a huge breath to enable her to scream and she choked back a sob when his weight jammed her against the wall. He was pressing himself against her.

'So, you call the shots?' he rasped.

Kitty felt her legs buckle with fear. Nevertheless, she could not allow herself to faint. *Not now! No . . . Please not now!*

Adrenalin charged though Frank's veins like bolts of electricity when he heard Kitty's terrified voice across the road. Moving slower than he would like, he felt as if he was wading through mud in his efforts to keep up, and not for the first time he cursed the war that, in his estimation, had made him less of a man than he had once been.

His eyes adjusted to the gloom and he could just make out the figure of a man grunting in his effort to pin Kitty to the wall. Frank's heartbeat was pounding in his ears and the adrenalin now gave him something of the agility he used to have. No longer could he feel the tin leg grating and slowing him down. He could do anything he had to do to save Kitty. He would not let her down.

Frank took the attacker completely unaware, his steel grip knocking the man off balance.

'Get away from her, you sewer rat!'

Kitty sank to the ground as the heavy weight was released from her chest. One side of her face felt wet and it stung when she touched the place that had scraped against the jagged red-brick wall. She half turned to see the huge figure of Frank Feeny. He was bearing down on her shadowy assailant. Even though he had the full use of only one leg, Frank had learned well how to utilise the other and he moved with the confidence of a lion going in for the kill. Remembering his boxing training, Frank adopted a combative stance and his strong, muscled arms lifted Kitty's attacker off the ground, throwing him from the alley into the street, where he landed in the gutter like a bundle of rags.

The street was silent save for the thud of the body as it hit the ground. Frank uttered not one word as he dragged the struggling man to his feet and slammed his enormous fist into his jaw.

Kitty could still feel the heavy weight upon her body, the gloved hand pressing against her lips, causing them to bleed, and she knew that had it not been for Frank's intervention there was no telling what this evil man would have stooped to.

It was only when she drew in a lungful of icy air, making her light-headed, that she realised she had hardly breathed since he laid his filthy hands on her. She made a super-human effort not to faint. Her heart was beating wildly, her legs felt like jelly and she could barely stand.

Kitty could just make out the determined set of Frank's jaw and the angle of his drawn-back powerful arm that he was ready to slam into the man's face. She knew Frank's clenched fist could deal a hefty blow, and she also knew that he could get into serious trouble – if he were caught.

'I'm sorry, I'm sorry!' the young buck cried, trying to shield his face from Frank's hammer blows and Frank suspected that this was the upstart who had been larking about in the canteen. 'It was my mistake, mate.' How pathetic he looked now, Kitty thought, as she heard the man who had scared her witless grovelling in the freezing hail of the November black-out, begging for mercy.

'It was a mistake, mate! Honest. I thought she were someone else.' The low voice was insistent now. 'It won't happen again, mister, honest! It were a mistake, mate!'

'I'm not your mate,' Frank growled through clenched teeth.

Kitty heard the man's body slamming against the wall. She worried that Frank might lose his balance although it sounded like he was doing exceptionally well.

'Put it this way – it would be the biggest mistake you ever made to go anywhere near her again.' Kitty heard a sickening crack and imagined it could be the other man's head hitting the wall. Frank's voice grew ever more intimidating. 'Have you got that – mister? If I ever see you around her again, mistake or not, I will knock you into the middle of next week. Right?'

At close quarters, Frank could see his face. He was right, it was the young upstart who had been full of bravado in front of his pals, and had obviously taken umbrage when Kitty put him in his place.

'I thought she were someone else.' The young squaddie's hand guarded his face as he tried to stay out of the way of Frank's powerful left hook.

'So that makes it all right?' Frank's growl became lower, almost a whisper. 'You think you can come around here and treat a woman like that?'

'No, I thought she were just some doxie, walking the dock road – some o' them like it rough . . .' He didn't have time to shield his face completely from the blow that came too fast to register, sending him reeling across the dock road and only narrowly missing being run over by an oncoming tram.

Kitty heard him squealing like a stuck pig as he landed in the gutter. Frank limped over to him, muttering something too low for her to hear.

'If you want a prostitute,' he growled in the squaddie's ear, wishing he could finish him off good and proper, 'go look somewhere else, you filthy scum. This is a respectable area.'

Dazed by the blow and obviously winded, the young soldier scrambled to his feet while Frank, towering over him, had retrieved one of his crutches and jabbed it into him as he made a run for it.

Kitty could hear the heavy boots skidding on the icy ground and the sound of stumbling in his haste to escape further punishment.

'That's right, you yellow-bellied coward,' Frank

called, 'you keep on running. And don't stop until you get to the gates of hell – where you belong! Because if you do stop you can be sure I'll catch up with you!' As the footsteps diminished Frank become aware of Kitty's gentle sobs.

'Kitty! Are you all right?' His voice was full of concern.

Putting a protective arm around her shivering shoulders, he waited until Kitty was able to raise her head and she said in a voice barely above a whisper, 'I'm fine now, Frank, thank you.'

'Are you sure?' Frank asked tenderly, his gentle eyes searching her face. 'You're bleeding.' He took a handkerchief from his pocket and gently dabbed at her cheek, his face etched with worry as he concentrated on cleaning her up.

'I'm fine, honestly.' Kitty's voice sounded firmer than she intended, and she could not gauge Frank's silence.

As he put his handkerchief back in his pocket Frank acknowledged Kitty was an independent woman through necessity; she'd had to be stoic from an early age.

'I've had more than that in me time – especially when I used to have to separate our Danny and Jack! Big buggers that they are.' Kitty wished she could show her gratitude to Frank more freely; maybe flinging her grateful arms around his neck and sinking into his kisses! Even in the blackness of the night, she could feel her face flush warmly at the thought. That might be how it works in those romantic books she borrowed from the library. In those stories the heroine was so thankful she threw all caution to the wind and she and her hero ended up in each other's arms, but it didn't happen here in Empire Street – people would think she'd gone mad.

Some birthday this had turned out to be. At least she would have a good tea . . . The pie! Where was the pie?

'Where are you going?' Frank asked, his concern turning to confusion.

As she retraced her steps down the back alley, Kitty knew she loved Frank Feeny with every beat of her heart, even more now than she ever had, and she always would. However, she did not intend to tell him that. Not when she was just a humble NAAFI girl, someone he treated like a kid sister, and he was a petty officer in the Royal Navy. He did not look at her in the way he looked at other girls. She knew that and so did everybody else. Talk about delusions! She must have a slate loose if she thought Frank Feeny would ever see her as his sweetheart.

'I've lost my pie!' Kitty called; the pie was a distraction from the emotions that threatened to overwhelm her – the attack and the nearness of Frank had caused an upswell of feelings that felt almost uncontrollable. 'I can't go home without my pie!' She retraced her steps as the clouds parted and the moon cast its silvery beam into the entry. Kitty saw the pie wrapped in its newspapers lying on the ground near the entrance and knew she had dropped it when . . . But she wouldn't think of that now.

'You're a case, Kitty Callaghan.' Frank shook his

131

head as they passed the bombed-out storage sheds and the rubble-strewn debris where houses had stood only days ago. Kitty did not know what he meant by that, and felt he was admonishing her. Suddenly she felt a bit woozy and had to grab his arm to get her balance.

'I just bent down too quick!' Kitty said when Frank put his hand out to catch her. He had always been there when she got herself into a scrape. But she should not depend on him now. She must learn not to. 'I didn't intend to cause you any bother.'

'You didn't,' Frank said abruptly as they neared Empire Street. He was going back to the naval base tomorrow. God, he would miss her.

'I'm going away tomorrow; I don't know when I'll be back.' The sound of a passing tram broke the silence, then nothing. Frank did not know what to say as the air hung uncomfortably heavy with their silence. He wished she would say something, even if it was only goodbye.

Kitty's senses were reeling! He'd been back for what seemed like only half a minute and now was going away again. She was glad the blackout was dark enough to hide her tears from him.

'So . . .' Frank said with a short mirthless laugh, but still she was quiet.

I love you, Kitty Callaghan. The words floated around Frank's head.

'Will you be home for Christmas?' Kitty asked eventually as they turned the corner.

'I'm not sure, everything is hush-hush . . .' There was nowhere else he would rather be.

'I can't wait to get back,' Frank said. Away from the adulation, like he had done something more heroic than getting in the way of a collapsing bulkhead that had shattered his lower leg. 'I'm getting the first train tomorrow.'

'I thought you'd be staying for a bit longer,' Kitty said, her insides dipping as they did when she was disappointed. She should have known he wasn't one for sitting around waiting for something to turn up – he made life happen. There was something about Frank that did not fit into the ordinary everyday world of Empire Street. His gentleness, given the power his athletic body still possessed, was not something he had been taught. It was far more subtle than that. Something . . . other.

Too soon they were outside her front door; the moment to tell each other their true feelings was lost.

'Will they let you continue to serve with your leg?' Kitty asked, unable to put her fears into more articulate words.

'They won't allow me to serve without it,' Frank laughed, and Kitty found that she couldn't stop herself laughing too, despite being genuinely worried.

'You're shivering.'

'I'm fine.' Kitty shrugged him away and then felt bad. He was trying to help . . . but he wasn't helping. His concern just made her realise all the more how much she yearned for him.

'Are you sure you're feeling better?' Frank's voice was gentle and full of concern.

'Yes, thanks.' Kitty flicked bits of soot from her

coat for the want of something to do. 'And for your information I don't make a habit of being dragged down alleyways!'

'I should hope not.'

'I'd better be getting in. Danny and Tommy will think I've got lost.'

'I'll wait until you are safely inside.' Frank did not want this moment to end. He would be gone when she got up tomorrow.

'I'm fine now, Frank.' Kitty knew his boxing training and the fact that he had been light-middleweight champion of his unit had helped him to recover from his surgery more quickly than someone less healthy. She edged towards her own front door. Then a thought occurred to her. Did she dare ask? Perhaps it was the shock she'd had but she couldn't think of anything worse than Frank leaving her right now. It would be agony. Perhaps she could get him to stay a little longer?

'Frank . . . there's plenty of food. I've got a pie and a stew. This is my birthday present and you'd be welcome to share it with us?'

Frank's heart was aching. He desperately wanted to tell her that he had always loved her but he did not want her to feel obliged because he had helped her. He wanted so much to tell her she looked beautiful; even now, with her ashen face and dishevelled hair, she still looked exquisite. More than anything right now, he wanted to walk into that house with Kitty. To sit with her and her brothers and to laugh and have fun and to gaze at that lovely face again. But, no. He had to be strong. It would never work.

'Sorry, Kit. But I'd better be getting back. Mam and Pop, you know . . .' He trailed off weakly, knowing it sounded like a terrible excuse.

Kitty was crestfallen. She was stupid to think he'd want to spend what little time he had with her. But she tried not so show it and kept her voice light.

'Well, good night then, Frank,' she said as she opened her front door, 'and thanks again.' She felt her heart wrench at the thought that she didn't know when she would see him again. If only he would stay a little longer. To Frank she would always be just the girl next door. Or in this case, the girl across the road.

'Good night, Kit, look after yourself.' He bent and kissed her cheek as a friend would do.

Her cheek was cold like silken marble. Her beautiful innocent blue eyes caught a flash of moonbeam. He saw the child in her eyes, the one who raced across the street with a newborn baby in her arms and who did not have a clue what to do or where to turn. As Frank turned away and tiredly made his way home he remembered those eyes again and the thought occurred to him, just briefly, that he was getting everything wrong.

Kitty tried to put the assault behind her by not thinking about it. She didn't want to worry Danny and she certainly didn't want Tommy to know what had happened. She had to come and go between home and the canteen so there was nothing for it but to carry on.

A week later, however, she received news that made

it very difficult for her to carry on as normal. She returned from the NAAFI one evening and entered the kitchen undoing her coat, her mind already on getting on the tea. She nodded to Danny who was sitting by the fire next to the new wireless that he had bought her for her birthday, which had been a wonderful surprise, though Kitty didn't like to ask where he had got the money from to pay for it. A little distracted, she paid no heed to the piece of paper that was in his hand. He was silently reading it, leaning forward in his chair near the dwindling fire.

'Didn't you think to bring some coal up before the fire goes out, Dan?' Kitty asked. But he didn't answer. 'Dan, did you . . . ?' Kitty looked at Danny's face and saw his furrowed brow and tight lips. His face was pale. 'Dan what's the matter?' She felt her stomach clench. 'What's happened?' she asked, though terrified of the answer that he was going to give her.

'It's our Jack,' Danny said. 'His ship's gone down. He's missing.'

'No! Please God, no,' Kitty let out a long, low agonised moan. 'Not our Jack, Lord. Please!'

CHAPTER EIGHT

'It's a letter from our Eddy!' Dolly called, sorting through the clutch of post and heading into the kitchen, where Pop, Rita and Sarah were sitting at the table. They looked up expectantly as Dolly ripped open the blue envelope with her thumb.

'Let's see! Let's see!' Sarah cried as the family gathered round, eager for news. Nobody knew exactly where Eddy was but his letters hinted at cold weather and Pop said nothing was colder than the North Atlantic at this time of year. They had not seen Eddy for nine months and they all missed him like mad!

'Shall I go and get Nancy? She's just put George down for a sleep.' Sarah knew her mother would not tell them anything the letter contained until she and Pop had soaked up every word. Pop looked at her now and a small shake of his head told Sarah to keep quiet.

When Dolly had finished reading the letter, she had a puzzled albeit happy expression on her face as she passed it to Pop, who always read out any news.

'Is he coming home?' Sarah was particularly close to her older brother and could not contain her eager questions. 'Where is he? Does he say?'

'Give us a chance to read it,' said Pop through a cloud of pipe-tobacco smoke while Dolly buttered a piece of freshly toasted bread and put it on a plate with the rest. Nancy, who had been resident at her parents' house since October, seemed to have no intention of going back to her mother-in-law any time soon. No matter how many hints Dolly threw or how many times Sid's mother came round to ask if she was ever going back, Nancy made some excuse to stay with her family. It was much livelier here than at that morgue Mrs Kerrigan called home.

'He says he is in good spirits! That's my lad.' Pop raised his head and Dolly, smiling, nodded. They both knew how important it was to keep things as happy as possible, for the family's sake. 'He says he will be home before Christmas if all is well and good, and he has a Christmas surprise for all of us.'

'He knows I love surprises!' Dolly was wide-eyed now and her smile almost went from ear to ear. She pulled up a chair and sat down, pouring some more tea into her cup and looking like the cat that had just devoured the cream. She liked nothing more than having her whole family around her and she knew that if her Eddy could make it home too, then it would be a good Christmas after all, even if there was less in the shops these days than there had ever been.

'He says this surprise item does not come with instructions,' Pop's black eye-patch rose along with his

138

silvering brow, a sign he was as baffled as everybody else, 'but don't worry, he says, it's not hard to fathom out, and we will all wonder how we ever managed to live without it.'

'I wonder what it is.' Sarah was wide-eyed while Pop, smiling, reread the letter.

'Our Eddy does love his puzzles,' said Dolly, 'and he knows I never get the clues right.'

'You won't have long to wait,' Pop laughed. 'He's always been blooming cryptic.'

'I hope he hasn't gone and done something daft.' Dolly's censorious tone did not fool anybody and they all laughed.

'So, what else does he say?'

'Not much, except, "Can you make sure my bedroom is not in the same untidy state I left it when I finished my last leave?" Well, I ask you!' Pop's heavy eyebrows knitted together.

'I'll give him *same untidy state*, the ejit!' Dolly's look of excited wonderment had completely disappeared now. 'I'll let him know I scrub this house from top to bottom every Friday!'

'And very nice it is too, my sweet!' Pop interrupted his wife's tirade, knowing she would forgive Eddy anything as soon as he stepped through that front door. Dolly got up from the table and, taking the tray of cutlery out to the scullery, she called over her shoulder, 'Do you think he's bringing home another lost soul, like last Christmas?'

'Oh, I remember, he brought home that Canadian sailor,' said Nancy. Then she pondered for a moment before saying in that little-girl voice she used when she did not get her own way, 'And does that mean I'll have to go back to Sid's mother?'

'I suppose so, love,' Dolly said, coming back and taking a fresh sheet from the ironing pile on the chair.

'You watch,' Pop said to the gathering of women, 'she'll have this house scrubbed and polished till it gleams now there's a possibility our Eddy is coming home.'

'Let's see what else we hear before we start counting our sheep.'

'Chickens,' Nancy said churlishly, refusing to be placated.

'Are there sharks in the North Atlantic?' Sarah asked, reading from the *Evening Echo*, trying to change the subject and then realising Mam would worry even more after that remark.

'There are more sharks round here,' Nancy shrugged. Supposing she asked Mam to let her muck in with cleaning the entire house? That might persuade her to let her and baby George stay. It wasn't fair that she would have to go back to that mausoleum with Sid's embittered old mother.

'Remind me I've got to check my dried fruit store, Pop,' Dolly said handing him the clean bed sheet, which had seen better days and which she had turned sides to middle to make a 'new' one that had a few more years' wear in it. With Christmas coming soon Dolly was busy preparing bun loaves to raise money for the Spitfire Fund and the Red Cross shop. She was always busy, never stopping.

'Will do,' Pop said, taking one end of the sheet Dolly handed him. Sarah would be able to make bandages with the offcuts.

'You've done a great job on this sheet, Doll,' he remarked. 'I'm sure you could teach the powers that be a thing or two about making do and mending.'

'I've had enough practice, Pop,' Dolly answered. 'The Women's Voluntary Service want me to recruit another street fire warden, so I asked Vera Delaney. She's the only one in this street who hasn't volunteered for anything.'

'What did she say?' Pop asked, not holding out much hope.

'What do you think?' Dolly mimicked Vera's plaintive tone. '"I couldn't possibly – I would be far too scared to go into a burning building." So that told me.'

'Never mind, Doll, everybody knows if you need a job doing it's best to ask a busy woman,' Pop said. There was not enough of his lovely Dolly to go round sometimes.

'That woman thinks she's the only one who is going through this war!'

Pop thanked the Lord every day for pointing him in Dolly's direction all those years ago. However, he knew that the more time she had on her hands the more she was inclined to ponder, which might lead to a fit of conniptions, so he thought it was a good idea that she was involved with everybody else's business instead.

'I'd think about doing more myself, but what with

my make-do-and-mend classes in the parlour every Monday and Friday, not to mention taking baby George's pram and collecting salvage,' Dolly said. 'And then there's the fire watching on a Wednesday night! Then, there are the bun loaves to make!'

'With your expert powers of organisation you're a boon to less fortunate women.'

'You're so right, Pop.' Dolly was glowing in the light of her husband's praise. 'There are some women who can't boil an egg, let alone make a pie.'

'Get away.' Pop's disbelieving tone encouraged her. 'You're having me on.'

'Straight up.' Dolly put the sheet on the table, watching her beloved husband tuck his thumbs into his braces and ease them from his shoulders before sitting down.

'Now you come to mention it, Mr Sefton said his wife couldn't boil water before the war started; now she's preparing bottled fruit like a good 'un.'

'Right,' Dolly said, 'we'll have to get cracking. Christmas is coming and bun loaves won't make themselves – we'll have to sort something out bed-wise in case Frank and Eddy do manage to get home, then we'll start looking for another fire warden.' Nancy knew her mother always said 'we' when she meant 'I'.

'You'll be putting your name down for a victory garden next spring, as well, I imagine?' Pop said. That would stop her worrying so much about her boys.

'Aye, if you like,' Dolly sighed. 'When our Eddy gets home there's going to be a houseful.' Her mind was now working overtime and her eyes gleamed with delight. 'I've got it all to do now,' she said with more than a hint of satisfaction, 'so if you'll all get out of my kitchen . . .'

Pop also knew that preparing for Christmas with her ever-loving family was the happiest time of the year for Dolly, although recruiting women for the Voluntary Service meant less time to get her household chores done.

'It's a good thing I still have some of that dried fruit left over from last summer,' Dolly cogitated aloud. 'A good rinse under the cold tap and it'll be good as new.' It was almost impossible to get dried fruit these days, due to shortages. Shipping carried only essential supplies and fruit was a luxury. However, Dolly had been canny when it was plentiful last summer. She had dried some and bottled the rest, which was now steeping nicely in the last of the brandy that Eddy had brought home last Christmas.

'I'll make a Christmas cake for us, and one to raffle for the Spitfire Fund,' Dolly said proudly.

'Mrs Kennedy will want to do a deal so she gets a Christmas cake,' Nancy said, knowing that rumours Winnie Kennedy was making a large profit out of the war could very well be true as the shop was very popular with women who had money to spare. It was amazing what Winnie was able to stock.

'As long as she buys a ticket she has as much chance of having a nice cake on her Christmas table as anybody else. But she's not getting one if she doesn't win it.' Dolly was now sorting through the cupboard, wondering if she had enough points for a jar of jam. There was word going round the street that one of the neighbours had seen a whole box of jam being delivered to the corner shop only half an hour ago.

Dolly knew Winnie Kennedy would save the jam for her 'select' customers, the ones who paid on the nail and did not ask for 'tick'. It was not right, Dolly knew, not when her boys risked their lives day in, day out. She sighed, predicting that this second Christmas of the war was going to be even grimmer than the last.

The German blitzkrieg had overwhelmed France, Holland and Belgium. British troops had been slain or, like her son-in-law Sid, taken prisoner. With constant rumours of an invasion, there would not be much in the way of Christmas festivities this year. No church bells – they were only to be rung if an invasion was taking place. No Christmas lights due to the blackout. The only joy she had was making sure she had a bit of bun loaf or Christmas cake for the family, and if they were all together so much the better.

'Well, I'll leave you to your kitchen duties, Doll,' Pop said, placing his flat cap firmly on his thatch of silvering hair, glad her mind and body were both occupied now. He gave her a loving peck on the cheek as she brought out her mixing bowl, then rolled up her sleeves for action.

The week after her discovery in the tearoom, Rita was back in Southport again. It was her day off and she was resuming her search for her children. She saw a crocodile line of schoolchildren turning into a tree-lined boulevard, obviously impoverished evacuees judging by the handed-down clothing they wore. Their jackets were either too big or too small, their short trousers held up with threadbare braces or a beloved snake-belt. The little girls among them looked slightly better, with their tightly braided hair and shiny faces. But the surprising thing was that one of the children was a Bootle boy, and he recognised Rita from her days working in the corner shop!

'Hello, Mrs Kennedy,' the young lad called. ''Ave you come 'ere to see your Mick and Meggie?'

Rita suppressed the urge to correct the names; this young lad was only being friendly and he was probably glad to see an adult's face he recognised from home. Rita confirmed that she was here to see her children but did not tell him she had no address.

'I don't see them much, though they live near me, but they don't go to our school.' The boy, Davey, proudly puffed out his chest as if by telling her he had achieved something wonderful.

'Sandy Avenue? So, which side are you on then?' Rita asked as nonchalantly as her thudding heart would allow. Surely, after all these weeks she must have some good luck.

'We're in seventeen and Mick is in thirteen, of course!' He looked at Rita as if she had gone doolally. Rita smiled. She could have hugged him. But she resisted.

'Of course! Yours is the one with the—'

'Apple tree!' he interrupted, obviously assuming she

had been before. 'Yes, that's ours.' His eyes danced with excitement and Rita opened her bag.

'I'll tell your mam I saw you,' she said. 'Is there any message?' She opened her concertina purse and took out a silver shilling.

'Yes, ask her if we can have an apple tree when I get home.' Davey laughed and Rita wondered if he was missing home half as much as his mother was missing him. She slipped the bob in his hand and his eyes lit up. Immediately he turned to show all his pals.

'Thanks very much, Mrs Kennedy!' he gasped, and seemed to grow a little taller as he proudly flipped the money into the air. 'I'm gonna save this to buy me mam a Christmas present.' Rita's heart swelled with admiration for the boy.

Rita hurried towards Sandy Avenue now she knew it was indeed where her children were. Her heart was beating so strongly she could hardly catch her breath. She was going to see her kids at last! And when she got there she was going to wipe the floor with Charlie Kennedy. How dare he do this to her? She was their mother. She had a right to see her children. This would be the last time he ever got away with something like this.

Rita approached the house. Outside there was a board in the window that announced 'NO VACAN-CIES'. The windows were closed. Taking a deep breath and steeling herself for the inevitable conflict, she rapped loudly with the door knocker. For a few moments she waited, but there was no answer so she knocked again, more persistent this time. She was damned if Charlie was going to elude her. Rita put her ear to the door but could hear nothing, so she bent down and pushed the letterbox open so that she could peer inside. In the gloom, Rita could see the staircase banister and a little of the way down the dark hallway. There were no lights on and she got the unmistakable sense that the house was completely empty.

Rita thought she would wait on the wall for them to come home. She looked at her watch: it was a little after noon. Well, she'd wait all day if she had to.

As she sat there, someone approached the house next door from the street, a refined woman in a tailored coat with a fox fur around the neck. Now she was closing her hip-high gate after pulling in a wicker basket on wheels. It seemed well stocked, Rita noted, although the little Yorkshire terrier that popped its head out of the top of the basket may have made it look full.

'Can I help you?' the woman enquired suspiciously of Rita.

Rita wasn't sure how to answer. Given the situation, she thought it would be best to play her cards close to her chest for now. Who knew what Charlie had told the neighbours?

'I've come to see Mr Kennedy,' she answered.

'Mr Kennedy is away for a few days, I'm afraid.' The woman rummaged around in her shopping trolley and the little dog shifted reluctantly as she delved underneath his little body, eventually retrieving her door keys. Rita noted that they didn't seem to be in the habit of leaving their front doors unlocked in this part of the world, unlike in Empire Street.

'Oh.' Rita's heart sank. She was so tantalisingly close to her children but now there was another stumbling block.

'Yes,' the woman continued. 'He and his wife and their children.'

'I'm sorry?' Rita thought she had definitely heard the woman say Mr Kennedy and his wife, but she was utterly flummoxed. The older woman repeated what she had said. Rita was shocked but tried to hide it. So, Charlie had shacked up with some woman, and was masquerading as her husband? Presumably the woman was this Elsie Lowe person. It defied belief.

'And who might you be?' the neighbour asked.

'Can you tell me when they will be back?' Rita's agony at this latest setback threatened to overwhelm her, but she fought back her emotions. It wouldn't do to attract attention for the wrong reasons. She must try and find out what she could.

'Not until you tell me who you are – you could be anybody. There have been a few strange faces around the place lately . . .'

She was too late. Perhaps he had somehow got wind of the fact she was looking for him and done a flit. The other woman looked dubious and Rita quickly explained that she was Mr Kennedy's sister.

'I didn't know he had two sisters,' the older woman said. Rita's brows pleated in confusion, but the woman didn't seem to notice.

148

'Young Ruby, your sister, is such a sweet thing, such a shame, a bit touched in the head, isn't she? But she gets along marvellously with Mr Kennedy's two – I sometimes see them playing in the Anderson shelter in the back garden.' She leaned forward. 'Suffice to say your brother has his work cut out with that wife of his – mouth like a fishwife, if you'll excuse me saying so. But as a widower, I suppose he has other considerations. Men don't like to be alone, do they?'

A widower? As if taking her children away wasn't bad enough, he'd obviously written her out of this new life of his and pretended she was dead. Were there no depths to which he wouldn't sink? God only knew what the children must be thinking.

'Well, I'm not very familiar with his wife – Elsie, isn't it?' Rita said, trying to glean as much information as possible.

'That's right. Elsie Lowe, as she previously was. A different class altogether, my dear.' She repositioned the fox fur. 'I mean, one can tell, can't one?'

'Most certainly,' Rita replied as a fresh westerly wind whipped along the avenue. This woman seemed to enjoy a good old gossip and it was working in Rita's favour.

'They've gone to her relations in Crosby, apparently.' The woman leaned forward again. 'They won't be back for a couple of weeks, maybe not until after Christmas, the child told me.'

'How are the children?' Rita smiled, though her insides were twisting at the thought that she now had no idea where they could be.

'You hardly ever hear those kiddies; even when they play in the back garden they play in whispers. They never mix with other children in the avenue. Such a pity, they seem like lovely children.'

'They are.' Rita was angry now. Charlie had lied to his mother about sending them to school, too. Or maybe Winnie Kennedy had lied to her as well? Charlie was probably desperate to keep his rotten little lies as secret as he could so keeping the children out of school would make sense. No chance then of their letting the real story slip out to a teacher or another parent. Horrified, she thought of her children cooped up all day. At home they were allowed to run in the street – let off steam, play with the other kids. Charlie was treating them like pet rabbits in a hutch.

'It's such a pity you missed them. They only went yesterday.'

'Thank you.' Rita could barely get the words out she was so choked up.

'Good day. Shall I tell them you called in?'

'No, don't worry. I'll track them down, you can be sure of that.'

As Rita set off towards the train station, the tears fell freely down her face. Passers-by stared at her and some even made to touch her arm and ask her if she was all right. But Rita wasn't all right. Nothing would ever be all right again until she had her children back, safe in her own arms.

That night, on her way home, Rita passed by Kitty's house. A cold chill crept up her spine as she found

Kitty on her own, holding the letter from the War Office and weeping over the cold grate.

'I'm sorry, Rita, but I can't stop crying.'

Rita's heart hammered in her chest as Kitty told her about the telegram. 'Danny said that it was the *Distinguished* that was sunk. They've all been talking about it at the docks. That was the ship that Jack was on.'

They weren't supposed to know where their men were stationed, but *Distinguished* had sailed from Gladstone Dock a few months ago. All the nurses had gone down to wave it off in a show of patriotic fervour and support. Jack Callaghan had been aboard. He had waved from the flight deck of the aircraft carrier.

It took every ounce of Rita's determination not to buckle under. She needed to be strong for Kitty. Was he . . . ? *He can't be dead,* she told herself firmly. *I won't believe it.*

She held Kitty and soothed her. Danny had a shift on the dock and Tommy was already over at Mam and Pop's. Brooking no argument, Rita scooped Kitty up and took her back to the Feeny household, where the warmth of the house and of its inhabitants wrapped them in a cocoon of security.

That night Rita had a dream. In it, water closed over her face and she began to struggle. Everything was black. She could not breathe. Her lungs would not take in air. Desperately she fought with everything she had to pull herself up to the light. If she got to the light she would be able to breathe. Fighting. Fighting. Struggling some more. If she could just . . .

151

'Jack, no!' Crying out, Rita awoke to find herself in her bed. Struggling to adjust, she switched on the little bedside lamp. The yellow light illuminated the shabby furniture and dingy curtains, all of which had seen better days. Rita felt desolate. How had she ended up here? No children, a marriage that was in tatters and now Jack, the love of her life, was missing. How could life be so cruel?

The air raid increased to a terrifying ferocity, a waking nightmare for everybody as the blazing timber yards and warehouses that lined the dock road lit up the port, making it possible for the bombers to pick out their targets with deadly accuracy. Danny thought last night's raid had been bad but this was even worse. Bridges, railway sidings and goods yards were being destroyed more quickly now, as the enemy were dropping wave after wave of high explosives. Parachute mines were bursting on impact and causing damage over the vast region of docks and surrounding community.

Last night's raid, as this one, started at tea time and if yesterday's was anything to go by, Danny thought, then it was going to be nigh on dawn before it ended.

Please keep Sarah and my family safe, Lord!

Danny headed through the dock gate, giving a perfunctory nod to the dock gateman who would be there right until the end of the raid whether his shift had ended or not – it was all hands to the job now.

Just on midnight, while the raid was at its height,

the decision was taken to abandon trying to unload the ships they were working on, as the fires raged all around. Men were ordered to join the fire crews in the hope of stemming the path of destruction.

'The railway's been hit,' one of the firemen said as he ran past. 'If it carries on like this there'll be nothing left in the morning.'

'Look at that!' One of the dockers pointed to a merchant ship next to the one they had been unloading earlier, now belching smoke. Danny knew the cargo was highly flammable and that if the fire took hold it would not only explode and cause devastating damage, but would likely burn for days, making the dock a Luftwaffe free-for-all.

'Don't be so bloody stupid, Danny,' Alfie Delaney said as Danny headed towards the ship. 'Danny, leave it! You'll get killed!' he shouted above the roaring flames and crash of the splintering wood of the timber yards and warehouses already hit.

'If it goes up it'll take half the dock with it,' Danny answered, getting his handkerchief out of his pocket to tie around his nose and mouth to try and lessen the effects of the thick black smoke that now filled the dock.

Men were fighting to put out the ship fire, knowing the five hundred acres of docks and twenty-nine miles of quays on this side of the river were busy with military and merchant ships. Anchored side-by-side, they were carrying munitions as well as much-needed supplies.

Even though Danny could not actively serve his

country, he kept up with what was going on around the world. Quiet conversations with Allied sailors in darkened corners of dock road alehouses were much more informative than anything he read in the newspapers or heard on the wireless. Newscasters were apt to give out the jolly old Britain-can-take-it attitude for the sake of American aid, but the men on the docks knew the real story. The one they daren't tell the rest of the country.

'You won't catch me being no hero!' Delaney called as Danny headed towards the stricken ship. Two hundred Allied ships had already been sunk by U-boats, and if it carried on like this Britain would be starved into submission. The likes of Alfie Delaney and Harry Calendar were doing a roaring trade with knocked-off imports and contraband, and even though Danny didn't mind the odd tin of unlabelled luxury, or bag of sugar to grace his table, he certainly didn't hold with the racket that Calendar and Delaney were running. But this was no time to stand around occupying the moral high ground, thought Danny. He had to get stuck in and help as best he could.

As he neared the ship he noticed an unconscious fireman being carried to an ambulance. Danny knew the oil drums on board the stricken ship were stored quite low in the hold and the fire was in the stern between the bulkheads. Upright walls within the hull separated the different sections of the ship and the oil drums. Even though the bulkheads were sealed to prevent fires spreading, Danny could feel the intense heat and suspected the drums were in danger of exploding because of the high temperature alone. He did not want to be here when they did.

Managing to haul the fire-fighting apparatus that had been discarded by the injured fireman towards the flames, Danny paused for just a moment to catch his breath. The heat was intense now as he clambered way down into the hatch, only to find the water supply had failed and he was driven back by the blistering heat, aware of the risk that the oil drums could explode any minute.

A bevy of burly fire-fighters pushed past just as Danny was having to retreat. They had a heavy-weight pump of some kind and several lengths of working hoses. Relieved, Danny stopped to get his breath and looked around for where else he could try to help.

Alfie Delaney was loading boxes of American and Canadian cigarettes behind wooden packing cases that had already been stowed and were bound for the south of the country. He would not drive the wagon off the dock himself; he was too cunning by half. If it was searched, and the smuggled goods were discovered, he would be in the clear.

He knew the driver on a casual basis so he didn't need to go into too much detail – loose lips and all that. This particular driver was well known for slipping into a certain roadside canteen and it wouldn't do any harm to slip him a few bob for a decent fry-up seeing as they weren't rationed – yet. This close to Christmas, Delaney thought, keeping a furtive eye out for anyone watching, it was odds on that this load would be interesting to Harry Calendar's lads while the driver enjoyed his breakfast. Job done.

Sarah took the Junior Red Cross motto 'Serve One Another' very seriously when she went as a VAD to the Liverpool Infirmary to study first aid and home nursing. When she was off duty she helped with hospital fund raising, knitting for the troops and providing 'comforts', proud of the fact she was serving as many people as she could possibly manage. This evening she'd been sent to join the first-aiders who manned the docks during air raids.

'Here you go, lassie,' said the leading first-aider, handing her a tin helmet. 'Try this for size.' The first aid post, north of Canada Dock, was no bigger than Pop's pigeon loft. It contained a Primus stove, a table, a couple of straight-backed chairs and a black box marked 'First Aid', which she was warned never to touch without the permission of the leading first-aider, a doctor from the nearby hospital who introduced himself only as McTaggart.

Learning she might be called upon to help with ambulance duties, Sarah felt ever so responsible. This is what she had worked towards in the St John Ambulance Brigade during that quiet time that everybody called 'the phoney war'.

'You must be prepared for every eventuality,' McTaggart, who was about the same age as Pop, informed her, and Sarah nodded. She wanted to be in the thick of it, saving lives, and getting stuck in, like

Mam and Pop would be doing with their fire watching and ARP duties now.

'Your first duty,' McTaggart said grimly, 'and one of the most important duties you will ever be asked to perform . . .' Sarah could hardly breathe she was so excited '. . . is to put the kettle on and make everyone a cup of tea. You never know when you'll get another.' Immediately her enthusiasm waned. She could stay at home and make tea!

'You will soon find out that the most welcome sight, giving fighting men and women the sustenance to carry on, is a hot cup of tea – you will be a heroine in no time,' he laughed, and Sarah pulled a truculent face.

However, his raised eyebrow expression told her not to argue. Ten minutes later, she was carrying a tray of tea things to the waiting medics at the ready near their ambulances, on standby to replace the last lot as the docks needed twenty-four-hour medical support.

The docks were burning now and so too were the sheds and warehouses as Sarah returned for more cups. Waiting for the kettle to boil, she wondered when it would be her time to shine. When the kettle boiled she replenished the pot and her face turned a warm shade of pink when one of the first-aiders told her not to use so much tea.

'It doesn't grow on trees, you know.' Sarah contained the pithy reply that it did, actually, as she left the first-aid post with a tray of full cups in her hands, and another enemy plane roared overhead just as she was crossing the cobbled road.

'Get out of the way! Take cover!' Men were shouting fit to burst as a basket of incendiary bombs exploded above her head. Sarah could not move. She was too stunned even to drop the tray. Looking at the ground, she waited for what seemed like eternity, frozen to the spot, waiting to meet her maker. Then suddenly she felt her feet taken from under her and herself being scooped up in strong arms and carried from the road. For a moment Sarah and her rescuer crouched in the shelter of an alley between two warehouses.

'Bloody hell, Sar!' said Danny Callaghan, breathless when they dared to raise their heads as thick, acrid smoke filled the cold night air. 'You pick your time to do a rabbit-caught-in-the-headlight impression!'

Sarah, open-mouthed, could not believe how close she had just come to being injured – or worse. Then she realised that she did not have a single cup left on the tray she still clutched. 'Oh, no,' she cried, 'I'm going to get into big trouble for breaking those cups.'

'I don't mean to alarm you, Sar,' Danny shouted over the general chaos of burning buildings, flying bombs and dropping incendiaries, 'but there is a war on, and we are right in the thick of it – who's worried about a few smashed cups?'

'There's no need to shout, Danny. I just made that pot of tea, fresh.'

'Well, it looks like you might have to make another one.' Danny shook his head. Sarah was a bit scatty sometimes. Then, out of the corner of his eyes, towards Canada Dock, Danny saw Alfie Delaney parking a covered lorry outside the dock gates. Jumping out and, looking both ways, Delaney crossed the road to Bent-nose Jake's, the public house opposite.

Danny watched Delaney slipping inside the pub, a notorious drinking hole for vagabonds and ne'er-do-wells. Danny knew that the charge hand should be on the twilight shift or on fire-watch, at least. When there were raids like this the dock workers could be here all night as nobody – at least not any man who had a conscience – would ever leave his mates to fend for themselves. Nobody in their right mind, let alone a foreman, would leave the dock to burn and go to have a bevvy.

'If you're all right now, Sar, I'll have to go and give the men a hand. Are you sure you're not hurt?'

'Thanks to you I'm fine, Dan,' Sarah said. 'A bit shaky, but I've no excuse not to get back to tea duty. But thank you again, and I'll see you later. Good luck.' The two of them exchanged a look for a brief moment and Sarah felt something unspoken pass between them. She wasn't sure that she could define it, but it caused her to reach out and squeeze his hand with her own.

Danny returned the gesture with gentle pressure of his own and one of his winning smiles. 'You too. Be careful.' With that, Danny sprinted towards the dock gate and disappeared into the smoke.

Sarah wished that he would tell somebody – Kitty, at least – that he had a heart condition. His ailment could kill him at any time, yet he would not hear of disclosing it, telling Sarah that an over-large heart would define him and cause people to pity him. Sarah could understand his reasoning. After all, her brother Frank thought exactly the same way about his amputated leg and continued to serve his country. Frank told Mam that there was nothing wrong with his brain and it might even come in useful one day.

However, Sarah felt that her knowledge of Danny's condition was becoming an increasing burden and wished she could tell somebody about it, especially when the likes of Vera Delaney gave free rein to her snippy comments. Sarah wondered how much longer she could bear Danny's secret alone. Many a time she had been tempted to tell Kitty the truth – but Danny had sworn her to secrecy.

CHAPTER NINE

December 1940

Two sleepless weeks of worry had passed since Danny and Kitty heard the news about Jack. They tried to keep it light for Tommy's sake, telling him that no further news was good news – but even they did not believe it wholeheartedly. Danny had tried telephoning for more news but it was difficult to get through to the number for the naval base that Jack had given him last time he was at home on leave, and then when he did speak to someone he was told that as soon as they had any more news, next of kin would be informed. Next of kin . . . Even the phrase sounded doom-laden.

'I suppose they've got to say that, Dan,' Kitty said one evening, taking the tablecloth off the table for the third time, shaking it and putting it back on again. There was not enough to do when she was in such an agitated state but she was trying to appear calm for the sake of her brothers. 'Anybody could say they were us.'

'What do you mean, Kit?'

'Well, how do they know we are Jack's family?' She wondered if Rita had rung the naval base from the hospital. 'We could be anybody, and the navy aren't going to give information out to people who are not family.'

'Don't talk so daft!' Danny answered, and immediately regretted the retort that sounded harsher than he intended. He took a deep breath. It was the not knowing that was getting him down, and he shouldn't take it out on Kitty. She was going through the same thing and handling it much better. 'I'm sorry, Kit, all I meant was, who else would be ringing to ask if our Jack was all right?'

'I know.' Kitty gave her brother's arm a reassuring pat even though she didn't feel too reassured either. However, she did not intend to tell their Danny about the letters Jack had been writing to Rita Kennedy. 'I don't know what I'm saying lately.'

A ran-tan on the front door had them skidding down the lobby, but they still did not want to take the telegram being offered by the young lad in the Post Office uniform.

Kitty held the telegram in her hand. Danny was standing on one side of her, Tommy on the other.

'Will there be any reply?' the young telegraph lad asked.

Danny took the telegram from Kitty's hands and sliced it open, both dreading yet eager to see the contents.

His eyes quickly zigzagged the page, his face expressionless.

Kitty hardly dared to breathe. Her heart was thumping

so powerfully in her chest it made her feel light-headed. Then Danny's face cracked into a huge smile and the agonising wait was over.

'He's alive, Kit! Our Jack's alive!' he shouted, waving the telegram in the air.

'What does it say?' Tommy yelled.

Kitty, hardly able to believe the news, snatched the telegram from Danny's hands and read the words.

'Battered stop Bruised stop Limping merrily home stop'.

She threw her arms around her younger brothers and as tears streamed down their faces they hugged each other, dancing around in circles until a small cough behind them sobered them slightly.

'Will there be any reply?' The telegraph boy had a wide grin on his face, relieved that he was a welcome sight this time.

'No reply, Sunny Jim!' Danny fished in his pocket and brought out half a crown. The young lad's eyes lit up.

'Have you got change of this?' Danny asked solemnly and, seeing the young lad's eager smile disappear, he laughed. 'I'm only having you on. Here, take it. All the very best to you and yours.' After all, it was nearly Christmas.

'Ta, mister,' the young lad called as he got back on his Post Office-issue bicycle and whistled down the street.

'Half a crown!' Tommy gasped. 'If I'd have known you were feeling so generous, I'd have gone to the post office meself!'

Ruffling his younger brother's hair Danny laughed out loud then said a silent thank you to his heavenly mother for looking out for Jack.

'Let's just thank our lucky stars, hey, Tom?' Kitty laughed, feeling suddenly that life could not get any better than this. She would have to run over the road and tell Aunty Doll and the rest of the Feenys. With a bit of luck Rita would be home from the hospital by now and Kitty couldn't wait to share the good news.

A few days later, Rita was on her way to work as she passed the door of the Callaghan house. It was early, so early that the sun hadn't yet reared its head and the purple hues of a cold and frosty dawn were just starting to make their way across the horizon. Despite the hour, Empire Street wasn't asleep. The baker's van had already passed on its way; the milkman was doing his round on his horse-drawn cart and was whistling a merry tune.

'Rita!' Kitty poked her head around the door – she was still in her nightdress and dressing gown and her hair was pinned up in a haphazard fashion. When she heard her name, Rita retraced her steps.

'Morning, Kitty. What is it?' Rita thought that despite the hour and her rather dishevelled morning appearance, Kitty still looked like peaches and cream. She could see why her brother Frank might be keen on Kitty.

'Have you got a minute, Rita?'

Rita hesitated. Her shift was due to start at 6.30am

and she was running a little later than usual. She had already worked an eleven-hour shift the previous day and had struggled to get herself out of bed this morning. As she readied herself in the dark she could hear Ma Kennedy's heavy snoring in the adjoining bedroom and reflected that her own mother would have already been up and about with a fire in the grate, a steaming hot cup of tea in the pot and something warm and filling for Pop's stomach to get him started for the day. With no such treatment in the Kennedy household, Rita was keen to get to the hospital so that she could have a warming cuppa before her shift started, but she always had time for Kitty.

'I've got five minutes,' she offered and stepped over the threshold where she followed Kitty into the cosy kitchen where a kettle was set to boil on the oven.

'Thanks, Rita. I won't keep you, but I thought you'd want to see this.' Kitty thrust a letter into her hands and Rita thrilled when she saw Jack Callaghan's distinctive handwriting on the front of the envelope.

Despite herself and her promise to put Jack out of her mind, the worry that something terrible had happened to him and then the welcome news that he was safe had brought everything back to the surface again. Rita didn't think she would ever forget the overwhelming sense of relief when Tommy had come tearing into the Feeny household and told them the news that Jack may be the walking wounded but that he was alive and well.

'I know it's early, but I thought you'd want to read it straight away. He sent us a letter too.'

Rita stuffed the letter into her pocket. 'I'll read it when I get to the hospital.'

Kitty smiled at her and Rita could see no sign of her friend's earlier misgivings. 'It's great news that Jack's safe, isn't it, Rita?' Kitty's eyes were shining. 'He says they might be sending him home. He doesn't know when but Rita, he might be home for Christmas, wouldn't that be wonderful!'

Rita traced her fingers over Jack's letter, 'I couldn't think of anything better, Kit.'

There was no time for the longed-for cuppa when Rita arrived at the hospital. A number of seriously ill patients who had been injured in raids on Ellesmere Port had been transferred to Bootle Infirmary and it was all-hands-on-deck for the entire morning. It was well into the afternoon before Rita could take a short break and she found a quiet corner of the staff sitting room to open the letter.

Dear Rita
I know that you said that you wouldn't write to me anymore and I understand why, but you didn't say anything about me not writing to you, so I've taken the liberty. Please don't ask me to stop. It keeps my mind off other matters and even though we can't share things like we used to, it gives me comfort to know that I'm putting words down on paper that you'll read and think about. I'll certainly be thinking about you.

No doubt you'll have heard the news about what happened out at sea. The censors will have a field day

166

if I say too much but it is probably enough to say that things could have been a lot worse than they were for me if it wasn't for the bravery and courage of my fellow men. It makes a man proud to serve with men such as these. We all wish this blasted war would end, but we'll keep fighting until we've wiped Hitler and his Nazis off the face of this earth.

I'm not sure when I'll be home again, but the people at home are always in my thoughts and I hope I am in theirs too. One day we'll be able to talk freely and to say the things that are on our minds. I look forward to that day, Rita. I know it will come.

Yours

Jack

Rita took the letter and brought it to her nose. Did she imagine that she could detect Jack's scent; that distinctive mixture of sandalwood and musk that she remembered so well? Rita folded the letter and put it in the pocket of her uniform. The rest of the day was as hectic and eventful as the morning had been, but every now and then, in quiet moments, Rita would reach into her pocket and touch Jack's letter. *Yes*, she thought, *keep writing Jack, I won't ask you to stop, not ever.*

CHAPTER TEN

'Will somebody answer that front door?' Dolly called from the back kitchen, where she was putting a folded sheet through the rubber rollers of the mangle and delighting in the amount of water that cascaded into the little galvanised bowl sitting on the floor underneath. The front door was usually open from first thing in the morning until last thing at night, but the weather had taken a turn for the worse and the thick December fog, mixed with the smoke puffing from every chimney, meandered up the thin lobbies, right through the little terraced houses and clung to the damp walls.

'If it's the coalman, watch what he's putting down that coal hole because I'm sure he diddled me last week. There was definitely not a hundredweight of coal in that cellar!' If Dolly thought she was being short-changed, she said so. The coalman would still expect his Christmas box even though there was not much coal to be had lately. Most of what they could get hold of was mixed with coke or even those awful coal dust 'briquettes', which were only marginally better than nothing.

'Mam!' Sarah, who had been having a dinnertime bowl of vegetable soup in the other room called from the front door. 'Will you come out here a minute, please?'

Sarah sounded a bit formal . . . Dolly felt a *frisson* of fear shoot through her, making her heart beat wildly. She hoped the official-sounding ran-tan on the front door was not a telegraph boy. Quickly she dried her hands on her pinny and headed towards the door, dreading bad news of Eddy, who was supposedly heading home in the North Atlantic, or Frank, who, although now shore-based in Southampton, was perpetually in danger of being bombed. Not today, Dolly prayed as she hurried along the narrow passageway, not a week before Christmas. Nor any day, for that matter . . .

'What's wrong?' Dolly tried to keep her voice light.

'Hello . . . Mrs Feeny?' A tall, willowy young woman in a grey two-piece suit, grey knitted turban, and stout black lace-ups held out a grey gloved hand. Dolly noticed that in the other hand the woman was holding a dark brown cardboard suitcase.

'Yes?' Dolly said. If this woman was selling something, she wasn't buying. It was coming to something now that it seemed they even had door-to-door sales ladies.

'I'm Mrs Feeny, too.'

It took a few moments for the information to sink in and, knowing that the accent was not local, Dolly was confused. She knew all of Pop's family – or what little there was of it. He had only a widowed sister who lived in London, and she had never had any children.

'What d'you mean? You're Mrs Feeny, too?' Dolly's question brought a response she never thought she would ever hear.

'Ay up, he's a rum bugger, is my Eddy,' the willowy woman rolled little eyes behind round horn-rimmed spectacles. 'I told him – I said, "Eddy, my lad, you'd best tell your mam we're wed. We don't want her goin' and having one of them there heart attacks when I turn up on her doorstep and her not having a clue who I am!" I thought he got the message an' all, but by the look on your face, Mrs Feeny, he obviously did nowt of the sort!'

Dolly noticed the woman did not even stop to take a breath, and seemed incapable of using one word where ten would do.

'Wait till I get my hands on him. I'll give him leave-your-mother-in-the-dark-my-lad! Anyway, where was I? Oh yes, I'm Violet – Vi for short, I come from Manchester, and my mam always said there weren't a bush big enough to hide my light under!' She then gave an ear-piercing, high-pitched laugh that ended on a snort. Dolly felt she had been verbally battered, and did her best to ignore Vera Delaney, who was not even trying to hide the fact she was gawping all the way from her own house three doors down.

'You'd better come in,' Dolly said, quickly ushering the tall woman up the narrow lobby and into the

170

kitchen where Pop was wiping a piece of dry bread around his soup bowl. He stopped when he saw the little shake of his wife's head.

'Pop, this woman claims she is our Eddy's wife!'

'That's raaght,' Violet's nasal twang echoed around the room as she stood by the sideboard waving her hand as if she was swatting a fly. 'And you're Mr Feeny, I tek it?' She offered her gloved hand.

'Someone get your mother a chair, quick!' Pop ordered, jumping up from his seat and knocking the plate of unbuttered bread flying in an effort to catch Dolly just before she fell to the floor.

'When did this happen?' Pop asked after settling Dolly onto the straight-backed chair. 'He's been at sea for over nine months!'

'Ahh, well, there's the rub,' said Violet almost apologetically. 'He wasn't at sea last August; he were in St Philomena's church marryin' me. It were a glorious day. We had Asti wine for the toast! Can you believe it?' She swatted the invisible fly away again. 'Didn't we think we were toffs – I ask you?'

The look on Dolly's face was thunderous enough to darken the brightest of days, Pop thought. He had never seen her quiet for this long before. However, she rapidly became her old self again.

'I don't believe it! You are living in cloud-cuckoo-land if you think for one minute I would believe my Eddy would enter into the holy sanctity of marriage without asking his own mother to the blessed wedding. You've got another think coming, you upstart you!' Pop suppressed a grin. The upstart was not the only one who could use many words – his Dolly was an expert!

'Ahh, right well,' Violet answered, as if she had already given the matter some thought, 'it were like this, our wedding . . .'

She stopped for a moment and Dolly, surmising this interloper was enjoying every single moment, said, 'Wedding indeed!' Their Eddy, the most reserved of all her offspring, would no more take himself off and marry a complete stranger than he would dance naked in the street with a cabbage on his head! 'You've got some explaining to do, madam, and quick!'

Violet took a deep breath and surprised everybody when she clasped her hands together and said with an air of pride, 'He won me in a raffle!' She nodded her head to verify her statement.

'You trollop!' Dolly spluttered. 'I've never heard the like of it in my life.' She looked quickly to Pop, who said nothing when the other woman opened her mouth and gave another of her braying donkey-laughs.

'Ay up, I'm that sorry, Mrs Feeny – I do get meself muddled sometimes. It's nerves, you know – they send me a bit doolally!'

'Do they now?' Dolly would not be mollified; their Eddy had not even hinted that he had a wife when he wrote home. And even though his shore leave was not frequent he did write regularly and this . . . this . . . *preposter* was not mentioned once – she would have remembered.

'What I mean is, he won a dance with me in some unexotic, far-flung NAAFI off Greatcoat Street in

172

Manchester! Oh, he were funny!' Violet said as Pop pulled out a chair and motioned for her to sit down while he put the kettle on again.

'Ee, I do love a good laugh, me.' She flapped her hands around her head and Dolly wondered if she had something wrong with her. 'Well, I knew as soon as he waltzed me round the dance floor! That's it, Vi, I said, this is the man fer me.' She looked as if she were about to throw back her head and give that raucous laugh again, but Dolly's steely expression may have prevented her.

'He said he'd made his mind up never to marry,' Violet continued at a more sedate pace now, 'as no woman could compare to his lovely mam . . .'

Dolly patted her hair and shifted in her chair.

'He could not shake me off for love nor money, though. He said to me once, "Vi, if you don't leave me alone you'll have folk talking—"'

'My son never uses the word "folk",' Dolly interrupted, giving Violet a chance to take a deep breath before diving right into her explanation again.

'Well, he might not have put it quite like that, I must admit. Anyroad, we used to go for little walks around and about; he were a right nice chap, we hit it off straight away! Then after we'd been writing to each other for a few months, and went dancing a couple of times, I got one of those special licences as a surprise for his birthday . . .'

'You got him a marriage licence as a birthday present?' Dolly could hardly believe her ears.

'He were right surprised, I can tell you!' Violet gave

173

a single clap of her hands, threw back her head, let out that terrible laugh again.

'It's always the quiet one's you have to watch,' said Sarah, keeping out of the way by helping Pop in the back kitchen. 'Our Eddy always said he was never going to get married.'

'It didn't look like he had much choice,' Pop whispered, 'but your mother won't see it like that.'

Violet was still talking when he took the tray into the cosy kitchen and placed it on the table.

'Getting married were the biggest surprise of his life – he told me!'

'It must have been so quick it made his head spin!' Dolly said acidly.

With no time to turn and run, Pop tried to suppress a grin that his new daughter-in-law's nervous enthusiasm encouraged. He could see she was going to be a force to be reckoned with. Dolly, on the other hand, was still looking a little shell-shocked, and, more worryingly, giving no indication of how she was ultimately going to react yet.

'Well, let's all sit down at the table and get to know each other a little bit better,' Pop said, trying to sound as normal as possible. If Dolly's putty-coloured face went any slacker she could be mistaken for a simpleton – and this woman, who was now his second son's new wife, would be given the completely wrong impression.

'He got . . . what?' Nancy's surprised voice accompanied a gentle thud as she pushed the brake on the

174

coach-built Silver Cross pram with her foot, parking it safely in the lobby.

Sarah put her finger to her lips and flapped her hand. 'She'll hear you!'

'I'll leave him there,' Nancy said. This was too good to miss and so she left baby George sleeping, cocooned under myriad-coloured woollen blankets against the freezing weather.

'It'd be a shame to disturb him,' Sarah smiled as she gazed past the covers her mam had crocheted and knitted with any spare wool she could get her hands on. She did not think her mother could cope with a newly woken and therefore fractious baby and Violet all at the same time.

Taking off her coat and hanging it on the coat hook above the pram, Nancy quickly followed her younger sister into the kitchen. She had to hear every bit of this! Their Eddy had gone and got himself wed and told nobody. The sly devil. When did that happen?

She knew sailors were supposed to have a girl in every port, but that definitely did not apply to their Eddy.

When she entered the kitchen, her mam and Pop were sitting at the table, opposite the long sash window by the back-kitchen door, and Nancy saw the narrow and straight back of the lady dressed in battleship grey. Nancy glanced from Mam, who looked indignantly shocked and clearly agitated, picking at the chenille tablecloth, to Pop, who offered a forced, almost apologetic smile.

'Hello, Nancy, love. Come and meet Violet – our

Eddy's new wife.' Pop said it as if it was the most natural thing in the world.

'Eddy's wife?' Nancy still couldn't take it in. Her brother had been writing as regularly as he could for months now and he had not said one word about having a girl, never mind marrying one!

'Violet's house has been damaged by incendiaries,' Pop explained. Violet had gone into some detail about how the vicarage she had lived in all her life had been hit by incendiary bombs, killing her parents. She had no family left. 'Violet's got nowhere else to go.'

Pop said it in a way that told Nancy not to say a word as it was obvious she was dying to say something. So Nancy kept quiet, busy thinking. There was no room in the house for any more people, let alone a total stranger! Mam and Pop had the front bedroom, she and George had the middle room and Sarah had the small room at the back of the house. If one of the brothers were home, or Tommy stayed when Kitty and Danny were both working late, then Sarah moved into the middle room. It was a bit crowded, but there was no other way.

Nancy and Violet were now eyeing each other. Nancy didn't at all like the way the woman was looking at her, like she was cataloguing her for one of Mam's clothing exchanges, such as were springing up in every church hall. How did they know for sure that this woman was who she said?

'She could be anybody!' Nancy blurted suddenly. Just then Violet opened her bag and took out a long envelope, handing it to Dolly, who withdrew a document and read it quickly.

'She's right,' Dolly sighed, handing the marriage lines to Pop to read. 'She is married to our Eddy.' Dolly scraped back her chair on the linoleum floor and went out to the back kitchen. Moments later, after an awkward silence, Nancy followed.

'So what does that mean?' Nancy asked, knowing exactly what it meant.

'There isn't enough room for everybody,' Dolly said quietly, turning on the cold tap enough for the sound to mask her words. Nancy knew her mother would not see anybody on the street. 'Violet has no home to go to, and no family to see to her. We have got to help her out . . . for our Eddy's sake, if nothing else.'

'Does that mean I've to go back to Mrs Kerrigan's house?' Nancy asked, though she knew the answer.

'I'm sorry, love, but I can't see any other way,' Dolly said. 'At least you have your own room at Mrs Kerrigan's and you are not cramped up like you are here.'

'But, Mam, she's worse than the Gestapo!'

'How do you know what the Gestapo are like?' Dolly asked, shaking her head, knowing their Nancy could be a trial sometimes.

'Nancy . . .' Pop's voice, behind her, held a warning note. 'You know we would never see one of our own stranded.'

Nancy nodded and left her parents to get on with making another pot of tea, knowing they wanted to talk in private.

'So, when did all this happen?' Nancy said, not taking her eyes from her new sister-in-law. There was no hope of her being able to stay here if this upstart was going to stay. Wait until she told Gloria.

'He did what?' Gloria echoed her friend's earlier response.

'I know! I've got to go back to moaning Minnie Kerrigan now!' Nancy was in no mood to be mollified by Pop. She had flounced out of the house and down the foggy street to the Sailor's Rest, above which her friend Gloria lived. 'I'll be like a caged canary! Sitting in, night after night, keeping that old bat company. I'll go doolally!'

'Oh, let's have a night out before you have to go and stay with old misery guts again – I've got tonight off.'

'Tonight?' Nancy wondered if she could wangle one more night in the middle bedroom, knowing it would serve Lady Muck right if she had to sleep on the couch in the parlour. She should have given them notice she was going to turn up. 'Fancy you having a night off!' Nancy would love a night out, it had been so long, but she wasn't going to let Gloria know that. Besides, Nancy certainly did not intend to show gratitude because her best friend could now fit her into her busy life.

'I've got something I want to tell you—' Gloria began, but her words were cut short.

'Miss Prim has brought her suitcase,' Nancy said petulantly. 'I notice that wasn't destroyed in the fire.'

Her nostrils flared. 'She talks laaak thaaaa,' she imitated Violet's flat, nasal tone, 'and looks like Popeye's girl-friend, Olive Oyl! And if she looks down that long nose at me again I'll have to say something.'

Gloria couldn't get a word in edgeways and decided, on past experience, that it was pointless trying to tell Nancy anything when she had a bee in her bonnet. The news would have to keep for now, because it was obvious Nancy was nowhere near finished moaning yet . . .

'She looked at me like I was something she trod in on a pig farm!' Nancy's face was almost as dark as her Titian victory roll, while Gloria opened her perfectly made-up, crimson lips and howled with laughter.

'Oh, I wish I'd been there,' she said eventually, patting her platinum-blonde curls.

'You can have that pleasure later,' Nancy said. 'I'll ask Mam if she will mind George while we go into town.'

Gloria put her hand up as if to stop her right there. She simply had to tell her own news.

'I got a letter: Romeo Brown isn't coming until next week.' She sounded disappointed.

'Who the heck is Romeo Brown, when he's at home?' Nancy asked. 'He'd have to be able to handle himself in our street, with a name like that.'

'Only one of the leading London impresarios – and he's coming to hear me sing next week.'

But as usual, Nancy seemed interested in only her own news. 'Going out then will work out better for me. If this upstart thinks she's going to pinch my bed she's got another think coming!'

'D'you think your mam will mind little Georgie next week?'

'I'm sure she will, especially when I tell her I'm meeting the famous Romeo Brown.'

'Oh, good show!' Gloria imitated the crisp tones of her RAF boyfriend, Giles, whom she had not seen since the beginning of the Battle of Britain, last August.

Nancy gave a tight smile. She wanted to be pleased for Gloria's success – really, she did – but how could she, when Gloria rubbed her nose in it every chance she got, with her glamorous clothes and blonde hair – and that voice?

Gloria's mother was a failed music-hall singer who lost her singing voice before marrying Cyril Arden. When she could not make it as a singer she was determined her daughter would. Gloria had it drummed into her from an early age that she was going to be a star, whether she wanted it or not. However, Gloria did want it – she took it for granted stardom would happen one day and revelled in the attention her mother lavished on her after a performance – which was, in fact, the only attention Gloria received from her.

'It looks like I'm really going places now, Nance!'

'Aye, well, just remember where you came from,' Nancy could not stop the envious words, 'Empire Street – the same place as the rest of us.'

'I'll never forget that, Nance,' Gloria said. 'This will always be my home.'

'And don't forget you're courting either.' Nancy could not push down the rising resentment of her friend's success, her freedom to go out every night and dine in the best hotels, or to be chatted up by the most handsome men.

'We'll go to the pictures today, if you like – save our troubles for another day,' Gloria said, and Nancy nodded, although she could not see what troubles her friend could possibly have.

'We'll call in at the Adelphi,' Gloria said, the following week. Nancy felt her spirits sink, knowing that if they went there Gloria was bound to be collared by somebody who wanted to talk to a local celebrity. 'I've just got to meet somebody, it won't take long . . .'

'You're not taking me on a blind date, I hope!' Nancy was peeved now, suspecting Gloria was only asking her to go for a night out because she was at a loose end. This wasn't a bit like the old days.

'No, I had a phone call from my agent.'

Nancy silently sneered. *Her agent, is it?*

'I've got this meeting with Romeo Brown – I told you about him last week. He's a famous London impresario and he really will be there this evening. If anybody can open doors for me, he can. He can make me a star, Nance!'

'Sounds phoney to me.' Nancy thought Gloria didn't half fancy herself these days.

'Honest, Nance, he's coming to hear me sing.' Gloria was checking there was no lipstick on her teeth in the mirror of her gold and mother-of-pearl compact.

'I hope you don't take all night.' Nancy pouted like a spoiled five-year-old. 'I'll feel a right lemon sitting outside your manager's office for hours waiting for you.'

'Don't be like that, Nance,' Gloria urged, linking her arm and doing that little wiggle she always did to show there were no hard feelings. 'You know we'll always be friends. You're like the sister I never had.'

'But I've got two sisters!' Nancy said. Had Gloria completely lost her marbles?

'I know, but you're the one I would have picked if I could choose one of my own.' The two of them suddenly started laughing and Nancy knew she could not stay cross with Gloria for long, although she could not hide her envious streak either.

'What will Giles have to say on the matter, I wonder. Swanning around top-class nightclubs and hotels and being fêted by London agents?'

Gloria said nothing now, Nancy noticed.

Nancy wondered what she had done so wrong to be in this position. Tied down with a baby while the Nazis were holding her husband prisoner! She did not even have a bed to call her own now that this new sister-in-law had turned up.

'Never mind, Nance, your turn will come one day.' Gloria gave her a hug. 'Your luck will come when you least expect it – you'll see!' Gloria knew Nancy was trying to burst her happy balloon but she was having none of it. 'I had a letter from Giles this morning. He said he might get some leave soon.'

'You caught Giles before he knew he was being

chased.' Nancy smiled, thawing now. Giles's family were a cut above Gloria's. His father bred and sold racehorses and his mother, a member of the Ladies' Guild, gave coffee mornings. They were a handsome family and Nancy knew Gloria would have fancied his father if she had not seen Giles first!

'Wouldn't it be marvellous if he managed to get home this weekend? I could tell him my good news!' The thing Gloria missed most about Giles was his masculine prowess – not to mention the divine champagne lifestyle and the swish out-of-the-way hotels. He treated her like a princess but she made sure he did not go without. Who could resist her feminine charms? *Oh, Giles, come home soon . . .* Nancy was not what she needed right now.

'What time shall I call for you?' Nancy said, looking forward to getting dressed up.

'Let's say half-past six – that way I'll be able to go over the songs with the band and, apart from my little singsong, the night and the dance floor will be all ours.'

'All yours, you mean.' Nancy knew there was no ration on male attention where Gloria was concerned.

'Your Sid won't always be a prisoner,' Gloria said, knowing Nancy had not been allowed to move out of her husband's sight before he was called up. 'He'll be back soon enough.'

Ruling your life as always.

CHAPTER ELEVEN

'Oh, it's ever so posh in here,' Nancy said as an attendant took her coat and showed her and Gloria to their table in the semi-circular booth on the raised balcony of the Adelphi Hotel. Above their heads huge glittering diamond-shaped chandeliers twinkled, and the girls' feet sank into the thick ruby-coloured carpet. Nancy sighed; she could get used to places like this. However, she knew if it were not that Gloria was singing here regularly in the evenings, she could never afford to come to such a grand place.

'You're going to make the most of the luxurious facilities, you mean,' Nancy laughed, soaking up the opulent surroundings when her best friend told her she was going to powder her nose.

The clientele were high-ranking servicemen escorting their dazzling wives or lady-friends, Gloria noticed, home on leave and out to enjoy the early Christmas party at which she had been invited to sing. It made a pleasant change from her dad's pub surrounded by beer-swilling dockers and their harassed wives.

'I'll tell you what, Nance,' Gloria said on her return, sliding into the plush banquette with the poise of a sensually stretching cat, 'those lavatories are immaculate. I felt so spoiled when the lady attendant gave me a fluffy towel to dry my hands on, then put a blob of hand cream into my palm.' She held out her elegant hand to Nancy and jiggled perfectly manicured crimson nails. 'Here, Nance, have a sniff of that. It's got a lovely perfume.'

'Oh, I must go and have a look later,' Nancy answered, engrossed in people watching. She had never seen so many diamond necklaces in one room. The fabulous function room, with its twinkling chandeliers, bejewelled patrons and candle-lit tables held the same enchantment as the first Christmas grotto she ever went to as a child. It was truly magical.

'This is the life, hey, Nance?' Gloria said, lifting her gin and lime but barely wetting her freshly applied cherry-red lipstick, savouring the perfumed atmosphere before getting ready for her big spot.

'Hello, Nance. How are you? I haven't seen you in ages. I buy you both a drink?' Nancy looked up to see a handsome man impeccably dressed in the uniform of an RAF flight lieutenant. Nancy's eyes widened! She had not seen Stan Hathaway since the week she got married.

'Fancy seeing you here,' she said, and was just about to tell him she would love a rum and peppermint when, to her utter astonishment, Gloria lifted an imperious hand.

'We're not here to be picked up, and we do not accept drinks from rogue males.'

That's a first! Nancy thought, unable to believe what she was hearing. Gloria would usually accept a drink from anybody.

Stan grinned and said in a very formal tone, 'Forgive me for being so forward. My intentions are honourable, I can assure you.' Then he made Nancy smile when he said, 'Anyway, you know me quite well, Gloria, so stop pretending.'

'Is that really you underneath all that RAF regalia, Stan? Well, you do scrub up quite well, I must admit. Now buzz off as me and Nance are waiting for someone, aren't we?'

'It's Lieutenant Hathaway to you, Gloria. Anyway, suit yourselves.' He winked at Nancy, then said, 'Catch you later,' above the rising notes of the band's opening music. Nancy scowled in Gloria's direction, the night losing a little of its lustre. She would have liked another drink and a catch-up with Stan. It had been a long time since she last saw him. What harm could it do? Gloria was only interested in herself and hated the idea that anyone should steal her thunder.

Looking at Gloria, who was surveying the room, her body perfectly poised to its best advantage, Nancy felt a well of resentment towards her friend. She's just a jealous cow, she thought as Stan went back to the company at his own table. How dare she dismiss her friend as if he was of no importance? Nancy watched Stan lifting a champagne glass in salute, acknowledging another RAF chum and leaning over to say something. Moments later, his pal was crossing the highly polished dance floor. Nancy nudged Gloria, who turned to look.

Gloria gasped in surprise, her mouth open, but nothing else came out. Nancy knew she could have any man she wanted – it had always been like that – but the one crossing the dance floor now was the man she wanted most of all.

'Giles!' Gloria squealed eventually as the officer she had been courting since last year neared their table. He was the only man who made her best friend's eyes light up like that, Nancy knew.

'Oh, Nance, Giles is home! He's come to see me!' Gloria gasped. As Gloria negotiated the balcony steps and then ran towards him with her arms open wide, Nancy felt a sudden urge to get up and leave. Unable to avert her gaze at this most intimate of moments, she realised that she would now be surplus to requirements. Gloria would not want her here now that her boyfriend was home, and Nancy felt a pang of severe envy.

She averted her eyes at last and met those of Stan Hathaway, who just so happened to be gazing in her direction. She gave him a dazzling smile. More than ever, she wanted to dance and have some fun, and as Gloria would now be completely occupied by Giles, Stan was the obvious choice of man with whom to have that fun.

But Gloria was back and had evidently seen the exchange of smiles between Nancy and Stan. 'Oh, Nance, are you all right? I didn't upset you, did I?' She looked to where Stan was sitting looking up towards the balcony. 'I must admit, he is very handsome, but I thought he was bothering you.'

Nancy knew her friend was saving her from doing something silly, more like. She sighed and relaxed a little. 'Gloria, you're hopeless. I can look after myself very well.'

However, their conversation was over when Gloria turned all her attention to her own boyfriend who had now followed her over with his drink in hand and took his place beside her in the semi-circular velvet-seated booth. Giles nuzzled her neck while Gloria, obviously lapping up the attention, snuggled closer. Nancy thought it was time to go and have a look at the ladies' room Gloria had been raving about earlier.

'If I don't move now, Giles, the band will never forgive me.' Gloria's hands slipped from around his neck, down his arm and, after a small clasp of entwined fingertips, she reluctantly moved away. 'I'd better go and get ready.'

Nancy wondered if she could make some excuse and go home as she made her way back from the ladies' room to the table. Gloria would not be interested in having a married friend around when her man was home on leave. Who could blame her? Nancy knew she would be just as thrilled to have her man home, keen to spend time and money on her and show her a fabulous time. She sighed, aware that it was an impossible dream; Sid was not that type of man.

'Knock 'em dead, kid!' Nancy said as Gloria went to change for her performance.

Just a few minutes later: 'Ladies and gentlemen, may I introduce Miss Gloria Arden!' The bandleader's voice rang out as Gloria leaned into the microphone to the rapturous applause of the audience. Dressed in a gold lamé gown, instead of the white-spotted navy-blue dress with the sweetheart neckline and puffed sleeves she had been wearing earlier, she looked every inch the successful singing starlet.

With her hair now expertly swept up into Betty Grable curls, replacing the victory roll she had recently taken to wearing in support of her loving aviator boyfriend, and graciously accepting the applause that greeted her, Gloria began to sing, holding the audience captivated with the emotion of her words.

'You have to admit, she is very good, isn't she?' Nancy turned to see the adoring look in Giles's eyes. He was evidently completely smitten.

'Can I let you into a little secret?' he asked, leaning towards Nancy.

He shuffled a little closer, then rummaged around in his trouser pocket and brought out a beautiful, tooled leather box. He held it out to Nancy.

'Do you think Gloria will like it?'

Lifting the hinged lid on the small navy-blue box, Nancy's eyes widened when she saw the most exquisite, dazzling diamond ring she had ever seen in her life. Her lips formed in a perfect 'O' and her gasp of surprise was audible.

'Like it?' she said when she could find her voice.

'I don't think she will ever let you out of her sight again!'

'I'm going to ask her to marry me,' Giles said. 'I've been thinking about her all these months I've been away and I vowed to myself to ask her the very next time I saw her.'

Without thinking, Nancy threw her arms around his neck and gave Giles a congratulatory kiss on the cheek, her eyes brimming with unshed tears, thinking it so romantic.

'I think we need a drink.' He sounded breathless, like he had been running up a hill, and Nancy was thrilled, hardly able to wait for Gloria to finish singing. Giles summoned an attentive waiter and Nancy felt herself relax, knowing Gloria was going to be delighted. This was the diamond she had been waiting for.

'Champagne?'

Nancy smiled and nodded, immediately returning her attention to Gloria's performance. She was certainly going to stay now. There was going to be a celebration and she would enjoy the night in style.

Looking over to where Stan was sitting she saw him nod and smile at her. She smiled back, giving him her best Rita Hayworth and secretly thrilled to have his attention. It was only a bit of flirting – where was the harm? She turned back to Gloria's stirring finale of the popular Vera Lynn song 'We'll Meet Again'. Her thoughts fleetingly turned to Sid, her husband, and then just as quickly she pushed them away . . .

What the eye didn't see . . .

* * *

'They're a bit earlier tonight,' Dolly said to Tommy, whom she was minding for the evening, as the wail of the air-raid siren cut through the freezing evening air. 'I was hoping to get my Christmas cake iced tonight.'

'I'll grab the baby, you grab the flask of tea!' Violet said, hurrying into the kitchen. There was no time to lose as the urgent warning sound, given by the police or air raid warden's short shrill blasts on a whistle, made them hurry.

Pop was out on ARP duties, while Sarah, in her capacity as a Red Cross volunteer, was helping at the hospital.

'I hope our Nancy and Gloria manage to get a bus home,' Dolly said as Violet snatched George's tiny siren suit from the sideboard and expertly slipped him into it.

'Looks like you've done that before, Vi,' Dolly remarked as she gathered her file of important documents comprising ration books, insurance papers and identity cards. Violet, despite her horrible laugh, was proving to be an asset. She would turn her hand to anything to help out and shared some of Dolly's domestic and voluntary load with a smile on her face.

'Can I go down the docks and have a look at the lights, Aunty Doll?' Tommy's eager eyes were wide until he saw the grim expression on Dolly's face.

Dolly could not believe her ears. 'Indeed you will not.'

'The idea of it!' Violet said. 'Have you no sense in that woolly head of yours?'

Dolly headed to the kitchen to collect the Thermos flask, and motioned for Tommy to pick up the spare blankets and stay close to her and Violet as they headed towards the brick shelter that had been built at the bottom of Empire Street, accessible to the people in the dock road, too.

'It's not fair,' Tommy grumbled under his breath. 'I never get to do anything exciting around here.'

'What was that, Tom?' Dolly asked, fastening her coat as she went.

'Nothing, Aunty Doll,' Tommy said innocently, knowing that the first chance he got he and Monty were going down to the docks. Since he had found the woolly mongrel wandering the dock road, his faithful companion had never left his heel. However, it did not matter how much he pleaded that his mate Ginger got some whopping pieces of shrapnel, Aunty Doll was having none of it. She would not let him out of her sight.

'Put your scarf on, Tom. We don't want that damp air getting on your chest.'

Tommy, sighing, did as he was told. He loved Aunty Doll and all the Feeny family, but they nearly smothered him with kindness, sometimes, especially since he'd come out of hospital after contracting diphtheria. Aunty Doll wouldn't let the wind blow on him – it was worse than living with their Kitty.

Although he knew he should be grateful. Aunty Dolly was a saint compared to that awful woman he had been billeted with in Southport who had treated him so badly he ended up in hospital at death's door.

But, no matter how much he told Aunty Doll he was all better now, she still made a big hoo-ha.

'Come on, we'll lose our place in the shelter,' Violet called as her long legs strode ahead. 'Didn't you hear your aunty Doll telling you to fasten that coat right up, Tommy?' she added.

Every inhabitant of Empire Street was hurrying towards the shelter now and Tommy could hardly see who he was in danger of bumping into over the blankets he was carrying.

'Come on, Tommy, no dawdling out here!' Violet called as huge searchlights arced across the black sky while the sight of a silent silver barrage balloon was caught momentarily in the flash of searchlights along with floating flares, their strange purple glow sailing gently to the ground like a promise of precious shrapnel to come. Tommy saw the air raids as a great adventure and was eager to be out. Billy Fisher had found a tail fin from an incendiary, he'd heard. He would have to wait until Aunty Doll and Aunty Violet nodded off, or they would stop him going outside before the all clear and spoil his fun, and he hoped that when the Luftwaffe came over they did not miss his school!

'Oh, we made it, Vi,' Aunty Doll said, panting, carrying little Georgie into the shelter.

Tommy thought he had been doing a good job helping Aunty Doll but now Violet was here she would take over as usual. Tommy shivered in the cold air of the shelter though he didn't bother to fasten the belt of his navy-blue gabardine mackintosh. Now he'd put

193

the blankets down he was having too many problems trying to fix his cap on straight while getting tangled in the long scarf Aunty Dolly had knitted for him.

He watched Violet take George, who had been waking because he did not like being disturbed and brought out on a cold night. Tommy thought Violet was being a bit too heavy-handed with the little baby for his liking. Wrapped in his little siren suit Aunty Doll had made from an old blanket, Georgie began to grizzle, just as Tommy knew he would. Aunty Doll had made him a siren suit too. It was meant to be easy to get on and off when you had to get to the shelter quickly in the middle of the night, but Tommy thought he looked like a big baby in his – even if Mr Churchill wore one himself. Tommy thought that once George was out of Violet's arms and back in the safety of Aunty Doll's, he would soon nod off, despite the sounds of the air raid.

Thunderous applause for Gloria brought Nancy out of her reverie and she clapped enthusiastically. The audience loved Gloria, it was obvious, and by the appreciative look on Giles's face, he did too. Standing now, the audience whistled and cheered as Gloria accepted the ovation with simulated modesty. Nancy could see she had it down to a fine art, but there was no getting away from the fact that Gloria was highly talented.

'She is rather special, isn't she?' Giles said, holding a huge cigar between his teeth and clapping enthusiastically.

'She could be as famous as Anne Shelton if this

agent signs her up!' Nancy said proudly as Gloria quickly made her way to Giles, accepting the salutations and acknowledging the hugs with a glowing smile honed by considerable practice in the dressing-table mirror.

Gloria watched Giles waiting impatiently for her and the thrill that shot through her was like nothing she had felt before as the hunger to be in his arms overwhelmed her.

'Oh, that was wonderful!' Giles said as he took her in his arms and they kissed for the longest time. Nancy thought that there was a time and a place for that sort of thing, and she was a bit shocked that Gloria could be so brazen in a room full of people. Gloria positively glowed when she slipped back into her seat beside Giles and was hardly able to take her eyes from him.

'Look what lovely Giles bought for us, Glor!' Nancy said eventually, trying to get their attention and feeling once more like a spare part.

'Champagne – what's the celebration?'

Gloria could barely believe what was happening as Giles went down on one knee and produced the small leather ring box. Her expression was one of absolute amazement as he spoke the words that she had been longing to hear.

'Marry me, Gloria, and you'll make me the happiest man alive.'

'Oh, Giles, of course I'll marry you!' she gasped as he slipped the ring on her finger and she threw her arms around his neck. Then, as the sparkling rock dazzled on Gloria's finger, Nancy felt a sharp pang of jealousy and realised that Gloria had done it again – she not only had a glittering career ahead of her, she also had an impressive fighter pilot to go with it! But Gloria was her friend, after all, and Nancy tried to push away uncharitable thoughts.

'Here, Nance, have some champagne. Let's celebrate!' said Gloria, twiddling her diamond-laden finger so that the beautiful stone flashed in the candlelight.

Nancy had never drunk champagne before and was dying to see what all the fuss was about. Gloria had once told her that it was ever so posh and film stars like Carole Lombard and Susan Hayward drank it all the time. She took a huge sip and spluttered as it hit the back of her throat. It was like liver salts with a kick, she thought. Although if she drank enough of it she might be able to relax a bit more. Nancy refused to be impressed as she took another sip . . . then another.

'Let's get Stan over to help us celebrate,' Giles said, beckoning Stan over to their table.

Her mother's words about being careful now echoed in Nancy's head but the words soon disappeared when the band's music filled the air and Stan asked her up to dance.

'It's lovely to see you, Nancy,' Stan said, taking her in his arms and gently guiding her around the highly polished dance floor. 'I heard on the grapevine that you'd married Sid Kerrigan. Away on duty, is he?'

'He's a POW. We don't know where he is.' Nancy affected a brave face, but the last thing she wanted to do right now was talk about Sid. It only brought her mood down.

'I'm sorry to hear that, for his sake, Nancy, but I always thought that you were too good for him and now you're all on your own, with no one to look after you.'

Nancy looked up into his eyes. She'd always liked Stan and he'd always liked her. She'd met him through her job in the George Henry Lee Department Store. The girls said he was a cut above the rest of the rabble around Empire Street because he had gone to university, but Nancy knew his granny lived near Empire Street; it was only his folks who'd put on airs and graces. He was as good or as bad as the rest of them. They'd indulged in a bit of flirting here and there but Sid had gone mad one night when he'd seen her dancing with Stan and that had been that.

'I think there is a bit of unfinished business between you and me. Don't you agree, Nancy?'

Nancy looked coyly away. It had been so long since she felt the thrill of a man's arms around her and, like a starving woman at a feast, she wanted more. Eagerly she listened as he plied her with compliments and enjoyed the feel of his strong hands as they gently caressed the small of her back. The music was loud and she was having trouble hearing what he was saying, so it was only natural she had to lean in to catch his words. Before long Stan was holding her so close, Nancy thought it was a good thing the lights were low. Nancy remembered how, even on her wedding day she had considered writing to Stan, as he had asked her to – just to be friendly, nothing in it – until their Rita persuaded her not to, that was.

'Shall we go on somewhere else after this?' Stan's cheek brushed Nancy's and his voice was warm and enticing. This was what she had dreamed about . . . yearned for . . . Yes, she would love to go on somewhere else, the night was young and why shouldn't they? She was harming no one.

'We could have supper in my hotel?' Stan asked. 'Or maybe just a nightcap – it's up to you.'

'You're ever so forward, Stanley Hathaway!' Nancy tried to sound shocked but she was thrilled; this was so sophisticated. The next time he turned her, weaving her so gracefully around on the dance floor, Nancy had to move to his right slightly, not being tall enough to see over his shoulder, just to see if her best friend was watching. Gloria would be so put out that she was not the only centre of attention tonight.

Maybe it was the effect of the champagne that caused Nancy to rest her head on his shoulder. Or, maybe it was just plain devil-may-care, she was not so sure. However, for a moment she was happy to entertain the thought that Stan was her man and she was his sweetheart.

Nancy felt as if she was the most desirable woman in the room when Stan, his hand still resting on the small of her back, accompanied her back to her seat. Pouring the champagne, Giles handed everyone another glass to toast his future bride. Earlier jealousy forgotten, Nancy felt her face glow, feeling proud and pleased to be in such glamorous company. As the night wore on Nancy got even more tipsy and could not help but giggle as the champagne bubbles went up her nose.

'You have the most beautiful laugh, Nancy,' Stan said in a dreamy voice, and Nancy had to crush the desire to gaze back into his eyes. He'd had a few, she was sure of that, and maybe he was a little merry, but why shouldn't he appreciate a nice-looking girl like her? These brave men needed all the encouragement they could get, didn't they? Who was she to dash his dreams?

She giggled some more, realising the champagne, which she had drunk far too quickly, had gone straight to her head. Stan moved towards her and for a wild moment, Nancy thought he was going to kiss her. She edged back in her seat. She was a married woman! She had a wedding ring on, for goodness' sake! But maybe just a little kiss wouldn't hurt . . . After all, if it hadn't been for Stan she would have been sitting on her tod, because Gloria wasn't taking a blind bit of notice of her now. Nancy decided that if Stan did try to kiss her, perhaps she would just let him have a little one: friendly, like. It wasn't fair of her to rebuff him completely, not after all his generosity. It was lovely that her admirer wanted to spend his money so lavishly when it was obvious he would get nothing in return!

Not used to being pampered, Nancy realised that she liked the champagne lifestyle – she liked it a lot.

'Another dance?' Stan asked, and Nancy could think of nothing she would like to do more.

* * *

Giles smiled into Gloria's deep blue eyes and Gloria returned his longing gaze, unable to speak when he looked at her like that. Suddenly she felt as if she was drowning in his eyes . . . and she did not want saving.

'I want to make love to you right now,' he whispered, and Gloria nodded. Tonight was the most special night of her life. She was going to be Giles's wife! Giles leaned in to kiss her and when the chair beneath her trembled she couldn't be sure it wasn't her whole body shaking with desire.

'Oh my God!' she gasped.

Breaking through her reverie was the banshee wail of the air raid siren, and the crash of masonry as it started to fall all around them.

'Ladies and gentleman, there is an air raid taking place and I must point you to the shelters . . .' Gloria's thoughts were now cotton wool. She was unable to think straight. The wonderfully magnetic gentle pressure on her lips made her hungry for more, much more . . . all she wanted to do right now was to be with Giles and nothing was going to stop her.

'Nancy? Nancy, over here!' Stan was standing on the other side of the dance floor – the explosion and the subsequent exodus of people had separated them.

'Stan, I've got to get out of here!' Nancy cried as he hurried to her and pulled her towards him protectively, leading her away from the rubble of the bombed dance floor with its fallen ceiling. 'Don't leave me, Stan!' she cried.

The air was thick with smoke and dust as she

stumbled through the debris, turning her ankle in the process, but that did not matter now. Within moments, as her legs no longer felt strong enough to support her, Nancy lurched forward and was relieved to feel Stan's strong arms around her, helping her to clamber over the rubble and make her way through a sea of people, all with the same idea. Escape.

Dear God, thought Nancy, this wasn't real. It couldn't be happening to her, not in this beautiful hotel.

'Oh, Stan!' Nancy could hold back the tears of shock no longer as another wave of bombers flew over the rooftops, drowning out any further words. Stan, holding tightly to her hand, pulled her towards the shelter where dozens of equally terrified and distraught people were all wanting to take refuge.

'Gloria!' Nancy said, suddenly remembering her best friend. 'I've got to find Gloria!'

'She was with her fella. He'll make sure she is all right. We have to get you somewhere safe,' Stan said, urging her forward.

'I can't stay in here; I have to get home to George, my baby boy!'

'It's too dangerous, Nance!' Stan took hold of her hand now and pulled her quickly into the shelter. 'We've got to stay here now.'

'He's with Mam.' Dazed, Nancy allowed herself to sink into the comfort of his arms. 'He'll be crying for me. He doesn't like the noise.' She should never have left him.

'He'll be fine with your mam, Nance,' Stan said. 'Just stay with me where it's safe, for God's sake!'

Nancy buried her head in his shoulder, but nothing could blot out the terrible thunder of the bombs that were crashing down outside. It sounded as if the world was coming to an end. Nancy clung to Stan, and prayed.

Gloria was aware of the crash of the ack-ack guns pounding away, and the sickening thud of bombs exploding somewhere close. Any minute they could be blown to bits! She felt a strange combination of fear and exhilaration; she had never experienced anything like it in her life.

Holding her hand, Giles pulled her towards the exit door.

All around them, women in furs and jewels picked up their skirts and raced for the safety of the exit doors. Chairs and tables were upended in haste as another blast brought down a glittering chandelier.

Gloria felt the ground shake below her and in the mêlée she lost one of her silk shoes. Hopping and hurrying she could still feel Giles's hand in hers. As long as she was with Giles she'd be safe. Another crash and she let out a small scream. Keep Calm and Carry On, she told herself, just like the posters said.

'Giles, I can't see!' Gloria's voice trembled as the lights went out. Distant cries and the rush of freezing air on her bare shoulders told Gloria that they were near the exit and within moments they were out in the street. In the darkness, with the dust and the noise, it was hard to get a sense of where they were or where they were going.

'Where's Nancy?' Gloria began to panic. The last

time she had seen Nancy she was on the dance floor just where that chandelier fell. 'Nancy!' However, her cries went unanswered as she and Giles made their way to the shelter. It was packed and there was no more room.

'We'll never get in there!' Giles said, seeing people crowding ahead of them round the door. 'Come with me. I know a place near here.' Gloria, having discarded her other shoe, did not feel the splinters of glass nor the hot cinders burrowing into her bare feet as she fled, dodging falling masonry and shooting flashes of flame, along Lime Street towards another shelter. A loud whoosh sped past her face and she ducked out of the way of a fiery piece of wood.

'In here!' Giles called, pulling her into the deep recess of a shop doorway. 'This will have to do, I'm afraid, darling.' They burrowed deeper into the long entrance, glad to be alive as Liverpool burned around them.

'We'll be lucky to get out of here tonight,' Giles said distractedly, leaning out a little to watch firemen desperately trying to contain the flames further down the street. A small whimper escaped from Gloria and he put his arms around her. She must be strong. She could not cave in now.

'It's all right, my darling. I won't let anything hurt you.' Gloria felt safe in his arms. If they were going to die tonight, surely it would be better if they died together, she thought as he whispered soothing words in her hair and stroked her tear-stained face. Giles removed his RAF greatcoat and placed it over them like a blankct. They sat in the darkness, and all the while he talked to her, soothing words about what they would do and where they would go once they were married. After a while, she didn't feel scared any more but she clasped herself around him tighter, enjoying the feel of his chest and back as her arms encircled him. The bombs continued to fall, but set back from the street the fugitives were well hidden, though there were now precious few people; just the occasional cry of an ARP warden or a fire watcher. Gloria felt Giles's lips search for her in the darkness. Then, gently, he folded her in his arms and her pliant body cleaved to his. She belonged to Giles now, that engagement ring on her finger said something more than mere words could. She was his. Yielding to his touch, she felt as if all her life had been leading to this point. She and Giles were bound together for ever now and she knew for certain that her life lay way beyond the limited confines of Empire Street.

Gloria could feel the passion rise in her and Giles felt it too. His hands moved across her body, caressing her breasts through the thin material of her gold lamé evening dress. Gloria hadn't led a sheltered life and had let men have their way with her when it suited her, but she had never felt like this before. As Giles gently but insistently lifted her dress she did nothing to stop him. The intense feeling was overwhelming and all she could think of was how much she wanted him; how much she wanted him to want her. As he entered her, Gloria clung to him, small cries escaping her lips with each powerful thrust of his body.

'Oh, Giles!' The ground shuddered beneath them, her body cleaving to him as another explosion matched her own climactic rapture.

Both spent, they gasped for breath as tears rolled freely down Gloria's cheeks. She had never felt anything like it. Giles, his eyes full of tender love, wiped away her tears with his finger.

'Gloria, my darling, are you all right? Did I hurt you?' He was leaning on his elbow, looking down at her through the flickering light of a distant blaze. Gloria leaned against the cool marbled doorway and shook her head. 'No, you didn't hurt me,' she whispered. 'It was wonderful, absolutely wonderful.' Her voice was hoarse, barely above a whisper, and he leaned down and, very tenderly, he kissed her tears away.

'Oh, Giles I do love you so much.' Gloria's lips were still tingling from his ardent kisses.

'I love you too, my darling, I have from the moment we met – even before I knew your name I knew you were the girl for me.' Giles took her hand and as her engagement ring sparkled he kissed her furled fingers.

'Everything is perfectly right,' Gloria smiled, and little rainbows of colour flashed in her tear-filled eyes. This was the happiest night of her life. Never mind that they hadn't used precautions, she was going to be his wife, wasn't she? Now she was going to be the wife of an RAF officer with all that it entailed. Her mother would have to take notice of her now, wouldn't she? Instead of propping up the bar every night she could help pick out a wedding dress. Her mother would like that. Being the mother of the bride she would be the centre of attention. Yes, she'd like that.

It was a pity she had not met the London agent before the hotel was hit and she wondered if he would still be around when the all clear went. She was sure that Giles would let her carry on with a singing career once they were married. They weren't like these small-minded types such as Nancy and Sid Kerrigan. Nancy . . . Gloria remembered the last sight of her friend and prayed that Nancy was all right . . .

Another explosion drowned her terrified scream as Giles moved forward, throwing his body against hers, protecting her from the blast. He was gallant, Gloria knew, so brave to protect her like this, risking his life as he so bravely did fighting to defend the skies above Britain, as he and men like him had done so successfully.

For the first time in her life she felt truly wanted. Her mother had always been too busy working behind the bar to give her much time, but things were going to be different now. She knew that tonight was going to be the beginning of something wonderful.

'We have to move. That fire is getting closer,' Gloria said. 'Let's make our way to the shelter.' If they were quick they would be away from here before this building went the same way as the rest.

'Shall we make a run for it, Giles . . . Giles . . . ?' He felt like a dead weight on top of her . . . so different from when they were making love. Gloria nudged him and tried to push him off her but he made not a sound. 'Giles, come on! We haven't got time to hang around now.' She wanted to get out of here; find Nancy . . . Poor Nancy, she could be anywhere, poor love, and she had only that gormless Stanley to get her out of the hotel. Gloria hoped she was all right. She didn't fancy going back to Empire Street and telling Pop and Dolly she could not find their daughter.

With a sense of rising panic, Gloria gave Giles another push and his body slipped a little. His chin was resting on the wings of his insignia badge and she could not see his face. Dipping slightly, she lifted his chin. Another cascade of roof slates crashed onto the pavement and Gloria winced, letting out a little squeak of distress.

'Giles! Wake up! We have to go.' Something was very wrong. There was something in the way he held his head that made Gloria shiver and the cold night air had nothing to do with it.

She could just make out Giles's smiling expression. However, the smile did not reach his eyes, which were wide open, and she quickly gathered that the light behind the blue eyes, making them sparkle only moments ago, had now gone.

She gasped in horror. What should she do now? There was no sign of life in the man who meant everything to her. Gloria was vaguely aware of a woman screaming. Then she felt a cold sting on her cheek and the screaming stopped! The screams had come from her. Now there were two men looming over her.

'He's gone, lass,' the older of the two men said as he moved Giles's body out of the doorway. Gloria stood in the recess, hardly able to take it in.

She watched, barely able to comprehend, hardly able to think straight while the warden put two fingers under Giles's chin and sadly shook his head. 'The shockwave sucks the life right out of them! Gone. Not a mark or a blemish!' They appeared to have forgotten Gloria was still there in the shadows of the shop doorway.

'This chap's lucky. Sometimes it rips the clothes right off their back and catapults them into walls. I've heard of this in London.' His tone was almost conversational. 'A bus full of people, just sitting there, all looking ahead like they were waiting for the next stop.' He shook his head as the younger warden hung on his every word.

'No way, Geoff!' the young man said, obviously impressed. 'Then what happened?'

'All dead, lad, every last one of them,' the older man said. 'Blast, it were. Blast. Never seen it before now, mind. But I'd stake our Gertie's life on this being blast!' He bent and closed Giles's eyes. 'I'm sorry, lass, there's nothing else we can do for him now. Best we get you somewhere safe while I try and find an ambulance.'

He guided Gloria past Giles's lifeless body, and turned to the younger warden saying, in a low voice, 'I doubt there's any going spare right now!' The girl looked too shaken to take in anything he was saying.

Another explosion brought more of the building down, and Gloria's fine-tuned sense of survival caused her to realise that if she wanted to live, she had to get out of there now.

She took one last look at the man who had given his own life for her before she allowed herself to be hurried away.

'Come on, lass, let's get you down to the shelter!' Gloria, dazed and feeling sick now, stumbled over masonry and rubble, her torn gown flapping in the sleety wind as she made her way to the shelter, her body trembling with the horror of it all.

'There's not a mark on him!' Gloria was talking to herself. 'Are you sure he's dead?'

'It's shock, is that,' said the warden to his pal as he guided her towards the shelter. 'It can send them doolally, you know.'

'He sacrificed his life to save mine.' Her hands covered her face as she tried so desperately to block from her mind the sight of Giles's lifeless body, and then she began to cry. 'I've got to find Nancy! I've got to tell her . . .'

'Aye, love,' said the warden, 'and you will, later, but now you've got to get to shelter.'

Utter devastation was all around. Cars lay on their roofs like toys tossed aside. There were huge holes where bullets and bombs had broken the roads and pavements. The sky glowed an eerie orange as incendiary bombs caused fires all over the city.

'The overhead railway has been brought down!' the warden continued. 'I've just come from fire watching on top of the Liver Building's roof.' He looked grave. 'A circle of light is surrounding the whole city as far as the eye can see. The whole of the docks to the north end are ablaze! Gladstone Dock is a come-and-get-me beacon to the enemy now. If they don't get it under control soon, the Borough will go the same way as Coventry! It's like Dante's Inferno down there.'

'Without a shadow of a doubt – God help them!' said the other warden.

But all that Gloria could think was that Giles was dead, and she thought that a part of her was dead now too.

CHAPTER TWELVE

'Mrs Kennedy! Mrs Kennedy!' Dolly Feeny coughed as thick black smoke from the burning roof began to seep down to the street. She had been in the shelter only for a few moments when someone said the corner shop was on fire. Dolly's newly learned fire-fighting skills came to the fore. The shop door had been locked when she'd got there and she'd had to grab a young warden to put his shoulder to the door and burst it open.

'What are you doing up here?' Dolly called as she climbed the ladder to the loft, having assured the spotty youth in an ARP uniform that was far too big for him that she could cope alone. 'I noticed you were not in the shelter,' she said, popping her head through the square opening to see Winnie Kennedy scrambling on all fours to gather valuables.

'I checked all the rooms and the cellar but you weren't there.' Dolly did not fail to notice the well-stocked storeroom, hidden, no doubt, from prying eyes and probing questions. And, even though Christmas was around the corner, Dolly knew the kind of luxury goods in Winnie's cellar were very hard to come by lawfully right now.

'You'd better get yourself down to the shelter. It's not safe in here.' Dolly had seen the flames licking out of the roof of the shop while she was hurrying from the shelter after making sure the children were safe with Violet. As the elected auxiliary fire warden for Empire Street, Dolly had a duty to make sure everybody was safe, and that all incendiary bombs were put out before they were allowed to take hold.

Hurrying up the street from the shelter, she'd noticed the incendiaries had gone right through Winnie Kennedy's roof and smoke was pouring out.

Having paid attention in her training, Dolly was keenly aware the incendiaries and the chemical bombs, with their brilliant white light designed to start signal fires, would alert enemy bombers. One large bomb could, and did drop hundreds of incendiaries, and Dolly knew there were many large bombs being dropped tonight.

Being only a few hundred yards from the docks, Dolly knew everybody was in peril. But it was now clear by the ever-increasing number of fire-fighters and the increasingly determined sound of the ack-ack guns that people were not prepared to sit around wondering what time they would meet their doom. Their Maker would just have to wait until the fires were out! The people of the dock road would do all they could to stop the enemy taking their houses and their livelihoods – or they would die trying!

'You just get yourself down to the shelter now, Mrs Kennedy,' Dolly ordered. She could not believe the stupidity of this woman who would rather save a few paltry insurance policies than her own skin! 'You could have been trapped up here and nobody would have known. You've got to get down to the shelter!'

Dolly knew her daughter Rita was on duty at the hospital in Linacre Lane, probably too busy to blink with all casualties being diverted from Bootle General on Derby Road. Winnie's son, Charlie – she refused to think of him as her son-in-law – was tucked safely away in Southport, thinking it far too dangerous for him to stay here.

That said it all really, thought Dolly: her courageous daughter would never shirk her duty, while Charlie would always get as far away as possible and then hide behind a woman's skirts. However, this was no time for opening old wounds, no matter how much the Kennedys aggravated her.

'You're not getting me in that filthy hole! Have you seen the state of them? They stink!' Winnie spat. 'I would rather die.'

'And you might just get your wish,' Dolly answered as she scrambled through the loft hole. Winnie never mixed with the locals unless she was taking their money. Dolly knew that to join the rest of the inhabitants of Empire Street in the communal shelter would give Winnie the vapours. She usually preferred to stay in the shop cellar and protect her stock. The cellar was big enough to hold a few people but Winnie never invited anybody to shelter there and now Dolly knew why.

After witnessing what she just had, Dolly suspected Winnie would not want the authorities mooching around down there when necessities were so scarce.

'I have to get my papers!' Winnie began throwing cardboard boxes out of the way and Dolly guessed that whatever the box she was looking for contained, it must be more significant than insurance policies.

'What good will they be if you're blown to bits, missus?'

'I must have them.' The other woman was insistent to the point of hysteria. Dolly looked out of the skylight and could see Heinkels coming over in droves so close she felt she could touch them. The glow of incendiaries, falling like rain, lit up the sky.

'Come on, we have to get out of here,' Dolly said impatiently. 'The place could go up in no time.'

'I'm coming now,' Winnie said, seizing the box she had been searching for, a yellow King Edward cigar box. In the corner of the loft, the blaze was devouring things that had been stored for years. Dolly, trying to keep her voice light, caught Winnie's hand.

'Come on now, Mrs Kennedy, you've got to hurry.' She guided the shopkeeper quickly and calmly to the loft ladder. All the while her heart was pounding. She was surprised when the stubborn shopkeeper did as she was asked to do, for once.

'Here you go; I'll take the box while you hold on to the ladder.'

'Don't go rooting.' Winnie's voice was stern as usual. 'Everything is private in there.' Dolly, if she had the time and the inclination, could have been offended by this haughty woman's suggestion, but she decided to treat her remark with the contempt it deserved and did not retaliate. Instead, she busied herself with the bucket of sand from nearby Seaforth shore, which thankfully Winnie had kept filled and ready on the landing since the raids began. Being so close to the coast, one thing these houses were not short of was sand, which was the best thing for putting out incendiary fires, although there was a stirrup pump downstairs in the shop, Dolly noticed.

Making her way back into the vast loft, which extended above the whole shop and living quarters, Dolly scrambled on her stomach towards the fire at the far end near the gable wall, pulling herself forward on hands and knees, staying low where the air was not so smoky.

Quickly, she spread the sand and watched as it killed the flames. Thankfully it had not burned through the floorboards. When she was sure the fire was completely out she rummaged around some more just in case she had missed anything. Satisfied, she headed to the loft opening and, taking the cigar box, untouched by the fire, she quickly made her way down the ladder. Not surprisingly, Ma Kennedy had already fled to the cellar beneath the shop. Lifting the trap door behind the counter, Dolly noted that Winnie had made herself very comfortable on a chair at the bottom of the wooden steps, while anti-aircraft guns pounded constantly above.

Dolly had to get back to the shelter at the bottom of Empire Street to make sure her family were safe. There would be many more casualties tonight without a doubt. Somewhere at the back of the shop, in the next street perhaps, Dolly felt the shudder of an ear-splitting crash and she made her way through the shop to the rear of the building, from where she could see that the back yard wall had collapsed. Even though the back living quarters seemed fine, she was taking no chances.

'You'll have to go down to the public shelter, Mrs Kennedy!' Dolly called over her shoulder. 'I can't leave you here. It's not safe.'

Empire Street, behind the blackout blinds, seemed bathed in a greenish-yellow glow and looked strangely eerie, but Dolly, dragging Winnie Kennedy up the wooden steps out of the cellar, did not have time to stand around pondering, as another explosion ripped through the next street.

'What if someone comes in and clears me out?' Winnie wailed as Dolly, the box still in her hand, urged her towards the shop door.

'And what will you do against the whole German army?' Dolly called to the stubborn shopkeeper. Although, if she had time to think on the matter, it was something Dolly would pay good money to see.

'I can't leave me shop!' Winnie said, dragging the box from Dolly as another explosion, closer this time, sent the stock falling from the shelves and shattered the back windows.

'Come on now; get yourself away out of here!' Dolly said as Winnie dived under the stairs clasping the oblong cigar box to her body like a shield that would save her.

'They'll rob me blind,' she whimpered. 'I'll be looted out of business.'

'There are no looters in these streets!' Dolly's rising fear was making her impatient now. 'They're all too busy saving themselves the bother of being blown up! Now come out of it!' Dolly did not have time to stand around chewing the cud with a stubborn woman who thought she was invincible to Hitler's bombs.

'Incendiaries will not only set your loft on fire – they will do the same to you – but they're not doing it to me!' Dolly shouted. 'Now you have to get down to the shelter!'

'But all my Christmas stock is in the cellar.' Winnie put the box back on the counter just as Dolly grabbed her bodily and threw her out of the door.

'Don't worry!' Dolly said with a hint of irony. 'I'll do a full inventory before we get blown sky-high!'

'Oh, that's good of you.' Winnie said just as mockingly, and Dolly shook her head.

Did this woman have no sense?

The young pimply warden had come back to the shop. 'Off you go with the nice warden,' Dolly said to Winnie as if talking to a small child.

Winnie glared at her. 'I'll hold you personally responsible for my stock, Dolly Feeny,' she said with menace. 'Make sure there is nothing missing when I get back.'

Dolly ignored the hysterical woman.

'Here! I left the box on the counter!' Mrs Kennedy's voice carried inside the shop.

'I'll make sure you get it, now go down to the shelter!' Dolly's heart raced as a parachute mine landed on Strand Road and caused a huge blast halfway down Empire Street. Nobody was injured as far as she could see, but she quickly picked up the box and locked the shop door as another explosion caused Winnie Kennedy to head for the shelter without another word.

At her own house, Dolly put the box on the table and then checked to see if Nancy was back yet in case she was too frightened to go to the shelter on her own. Then she locked her front door and at last headed back to the shelter herself.

When Dolly had left to do her fire warden duties, Tommy knew that, with fewer pairs of eyes on him, this was his chance to escape the shelter. When Violet was attending to George he muttered something about having seen a school friend at the front of the shelter and he sneaked out and into the street to watch the brilliant light show in the night sky. He was bored stiff in that shelter and wanting a head start on shrapnel collecting before the all clear sounded.

Watching the anti-aircraft shells zip overhead Tommy, thrilled, gasped in wonder as the tracer bullets streamed across the inky blackness in lines of vibrant orange and brilliant yellow flame. The delight of listening to the army defence attempting to shoot out the flares with anti-aircraft guns before they could assist the raiders was like nothing he had ever felt before. It would be a shame to miss all this because he was stuck in an air raid shelter.

'Monty!' Tommy hissed through gritted teeth as his faithful canine friend sniffed walls and gateposts. 'Get over here, now!' If the air raid precaution warden caught him out of the shelter, he would be marched straight back home again and miss the fireworks. Tommy automatically ducked when a mine dropped nearby, his heart thundering like a speeding train. The noise was incredible. It set his ears ringing and sent a pain shooting through his head. He put his hands over his ears and shook himself. The ringing wouldn't stop.

'Phew! That was close, fella,' he said to his dog, who was now pushing against him so snugly that Tommy felt he would be pushed over. 'All right, we'll get going now! It's getting a bit too close for comfort.' Immediately there was another explosion and, seeing a half-open door of a warehouse Tommy slipped inside, but no matter what he tried to do to coax his canine friend inside Monty would not go into the warehouse.

'Come on, fella, here's a treat,' he said in a whispering voice, which usually brought the dog running. But not this time. Tommy did not know where the blast and the huge ball of light came from. All he knew was that Monty was acting very strangely now, jerking his head in that daft way and looking up to the sky.

Almost immediately, Tommy realised that the whole world had fallen silent. There was not one single sound. He opened his mouth to call Monty to him but no sound came. He yelled at the top of his voice but there was nothing. Not even a little squeak. He had lost his voice! Monty was jerking his head in that strange way again and Tommy realised he was barking! A spike of fear shot right through him when he realised he had not lost his voice. He had lost his hearing!

'Kitty!' He opened his mouth and he yelled his sister's name as loud as he could – but there was nothing – no sound at all. For some strange reason tears began to fill his eyes. Aunty Dolly would be worried. Pop would probably be out looking for him. He was in big trouble now, for sure.

His face was soaking wet with tears, and Tommy felt his shoulders shuddering, but still he could not hear anything. Not even the bomber overhead that had just dropped another load of high explosives onto the back of the warehouse. Turning quickly, Tommy saw the roof disintegrate like lit paper as the walls plummeted at the back end. Flaming stanchions of wood fell, blocking his path and one wooden girder landed just in front of him so close that his foot was trapped under it. Tommy was too far away from the door to get out. He was going to die! He was going to perish in a disused warehouse on the dock road, because he was too stupid to stay in the air raid shelter and help Aunty Violet with little George.

'My box!' Winnie Kennedy said, and made a beeline for the exit of the air raid shelter. Dolly took hold of the sleeve of her coat and, with her strident Irish inflection, ordered Winnie to sit down and behave herself.

'You'll have them all panicking – now put yourself in that chair and we'll have less of the ructions!'

Dolly was impatient now. Little Georgie had been fractious all night, and she'd been too preoccupied with him and Winnie's whingeing to see where Tommy had got to, though Violet said something about him seeing a school friend in the crowded shelter. She watched as George's little body shuddered under the force of a dry sob and her heart went out to him. An air raid shelter was no place for a teething baby.

The sound of explosions ripped all through the night, making tired neighbours impatient. When they took to shushing the irritable child, Dolly sang him lullabies and eventually, exhausted, he nodded off. Nevertheless, she could well do without the likes of Madam Kennedy coming over all hysterical and waking the child up again. Dolly, like a lioness protecting her young, knew that if this child made one peep of protest at Winnie's whingeing, she was going to sling Madam Kennedy out to the Germans herself!

'I forgot to pick up my box of policies.'

Dolly sighed. Those policies must be worth a small fortune. Dolly had never seen anybody get so aerated! However, it must be awful for Ma Kennedy being on her own night after night, Dolly mused, now Charlie had done a bunk to Southport, and Rita could hardly give up her job at the hospital to stay at home and look after the cantankerous old so-and-so . . .

'This raid can't go on much longer,' she whispered,

omitting to tell Mrs Kennedy she had put the box on her table and forgotten all about it when she left. She had a bit more to think about than stupid policies – like the welfare of her family, who were all out there, in the thick of it.

CHAPTER THIRTEEN

'Is that bloody dog going to howl all night?' a huge man with a flat, broken nose said as they loaded another carton onto a flat-backed wagon. 'It'll have the bobbies here in no time.'

'It's a bit late to worry now,' Alfie Delaney said. 'They're on their way over.'

They both watched the dock police hurrying to a burning warehouse, from which Delaney and his oppo had just relieved numerous crates of booze, which would be gratefully received at this time of year, no questions asked.

Delaney decided he would get the knocked-off booze out of here while everybody else's attention was on the warehouse.

'It's only Monty!' he said. 'He follows Tommy Callaghan everywhere.'

'If he doesn't pipe down he'll attract attention. You'll have to shut him up – he knows you,' Harry Calendar said through gritted teeth.

Alfie Delaney hesitated only for a moment. He knew

that if the dog was howling then Tommy would be lurking around somewhere. Probably up to no good! Leave him to it, Alfie thought, aware that his share of the money was at stake.

'He'll have the rozzers here any minute – go and shut the bloody thing up!'

Alfie decided he would rather take his chances with the dog than with Harry in a strop and he headed across the road towards the howling dog. The warehouse was blazing away but no matter how much he tried to lure the snarling mongrel from the doors Monty was not budging.

'Come on, fella,' Alfie said as the scorching heat made the buttons on his braces too hot for bare skin. 'Where's Tommy – hey? Where is he, fella?' Something akin to cold dread now filled Alfie's body. No! Tommy could not be in there, surely.

'Tommy! Tommy, are you in there, you daft little bugger?' Alfie called through the huge wooden doors while Monty jumped and bounced eagerly, yapping around his heels.

There was nothing for Alfie to do but go in to check. 'Tommy!' he yelled, his voice cracking under the effects of the smoke. Suddenly he caught sight of the young lad lying on the floor. His foot was jammed fast under a girder and flames were beginning to lick around the bottom of the wood. Alfie knew he had to act fast. The wood was paper dry. The flames would not take long to run up the scantling. Gathering his strength again, Alfie kicked the log with the heel of his boot. It did not budge.

Tommy, obviously overcome by fumes, wasn't moving now.

'Over here!' Alfie yelled to the dock police, who were now battling with a fire hose. A crowd of dockers surged forward, piling into the warehouse. Alfie was flung to one side as two burly stevedores heaved the wood from the little boy's lower leg, while another man slid Tommy out of the way.

'Is he all right?' Alfie asked, but the docker, picking Tommy up, ran without a word towards the hospital.

Pop, heading back towards Empire Street along the dock road, knew it was far too dangerous to try to get back now. The docks were burning. He directed the stragglers who had yet to seek shelter to the railway arches in Bentinck Street, used as an unofficial shelter by the people of Vauxhall.

Someone told him that Blackstock Gardens had taken a direct hit and that there were hundreds killed. Dolly's sister lived in Blackstock Gardens!

'Get in here!' he shouted. 'You'll get killed out there!' The arches were considered a safe place, given their reinforced structure.

Soon the shelter began to fill up and it wasn't long before the German bombers' approach caused everybody momentarily to hold their breath and look up towards the concrete dome. All they could do was wait and pray. Pop, who had just got everyone in before the bombers appeared, and so had sheltered there along with everybody else, let out a relieved sigh as the planes passed over without dropping their load.

However, they were now heading towards the docks. Along with everybody else, Pop began silently to pray again when the distant thud of dropping bombs sounded once more.

'Jesus, Mary and Joseph, pray for us this night.' A woman of indeterminable age pulled her shawl more tightly around herself and the baby sitting on her hip, blessed herself and looked to the heavens, while a young lad of no more than nine darted towards the street.

'Joey. No!' the woman cried, not quite quick enough to grab the excited youngster's collar. He wanted to see the 'fireworks'.

Instantly, Pop was after him.

'Come here, you young fool,' Pop called as he hurried out of the shelter along Bentinck Street heading towards Regent Road. Along with the Athol Street gasworks, the railway and the nearby docks, this was probably one of the most dangerous places in Liverpool right now. 'Get back, lad! You'll get yourself killed!'

But the young lad either didn't hear or didn't want to as he carried on down the street.

Just then, Pop heard another wave of bombers approaching only moments before they came into sight. All of a sudden, they were overhead, strafing the ground with bullets.

'Come back, lad.' Pop could feel the cold rivulet of perspiration trickle down his back. 'You've got to get back to your mam!'

He watched the lad stop dead in his tracks, twisting

as he did so that he was now facing the shelter. A look of horror swept his dirty face. There was a sickening thud. A deafening crash. The fall of masonry.

Turning, too, now, Pop watched the railway arches crumble and fall as if in slow motion. They were full of men, women and children and they had just taken a direct hit! The little boy opened his mouth and for a moment, no sound came. Then his horrified scream pierced the freezing air.

'Mam!'

When the all clear sounded, Winnie Kennedy got out of the shelter so fast she elbowed aside small children in her way. Dolly could only shake her head in wonder. Everybody was in the same boat. It was a rare person indeed who had nobody to worry about except themselves.

Back in the familiar surroundings of her sitting room at the back of the shop, Mrs Kennedy noticed the cigar box was not where she had left it. Alarm shot through her like an electric shock. The story of her life was inside that box. She would never be able to hold her head up again if anybody got their hands on that lot.

'I wouldn't have known he was there if it hadn't been for Monty!' Alfie said later as he gave Dolly and the rest of the family the news. He had hoped to see Kitty, to wallow in her gratitude, but she was at the hospital with Tommy. However, he did wonder what had happened to Danny, who had not been seen for ages.

* * *

'Tommy has a perforated eardrum, but we're hopeful his hearing will eventually return,' the doctor told Kitty when she arrived at the hospital. 'We're just not sure how long that will take.'

'Can I stay with Tommy until he has calmed down a bit?' Kitty asked, knowing he did not like hospitals after spending last Christmas in one.

'We've given him something to help him sleep,' the doctor said. 'We will keep him in for observation because of the deafness . . .' Dr Fitzgerald saw Kitty's look of alarm and assured her Tommy would be fine after a few days' rest.

'He's like a cat with nine lives! I've never come across a kid so lucky,' Dr Fitzgerald smiled.

'He scares the life out me,' Kitty sighed. She was surprised that Alfie Delaney had actually done some good for a change. 'Tommy must be well on the way to his ninth life by now, the scrapes he gets himself into!' She noticed the doctor's kind eyes. They were blue, like Frank's.

'We'll throw him out when he's good and ready, don't you worry.'

Dr Elliott Fitzgerald made a stab at humour even though he was exhausted, though he tried so hard not to show it. He had been on duty for three days straight, catching moments of sleep only when the influx of injured people eased. However, the snatched catnaps were not enough to sustain him as a new influx of casualties filled the corridors, and he was ready to drop. He remembered Kitty Callaghan from when she had visited Tommy and Frank Feeny, the young naval officer who had lost his leg when it had become infected. There was something about her that he was drawn to. He could see that Kitty was no longer the shy awkward girl she had been a year ago, but there was still an innocence about her that was refreshing. Catching sight of himself in the glass of the door to the ward, the doctor thought Kitty must think him a sight. He did indeed look like a man who hadn't slept for three days.

'Come and sit over here where it's quiet,' he smiled, guiding Kitty to a bench beneath the spiralling stairway. The girl looked exhausted too. She told him she worked in the NAAFI canteen, keeping the men and women of the forces supplied with food and drinks while they battled with the dock road blitz. Kitty was consumed with guilt once again as she told him that Dolly, their family friend, had been looking after Tommy while she had been at the NAAFI.

'It isn't Dolly's fault that Tommy went missing. He's a handful and runs rings round us all, and what with everything that's been going on . . . but I don't want to send him away again, Doctor.'

'Don't feel that this is your fault; there is no one as resourceful and wily as a schoolboy, Kitty. Your job is important, too.'

'I've been dishing out tea and sympathy, that's all,' Kitty said, feeling now that the NAAFI wasn't half as important as her little brother.

'Tea and sympathy sounds just right to me.' Dr Fitzgerald knew the docks were the main artery for the import of essential supplies from America and the

Colonies. Liverpool was always going to be a major target.

The fact that the authorities refused to give out any information regarding Merseyside, the newsreels stating only that a town in the North-West was lightly attacked, and there were a few minor casualties, was a bone of contention amongst the locals. They felt the rest of the country did not understand their plight and had less admiration for the people here than for those in places that were well publicised as 'going through it'. The doctor was astounded at the grossly understated way the news was delivered: an 'incident had occurred' it was reported, when in fact the port had been all but annihilated. He suspected that if the authorities could have got away with it, they would have made no reference to Merseyside at all.

Who could blame these brave, stoic people for feeling aggrieved when they were being battered, maimed and killed on a daily basis? Their homes were being blown from under them and razed to the ground in 'incidents'. Outside of London, Liverpool was the most frequently bombed port in the country.

His London home had suffered the same plight as Liverpool, but London citizens at least had the sympathy of the whole country as well as America.

However, Dr Fitzgerald never failed to be amazed at the enduring way that these people 'took it'. Night after night, they balled their fists at the skies and carried on regardless. They must, they said – what else could they do? Let the Nazis defeat them? He remembered one proud woman who had come into the hospital without her left hand after a raid and thanked God that she was right-handed.

'I'm off duty now; can I walk out with you, Kitty?' he asked. Kitty nodded, suddenly shy. Dr Fitzgerald had been good to her family. She credited him not only with saving Tommy's life but Frank's too. She was a little over-awed at his friendly overtures. Why would a doctor want to talk with a NAAFI canteen manager like herself?

They walked the half-hour journey back to Empire Street. They were surrounded on all sides by the devastation and destruction that had been inflicted by the Luftwaffe. As they passed the smouldering wreckages of houses, shops, churches and schools, it seemed that there was no part of the city that had not been affected in some way. As they got to Southey Street, nearer to the dockside, Kitty let out a gasp of shock. A whole row of houses that had stood yesterday were now gone, just heaps of rubble in their place. Kitty could see the upstairs floor of one house, the entire side wall destroyed and the contents of the bedroom exposed for all to see: a wardrobe; a bed; the mirror on the wall. She felt it was almost indecent to look at such an intimate scene, bared to the world. As they walked slowly by, something caught her eye. A little brown bear. This must have been some beloved toy – but where was the child it belonged to? She and the doctor looked at each other, each thinking the same unbearable thought. At that moment, a woman passed them, pushing a giant pram filled with what was left of her belongings. Trailing behind her were two children, both toddlers, looking bewildered and tired. One of them, a little girl, wore a dirty grey coat, covered in soot and ash. She was grizzling and Kitty's heart went out to her. She bent down and held out the little bear. The child immediately stopped crying and reached out for the tatty toy.

'Teddy needs a cuddle,' said Kitty, and the little child took the brown bear and hugged it to her, giving Kitty a gummy little smile.

'Thanks, love,' said their mother. 'We've been bombed out.' She nodded towards the pram. 'This is all we've got left.' For a moment, she looked as if she was going to cry. Kitty couldn't even tell how old the woman was, so wretched did she look, and Kitty thought that the experience must have added years to her.

But then the woman raised her eyes to heaven and said, 'Bloody Jerry. Well, if he thinks he's got us beat, then he can think again. Right, kids?' She turned to her children and held out her hands. 'Come on, let's get to Auntie Jill's. She'll have a nice cup of cocoa and a slice of buttered toast for us.' And with that she went on her way.

Kitty felt her heart would burst with pride at what the people of Liverpool were coping with. They'd show Hitler yet.

'That was kind of you, Kitty,' said the doctor.

'Anyone would have done the same, Doctor.'

'Please, Kitty, call me Elliott. It seems silly to stand on ceremony this morning.'

Kitty blushed. She wasn't sure how she felt about calling him by his first name. She stole a glance at him as they continued on their journey. The name Elliott suited him; it was strong, yet gentle.

They neared the docks, where another Atlantic convoy of about fifty ships was sailing out, bringing a lump of patriotic pride to the doctor's throat.

'I'm toying with the idea of joining the navy,' he told Kitty. 'Then again the army is quite appealing. Of course, I could stay here in Liverpool – they need all the doctors then can get – but it wouldn't seem right.'

'I should think they'd be glad to have you in either. You're a very good doctor.'

'No better than any other, Kitty. But thank you.' Elliott Fitzgerald wasn't a vain man but he couldn't help but feel a *frisson* of pleasure at her praise. 'My brother is in the Fleet Air Arm,' Kitty said, and then quickly covered her mouth with her hand, knowing that loose lips sank ships. The young doctor wasn't about to go over to the enemy, that would be ridiculous, but he would think her a silly blabbermouth for saying it. Briefly, she wondered why it mattered what he thought of her. 'Do you live far from here?' he asked, politely ignoring her indiscretion.

'Empire Street,' Kitty answered, quickly trying to cover her embarrassment. She suddenly felt awkward, as he was watching her now.

'Ahh,' Elliott said knowingly. 'Yes, I knew that. I'm staying in digs on the other side of the city, in Walton.'

'It's nice there,' said Kitty. 'Or was.' She knew that the suburb had also taken its fair share of bombardment.

They continued on past more of the docks, now harbouring another vast armada of ships docked, refitted, reloaded and repaired on a daily basis.

Men were unloading the cargo the country depended upon for survival, while others mended the sheds and the roofless warehouses that had been bombed. They were turning the ships around to sail right back out as soon as was humanly possible, to do it all again.

Elliott and Kitty watched in silent fascination as huge American bombers were unloaded from the ships. They would be down the other end of the country by teatime and probably over Germany tomorrow.

Of course, Elliott thought, women like Kitty propped up the men who fought the war. They were the ones who did much more than offer tea and a sympathetic ear, when the troops visited NAAFI all over the country for a well-earned rest. These women were the backbone, keeping everything ticking over with the least amount of fuss. He had much admiration for women like Kitty Callaghan . . .

'Will Tommy be all right, Doc— Elliott?' Kitty asked.

'Oh, yes!' he answered, 'we have given him something for the pain.' He put his hand on Kitty's arm in a gesture of reassurance when he saw the look of panic cross her face. 'He will be fine in a few days; he will still be with us for Christmas, in which case Santa will visit him at the hospital.'

Christmas! Kitty did not know what to say. This would be the second Christmas Tommy would be in hospital. It was getting to be a habit!

'I'd hardly given Christmas a thought, what with the bombings. I'm not sure anybody else in our street has either.' The best present of all was getting away with their lives.

Kitty could not stifle the long yawn no matter how she tried. Quickly she put her hand over her mouth. 'I'm so sorry. Like everybody else I've hardly slept for the last few days. We're all exhausted.'

'He's a tough one, is Tommy,' the doctor said. 'He'll be right as ninepence in no time. Now I think you should get some rest or you'll be no good for that tea and sympathy that we all need.'

'You look like you could do with a good night's sleep yourself,' she chided gently. Kitty thought Elliott Fitzgerald looked like he needed a good scrub as well. His hair was ruffled and his suit looked as though it had been screwed up in the bottom of a wardrobe for a few months.

Elliott was aware of her scrutiny and looked down at himself, smiling ruefully.

'I don't always look like this, you know. You've caught me on a bad day.'

Kitty returned his smile, thinking all men were little boys really. 'You need someone to look after you, like our Tommy.'

'Maybe you're right.' Elliott remembered again that Kitty had been visiting a young naval officer who'd suffered an amputation after a nasty infection had taken hold. He'd noticed how attentive she had been at the time, but the patient had been transferred out to a specialist unit down on the South Coast and he hadn't seen Kitty after that. He wondered if they had been sweethearts.

'How is your friend? Frank Feeny, wasn't it?' Her devotion was admirable. He was one lucky man and Tommy was one lucky brother. Kitty was more attentive than some mothers. Even when she could only talk to her brother through the glass window of the isolation ward last Christmas she was there day and night. 'I noticed that you were by his bedside as often as you could be.'

Kitty thought of Frank and how she had prayed fervently that he wouldn't die. 'Yes,' she answered. 'He's . . . he's a friend of the family. He's doing very well. He's got a new leg now.'

'Oh, I see, that's good news. It can be very hard for a young man like Frank to cope but he is strong and he'll adapt.' Dr Fitzgerald wondered if it was true that they were just friends. He had seen the way Kitty looked at Frank when she thought no one was watching. The thought popped into his head that he'd give anything to have Kitty look at him like that too.

Kitty thought of the time and mentally calculated if she had long enough for a sleep before she had to be back on duty at the NAAFI, where she had promised to put up the manger in the mess hall . . .

They had now reached the turning for Empire Street. Kitty turned to Elliott and said, 'This is where I live. If you don't mind I'd better be getting on now. Thanks so much for everything you're doing to help Tommy.'

The doctor realised that he'd managed to walk

236

Kitty almost to her door. She must think he had lost his head, wandering around like this.

Embarrassed, he said, 'Yes, of course, Kitty, I must be getting on myself. I've only a few hours off and then I need to be back at the hospital.'

'You work so hard.' Kitty smiled. 'Goodbye then, Doctor . . . sorry, Elliott.' It still sounded funny calling him that.'

'Goodbye, Kitty. Tommy's quite safe with us.' Kitty gave him a smile and it seemed to light up her whole face; Elliott thought again how beautiful she was and decided that he would very much like to see her again – very much indeed.

The champagne had long worn off when the all clear sounded and Nancy's head was thumping. Somehow, among the crashing explosions and the singing crowd whose strangled notes failed to rise above the splintering sound of crashing buildings, she had managed to fall asleep on Stan Hathaway's shoulder.

The wail of the all clear siren woke her with a start and Nancy looked around, trying to gather her thoughts. Her mouth was dry and she longed for a drink of water, a cup of tea, anything to rid her mouth of the awful taste. As she lifted her head, she felt as if her eyeballs were spinning in their sockets and, standing now, she stumbled to stay up straight.

'Oh my . . .' she groaned as she put her hand to her hair, now matted with something sticky but she was far too head-sore to untangle it all. Nancy shivered and hugged the warm overcoat that somebody had kindly put around her shoulders, trying desperately to gather her thoughts as she was carried along by the crocodile line of people who were leaving the shelter. Outside the sleety rain struck Nancy's face with little needles of ice, but she ignored it as she caught sight of her best friend.

'Gloria!' Nancy called. Somehow, she thought, she and Gloria had been in the same shelter, but in the gloom and with all of the crowds, they had managed to miss each other.

'Wait!' Stan caught Gloria's arm. She looked dazed and Nancy felt a chill run through her that had nothing to do with the icy weather when she saw her best friend walking barefoot down the cinder-strewn street.

'The shelter was full,' Gloria whimpered. She had been wandering aimlessly, her shoes lost and the bottom of her torn dress in her hand. 'I didn't care if I was killed too.'

'Oh, thank God you're alive!' Nancy stumbled over the rubble of a fallen building and threw her arm around Gloria's shoulders, vaguely wondering where Giles had got to, but for now it was just so important that Gloria was safe.

'I tried to find you,' Nancy cried above the constant engine noise of the salvage wagons, and the roar of water shooting through the fire hoses, which seemed to be making little impact on the hungry flames devouring everything in their path.

'Here,' Stan said, removing the jacket of his RAF uniform and slipped it around Gloria's shoulders. 'You are perished.'

'We looked everywhere, didn't we, Stan?' Nancy cried, hugging Gloria, who seemed strangely unmoved by all the commotion around them. 'I thought . . . Oh bloody hell, I thought you'd copped it! Where's Giles? Did you lose him? Is he in another shelter? Why aren't you with him?'

'Giles is dead!'

Gloria's low voice held no tone; it was just a string of monotonous words as she recounted the story of his death.

'. . . There wasn't a mark on him. He looked like he was asleep when I left him.' Suddenly, as if the words brought home the full horror of what she had just gone through, Gloria burst into tears and was shaking uncontrollably. 'Oh my God!' She buried her face in her hands as racking sobs shook her whole body.

'No!' Nancy immediately drew Gloria closer, hugging her as she would a child.

Nancy had a million questions but knew instinctively that Gloria did not have the ability to explain any more. And who could wonder?

'We've got to get you home!'

'The warden said the docks are in a terrible state and some of the buildings are still ablaze,' Stan informed them.

'We've still got to get back along the dock road,' Nancy answered, knowing the bombers would have had a clear view of the whole area as all around them was devastation and destruction. Her thoughts were racing. Her baby boy! Why hadn't she taken Mam's advice and got him away to somewhere safe? And what about Mam, Pop, Sarah? They would be out in this . . . doing all they could to help people.

A collective groan went up from a group of people gathered in a huddle near the station when they were told by a passing policeman that the line had been mangled and there would be no trains today – or even tomorrow, come to that.

'I wouldn't advise going anywhere near the dock road, either,' he said grimly.

'We have to go that way, we live there!' Nancy cried, and the policeman sadly shook his head. 'Nothing can get in or out . . . The Royal Infirmary took a big one, too – they say there are people dead – and you'll never get through London Road.'

'Sarah is working at the Royal!' Nancy cried, looking helplessly towards Gloria as Stan put his arms around her.

'Come on, we'll try and get through.'

'Oh, me mam will go mad if anything has happened to Sarah.' Nancy's voice was getting higher and, desperately trying to calm the rising hysteria, she took a deep breath. 'Come on, Glor, we'll get you home and find out what we should do next. Oh my God!' Nancy used the words like her own personal mantra, begging for some respite from the horror of it all. It had been such a fabulous night earlier, the best she had ever known . . .

'I'll never see Giles again!' Gloria let out a strangled cry of anguish that rent the air of the breaking dawn. Suddenly she wanted to be back at home. If she stayed a moment longer, she would cave in; give way to the hysteria now building up inside her.

'I've got to go!' she cried. 'I've got to get back to Empire Street!'

Looking around at the devastation, Nancy could hardly believe that this could happen to her home city. Fires were ripping through nearly every building in Lime Street and Ranelagh Street. There would be nothing left of Liverpool at this rate. Nancy knew that getting home would be no easy task.

'Get some water down here now!' Danny shouted, cupping his hands around his mouth. The all clear had gone a while ago but there was still work to be done. Moments later, he felt the violent jerk as the water burst through the hose in a jet so powerful it nearly knocked him off the steel ladder. He was relieved to see more men making their way down the hatch and they worked together steadily to get the cargo out before it was consumed by the greedily licking flames.

The searing heat was making Danny feel unsteady. His head felt as if it was full of air and the hold began to shimmer in the intense heat. But he could not give up. Too many people were depending on him and he could not let them down.

'You all right there, Dan?' The fireman, who had known Danny for years, looked concerned. Danny raised his thumb in acknowledgement. He would offer all the help he could give even though the work was hot and dangerous. If he was on board ship as part of a convoy, he would have no choice but to put out a ship's fire – this is what it would be like, he reasoned as adrenalin pumped through his body.

Moments later, he was released from his precarious foothold by one of the fire-fighting team, who gave him a big thumbs up and an encouraging nod of his head. Words were useless with the noise around them as he and Danny positioned the hose onto the flames. The men, ringed by a wall of fire, fought and eventually managed to extinguish it. They were half-blinded by the fumes and smoke before they were able to clamber from the hatch.

'You took your bloody time!' Alfie Delaney said as Danny's thick-soled, steel-toecapped boots touched firm ground. 'I had to give your wagon to somebody else.'

'I had to help out,' Danny said. 'That ship going up would have been a disaster.'

Moments later, as he made his way across the dock, he felt light-headed. His chest felt as if all the air was being squeezed out of it and his left arm grew so heavy he had to hold it up.

'You all right, Danny?' one of the dockers asked. 'You don't look so good.'

As Danny tried to speak his legs gave way beneath him. He opened his mouth to gasp the smoke-filled air, but collapsed onto the quay as the strain of his heroic effort got the better of him.

'Someone get first aid over here!' the docker shouted, and moments later Sarah was kneeling over Danny's stricken figure.

Nobody noticed Alfie Delaney slipping back to a nearby warehouse.

CHAPTER FOURTEEN

A docker went hurtling to the police box to bring emergency help. All the time Sarah prayed like she had never prayed before.

'Oh my days!' she gasped. She was the only person, apart from his doctors, who knew Danny had a heart condition. When she saw him lying on the quay surrounded by a small crowd of men, her own heart pounded with a fear she had never known before.

Sarah pushed herself through the throng and kneeled beside him, shutting out the cacophony of voices that surrounded her. She tried to focus on what she had been taught in her training. She felt his pulse. It was faint but she could see clearly that Danny was not breathing. *Dear God, please don't let me mess this up*, she prayed. Tilting his head back and opening his collar, Sarah started rhythmically to pump his chest, interspersing it with puffs of air through his mouth and into his lungs.

She carried on doing this until the ambulance arrived.

'Went out like a light, he did,' said a man in baggy

corduroys as he pushed his oil-stained flat cap to the back of his head. 'One minute he was talking away and the next he went down like a pack of cards.'

As the ambulance man parted the throng Sarah said determinedly, 'I'll go with him. I'm . . . I'm . . .' She could not bring herself to say 'Danny's best friend'. 'I'm a friend of the family.'

'In that case you will be able to give his details for the hospital,' McTaggart said, grimly, arriving at the scene from seeing to a fireman with burns. 'But make sure you come straight back and let us know how he is.'

Sarah nodded.

Fear pumped in her throat and tears rolled down her cheeks as the ambulance men worked on Danny's unconscious body. He had to be all right! He just had to be!

She would never be able to face Kitty if anything happened to Danny . . . Sarah knew now she should have told somebody about his heart complaint. Danny should not have been doing such heavy labour with a serious heart problem. The dock work was far too strenuous.

'Might be the effect of smoke after saving that ship – he deserves a medal for what he did!'

'What do you mean?' Sarah could hardly believe what she was hearing.

'The fire guard took bad, collapsed; this lad took his place,' the docker said. 'Not a minute's hesitation neither!'

'Please, Holy Mother of God, let Danny be all right.'
Not only had Danny heaved essential cargo all over
the dock, he also saved a ship from being blown
sky-high.

Won't you ever learn to say no, Danny?

The windows and the fronts of every shop in Church
Street were blown in, Nancy noticed as they scurried,
heads down, towards the Pier Head. Lewis's was lost
in flames. Blackler's had also copped it. In the distance,
they could see the orange glow of light in the sky
above the Pier Head. It was going to be a long trek
home – if they could get through.

Every road was blocked. Scotland Road was impass-
able. Stanley Road was too dangerous with falling
buildings and raging fires.

'We'll just have to try the dock road. It's the only
way,' Stanley said, and both Nancy and Gloria looked
at him as if he was quite mad. The docks were on
fire from the south end to the north.

People, visibly shocked and dazed, were hurrying to
places they were once familiar with, knowing tomorrow
the city centre would be barely recognisable. Nancy
moved automatically. Putting one foot in front of the
other she held Gloria and Stan's hands as they stag-
gered through the wreckage of the places she had
known all her life. A short while later, they reached
the part of town that led them to the river.

'We'll never get through here,' Stan said as fire-
fighters were desperately trying to quell the flames.
All around them intense heat fought with freezing air.

Sparks fanned into the black sky from a hundred different fires. Merseyside was alight!

'Here, cut down this way!' Stan had to shout above the fire's roar, his handkerchief over his face as the thick, suffocating smoke burned his nose and throat. The whole place smelled like bonfire night.

'Are you related?' the nurse asked kindly, and Sarah shook her head, her uniform bearing the evidence of Danny's sickness as the ambulance had headed to the hospital.

Sarah could not speak, aware that in the next room they were doing all they could to save Danny's life.

'Has anything like this ever happened before?' the nurse asked.

Sarah wasn't sure what to say.

'All I know is that he has been excused military service, but I'm not sure of the details.' Sarah knew this was a half-truth.

'Between you and me, it will be a miracle if this boy survives the night.'

Sarah's gasp of anguish told the nurse she had said more than she ought, and she realised too late that Sarah wasn't here in a professional capacity but in a personal one.

Please Lord, let Danny live. I'll die if he dies.

'Oh, Kitty, thank God you're here!' Sarah cried, feeling relief that she no longer had to carry the burden of responsibility and worry alone.

'How is he?' Kitty asked, looking almost grey with

the strain of both of her brothers now being ill in hospital while doing full-time work at the NAAFI. She had heard about Danny's accident as she'd turned the corner into Empire Street, after saying goodbye to Dr Fitzgerald, and the wife of one of the dockers met her as she went to the door to tell her the grim news. It had taken Kitty an hour to make the journey back to the hospital as many of the roads were now closed and much of the city was alight. She had just left Tommy in the children's ward – now here was Danny, his life hanging by a thread.

'They wouldn't tell me anything except he'd had an accident on the dock!'

Sarah explained about Danny saving the ship, making Kitty swell with pride, but what she heard next made her blood run cold in her veins.

'Kitty, he has heart trouble.' Sarah knew it was better not to sugar-coat it. She felt guilty enough at not telling Danny's older sister before now. She should have told her – she might have been prepared.

'Heart trouble?' Kitty asked, a look of horror widening her eyes. 'Since when? He never said anything.'

'Something to do with rheumatic fever, apparently. He only found out when he was excused military service.'

'Excused? How do you know all this, Sarah?'

'He told me not to say anything. I'm sorry, Kitty. He didn't want to worry you.'

'I wish people would stop trying not to worry me,' Kitty said angrily. 'I'm a big girl now; I can take it!'

As they waited for news Sarah told her everything she knew.

'I am so sorry, I really am – I didn't mean to keep anything from you but . . .'

'I know,' Kitty said gently, 'but you know what maddens me? The likes of Vera Delaney squawking about how good her Alfie is compared to a waster like Danny Callaghan!' How dare she?

'I heard that Alfie saved young Tommy,' Sarah said, and Kitty nodded.

'Yes,' she said. She was grateful to Alfie for raising the alarm but she knew he would want some kind of reparation for his good deed. Because Alfie Delaney did not do anything for nothing.

'Don't think about it now, Kit,' Sarah said quietly as Rita, who was on duty there, came into the corridor. Immediately she threw her arms around Kitty's shoulders; her trouble was their trouble – they would share it equally.

'I'll go and see what I can find out,' Rita said. 'They'll tell me before they tell you.'

'Thank you,' Kitty murmured and resumed her wait in the cold corridor with Sarah.

Whatever next? she wondered.

CHAPTER FIFTEEN

'Oh, Mam, it's hell out there.' Nancy ran into her mother's arms. She felt five years old again and she could not utter a word without sobbing. Trembling, she buried her head in her mother's shoulder and after a long while, her sobs lessened, leaving only small shuddering intakes of breath. 'Gloria's boyfriend was killed. They got engaged last night and he was killed saving her.'

'Holy Mother of God!' Dolly blessed herself and urged Nancy to a chair at the table. 'Is Gloria all right?' Nancy nodded as her mother poured her a hot cup of tea she'd just made after switching the gas and water back on, and then she noticed Dolly pouring a generous amount of something alcoholic into the tea. 'For the shock,' Dolly said, taking Nancy into her arms and clasping her bedraggled daughter to her bosom. The clock struck six a.m.

'Where's Pop?' Nancy asked, her voice still trembling. 'Has he gone to the Royal to see if Sarah is all right?'

'Sarah? She's fine, but Danny Callaghan collapsed after helping to save a ship from blowing up Gladstone Dock.' The devastation of surrounding streets was so bad there were many confusing stories circulating.

'And Pop?' Nancy asked again.

'He's out there somewhere,' Dolly answered, knowing she would not see her beloved husband until he had done what he could to help anybody in need. 'George!' Nancy had to hold him in her arms. 'I have to see my baby!'

'He's all right Nance, he's safe,' Dolly said, filling cups, lined up like soldiers on parade. 'Violet took him into her bed; he's been there since we returned when the all clear went. He slept right through it.'

'Maybe I should think about having him evacuated,' Nancy said. She had not been able even to contemplate it before this latest raid.

'You're right, Nance, the raids have never been this bad before.'

Nancy looked up to her mother now and noticed she looked more tired than usual; she was just about to comment when Sarah came into the room.

'Sarah, love, you look done in!' Dolly said as her youngest daughter dragged herself into the fireless kitchen and shivered. Dolly was just putting a match to the corkscrewed newspaper threaded through the kindling and cinders that still had some burning left in them.

'I'm wiped out, but I'll never sleep,' Sarah said as her mother added a few select pieces of coal before balancing the shovel on the fender, then covering the whole thing with a sheet of paper. The draught drew the kindling and the fire soon cast a weak glow to the kitchen.

'How's Danny?' Dolly asked Sarah as she busied herself.

'They won't say anything just yet – well, not to me anyway.'

Sarah was so worried about her friend. She knew his heart was enlarged but she didn't know he would keel over like that. What chance did she have of becoming a nurse if she couldn't see that coming?

'If he saved a whole dockyard from being blown up he deserves a medal,' Nancy said.

'You're not the first to say that, but Danny won't want any fuss,' Sarah replied.

'Poor Kitty.' Dolly, in time-honoured fashion, wrung her hands in despair. 'Poor, poor Kitty, she has it all to do now.'

'The doctors said Danny will need as much rest as he can get.'

'Good luck to him with that one, around here,' Nancy said unthinkingly, and when her mother and sister glared at her through tear-filled eyes she looked away, saying petulantly, 'I'm sorry, it's been a terrible night and I'm tired.'

'You go to bed, love,' Dolly said with a sigh; everybody was feeling the strain now.

Sarah got up from the ladder-backed chair. 'Let me make you a sandwich.'

'Oh, well,' Nancy sat back down on her chair at the table, 'if there's a sandwich on the go I might as well take it up with me.' She did not see her younger sister's scornful expression or the shake of her head. If Sarah had not witnessed her sister's absolute thoughtlessness first-hand, she would hardly believe it credible.

Rita had always done the right thing, the decent thing, never bringing shame or worry to her mother no matter what the cost to herself. She had even married Charlie when she knew she did not love him – although, there was a huge price to pay for her deception and she had paid every day since. What else could she do? She had no choice but to marry Charlie. Pregnant, desperate and backed into a corner, her only option was to marry him to save her family name.

'He was put on this earth to torment you,' her mam would say, 'as if he blamed you for his own reckless deed.' Her mother was talking of Michael's conception, Rita knew.

The premature birth of her son, discussed only on the day of Michael's delivery in Mam's front parlour, never came up again. What would be the point in talking about it, Mam said in that rapid no-nonsense kind of way that brooked no argument, during Rita's confinement? The Good Lord had seen fit to give her a fine healthy child, so he must have been pleased about something.

Thinking of her mother's illogical philosophy, Rita knew that carrying the burden of her secret was becoming more difficult now she did not have the children to occupy her.

Turning into Empire Street, her heart raced when she saw the effects of last night's raid, especially when she saw a large hole in the shop roof, the boarded-up windows and the scorch marks around the windowless skylight, realising how close the street had come to being devastated. Picking up her swift pace, she hurried into her mother's house on the other side of the entry from the shop.

'Mam, is everyone all right?' she asked when she saw her mother sitting at the table, her forefinger outlining the lid of a yellow cigar box on the table, in a world of her own by the look of it. Dolly jumped visibly.

'Holy Mother of God!' she said in her inimitable Irish brogue, dramatically clutching at her buttoned-up cardigan. 'You frightened the bejesus out of me!'

'Sorry, Mam,' Rita said, giving her mother the customary kiss on her upturned cheek. No matter how many times they came into the house during the day or night, the family never failed to greet Dolly this way. 'I saw the scorched roof of the shop and the door still shut!'

'Incendiaries . . . Lady Matilda's fine,' Dolly answered, referring to Mrs Kennedy. 'She spent the night in the shelter, would you believe? Amazing what a few bombs can reduce a person to, isn't it?'

'Is she all right?' Rita asked, and Dolly nodded wearily as she got up and headed to the back kitchen.

Rita sat for a while listening to her mother bustling about, opening the tea caddy, pouring boiling water into the pot. She would have offered, but her mother would not hear of it – not after Rita had worked all night, and Dolly never thought of herself.

The only sound in the room was the incessant ticking of the clock on the mantelpiece . . . The quiet of the morn after the deafening roar of the night, Rita thought. Suddenly she noticed the box.

'Who does this belong to?' she asked, turning over the unfamiliar cigar box sitting next to the empty sugar bowl.

'That's her ladyship's,' Dolly called. 'She was in a right pullover about that box!'

'Palaver,' Rita absent-mindedly corrected as she slowly drew the box towards her, promising herself she would not pry. Nevertheless, the lid was slightly ajar . . . She felt tempted to peep; it was human nature.

'Ma Kennedy tried to go back inside the burning shop!' Dolly said, coming into the kitchen carrying a fresh pot of tea, nodding her turbaned head. After donating her Dinkie curlers to the Spitfire Fund, she, like many of England's women, regularly wore a scarf fashioned into a turban around her head now.

'I wonder why it is so important.' Rita said as Pop came into the kitchen from the privy.

He had been out all night, and having come home to see that his family were all all right, he was keen to be off again. Fires still raged across the city. Pop knew that there were many people still buried amongst the rubble. Some of them could still be saved, though for many it was already too late. He didn't say any of this to Dolly.

'I'm off, Doll.' Pop kissed Dolly's cheek. He had

not told his wife about the railway arch bombing either – she would only worry if she knew how close he had come to being killed. 'Shall I take the box into Mrs Kennedy?'

'No, it's fine,' Dolly answered innocently as she headed to the kitchen for saccharine tablets. 'Our Rita can take it in when she's ready.'

While Mam was in the back kitchen, Rita could not resist a quick peep under the stiff cardboard lid. What harm could it do?

'Wait until you see what's in there,' Dolly said as she came into the quiet kitchen, making Rita jump.

'Mam!' She let out a guilty laugh, her heart pounding. 'You frightened the life out of me.'

'I did so.' Dolly gave Rita a knowing look. Then, her voice softening, she said conspiratorially, 'Have a look. You'll dance on a dung heap when you see what's in there.'

Rita, used to her mother's quirky sayings, raised the lid a little . . . and then some more . . . until it was lying on the table exposing the contents. Her fingers itched with curiosity to delve right in. What would cause her mother-in-law to panic about a battered cigar box – to the point of endangering her own life to save it?

'Mam! Have a look at this!' Rita's eyes widened when she saw the official documents.

Dolly put down the teapot with a satisfied nod. 'Didn't I tell you!'

'You didn't tell me this, Mam!' Rita could hardly believe her eyes. 'Have you seen this lot?'

'Not all of it . . .' Dolly looked a little uncomfortable. 'Your father came in.'

Dolly took the papers and her eyebrows pleated while Rita urged her to read them.

'Well, I'll be!' Dolly exclaimed, her eyes wide in amazement. 'Of all the sneaky, two-faced trollops! That Winnie Kennedy takes the big prize, doesn't she?' Opening the other yellowing documents, Dolly quickly realised they were deeds! Deeds to three properties.

'Deeds to the shop, with large living accommodation behind and above it . . .' Dolly gasped and looked at another one. 'Then there are premises in Southport . . .'

'A boarding house . . . apparently,' Rita added, 'and then there is a house on the seafront at Crosby.'

Crosby! Rita knew it was a long shot but it was possible – Could Michael and Megan be there?

'Surely this doesn't mean those big double-fronted villas?' Dolly's eyes widened. Rita looked at the address again and nodded. 'Well, I never did . . .'

'For years, Charlie and me dreamed of a place of our own.' Rita was so angry she almost choked on the words. 'And all the while his mother had all this fabulous property and never told anybody. While my children were cooped up in that shop she had houses and gardens . . . Oh, Mam, how could she be so cruel?'

'Spiteful, more like,' Dolly said, 'but where did she get the money for such property?'

'I've no idea,' Rita said.

'She didn't want to see you two happy, never did,'

Dolly said, 'and while Charlie was under her roof she had a say in his life, because he was spineless. He was always beholden to her, and would be while he had nowhere else to go.'

'Do you think that's why he turned out as bad as he is?' Rita asked. It was too late to keep up pretences now. The damage was done. He had cheated her of a happy family life, a loving marriage, and now he was cheating her out of being a mother to her own kids! 'But I'm not going to say anything just yet. If I do she will be off like a bullet from a gun to warn her beloved son.'

'What's in the cat is in the kitten, I say,' Dolly answered, knowing Charlie had always been a sly one. The war had allowed him to show his true colours.

'She could have let us live in one of the properties.' Rita felt cheated. 'We didn't want them buckshee!'

'I doubt the money had anything to do with it.' Dolly poured the tea into two cups. 'She would do anything to keep her son.'

'But in the end she couldn't keep him – nobody could,' Rita said sadly. 'Do you know what, though, Mam? I don't miss him one bit, but I miss my kids so much it hurts.'

Dolly looked at her daughter questioningly. 'What is it, Rita? Is there something you're not telling me?'

Rita sighed. 'I didn't want to say anything, Mam, but you know Charlie has taken the kids? Well, he didn't tell me where and I don't know where they are. I've been looking for them in Southport, but now I think they might be in this house in Crosby.'

Dolly's lips tightened and she thought for a moment before saying, 'Do you know what has just struck me? All the while you were missing your kids, I bet she knew exactly where they were.' She shuddered. 'It brings a chill to your bones just thinking about the evil in that woman.'

'How could one mother do that to another?'

'Aye,' Dolly sighed. She looked down at the box and her eye caught another document, a smaller, less aged one.

'What's this, I wonder,' she mused, unfolding the sharply folded paper. Her eyes flicked across the page. When she finished reading she looked up to her daughter, her voice solemn. 'I think you'd better have a look at this, Rita.'

'This is the birth certificate of someone called Ruby Kennedy.' Rita remembered something the neighbour in Southport had said about a sister called Ruby although she had never heard the name mentioned in the Kennedy household. 'So, Ruby is Mrs Kennedy's daughter, according to this,' Rita said after reading the birth certificate. 'It gives the mother's name as Mrs Winifred Kennedy.'

'The girl will not be a child now,' Dolly answered, sitting in the straight-backed chair. 'The date on this is 1920.'

'Oh my word!' Rita gasped. 'Mrs Kennedy has a daughter!'

'There's the proof.' Dolly stabbed her finger on the line that said 'Mother's Name: Mrs Winifred Kennedy' . . . 'But look now, there! The father's name.'

'It says her husband's name!' Rita answered. 'And the date is . . .'

'Two years after he passed on.' Dolly nodded.

'The lying hypocrite – that's what she is, Mam!' Rita could not hold her anger in. For all the time she had been married to Charlie Kennedy, his mother had looked down her nose and treated her no better than a common servant, always casting veiled accusations and begrudging her children, especially Megan, the time of day.

'Of all the rotten . . . she's got the cheek to call anybody!'

Dolly put her arm on her daughter's.

'Mam, don't say anything, please!' Rita begged. She knew she would cry. 'Not yet.'

Dolly stretched her face with both her hands and sighed. Her daughter had felt so much heartache because of that family.

'You know I won't say anything, acushla,' Dolly said, shaking her head, 'but don't expect me to be anything but merely civil to her – and she doesn't even deserve that!'

'Thanks, Mam. She'll get her comeuppance one day, I'm sure.' Rita knew that her own family might not have much, but compared to the Kennedys they were rich in something Charlie and his mother would know nothing about – being a proper family.

'I know why she didn't come for the box,' Dolly said. 'She'll be too ashamed.'

*   *   *

259

Dolly did not give in to her desire to cry later that afternoon when she saw the destruction of last night's raids. She had finished her stint at the Red Cross shop and after a spot of dinner with Pop she was out of the door before she even had her coat on to see Tommy and Danny.

The news had now got around that Danny had something wrong with his heart. She knew he had always had a soft heart but she never thought there was anything wrong with it really. Pop caught up with her minutes later and they made their way along Linacre Lane on his cart together.

The Callaghans were like her own kids and Dolly had made a promise to her poor friend Ellen, Danny's mam, that she would look out for them if ever she could. Thankfully they had all survived the awful night – but nobody had got off lightly.

On the way to the hospital Pop relayed for a second time the tale of her sister to Dolly who wanted to hear it again now that it was just the two of them. Dolly wanted to make sure she heard it right and her sister was all right.

'Your Cissie heard the sirens and made her way to the shelter, as usual,' said Pop. 'Everyone was rushing to the large concrete shelter in the middle of the courtyard, and two trams stopped along the road to let the passengers off.' He sighed now as Dolly silently wiped her streaming eyes at the horror of it all. 'The shelter was packed to bursting with people and your Cissie was turned away.'

Dolly made the sign of the cross. 'Glory be to God,'

she said. 'You know what our Cissie's like, stubborn as a mule and thank the Good Lord too . . .'

'She went home and got back into bed,' Pop said. 'Not a scratch on her.'

'And poor Danny gets knocked sideways saving the entire docks from deviation.'

'Devastation,' Pop said in a very low voice.

'I know what I mean, Pop.'

Pop nodded, puffing on his pipe. Dolly always had the last word.

For the third night Kitty was busy giving out cups of tea, buckets of water and words of sympathy to the men in uniform, who were helping the civilians of the area to put out fires. She had not slept much, and knew that when she did finally get to bed she might never get up again. With Danny in hospital and Tommy, too, she was too frightened to stop running here, there and everywhere in case the Good Lord caught up with her as well. However, she knew that Dolly and Pop, along with the Feeny sisters, were all visiting the hospital, jumping in to help where they could. Kitty didn't know where she would be without them.

The docks were battered but not beaten, and fire-fighters, dropping with exhaustion, were still battling to save what they could. Many crews came over from miles around, even from the other side of the Mersey, desperately trying to put out fires that had been blazing all night. By the look of them, thought Kitty, the docks would be burning a long while yet, as they were full of oil and wood.

'St James' Church copped it,' one fire-fighter said as he took a well-earned cup of tea from her in the NAAFI canteen.

'Gladstone Dock warehouses are still burning, and the oil refinery works will blaze for days, by the look of it,' his pal said as he pinched a few strands of tobacco from his tin to roll his own cigarette, lit it and inhaled deeply.

'Your Danny did the business – he's a hero, that lad.'

Kitty felt so proud, but she was going to give him a good talking-to when he was on the mend. Fancy not telling her he had a wonky clock! She knew that there were many heroes last night, and the night before that, too.

'There but for the grace of God,' she whispered. Her little house was only a spit away from the dockyard devastation and not a window broken. Swallowing a painful lump in her throat and feeling the tears well up in her eyes, she turned to get more cups. She didn't want anybody to see her tears – their Danny would go mad if he thought she was crying over him. He didn't like a fuss.

Like everybody else, Kitty would never give in, even though many dwellings round about had been levelled by the bombs. There was word going around that people would have to move out of the area if it got much worse. But when she'd seen Tommy this afternoon he'd been adamant he was not going to be evacuated again, no matter what.

Kitty could not see how much worse it could get.

Nevertheless, while she was needed here, she would carry on, because that was what she had to do.

'You won't catch me giving in to a jumped-up little Charlie Chaplin impersonator!' Dolly said with feeling the next day, and the rest of the women on the WVS van laughed. They were all exhausted, but still managed to brew huge pots of tea and serve it with smiles on their faces – albeit weary ones – and comforting words. Everybody was done in, so there was no point in moaning about it.

A determined woman and a dedicated member of the WVS Housewife Section, Dolly felt she had the capacity to carry on no matter what, because that's the way she had always lived her life. She took nothing for granted. And, strangely, she seemed to have the energy of a lively two-year-old who could not sit still for five minutes without fidgeting.

'Sure, it's hard to sit around doing nothing,' she said, pushing up her sleeves, 'when there's plenty I could be getting on with.' She handed a mug of hot tea to another fireman. 'I have to thank God that I'm able, as there's many who cannot help themselves.'

Eventually, after making countless cups of hot sweet tea, the WVS ran out of supplies.

'Dolly, you look done in, love.' Pop had just come from Balliol Baths where there had been a collection of cardboard coffins ready for use a few weeks ago. Now they were filled and the dead had been put in the drained swimming pool ready for collection and burial. His weather-beaten face looked as weary as everybody else's as he beckoned his wife from the tea van.

'We haven't seen each other since you took me to visit Tommy and Danny in the hospital.' Last night had seen the third consecutive night of bombing and terrifying raids. Christmas was fast approaching and there had been no let-up so far.

'I heard the Royal Infirmary was hit again,' Pop said. 'I went along there and saw Sarah; she was fine – stoic as always, like her mother.'

'Rita's supposed to be at Linacre Lane hospital but I gather from someone who came by earlier they haven't seen her. Bootle General is taking casualties and then sending the injured elsewhere.'

'Aye,' said Pop, 'and they're using the clinic across the road for emergency cases, so Rita might be there. I'll check it out just as soon as we get you sorted.' He beckoned her from the van and she did not protest. She had been so busy looking after everybody else – now it was Pop's turn.

Pop put his arm around Dolly's shoulders. 'Nancy's back at the house making something to eat – you never know, it might be edible.' They laughed: Nancy was a terrible cook. 'But at least it will be hot. Violet's helping out at the town hall. And I went to see Tommy again. He's going mad because he can't go collecting shrapnel.'

'What about his ears?' Dolly sighed, partly with relief and partly with exhaustion.

'Aye,' said Pop as they sauntered back to Empire Street, 'he's still got two, and they're beginning to work, but he said the volume is still a bit low.' Pop smiled and Dolly laughed. Their sense of humour had not been injured, thank the Lord.

'Kitty's kept the NAAFI open for the last four days,' Pop said, puffing away on his pipe. 'She and the other NAAFI girls are doing a sterling job down there on the front line of the docks.'

'I've told Nancy to make a few pans of stew; we're going to need them with everyone working so hard. Even Nancy can manage stew.'

'Where are we getting the ingredients for a few pans of stew?' Pop asked, and Dolly gave him an old-fashioned look that told him to ask no questions and he would be told no lies.

'They'll all be exhausted when they get back.' Every street, every neighbour, every household was being used to the full in this awful time. People were dropping with the want of a sleep. Some were sitting on the pavement with their feet in the gutter, while others were wandering aimlessly. Last night's raid had been the worst yet. Houses were gone, schools, factories, parts of the docks had burned for three days, but thankfully all the houses in Empire Street had escaped except for a few shattered windows. However, the corner shop and the pub had taken a bit of a battering. They dodged cracked and broken paving flags.

There was still much to do and Dolly had not only dished out tea on the WVS van but also good advice – telling the homeless where they needed to go to get their ration books renewed, or sorting out burial arrangements for those that needed to know.

'Come on, Doll, you've done enough for now,' Pop said. 'An empty sack won't hold up, you know.'

'You're right, Pop, I won't argue with you there,' Dolly said, waving goodbye to a woman she had helped out this morning.

'Come on, love, let's get you home and get a bit of food inside you,' Pop said.

Dolly, noticing the concerned look in Pop's eyes, said in return, 'I didn't do it alone. Let's go and get some breakfast.'

'You haven't slept for three days, Doll,' Pop said, knowing his wife would carry on until she dropped if need be, 'and breakfast time came and went long ago.'

'Everybody's in the same boat,' Dolly said wearily. Her bed would be a welcome sight if the raids kept off. Surely the Germans must be running out of bombs by now.

'I'll just nip home for half an hour. Make sure all is as it should be,' she said, and Pop sighed with relief.

When he brought her a hot cup of tea and a sandwich from the back kitchen, she was fast asleep in the chair by the fire – and she still had her coat on.

CHAPTER SIXTEEN

Even the raids could not wipe all thoughts of Jack Callaghan from Rita's mind. And as she now said another quick prayer of thanks to anybody in heaven who might be listening, for sparing her and her family, she automatically said one for Jack as well. Since the last letter from Jack, he had written to her twice more. He had told her about his injured arm which had caught a bullet from the strafing when his ship went down. It was his left arm which had been injured so he was still able to write, thankfully. From the dates on the letter, Rita thought he couldn't be too far away now as they didn't seem to have taken that long to reach her. She had prayed fervently for the Lord to protect him and bring him home safely.

She knew Bootle was no place for children right now, but neither was that place where Charlie was playing happy families. She had pleaded with Matron for time off so she could go and see Michael and Megan, but as the raids grew heavier – last night being the worst and the one people on the wireless were now calling 'the Christmas Blitz' – she knew her place was at the hospital. Her children were safely away from the raids. That's all that mattered for now and she had to put her own selfish longing to one side until she could get to see them.

She hoped she would manage to get to Southport to give them their presents on this, the second Christmas away from home, if indeed they had returned to Southport.

Christmas? A time of goodwill to all men. Rita sighed; there had not been much evidence of it when the Luftwaffe did their best to wipe them out. She realised that this war might have broken some people's sleep but it didn't break their spirits. Houses destroyed and shattered families were now a common sight, but life had to go on. They must not lie down and take it – they weren't made that way, as Mam would say. Most people had nothing to begin with after the Depression of the thirties. God alone knew if the forties would kill them or make them stronger.

No, Rita decided, she must not be selfish. At least she still had a loving family. There were people caught up in the bombings who needed round-the-clock care. She could not desert her post at a time like this. There were just not enough nurses here to cope, even if there were trains to Southport, which she doubted.

Michael Kennedy was keeping himself busy making paper aeroplanes out of old bits of his father's newspaper. It was dark. The lights were off as both he and Megan were now in bed, but he'd managed to find an old torch in the cupboard under the stairs of the boarding house in Southport and most nights, when he knew no one was prowling around he would be underneath the covers of his bed either reading his favourite comics, *The Beano* or *The Dandy*, or drawing pictures of his favourite planes: Lancaster Bombers or Spitfires.

Tonight, both his dad and Elsie had gone to the pub up the road and left them both alone with Ruby. He liked Ruby, she was a bit odd but you could have a bit of fun with her, though even Michael was sure that she wasn't the best person to look after them if anything went wrong. What if the bombs starting to fall again like they had back home? His father said that they were safe in Southport but he had heard some bombers passing over the other night and the noise from the incendiaries had seemed quite near. Michael wasn't scared, but he did want to do the right thing and look after his sister. He'd promised his mam he would!

He hadn't minded coming to Southport. When it had been warmer, he would go with Elsie, Ruby and Megan along to the seafront and sometimes meet up with other boys and have a bit of fun larking about. But since he and Megan hadn't yet started going to school – his father kept promising but it never seemed to happen – and the stream of visitors to the boarding house had dried up, things had started to become very dull.

He was disturbed by a small noise from the bed next to his. He immediately recognised it as his sister

Megan having another bad dream. Michael threw his own covers off and using the torch to guide him made his way over to his younger sister's bed.

He could see by the light of the torch that her little face was creased and anxious. Tossing and turning, she let out small cries which sounded like *Mam*. It had been like this for a while now. Michael thought that far from getting used to being away from home, Megan was finding things harder and harder. Why couldn't they just go back to Empire Street?

'Hey, Smidge,' Michael whispered and nudged her gently awake. Megan rubbed her eyes and looked around her, almost as if she wasn't sure where she was.

'I had a bad dream that we were lost and Mummy couldn't find us.' Megan's cheeks were flushed as she sat up in bed. Michael thought she might cry and decided it was best to distract her.

'Here, let me show you this.' He grabbed his comic and started to tell her all about the characters in *The Beano*. His favourite was Lord Snooty and he always enjoyed seeing him get his just desserts.

'When Uncle Eddy wins the war, can we go home?' Megan asked her brother, her big eyes looking up at him imploringly. 'I miss Mummy and don't like Elsie. She tells me off if I don't eat the rice pudding, but I don't like rice pudding.'

Michael thought for a minute. Maybe he and Megan could write to their mam and ask her to come and visit? He had a shilling that one of the boarders had given him for helping to fix a puncture on his bicycle and he hadn't spent it yet. Perhaps he could get Ruby to take them to the post office where they could buy a stamp?

'Let's write Mam a letter. You can tell her all about Southport and ask her to come and see us. She'd like that.'

Megan's eyes lit up. 'I can draw a pretty flower for her.'

Michael dived under his bed and fished out some paper and a pencil. He'd also ask Ruby if they could buy an envelope.

By the light of the torch, the two children wrote their mother a letter.

Nancy, Sarah and Dolly were just finishing off the last of the toast when the letterbox shut with a thud. Sarah, who had not long come in after a night's duty at the hospital, headed to the back kitchen to get the tray to collect the breakfast dishes while Nancy, at the sound of envelopes scattering across Dolly's highly polished linoleum, scurried to the lobby.

Tomorrow was Christmas Eve and there was still much to do.

'I've got supplies for the Red Cross parcels, Mam,' Sarah said, coming in with the tray as Dolly cleared the breakfast things from the table and put them on it. 'People are so generous,' she told her mother. 'Even now, when they have so much to worry about, Christmas seems to bring out the best in people.' She watched as her sister came in reading a letter, another envelope sticking out of her cardigan pocket. Nancy dropped the remaining mail on the sideboard near the door without looking up from the blue lined paper.

'Well, it brings out the best in some people,' Sarah added, emptying the brown carrier bag of supplies that had been donated to the hospital and would be added to the Red Cross box ready for distribution later.

'I'll sort them out in a minute, love,' Dolly told her daughter.

Sarah's latest pursuit when she was off duty was, like Dolly, collecting and sending comforts to prisoners of war. Nancy's husband, Sid, was a prisoner of war, which gave Sarah and Dolly more incentive – as if they needed any – to collect for men who would not be home with their families this Christmas. She knew Sid would not mind when he received a parcel or a letter, just as long as it was something – it would be a little more like Christmas then, no matter how late.

'She's eager this morning,' Sarah said in the back kitchen to her mother after eyeing the Forces mail notepaper. 'I didn't know Sid would manage to write from the prison camp.'

'It must have been written months ago – they take ages to get here,' Dolly said, busy at the sink. 'Mrs Simpson's son is a prisoner and they've never yet had a letter.' Dolly had noticed that Nancy rarely wrote to her husband. When Dolly questioned her about it, Nancy said she was trying to steel herself against bad news. What a lot of tosh! The girl could not be bothered – out of sight out of mind, by the look of it. No wonder Mrs Kerrigan got annoyed with her.

Collecting the items that would be sent to Geneva and then on to the POW camps in Germany, where Sid had been held since the Germans overtook France last June, Dolly was certainly concerned about her daughter's increasingly carefree ways. However, as a caring mother, she tried not to show it. They had a lot on their plates and it was hard to know what to deal with first.

'You'd think she would be a bit more interested in helping out with the war effort.' Sarah knew their Nancy had her silly head in the clouds most of the time, listening to dance tunes on the BBC Forces Programme on the wireless. Sorting the donations into different categories Sarah added, 'If that letter's off Sid she doesn't sound happy about it – there isn't a peep out of her.'

'She'll tell us in her own good time,' Dolly answered, and Sarah nodded.

Nancy's heart was now beating wildly as her eyes flew across the page for the third time. Stan, who had helped her so gallantly after the raid, had popped a note through the door. She was so glad she had gone to fetch the post because Mam or Sarah would have asked questions if they'd seen the envelope without a stamp.

He wanted to meet her! Stan said in the letter that he could not stop thinking about her! Nancy's mouth was dry with excitement. She wondered if she dared. It had been so wonderful snuggled up against him when she had the excuse of being in shock after that raid, but she was a married woman – and if she was caught fraternising with another man when her husband was in a prisoner of war camp her name would be mud. She hadn't even opened her other letter yet, although she had recognised Gloria's handwriting.

As Sarah put a tin of pilchards into a brown cardboard box on the back kitchen table, along with tinned peaches and a packet of cigarettes, she knew Sid wouldn't get these for many weeks or months – if at all! But some poor soldier would.

'I reminded her to write this morning but she just shrugged,' Dolly whispered, hearing Nancy coming into the kitchen.

'I don't know if Sid will receive the actual parcel we send,' Sarah said in a cheery voice so as not to let Nancy know they were talking about her, 'but I have it on good authority he will receive something.' Germany was bound by the Geneva Convention in the same way as England. Nancy sighed; she knew they had been talking about her – their Sarah was trying too hard to include her in the conversation.

'D'you remember our Rita telling us about that young German pilot who died in the hospital?' Dolly asked, and the two girls nodded. 'She mentioned him again yesterday. He was just a bit of a lad.' War was a terrible thing, especially at this time of year.

'A bit of a lad who came to kill as many of us as he could,' Nancy said, her mind on other things now. 'I'm going to see if Georgie's awake.' With that she flounced out of the room with her letter and into the parlour where she could read it again.

'She could have given us a hand with this lot!'

Sarah stared at the closed kitchen door. Dolly patted her hand and gave a gentle shake of her head.

'We all know our Nancy's a bit scatty, love,' she said, 'but she's not a bad girl.' Dolly would hear no criticism of any of her offspring, no matter how unruly they appeared to be. It was her prerogative as a loving mother to pass judgement, and nobody else's. She said so – often.

'Has she heard from Gloria lately?' Sarah asked. She had been so busy at the Royal Infirmary she hardly had time to catch up on what was going on in Empire Street.

'She's gone to see her aunt in London,' Dolly said. 'I did think she might write to Nancy, but there's time yet.' Dolly picked up a roll of brown tape left over from the time she and Pop put Xs on every window, and sealed the cardboard box of comforts for the troops.

'She took Giles's death very badly. It must have been devastating for her,' Sarah said.

'A few weeks away from this place will do her good,' Dolly answered, opening the lid of another cardboard box and putting in things that might bring a bit of relief to some poor soul. 'Though she might need more than a few weeks,' Dolly said as if to herself. 'That kind of thing can have a terrible effect on a girl's mind.' She paused and leaned on her box. 'I remember a girl back in Cashalree Bay; she threw herself into the River Shannon and was never seen again.'

'Gloria wouldn't do that, surely, Mam!' Sarah gasped, and Dolly reassuringly patted her arm.

'No, my darling, Gloria would never do such a thing – it would ruin her hair!'

'Mam! That's terrible!' Sarah's eyes widened; her mother said some very inappropriate things sometimes. 'Now I know where our Nancy gets it from.'

'I know,' Dolly said with contrition. 'I'll confess to Father Harding when I see him – although he's a bit busy. A barrage balloon snapped, caught fire and set the church alight.' There had been so many buildings destroyed around the dockside, it was a wonder there were any standing. 'We'll have to go to Midnight Mass at St Winnie's.'

Sarah's chin rested on her chest in an effort to hide her face. She'd seen the devastated, skeletal remains of the church and thanked God that there was nobody in it at the time. But however hard she tried she could not stop smiling. Her mother said some daft things, but sometimes a little levity was called for in the grimmest of situations just to keep sane – they did it all the time at the hospital. She knew that most people around here, no matter how bad the circumstances, found solace in dark humour.

'So you will be going to Midnight Mass on Christmas Eve as usual, Mam?'

'We all will if God spares us,' Dolly said stoutly, 'including your father!'

'Once a year whether he likes it or not,' Sarah laughed. Her father was a good man with a heart so big he would give you his last penny. However, not a regular churchgoer, he told Mam he could talk to the Big Man upstairs anywhere. Sarah thought about people like Vera Delaney and Mrs Kennedy, wearing their knees out at eight o'clock mass every morning, but who would not give a body a push off the pavement if it meant they would not benefit. Pop was right, as always.

Picking up the post from the sideboard, Dolly's brow creased in puzzlement.

'Did Violet say she had any family back in Manchester?'

'No, she said there was only her and her parents before they were killed,' Sarah answered, looking up from the box she was filling. 'You remember, that's why she came here; she has nobody left to call family. It's so sad to have nobody, isn't it, Mam?'

'Well, there must be somebody because she's got a letter here.'

'It might be from a friend,' Sarah answered, 'although she did say they were a very quiet family who did not mix much.'

'Aye, you might be right,' Dolly said, putting the letter into the cut-glass bowl on the sideboard, which was where she put all of Violet's mail.

Kitty was pleased to see that Danny's colour was a lot better than the last time she had seen him. Danny was confined to complete bed rest for now and there was no chance that he would be home for Christmas, but the doctors had said that he was doing well, despite it being a very close shave.

'Why didn't you tell me that there was something wrong with your heart, Danny?'

Danny's voice was still a little weak and Kitty had to get nearer to him to hear properly what he said.

'I don't want to be treated like an invalid, Kit. All I've got is my pride.'

'Oh, Danny. I couldn't be prouder of you. Look at what you've done – saved the lives of all of those dockers and nearly killed yourself in the process.' Kitty took his hand. 'I'd rather have an invalid brother than a dead one.'

Danny squeezed her hand and looked at her intently. 'And I'd rather be dead than stuck in an armchair for the rest of my life.'

Despite her own fears, Kitty understood what he meant. Danny was more 'alive' than anyone she knew and he would never take this illness lying down.

'Anyway, I've made a friend in here, Kitty.'

'Really, who is it?'

'Well, I've been going out of my mind with boredom, but there's this army officer chap who's in here too. He's been bringing me crossword puzzles and the like to do. He's been keeping me company.'

'That's good, Danny. You've always been good at that sort of thing.'

'It's stopping me going mad, Kitty.'

'Going mad is the least of your problems.' Kitty looked at the clock on the wall. 'I'd better get a move on if I'm to see Tommy before visiting hours are over. Anyone would think you two had cooked this up between you!'

'Maybe we did, our Kit.' And Kitty was pleased to see Danny's cheeky grin spread across his face.

'Danny, what shall I do about our Tommy?' Kitty chewed on her nails. The vexing question of her little brother had been preying constantly on her mind. 'We can't keep him here anymore, it's just too dangerous, but I'm worried about what will happen if we send him away.'

'What about sending him to Ireland? He could stay with Mam's family.'

Kitty thought for a moment. 'It's an awfully long way.'

Danny nodded. 'It is. But they'll think the sun will shine out of his posterior and, more to the point, he'll be safe and there'll be no running away.'

The idea that Tommy would be so far away tugged at her conscience. She'd have to think about it, but Danny was right – being safe was the most important thing for Tommy now, and it was her duty to make sure that happened.

'They might not send you home today, Tommy.' Kitty didn't know what she would do if the hospital did discharge him today. She knew she could not let Tommy freely roam the streets. And every time she mentioned evacuation he was adamant he wasn't going again.

'It was bad enough being in hospital last Christmas,' he said. 'I missed the party last year, as well.' Tommy's mouth was downturned.

'So you heard me talking to Dr Fitzgerald then?' Kitty asked, knowing their Tommy was trying to stay at the hospital long enough for the Christmas party.

'He said he'd see what he could do.' Tommy gave her a sheepish smile and she ruffled his thick mane of dark hair. It would be easier for her if Tommy was in hospital over Christmas, she thought, feeling guilty. With Danny being in hospital too there was nobody at home to look after Tommy as she was on an early shift – and she didn't like leaving him on his own.

'Aunty Dolly could mind me,' Tommy said, 'but I'd rather wait until after the Christmas party.'

Kitty nodded. She didn't like putting Aunty Dolly out, especially at this time of year – she was busy enough and would probably have a houseful. There had been talk of Eddy coming home at one time.

'What are you doing on Christmas Day, Kit?' Tommy asked. He looked all clean and shiny, for a change, sitting up in bed in his striped pyjamas with his hair neatly combed and still wet from his bath before visiting time.

'I'll be working in the morning and I'll come and see you a bit later, then Danny.' Kitty didn't want to sound self-pitying. 'Then I'll get dolled up and go dancing.'

Tommy gave her a sidelong, disbelieving smile. He knew their Kitty never went dancing. She was too busy working or looking after him and Danny. Just then a nurse came onto the ward and rang one of those huge hand bells Tommy had seen in the school playground.

'I'll have to go, sunshine,' Kitty said, giving him a hug and ruffling his hair again. 'There, you look more like your old self now. See you later.'

'Aye,' Tommy said with a quiet smile. They both hated this time, when she had to go. 'See you later.' They never ever said 'goodbye'.

She was just leaving the hospital by the Fernhill Road gate as Dr Fitzgerald was coming off duty. He caught up with her rapid pace and walked alongside her now.

'He's a fine little chap, your Tommy.'

'He's got a family who love him,' Kitty answered, 'and I know he's a little tinker at times, but he doesn't mean any harm.'

'Everybody is so busy doing war work, it can't be easy.'

'Oh, I know it. If there is a scrape our Tommy will find a way into it.'

'You can come in and see him later if you like.' Dr Fitzgerald gave her a warm smile. 'I'm back on duty this afternoon.'

'Thank you, I'll be there.'

They chatted and walked, and the half-hour walk from Linacre Lane to the dock road flew past.

'I'm sorry, my chatter means you've missed your lift back to your lodgings.'

He had told her he moved from London just before the war when he was offered the job at the general infirmary known locally as the dockers' hospital.

'You can keep me talking anytime.' Dr Fitzgerald was as different from the rough-and-ready men of Bootle as it was possible to be, Kitty thought, taking in his fresh, clean-shaven complexion, which now looked so much better than the last time she had seen him, tired and careworn. He had a healthy glow as the west wind whipped around them, giving her cause to shiver.

'Here, have my scarf,' Dr Fitzgerald said, but Kitty shook her head.

'I couldn't possibly take your scarf!' she declared, knowing what people would say if they saw her walking down Strand Road in a fancy woollen scarf.

'I'll soon be home,' she assured him as they crossed the canal bridge. Just then his hat flew off in the gusty wind. They scrambled to retrieve it from an icy puddle before it blew into the canal, both bending at the same time and almost knocking heads. The doctor looked sheepish as he slicked down his unruly hair before replacing his hat.

'I really don't mind,' he said as he wound the scarf around her neck, and the instant warmth caused her to snuggle into the luxurious comfort.

Kitty suppressed the urge to giggle, although not unkindly as the heat of embarrassment crept from her throat to her cheeks and she hoped the fog from the smoke-filled chimneys was enough to hide her blushes.

Dressed in a navy-blue bib and brace overall, and looking like something the moggy dragged in, Kitty wondered what he must think of her. Then she wondered why she thought that. Surely, he meant nothing at all by the kind gesture. He was just being considerate.

'I'll try and get something sorted about Tommy being evacuated, but I can't promise anything. He's really not keen.'

'We don't want him coming to any more harm.'

What he meant, Kitty thought, was he didn't want Tommy turning into one of those latchkey kids. Kitty experienced that sinking feeling of dread. Tommy was already one of those latchkey kids. He went over to Aunty Dolly's every day, but she could not know for certain that he would stay there. Aunty Doll had a lot to do, too. There was her family to take care of, little George to look after, as well as her WVS work. Kitty could not expect her to take Tommy on indefinitely.

'I'm not surprised he doesn't want to go, given the last place. But there are good people, too.' Dr Fitzgerald liked this beautiful girl, whom he recognised had worries beyond her years. He would like to ease her burden.

'We have relations in Ireland . . . Mam's family.' Kitty knew her maternal grandparents would be glad to look after Tommy, the final link to their beautiful daughter who had died giving birth to him.

'I was wondering . . .' Dr Fitzgerald said as Kitty turned to go. She stopped and waited for him to continue. 'I was wondering . . . if, er . . . if you . . .' He hesitated and then in one breath the jumble of words tumbled from his lips. 'I was wondering if you would like to go to the New Year dance at the town hall?'

'Oh!' Kitty didn't know what to say. She had never been anywhere as posh as the town hall before, especially with a doctor. What would they talk about? She was a girl from the backstreets of dockside

Bootle and he was a doctor who came from a privileged background. They were worlds apart.

'I'm sorry, I sprung that on you. I didn't mean it to come out like that.'

'Does that mean you are withdrawing your invitation?' Kitty felt bold all of a sudden, perhaps because she was tired to the point of dropping. She was off duty at New Year and it had been such a long time since she had gone anywhere that wasn't the NAAFI. She was tired of the war, tired of rationing, tired of falling into bed only to wake up what felt like moments later and have to start all over again. Why shouldn't she have a night out? The doctor was just asking her to be friendly, wasn't he? Where could be the harm in saying yes? As she reached the broken kerb, before crossing the road, she stopped and turned to where he was standing.

'I'd love to,' she said, and a smile broke out across his handsome face.

What did women wear to go to dances at the town hall, she thought as she wound her way through the horse and carts, wagons and trams across the cobbled road, heading for her home. But before she put her foot on the first stair to go up for a nap there was a knock at the front door.

After night duty at the hospital, Rita returned to Empire Street tired although too unsettled to sleep. It was after 7 a.m. and as she passed by the family home, she couldn't resist popping in despite being dead on her feet. The hearth was blazing and the prospect of a slice of toast with jam and a hot cup of her mam's freshly brewed tea, strong enough to stand a spoon in, was just too hard to resist.

'I'm glad you popped in love,' Dolly poured Rita a cup of hot tea as she warmed her cold legs by the fire. 'Something arrived for you this morning which I'm sure will put a smile on your face.'

'What is it?' Rita asked, intrigued by her mother's barely suppressed grin.

'Look at this! It arrived with the post this morning.' Rita took a small grubby little envelope from her mother, which was addressed in a tidy but childish scrawl to: Mrs Rita Kennedy, Empire Street, Liverpool.

'Mam!! This is from Michael! How did it get into your hands rather than Ma Kennedy's?'

'Well, I think the postman must have decided that you were still living here. It's got no number on it and he must have decided to drop it in with our post rather than hers. Perhaps he owes her a bit of tick or something? You never know around here.'

Rita was barely listening to her mother as she tore open the letter. Her heart was in her mouth and tears immediately sprang to her eyes as she read the words written on the page.

Dear Mam
We hope that you and Nanny and Pop are OK and not getting bombed. We are not, it is mostly quiet here but sometimes you can hear the planes. Dad says that we will both get a present from Father Christmas if we don't make too much noise and are good. We wish

we were with you at Christmas and hope that you will come to see us very soon. Megan has drawn you a picture.
Love from Michael and Megan xxxx.
PS. Ruby helped us to post this.
PPS. We have chickens in the back yard and we will be eating one on Christmas Day.

Tears streamed freely down Rita's face as she looked at the little flower which her beloved daughter had drawn.

'That's it, Mam,' Rita said through her tears. 'My children need me and I'm going to get them back.'

Somehow, Rita didn't care how, she was going to get to Southport. She would walk if she had to. She desperately needed to see her children, and now it was clear that they really needed her too.

CHAPTER SEVENTEEN

'I agree we should give as much as possible to the war effort,' Mrs Kennedy said to Vera Delaney while the shop was full. However, a short while later, when it emptied out to just the two of them she said in hushed tones, 'I think it's a bloody disgrace we should have to give up so much of our household stuff.'

'I know,' said Vera. 'Only the other day that busybody Violet Feeny came round and asked if I could possibly spare another pan for the Spitfire Fund. I said to her, "Look, I could build a spare Spitfire for the amount of pans I've handed over."'

'The chandlers are full of them and they don't come cheap, yet they want ours for nothing!'

'That's not very patriotic, Mrs Kennedy,' Dolly said, catching the end of the conversation. Vera Delaney stood back to let her get served. Vera had put her best pans in the attic. Nobody was getting hold of those.

'I'm keeping hold of everything now,' said Mrs Kennedy. 'They've had all they're getting out of me.' Consumer goods were becoming scarce now.

'Just a loaf – if you can spare one,' Dolly said drily. 'Oh, by the way. Here's that precious box of yours.' Dolly passed it pointedly over the counter and the two women exchanged a long look before Mrs Kennedy took it from Dolly who then left the shop with a secret smile on her face.

'Their Rita got me a war bond for Christmas – I ask you . . .'

'I got war bonds off our Alfie,' Vera said, looking pleased. 'I've knitted him a pullover with wool I managed to get at Dolly's bring-and-swap day at the church hall – you don't need coupons for that.'

'America donated a lot of toys for the hospital,' Mrs Kennedy huffed, 'which was just as well because there was nothing worth buying. The wholesaler isn't stocking toys any more. I have to write directly to the manufacturers if I want toys, the manager said. Snooty so-and-so he was, too.'

'The old postman told me he's sick of trying to deliver cards and parcels to houses that are no longer standing. They put a notice up in the post office: check daily if you've been bombed-out!'

'As if that's all they've got to worry about – a Christmas card – when they've got no homes to go to.' Mrs Kennedy let out a long stream of dissatisfied air.

'I'll miss the church bells this year, though,' Vera said.

Mrs Kennedy glared at her: if the church bells rang it meant they were about to be invaded.

'Aye, I suppose you're right,' Vera sighed heavily, 'but it won't seem like Christmas without the bells.'

After a moment's thought she asked with a shrug, 'I see you're getting your roof mended pretty quick.'

'Your Alfie said he'll see if he can get me some wood and slate off the dock.'

Rita was surprised to see workmen already up fixing the corner shop roof. It hadn't taken Mrs Kennedy long to grease a few palms to get what she wanted. She decided to go through the side door halfway up the entry, instead of going through the shop. If only her precious friend Vera knew what kind of a person Winnie Kennedy was. Her mother-in-law would not be so high and mighty then, would she?

'You wash your mouth out, Vera Delaney,' Mrs Kennedy was saying behind the counter of the shop, which never closed when profits beckoned. 'My son would never stoop so low!'

It was unusual to hear Winnie talking like this to one of her oldest friends. Rita clenched her hand, quietly closing the side door at the bottom of the stairs near the adjoining shop door. On hearing the raised voices, she stepped back into the shadow of the small vestibule. She did not know why she was still here. Mrs Kennedy was hardly ever civil. If it had not been for the possibility that Charlie might bring the children back here she would have gone long ago.

Placing her bag on the hall table next to the empty sherry bottle, which Mrs Kennedy had forgotten to put in the salvage bin, Rita shook her head, suspecting her mother-in-law had taken to drink of late. However, that would be no concern of Rita's soon, as she had no intentions of staying here. As soon as she could find other lodgings she was moving out.

Maybe Mrs Kennedy needed the alcohol to help take her mind off the terrible wrong she had done – like forgetting she had a daughter and three paid-up properties.

From the way the mirror was positioned, at the bottom of the stairs, Rita could see everybody in the shop without being seen in turn. Vera Delaney, who liked nothing better than spreading malice and misery, was rearing up indignantly and Rita intended to hear what she had to say. Vera's Christmas spirit had given up the ghost long ago.

'So where has your Charlie got to, then?' Vera's voice held a note of accusation. 'Everyone has been speculating. He's the talk of the neighbourhood!'

'They're billeted with an old woman, I tell you,' Mrs Kennedy said stiffly and Rita's heart began to thunder in her chest. She might be about to learn something useful for when she went to Southport to claim the children and confront Charlie.

'Well, my cousin Tilly lives two doors down from them in Southport and ran into him one morning in the street with some other woman, and she certainly wasn't old,' Vera said, and Rita could hear in her voice that she was revelling in recounting the story to Ma Kennedy. 'She's not in the first flush of youth, by any means, but she's not on her last knockings neither.' Vera hugged her shopping bag and pursed her lips. 'Bold as brass she was . . . Bottle-blonde, mind, so what d'you expect?'

Rita knew Vera liked everyone to think her cousin owned property in the affluent seaside town of Southport, but what she failed to divulge was that her cousin was the cleaner to a wealthy doctor.

Vera gave Mrs Kennedy a knowing look that said women who dyed their hair were no better than they ought to be. 'Linking her arm with your Charlie's like she owned him, she was, and ordering those little kiddies to get a move on . . . She heard it as clear as I can hear you now.'

This confirmed what Rita had learned from the neighbour in Southport like nothing else could. He had lied and cheated on her regularly, but she had never imagined when he'd left here nearly three months ago that he would stoop so low as to take up with a fancy woman in a new life of his own and deny her, Rita, the right to visit her own children.

Well, Rita intended to get them away from their cheating father as soon as she could. There was no chance of her bringing them back here to Empire Street, though, with such ferocious air raids almost every night. No, she could not bring them back to this – but she did know where she could take them if she had to, somewhere they would be safe and happy.

'You are mistaken, Vera.'

Mrs Kennedy's haughty tone carried to the hallway. She would have her nose so high in the air she would be in danger of drowning if it rained, thought Rita.

'Charles would have been in his place of employment at that time of day.' Mrs Kennedy's voice was becoming shrill now.

Charlie was seldom at work, and his work was not like that of all the other men in the area who had to graft on the docks and in the factories – when they could get work at all, that was, Rita thought acidly.

If only Vera Delaney knew the whole truth about her so-called best friend and the child she never mentioned – she'd have spread it around Empire Street in no time; anything to get one over on Winnie Kennedy, who wore her snobbery like a badge of office.

'I'll go over and see Kitty when I've finished this,' Violet said busily as she cleared the dinner dishes from the table and noticed that Nancy had not done a hand's turn all morning. All she did was mope in the chair by the fire, hogging the precious heat and nursing baby George, who had fallen asleep ages ago.

Nancy was such a lazy individual, thought Violet, who wondered how the woman could sit idly by and let everybody else do the grafting. If she didn't move soon she would need dusting!

'Let's hope there will be no raids tonight, touch wood.' Violet was supremely superstitious and her life seemed ruled by little rituals that she believed would save her from harm.

'Touching wood won't save you if a bomb's got your name on it!' Nancy said, recalling the devastation she had seen. It was as if nobody else had been involved in a raid except Nancy.

'Well, that acorn on the window-sill did the trick!' Violet said with a satisfied nod of her head. 'We weren't set alight like the corner shop.'

Nancy lifted her eyes to the ceiling and refrained from telling her sister-in-law that it was just a coincidence. And who the hell did she think she was, telling everybody that she would go over and see poor Kitty? She had only been here five minutes! Nancy had never seen anybody stick their nose into other people's business so quickly.

And, Nancy thought churlishly, she was sure that if you wanted news spreading you only had to tell Violet and it would be around the street in no time. She could not keep her big gob shut! Nancy was in no mood for her today.

'Did you get your letter?' Nancy asked, and a ripple of curiosity made her wonder when Violet suddenly became animated, pulling the shabby brown cardigan she wore over a flowered apron that hung on her scrawny frame.

'Shall I put George in his pram while you get changed?' Violet asked, her arms outstretched already, heading towards the chair.

'No, thank you.' Nancy's voice was stiff and her manner cold. 'I can do it myself when I am good and ready.' She only mentioned once that she *might* go to Strand Road to see if she could get Gloria a little Christmas present in case she managed to get home for the day. She didn't say she was definitely going. It was more than likely that Gloria wouldn't make it home until after New Year. In her letter she said she was having such a good time. The anger and the disappointment ate away at Nancy. Fancy her best friend going to London – and staying there!

It didn't take much to make Violet aware of the warning note in Nancy's voice. Nevertheless, she felt it was her duty to broadcast advice for Nancy's own good.

'You'll spoil him if you sit with him on your knee all day,' Violet said. 'You'll be mithered and get nowt done, because he'll want holdin' all of t' time.'

'And what's it got to do with you if I'm *mithered*?' Nancy almost spat the words. 'We didn't know you from Adam this time last month and now you're telling me how to raise my own son!'

'I didn't mean owt by it . . .' Violet replied, visibly shaken, obviously not used to being spoken to in such an abrupt manner.

Dolly came into the kitchen and quickly intervened.

'Everybody's going through a rough time,' she said. 'Nobody's getting much sleep and nerves are stretched to breaking point, but it's Christmas – there's enough fighting going on outside without bringing it in here.' Nancy had no right to take her mood out on poor Violet. 'I'm sure Vi was only trying to help you, love,' Dolly added in a gentler tone.

'Well, she's got far too much to say for herself in this house lately,' Nancy pouted. 'She must think we're as thick as two short planks, coming in here telling me how to raise my own son!'

'All right, Nance.' Pop's usual calming tone held a worried note. He didn't usually interfere in what he called 'women's talk', knowing it was best not to meddle in things he knew nothing about – though it was his duty as a peace-loving man to put a stop to his daughter's tirade before tears were spilled.

But it was too late, already the tears were flowing down her cheeks and Pop knew she wasn't coping at all well with the hostilities. Nancy always did have a delicate constitution where duty was concerned. She was more of a happy-go-lucky kind of girl who liked to enjoy herself. It was a pity she had to face reality and get on with it like the rest of them, he thought.

Violet noticed something different about Nancy today. She could not put her finger on what it was just yet. However, in time she would.

'Why don't you come to the church hall with me later this afternoon, Nance?' Dolly said, trying to calm troubled waters. 'We are sorting the POW parcels: maybe you'd like to send one to Sid?'

'And they are recruiting for the Voluntary Service – you'd be a godsend to the WVS,' Vi said with a hint of acid, knowing there was nothing the Voluntary Service could learn from Nancy – unless they needed a crash course in nail painting or lipstick pouting.

'Aye, jam making and knitting boot socks might be right up your street, Vi,' Nancy said peevishly, wishing they would all go away and leave her alone, 'but I've got better things to do with my time.'

One of the reasons why she was so irritable and snappy was that Stan was supposed to be taking her to the pictures tonight – and she really wanted to go with him. In the days since the bombing of the

Adelphi she and Stan had been seeing quite a bit of each other. His granny lived just round the corner and he'd been to visit surprisingly frequently these last few days. Nancy had started visiting Mrs Hathaway in the evening, just to keep her company, like – in the hope that Stan would call in to see his dear old gran. He had not let her down so far, and luckily for her visitors Mrs Hathaway was hard of hearing and a bit doolally. Nancy knew that Stan would like them to be more than friends and he had told her often enough. Nancy knew that she was treading on dangerous ground but felt that she deserved a bit of fun. If things got too serious with Stan, she'd pull the plug on it.

This morning's letter said he couldn't make it, as he was taking his dear old granny to Mass. That was a big fat lie if ever she heard one, she thought peevishly. Nancy decided to keep a lookout to make sure he wasn't stringing her along.

But being the wife of a prisoner of war, she knew she had to behave herself. Her mam would not take too kindly to any kind of gossip that might grow into a scandal, and there were some, like Violet, who would not be slow to tittle-tattle given half the chance.

A short while later she put baby George into his pram and after dressing in her best woollen coat and making sure her hair was looking its best she smeared her lips with a slick of rosy lipstick and made her way to the telephone box to ring Stan. She only hoped the Post Office lines weren't down.

* * *

'You look as miserable as I feel,' Rita said to Kitty when she saw her standing on the step, her cardigan folded around her body and her arms tucked tightly around her slim frame.

'D'you fancy a cup of tea?' Kitty asked before heading into her warm, cosy kitchen. 'I wanted to give you this.' Rita took the latest of Jack's letters and put it away safely in her coat pocket where she would read it later.

'I was thinking of sending our Tommy to me Mam's people in Ireland, and I wanted to talk to you about it, seeing as Danny has to stay in hospital and not worry about anything. At least I'd know he would be well looked after by people who care for him but the little sod's having none of it.' She gave a hollow laugh. 'Every time I mention going away he takes a turn for the worse. He's a better actor than Randolph Scott!'

Rita laughed; her friend's dry wit was a tonic on a day like this.

'Will he be in hospital on Christmas Day?' Rita was on duty on the children's ward, and there was going to be a party for the kids.

Kitty nodded.

'I'll make sure he gets a good present,' Rita smiled. 'You can come in and see him in the afternoon, if you like – we're quite flexible on Christmas Day.'

'Oh, Rita that would be great!' Kitty was thrilled. The prospect of the party was the only thing keeping Tommy there. 'At least he's conscious this year and he's not as deaf as he makes out either. He could hear the grass grow if he had a mind!'

'You never know, *he* might like a trip to the countryside too, all that fresh air and open space to run wild in,' Rita said, recalling how her own children loved the farm. She had decided she was going to send them back to the farm in Freshfield at the first opportunity. Joan and her husband, Seth, had written telling her they would love to have Michael and Megan back.

'I'll see what I can do – but for now all he can think about is the Christmas party.' Kitty felt better for the first time since Tommy had been admitted to hospital.

'Dr Fitzgerald is playing Father Christmas,' Rita smiled, knowing that the young doctor always tried to be on the ward at visiting time so he could have a few words with Kitty.

'Is he? That's nice for the children,' Kitty said innocently, feeling her face flush at the mention of the doctor's name. She watched Rita pull on her gloves and fasten her woollen scarf more snugly around her neck before tucking it inside her heavy woollen coat.

Kitty thought of Rita almost like the sister she had never had and, indeed, the whole Feeny family were an extension of her own – all except Frank. The feelings she harboured for Frank were far from sisterly, but it was no use longing to see him. He had built such a solid, invisible wall of independence around himself that Kitty could not get through to him however much she longed to. It would be a dream come true to look after him and care for him. However, that was exactly the type of thing he did not need to hear.

As if Kitty's thoughts of him had conjured his name Rita said blithely, 'Mam hoped that our Frank would get a bit of Christmas leave, but there's no sign yet, not even a letter.' She stopped talking when she saw Kitty flinch slightly at the mention of his name, and her hand flew to her mouth. 'I'm sorry, Kit, I didn't mean to open old wounds.' She knew they had been sweet on each other for a time but she wondered if that had fizzled out now.

'You didn't open an old wound.' Kitty forced a smile. 'Frank and I are just like family and that's all we'll ever be.' Kitty knew he did not feel remotely romantic towards her and the most cutting thing of all was that he probably never had. However, there was no use worrying about what might have been. No, Kitty took a deep breath and forced a stiff smile, better to live in the here and now – let yesterday take care of itself.

'Your mam will be made up if Frank and Eddy manage to get home for Christmas.' Kitty thought that Eddy still had some explaining to do regarding his decision to wed on the Q.T., and he would have to answer his mother, Christmas or no Christmas.

'Is something else wrong, Kit?' Rita asked, concerned that her friend looked so out of sorts.

Kitty shook her turbaned head.

'Not really, I'm just worried about Tommy going to Ireland, and about Danny.' She gave a little smile, but the warmth of it did not reach her eyes.

'I know how you feel, Kit,' Rita said as Kitty poured the tea. It wasn't easy these days for mothers, not only worrying if their kids would have a home to come back to, but also worrying if they were being well looked after – and if they were, would they have changed by the time they got back home?

'I wanted Michael and Megan home for Christmas but after the last few nights' raids I know I can't bring them back here.'

'Do you know where they are now?' Kitty stopped pouring and pulled up a chair.

'Back in Southport. I got a phone call from Charlie's next-door neighbour this morning,' Rita explained. 'I can't get the train because the railway lines are down after the raids. I wish I could bring them home. I miss them so much. I've got them some toys – nothing fancy, there's not much to buy – and Pop has made Michael a smashing wooden train set and a little doll's house for Megan – if they ever come home.'

'There's a woman down Trevelyan Road who's got some American comics,' Kitty said. 'I would have got you some but they're more for older boys. I got our Tommy a couple and I think Danny would enjoy them, too.'

Rita smiled. If life was hard for her it must be even worse for Kitty. Looking at the time on the mantelpiece clock, the only thing to adorn Kitty's fireplace, Rita knew it was time to make tracks. She had spent far too long talking and must be off. Sitting here talking to Kitty and drinking her tea ration was getting nothing done.

'Have you heard anything from Charlie?'

Rita was quiet for a moment.

'You remember what I told you I'd heard from the lady next door when I went to Southport, about Charlie and "his wife" living there? Well, I only had her word for it, of course, but I've just overheard Vera Delaney telling Ma Kennedy that Charlie and this woman are living as man and wife.' Rita wondered how it affected her children. Did they call this new woman 'Mam'?

'You know what Vera's like, Rita.' Kitty patted her friend's arm. 'She's probably got the wrong end of the whole situation and is making a forest out of a stick.'

Rita knew that Kitty, the eternal optimist, was trying to make her feel better, but it was too late to bury her head in the sand. 'I doubt it, Kit, and I intend to find out and claim my children back.'

'Good for you, love.' Kitty's expression became concerned. 'Are there any trains running out that way today?'

'No, there aren't. I shall have to wait.' She got up from the straight-backed chair at the kitchen table. 'I'll see you later, Kit.'

'I hope you don't mind me saying, Rita,' Kitty said as they reached the front door, 'but if I didn't know you, and someone told me you and Charlie Kennedy were man and wife I would never believe them. You're far too decent for the likes of him.'

Rita hugged her and wished her all the best for the Christmas season, feeling Kitty's innocent warmth radiate towards her along the narrow hallway as she left.

*   *   *

Violet made her way through the back ginnels towards one of Salford's three-up three-down terraced houses that looked much the same as Empire Street, with their front parlours and their outside lavatories. She came under cover of the early morning darkness to prevent tongues wagging, and she closed the back gate very carefully and very quietly behind her.

'It's only me!' she called softly as she opened the unlocked back door that led to the kitchen beyond. The difference between this and Dolly's cosy kitchen was stark. This one possessed hardly a stick of furniture, the table under the thin, scarred window had been second- or maybe third-hand when her mother took possession of it, and Violet noticed the dilapidated couch was in need of some kind of cover to hide the bulging horsehair stuffing. The ash-covered coals threw out no heat, making the poverty-stricken room drab and cheerless.

'Hmmph! You took your time, I must say.' A toothless woman in a faded old pinny, ragged slippers and a woollen headscarf tied in a knot below her chin, did not look in the least bit pleased to see her daughter.

'I came as soon as I could, Mam,' Violet said quickly. Automatically she felt the brown clay teapot that sat in the middle of the old-fashioned square table covered in soiled newspaper. It was cold, as she expected.

'Shall I make a fresh pot of tea, Mam?' Violet said as if she had last seen her mother recently instead of the morning of her wedding last August. 'I came as soon as I heard about the raid.'

'There's nowt in. I've got no tea,' Mrs Brown told

her daughter, who for as much as she could not stand the man her mother had married, still loved her mother. 'I had to hitch a lift from the Mersey docks. There's no public trains, only troop trains.'

'Oh, is that what I am? The public – grand,' Mrs Brown said miserably, and Violet wondered why she took everything so personally. However, she tried to keep the conversation on a positive footing. 'The railway people don't mean you, Mam, they mean people who are not in the Forces. They need space to get supplies across the country.'

'We got it full belt last night,' Mrs Brown said in a dull voice. Violet took it to mean an enemy raid. 'I were on me own most o' night – until he came home stinkin' drunk from t' pub.'

While Liverpool had suffered a lighter raid, it seemed that Manchester was now the main target for Hitler's wrath.

'I had to come and make sure you were all right, Mam,' Violet said, pulling a rickety chair from under the grimy table. She grimaced when she saw the half-filled bottle of brown sauce, which had no lid to prevent the crusty residue attracting God-knew-what. Although Violet doubted the mice would grow fat in this place. The saltcellar was perched in its usual place on the black, almost fireless range, to prevent it going damp.

'I wish they'd bombed the hell out o' that pub,' Mrs Brown said bitterly.

'Have you heard anything from the kids?' Violet had two younger half-brothers and two half-sisters.

She had told Dolly and Pop – even Eddy, her husband – a complete set of lies when she'd said her beloved parents, a vicar and his wife, had been killed when their pristine house was bombed. She was not the only child of devout parents at all.

She was one of eight. Three were her own full brothers and sisters, all older than she, and who had now left home and had families of their own. They had little time for the family they had left behind. The other four were the living product of her mother's second husband, whom she had married fifteen years ago when Violet was only five. Her mother had a baby every year almost, lost many, kept four, while he spent as much time as possible in the alehouse because he could not stand the noise – not that it had anything to do with him, Violet thought drily. When he had started to look at her in a leering way each time he came home from the pub, she vowed to get away as soon as possible.

Shuddering with disgust, she came back to reassure herself that this place was as bad as she remembered. It was. Life had been unbearable!

Once the kids had been evacuated, the oldest being almost fourteen and the youngest seven, Violet set her cap at Eddy, refusing to be her mother's support any longer. It was a shame her mam suffered with her nerves, but Violet could not bear to be in the same house as that hateful man much longer, and was of the opinion that her mother had married him so she was welcome to him.

She had been writing to the each of her siblings

and they all said the same: they were much happier now, away from this miserable hovel. Looking at her shrivelled mother, not much older than forty and married to a belligerent drunk, Violet knew exactly what she did not want in life. If Eddy or his family ever found out about this, she would die of shame.

'Is everything all right, Mam? You sounded upset when you wrote.'

'Upset? Did I?' Mrs Brown said miserably, staring into a fireless grate. 'Is it any wonder when I'm married to a feckless waster who is neither use nor ornament? Not a care for me.'

Violet fought the urge to remind her mother that nobody had forced her to marry him. It would not do either of them any good raking up the past. It was the here and now they had to worry about.

'Wouldn't you think about doing a bit of war work instead of scrubbing other people's houses, Mam? It pays more.' Violet broached the subject with caution, knowing her mother did not take kindly to being told what to do, even if it was for her own good.

'War work? War work! I wouldn't know how to do war work!'

'No,' Vi said, remembering, 'I know.' Her mother had never been a good mixer, and the solitary toil of domestic drudgery was all she had ever known.

Her thoughts now turned to Dolly, who could not find enough hours in the day to do the things she wanted to do. And here was her own mother, sitting in the same sagging chair by the dead fire, her cardigan dragged around her hungry body.

'I've brought you a few bits,' Violet said, opening her bag. She knew Dolly thought she was mean with her own rations, but she had been saving to bring her mother a bit of Christmas cheer, knowing she would not have any spare.

She put some bread, cheese and bacon on the table. The sight of the food lit up her mother's eyes for a fleeting moment. However, if things were still the same as they used to be, Violet doubted her mother would get to taste any of it.

'He'll enjoy that for his Christmas breakfast,' Mrs Brown said wearily, wiping a dewdrop from the tip of her nose with the cuff of her cardigan sleeve. Violet sighed in exasperation. She had forgotten the time when her mother laughed, really laughed like the Feenys or the Callaghans did. Her mother, not one for demonstrations of affection at the best of times, would not think of passing a compliment, or giving a hug as the Feenys did so automatically.

All this was the reason Eddy had never met her family. Violet's heart lurched now at the thought of Eddy. He would not look down his nose if he found out she came from this . . . this hellhole. However, he would then know he was married to a liar.

'Mam, the bacon is for you too. It'll be a nice treat on a butty for Christmas morning.' The least her mother deserved.

'Nice I'd look eating bacon, when he'll be watching every mouthful,' Mrs Brown huffed. 'No, I'll dip me dry bread in the fat, same as allus! That'll do me.'

'Mam!' Violet protested. 'That won't do!' Even the

warning glare was not going to stop her having her say this time. 'You bent over backwards for that man and what thanks did you get?' Even now, Violet refused to call him her father – because he was not.

'You mind yours and I'll mind mine, if you please.' There wasn't a sniff of thanks for the rations and Violet knew that's all her mother would get of them – a sniff, because when he came in this lot would be gone in one sitting – the greedy fat pig!

It was Christmas but there was no sign of cheer in this house, not because of the war but because there never had been a celebration of any kind. That would mean him spending money on somebody other than himself. It was a far cry from the days when there had been just the two of them, happy in their own way, after Violet's elder siblings had gone to school. 'Here, let me make you a cup of tea and something to eat.'

Violet was determined that her mother was not going to give all this away to him.

A short while later, she watched as her mother devoured the bacon sandwich, and wondered when she had last eaten. Only when she was quite satisfied her mam had had her fill and was now on her second cup of tea, did Violet stand up and put on her coat. It was growing dark and she still had to get all the way back to Liverpool.

How she wished that fat drunken upstart had come back from the pub early so she could have it out with him. Her poor mother was half-starved while he drank all the money for which she worked her fingers to the bone. He needed reporting! And she would do it, too, but her mother, frightened of her own shadow, would never forgive her. She drank her black, weak, sugarless tea and could tell her mother was on pins – she did not want *him* coming in and catching her there.

'Well, I'll be off Mam.' Violet could see that she wasn't going to be offered so much as a piece of dry bread after her long journey. How she was going to get back to Liverpool again she did not know. But get back she must, because if she stayed in this place one minute longer she would scream until her lips turned blue – the way she used to.

'Try and get out a bit more, Mam.' Violet turned to her now and her heart went out to this woman who had sacrificed everything for a man who could not care less. She put half a crown on the table. 'Don't give it to him, Mam. Save it and buy yourself something nice.'

'Aye,' her mother sighed. 'I will that.'

There were no hugs or fancy words before Violet left the same way she came. But the grateful look in her mother's eyes said everything that was needed.

'Look after yoursel', Mam,' Violet said, looking up the back yard towards the cheerless house before she closed the back gate and hurried up the ginnel.

The air-raid siren started as she headed out of Manchester. Luckily she managed to get a train, which was full of soldiers on leave. One even offered her his hip flask but Violet refused. They deserved their drinks after what they'd been through. Suddenly Violet realised how soft she had got since she moved to Empire Street. A short while ago she would have turned her nose up at such public displays of merrymaking.

The soldiers' chatter was about pubs of mutual interest and who was going to win the league, unaware that teams played twice a day, to make the numbers on the football coupons, each team taking turns to play at home in the morning and away in the afternoon.

As the train journeyed towards Liverpool, Violet was unaware that the Manchester raids were of the same magnitude as the ones suffered by Bootle the previous nights. Nor did she know that the meal she had lovingly prepared for her mother would be her last, as the gable end of the house crushed the last breath from her malnourished body.

CHAPTER EIGHTEEN

'Look, there's no risk,' Delaney said when he visited Danny in hospital. For a time, Danny had been warned not to do anything more strenuous than breathe in and out, but at last his fitness was gradually improving. He couldn't wait to get out of here and refrained from telling the doctor he had a family to support.

However, he knew he would not be strong enough to return to the docks for a while yet. And with Kitty working he would not be entitled to means-tested National Assistance money. But he would not live off his sister when he got home.

He had his pride and would not accept hand-outs. Danny had no illusions; he had more about him than his deluded father, who always thought there would be something better around the corner. Well, all he could say was it must have been one hell of a big corner, because his poor ould fella never did see the 'something better'.

'Of course there's a risk, Alf.' Danny had to be careful what he said; Delaney could make life unbearable if he thought Danny was not on his side. He spoke in a whisper. 'You're asking me to take the medical test for you. That's fraud, that is, and we could both go to prison.'

This wasn't the first time that Alfie Delany had mentioned that he wanted Danny to take his army medical test for him. Despite all of this big talk, Alfie was a coward and would do anything to avoid his call-up. Danny knew that there was nothing that would have made him prouder than to have fought for his country, but that wasn't to be. He couldn't believe that Alfie had the nerve to ask him to do it again. He had no intention of doing so, but Alfie was persistent and used to getting his own way. By hook or by crook.

Danny had a few bob saved, and Kitty was earning in the NAAFI. Something was bound to turn up in the New Year. He did not want to get mixed up in anything dodgy, especially when dodgy also meant dealing with Harry Calendar, a notorious spiv who lived in unashamed luxury in the Dingle Mansions and who was behind most of Alfie's dodgy deals.

'How's that little brother of yours doing? It was a good thing I was passing that warehouse when I was. Things could have gone very differently if it wasn't for me, you know.'

Danny knew it was only a matter of time before Delaney brought up his supposed rescue of Tommy. He was going to use this as emotional blackmail and if that didn't work, he'd try something else.

'Anyway, you have a little think on it, Danny boy,' Delaney said, 'I know you'll come right in the end.

Besides, Mr Calendar and I both know a few things about you that might surprise a few people.' Alfie's voice was light in tone, but there was no mistaking the menace behind it. This was a veiled threat. If Danny didn't take that test, then Aflie was likely to fit him up for something. He was between the devil and the deep blue sea. He watched as Delaney opened a newspaper parcel he had brought in.

'What do you think about these, Dan?' Delaney showed him a brand-new pair of leather football boots. 'Would your Tommy be made up with these?'

Danny eyed the boots cautiously.

'Any player in the Northern League would be made up with those, Alf.'

'Here, give them to Tommy for Christmas with my compliments.' Alfie thrust them into Danny's hand. 'As a pal, I wouldn't dream of taking a penny for them.'

'Hang on, Alf . . .' Danny would never be able to afford these in a million years. They were beauties. However, he would rather Tommy went without and he himself not be beholden to the charge hand and his sneaky practices.

'Now, don't bite your nose off to spite your face, Dan,' Alfie laughed as he got up to go. 'I'm sure you can always do me a favour one day. Now, I must be off . . . people to see, things to do, etc.' Alfie tapped Danny's arms lightly. 'Remember what I said, Danny boy. I'll be seeing you.' And with that he was gone.

Danny knew that Alfie was setting him up. But

from his hospital bed, it seemed like he was a sitting duck for Alfie's machinations. Accepting the boots confirmed he was obligated to Delaney now – if he tried to put a bit of distance between them, no doubt Alfie would use his connections with Harry Calendar to rope him in and Danny had a good idea where that would lead.

He needed time to mull things over. He would need every ounce of energy he had to outwit Delaney . . . it wouldn't be easy. Danny might be cleverer than Alfie, but Alfie was persistent and had his health . . .

A friendly face at the porthole window curtailed any further cogitating.

'Are you decent, Danny?' Sarah laughed as she came in carrying an armful of brown paper carrier bags. 'I brought you something to cheer you up.'

'You didn't have to do that, Sar.' Danny was thrilled to see Sarah Feeny all decked out in her Red Cross uniform, looking lovely. He knew she must have been busy with incoming casualties and didn't expect to see her here today. 'But I'm glad you did.'

'Have you walked from town?' Danny asked, knowing work was being carried out on the dock road tramlines. As she came closer he was admiring her slim, shapely legs beneath her navy-blue woollen cloak.

Sarah nodded, she was tired. But she could not go home without popping in to see her old pal Danny first.

Anyway, she thought, he had always been her one true friend and they could talk about anything. Danny was a man and she needed a bit of male advice. In fact she could think of nobody better she could discuss her problem with.

'I brought you some American comics. We had some Canadians visiting an injured pal and they left quite a few,' Sarah said.

Danny's eyes lit up when he saw Superman, Batman and Captain Marvel among the comic strips. 'This is the life, hey, Sar?' He didn't tell her their Kitty was bringing some in later – and he hoped they weren't all the same.

Sarah was thrilled she had made his day. She wouldn't stay long because she didn't want to tire him out, nor did she feel she had the energy to keep her own eyes open much longer. There had been over fifty air raids on Merseyside since they began in August, with each raid lasting anything from a few minutes up to ten hours. Sarah was glad there had been no raids last night, but there was still plenty of clearing up to do and many casualties from the raids.

Danny looked deadbeat now, and she still worried about him and the strain that had been put on his heart. He had always been a grafter when he could get work, even more so now. The docks had to keep going no matter what aggression the men faced. Loading and unloading the ships was of paramount importance for the whole country and Danny, along with every other man in the reserved occupation, would not shirk his duty.

'Are you on duty tonight, Sar?'

'No, I've got the night off, unless there's an air raid.

I hope there isn't. It seems ages since my last night off.'

'I hope Father Christmas brings you something nice,' Danny said, rolling the comics into a tube for the want of something to do – he had always liked Sarah, he found her so easy to talk to. But he did not want her to see him as an invalid. Now he knew what Sarah's brother Frank felt like when he lost his leg, but Danny was just as determined to get back to work. If he didn't work he didn't eat – simple. 'I hope you get everything you wish for, Sar,' Danny said tenderly. She deserved it.

'Just forty winks will do me.' Sarah gave a tired laugh. 'I'll sleep without rocking, that's for sure. Are you going up to see Tommy today?'

Danny nodded. 'Maybe this afternoon.' Danny was now allowed to walk over to see his little brother, but the effort was sometimes too much. He could feel the energy draining from his body, but he did not want Sarah to leave on his account.

'How is he doing?' Sarah asked, concerned.

'Swinging the lead, I think,' he laughed tiredly. 'He's got those doctors fooled into thinking he's worse than he is because he got wind that there's going to be a party.'

Sarah laughed and Danny gave a contented sigh. She had a nice laugh . . . His eyelids grew heavy . . . Now what did he go and think a daft thing like that for? 'I can't wait to see his face when he sees his new football boots.'

'He's football mad, your Tommy,' Sarah answered.

'He's broken more windows than the Luftwaffe.' They both chuckled, knowing Tommy had taken the toes out of more left shoes than any other kid he knew.

'Our Kitty says he's the only kid with a mouth on his left foot!' His speech was slurring and Sarah knew it was time to go when his eyes closed. She made to get up and suddenly Danny was wide-eyed and continuing to talk as if he hadn't stopped.

'The boots are two sizes bigger than Tommy's normal shoes,' he gave a tired chuckle, 'but due to the shortages, they were all I could get.'

'I'd best be off, let you get some rest.' Just the sight of Danny's heavy lids made her want to curl up and go to sleep too.

Danny raised a heavy finger. 'All the best, Sar . . .' He was fast asleep before Sarah reached the ward door.

'Same to you, Dan.'

The children's ward was decorated with bunting of colourful crepe paper gleaned, borrowed or begged over the last couple of weeks, and making it had kept the children quiet for days. Now it adorned the middle of the ward between the iron beds and cots. Rita and the rest of the nurses sang Christmas carols, encouraging the excited children to do the same, while some, like Tommy who were not so badly injured or ill, had been allowed to help with pinning up the decorations. Afterwards the staff and the children looked on in wonder at their splendid efforts.

'Ho! Ho! Ho!' A booming voice resonated down

the corridor after the children had finished their lovely chicken dinner and Christmas pud. The jolly greeting alerted the twenty children, who sat up in bed with polished faces and not a hair out of place, eagerly anticipating a meeting with 'him'! Some of them actually squeaked with excitement.

Father Christmas was on his way!

A five-year-old boy looked troubled as he sat stiffly in his cot, showing the blistered effects of an incendiary bomb fire, his face partly bandaged. 'But what if he doesn't know it's me?' he said.

'Don't you worry, Sammy, Father Christmas knows all the good little boys.'

'And girls!' a determined voice came from the other side of the ward, and Rita laughed.

'He won't forget the girls either, Mary!'

'Just as long as he doesn't,' Mary replied indignantly as all eyes focused on the ward door. However, there was a collective groan when the janitor came on to the ward with a shovel of coal for the fire.

'Oh, you're not happy to see me?' the janitor asked and, sensing a bit of fun, the children chorused in unison, 'We want Father Christmas! We want Father Christmas!'

'I bet you'll want to see what I've got for you,' the janitor said, and the children nodded. He left the ward and moments later they were rewarded with a Christmas tree, which was put in a bucket at the end of the ward.

'Who wants to help me decorate it before Father Christmas gets here?' The janitor, a Great War veteran, laughed when those who could, jumped up and down with their hands in the air.

'Me! Me! Me!' They jumped from the beds as regimentally straight covers were thrown back and pyjama-clad children in bare feet bounced around the ward.

'This is much better than last year,' Tommy told Rita, whose recollection of Tommy at death's door with diphtheria was still fresh in her memory. Thankfully the traumatic episode was well behind him – except that now he was getting in the way of burning buildings and high explosives instead.

'You little hooligans should not be out of bed! Matron will have my guts for violin strings!' Rita laughed, clapping her hands, and all the kids talked at once, excited at the sight of coloured glass balls, which, she presumed, had never graced many poor homes.

The little girls, emboldened by the boys' forthright eagerness, were now cooing over the manger in the corner, which the nurses had set up while they were all asleep last night. Rita and Maeve watched the boys, Tommy Callaghan among them, who were deadly serious in the positioning of tree decorations. Hopefully they would have it finished by the time Father Christmas got here.

It was a wonderful sight and Rita wished she had a camera. Such a peaceful scene. Somebody should make a Christmas card of it and sent it to Hitler, she secretly reasoned. She missed Michael and Megan so much it caused physical pain. What would they be doing now, she wondered.

However, she had no time to dwell as a little voice called, 'Nurse, Nurse! Come and have a look at this.' One of the little girls beckoned her and, thankfully, Rita's mind returned to the matter in hand.

'Do you think baby Jesus will have a party for his birthday, Nurse?' one of the little girls asked, slipping her little hand into Rita's, and she nodded, unable to speak now for the lump in her throat.

'I'm sure, when we have our party later,' said Maeve, sensing that Rita could not speak right now, 'we can all sing "Happy Birthday".' All the children gleefully nodded, even more excited now.

'Is our Kitty coming in this afternoon, Nurse?' Tommy was careful not to call Rita by her Christian name on the ward, even though he knew her as well as he knew his own sister, as Kitty had told him she must be called 'Nurse' at all times and afforded the respect her uniform deserved when she was on the ward.

'I'm sure she'll be here as soon as she can, Tom,' Rita smiled. She loved Tommy like one of her own and was glad she had been put on the children's ward, where she could keep her eye on him and reassure Kitty and Danny.

After their arranged afternoon nap, which none of the children could manage as they were so excited, tables were brought in. The nurses arranged them in a long line down the centre of the ward, and covered them with brilliant white cloths. Delightedly the children watched with hardly a sound as the paste sandwiches, jellies, cakes and biscuits, which had been donated

319

from all over the borough, were ceremonially brought in and placed on the long table.

Jugs of evaporated milk to pour over the jelly and tinned fruit, and beakers of orange juice and lime cordial, which some of the children had never tasted before, were placed on the tables alongside paper hats and whistling streamers.

At last the children were allowed to get out of bed and hobble, hop or hurry to take their places at the table.

There was an air of expectation when one of the children said he heard the sound of a ringing bell coming from far away. Rita prayed that, as dusk was closing in, there would be no raids this afternoon.

Let the children have their day.

Moments later Father Christmas, complete with a soft pillow for a bulging tum, ho ho ho'ed his way onto the ward, much to the delight of the waiting children.

However, their delight was nothing compared to Rita's when she saw the distinctive outline of Jack Callaghan. She felt her heart jump so sharply she could not catch her breath! Jack entered the ward behind Father Christmas with Kitty and Danny following.

It took all of Rita's professional reserve to stop herself from calling his name aloud and she only just managed to silence the gasp of appreciation his dignified presence evoked, looking more handsome than ever in the uniform of the Flight Air Arm. For the moment Rita was speechless. His presence seemed to radiate out across the whole ward. Rita wondered if everyone else could feel his strength and goodness too. But no one felt for Jack the way that she did.

'Hello, Rita,' Jack said eventually, and she knew it was not her imagination when she saw his eyes soften.

Rita, standing beside him, almost touching but not quite, longed to feel his arms around her.

There was no need for words, just to have him standing next to her was thrilling enough for Rita right now. Their letters to each other had become more intimate as time went on and Rita found she had opened up her heart to Jack in a way she would once never have thought possible and – even more thrilling – he had done the same.

Kitty noticed that her brother's gaze lingered on Rita's face for a long while longer than was necessary and, if she had not guessed by the enthusiasm with which Rita had received Jack's letters, she quickly realised that Jack and Rita had lost none of their mutual affection for each other. Kitty could see the two of them were still very much in love. Why did life have to be so complicated, she wondered?

'It's good to see you home, Jack,' Rita smiled, willing her thundering heart to slow down, glad the children, staff and families were preoccupied with Father Christmas. 'The hospital has been bursting at the seams this week.' Her voice, even to her own ears, sounded high-pitched and unfamiliar.

Kitty now knew there was still something special and the letters that went back and forth between her brother and Rita were, as she had guessed, more than just neighbourly. Jack was playing with fire now. Rita was a married woman. There would be repercussions to a special friendship like theirs.

Rita knew she must think of something more mundane than Jack Callaghan's perfect brown eyes. She had not greeted him with a wide smile and a cheerful hug of welcome as she always had done before and she told herself she was on duty and must behave accordingly. However, she had hugged Kitty and even Danny. Rita was finding it difficult to breathe now.

Rita knew now that she loved Jack Callaghan with every beat of her heart and she always had. But even though she acknowledged her marriage to Charlie was over and done with, she could not shake off the feelings of guilt eating away inside her. She felt wicked just thinking about Jack the way she did . . . She could never love anybody the way she loved Jack. However, any dalliance was out of the question, it would bring shame to her family.

It was a crying shame she had married Charlie. Her mother had said many times right from the beginning that Charlie did not deserve her consideration and, like the wily fox he most certainly was, he had shown Rita his true colours only after the wedding ceremony. Her frustration was the price she had to pay for marrying Charlie, a life of wondering what could have been, and Rita knew that the feeling would eventually destroy her if she let it. She shivered.

'Are you cold?' Jack's concern was obvious now and Rita felt a flood of heat rush to her face. There was nobody else in the whole world for her except him. How she longed to run into his arms and tell him how much she had missed him. How much she had worried about him. How much she longed to feel his arms around her once more. But she couldn't. It was impossible.

'I'm fine, Jack,' she smiled gently. 'But what about you? How's your arm?' Rita was trying to keep her voice steady as Jack removed his greatcoat with one hand and she saw his other arm was strapped in a sling across his chest.

'Gunshot to the shoulder, right through there!' He pointed proudly to the place just below his shoulder between his neck and his heart as Tommy proudly looked on, eager to know every detail. 'A bit further and I'd have been going to see Ma.' He grinned at Tommy. 'I was ever so brave though, Reet. You'd have been proud of me.'

I'll always be proud of you, Jack.

Kitty clicked her tongue and joked, 'Going to Ma indeed! Don't you know that only the good die young, Jack Callaghan? They'll have to shoot you with a twelve-bore shotgun!'

'I didn't expect my own sister to ruin my hero image!' Jack laughed, and Rita laughed too as the children busied themselves with eating as many goodies as they could muster because this kind of feast did not come every day.

'You are a hero, Jack.' The words were out of Rita's mouth before she could stop them. Then, quickly regaining the no-nonsense persona of a ward sister she said brusquely, 'And don't let anybody tell you different.'

'That's my girl, Reet!' Jack said quietly, looking straight into her eyes, and Rita felt that old familiar *frisson* of electricity shoot through her. He was the only person she allowed to call her Reet. However, she had duties to perform and she could not stand around here, no matter how much she wanted to.

'I'll catch up with you later.' She aimed the remark at Kitty, who nodded.

'See you later, Reet,' Jack answered with a smile.

CHAPTER NINETEEN

'Vi, where've you been? We've been ever so worried, love.' Dolly hurried forward as Violet entered the warm cosy kitchen and gave her daughter-in-law a hug. Not usually one for shows of sentiment, Violet gladly accepted the motherly embrace, knowing her own mother had looked so worn out yesterday.

'I just went for a little walk,' Violet said. She needed time to sort things out in her head. She decided that she was going to write to tell Eddy the truth if he didn't make it home for Christmas, and seeing it was nearly dinner time she didn't hold out much hope of him arriving today. However, it wasn't fair that her brave sailor be married to a liar.

She would have to take the consequences of the underhand way she had trapped him into marriage. He thought she was married to the only daughter of a respectable, decent couple who had been killed in an air raid. The good thing was that Eddy had not seen where she came from. The bad thing was she had told him so many lies she didn't think he would ever trust her again.

The reason she had lied to him was because she didn't want to lose him. From the first time they met she loved Eddy with every fibre of her being. But, she recognised, he was entitled to know the truth if they were to have any kind of life together when the war was over.

A heavy ran-tan on the front door postponed any further questions.

'I'll get it,' Violet said, still in her coat. Moments later, after closing the blackout curtains across the door and turning on the light she called from the hallway, 'Pop, it's ARP business for you!'

Dolly looked at her husband and he looked back, his brows puckered before he shuffled out in his carpet slippers. Dolly was about to put the chicken in the oven and start the dinner, seeing as there was no sign of her sons coming home. A little disappointed, she had refused to peel the vegetables in case they turned up, but time was getting on now. They'd had the King's speech and everything.

Pop wondered what he was about to face. Dolly said Christmas dinner would be a couple of hours yet. Anyroad, he thought, looking forward to his chicken dinner, they were lucky to get any kind of Christmas this year.

'Who is it, love?' Dolly asked Violet when she came back into the kitchen.

'I don't know. The man says he's from the Salvage Corps,' she shrugged, 'but don't they usually go around with the fire brigade?'

Dolly's face darkened, mentally working out what

326

to do next. She knew why the Salvage Corps was here.

'Everybody, collect your things. There's an unexploded bomb at the bottom of the street – we're being evacuated to the church hall,' Pop said in that calm, measured but determined tone he used to urge people into air-raid shelters.

Dolly and the rest of the family quickly and quietly gathered all that was necessary for their evacuation.

'I should have cooked earlier,' Dolly said apologetically. 'Now we'll have to have sandwiches.'

'They'd better be ready because we've got no time to make them now,' Violet said, and Dolly grabbed the bread and some meat paste and then, as an afterthought, the Christmas cake, and an armful of tins, while Violet slipped baby George into his siren suit.

'The bomb could have landed at this end of the street,' Pop chuckled. 'Then we could have sheltered in the pub.' He chivvied them along, trying to keep everybody cheerful, without panic, while ignoring one of Dolly's raised-eyebrow looks. Any minute now he would disappear to see if any stragglers were left in the houses on Empire Street. However, it did not take long to get everybody out and down to the street.

The church hall was quite festive, with paper chains and Tilley lamps. Dolly took provisions of tea and sugar from the extra ration they had received for Christmas, along with some condensed milk.

A short while later Dolly and her friend Mrs Mawdsley, who served with her in the WVS, were organising cups of tea and exchanging information with other families from Empire Street. Pop was having a pow-wow with Cyril Arden from the pub, while Violet was shushing little Georgie, who was teething and fretful. Sarah had to be back at the hospital for six and Nancy was off visiting Gloria, who she said was joining some friends from George Henry Lee for the day and needed her to help get her through losing Giles.

It wasn't unusual for Nancy to spend all of her time with Gloria, especially given the circumstances, but she was amazed at Nancy leaving all the babysitting to Violet. Violet didn't mind at all – but that was not the point, Pop said.

'Vi's so good with the baby,' Dolly quietly remarked later to Pop when they got a minute and, puffing on his pipe, he nodded.

'Even if she's not so good with his mother,' he replied even more quietly. 'Has our Nancy gone to meet up with Gloria at a friend's house again? That's the third night this week.'

Dolly made a mental note to have a word with Nancy when she got back, and just hoped that Christmas would not be spoiled any more than it was already. Her daughter's dramatic tantrums could be quite unnerving when Dolly broached the thorny subject of looking after her own baby for a change, instead of depending on Violet all the time.

As the night wore on and the hands on the church hall clock ticked round to midnight, somebody started to sing a Christmas carol. All the children joined in and in no time at all, the church hall rang with the voices of Empire Street. Everybody joined in, even men who had not been to Mass for years. This was the second wartime Christmas and since last year the rest of Western Europe had been overwhelmed by the German blitzkrieg. Thousands of British troops had been killed, wounded or taken prisoner. Then there was the invasion scare and the blitz. It was a wonder anybody remembered Christmas at all! However, they were surviving. It was hard but they were doing their best.

This was not the best time of the year for some families, not because of the shortages of food or goods, but because some of their men were not here. Nobody wanted to leave their firesides at this time of the year, remembering a time when the kids could play with their toys in peace. Now, it seemed like one long relentless slog without husbands and brothers who had not been seen for such a long time.

'We must be grateful for small mercies, Doll,' Pop said in the lull of a carol. 'At least our house is still standing – well, it was the last time I looked.' He gave Dolly a loving kiss on her upturned cheek.

'You're right, Pop,' Dolly smiled. The papers and magazines encouraged a 'Christmas as normal' attitude and she was trying to make the best of it.

However, a festive cheer went up when Pop and Cyril Arden braved the unexploded bomb, sneaked into the back of the pub and came back with a couple of wheelbarrows loaded with crates of stout and pale ale, which went down a treat and made everyone mellow for bygone days, as did a few schooners of sherry for the ladies.

'You can settle up tomorrow, if we're still here,' Cyril laughed. 'After all, it is Christmas.'

'Here, Cyril,' Vera Delaney called, sitting at a table with Mrs Kennedy, who was knocking back the sherry like there was going to be a drought – and there would be if the two of them didn't hang fire. 'I haven't seen anything of your Gloria lately. I thought she was back.'

'She's staying in London for Christmas,' Cyril answered, taking a seat next to Pop and Dolly and saying in a low voice, 'Nosy old bag!'

Dolly's ears pricked up. Gloria gone away? Then where had Nancy been going recently? What was she up to? Dolly felt an anxious knot in her stomach. How many times had she told Nancy to stay out of trouble? Rita had said something about Nancy and Stan Hathaway a while ago, but she hadn't really been listening. If Nancy was playing fast and loose with her morals . . .

Mrs Arden sat beside her and put her sherry on the table. She informed Dolly that Gloria had gone to stay with one of the other singers at the Adelphi with whom she had become friends. They were doing a few shows in London too and Gloria hoped it would help her take her mind off her loss.

'She didn't half love him, you know,' Mrs Arden said fervently, as if half loving somebody was an option. Dolly knew exactly what she meant, though, and she nodded tiredly, thinking about Nancy and Sid.

'Will it take long d'you think, making the bomb safe?'

'I couldn't say,' answered Pop. 'Depends on the bomb disposal lads.'

'I wonder what the boys are doing,' Dolly said, thinking of her sons and the times when they were all together. They had been a happy family – they still were – if only it wasn't for this blasted war. 'I wonder where they would be if there was no war?'

'If you "wander" any more, Doll,' Pop laughed, 'we'll have to send a search party out looking for you.'

'I beg your pardon?' Dolly laughed even though it was heartbreaking for her knowing her sons were out there somewhere, like many other women's sons from all over the world. Nevertheless, as long as Pop was here, she knew everything would be fine. As the time wore on they found they were having a good time, singing and swapping stories they did not usually have time to tell.

Violet told them about her family back in Manchester. She never spoke of her parents usually, and Dolly could see why when she saw how upset she got when she talked about them. It was such a shame she was an only child, Dolly thought, and that her parents, her only relatives, had been killed. She must have been so lonely . . . Little Georgie was sound asleep in her arms now and Violet looked so content.

When he was suffering with his teething, Violet seemed to be the only one who could comfort him, much to Nancy's irritation. But what could she expect when the child had seen hardly anything of his mother lately?

When everyone was feeling mellow, somebody opened the piano lid and Pop, ready for any occasion, had brought along his accordion, which he played with gusto. Somebody from round the corner on the dock road had brought a revolting concoction he had brewed himself. However, after a couple of glasses, it tasted quite palatable and it didn't cost as much as Cyril Arden's beer, although one wag said it would run his motorbike and sidecar a treat. The songs went on well into the night.

A miniature Christmas tree with a fairy on top sat on the stage. Dolly and the rest of the Empire Street women had brought a feast between them, including sandwiches, bun-loaf and Christmas cake. It was a strange gathering, but these were not normal times.

As the night wore on, neighbours remembered the loved ones who were still away, or the ones they had lost. Even later still, when the ale was on the wane, Vera Delaney piped up, 'I wonder who will still be here next week!' Luckily Pop would not allow the company to dissolve into maudlin wrecks and he opened up his squeeze-box again. In no time there was dancing in the church hall.

'Well, this is a fine how-do-you-do, I don't think!' a mock-stern voice boomed.

All heads turned to the door, not in the least bit tired now, and were thrilled to see Eddy standing in the doorway. Instantly the return of one of their own raised everyone's spirit.

'Hello, playmates,' Eddy said, doing his Arthur Askey impression. Nobody knew who screamed the loudest when Dolly and Vi each made a beeline for the door.

'My boy is home!' Dolly laugh-cried and looked at Pop as if he had done something wonderful. Violet got her husband in a stranglehold and his proud father, who shook his hand until it went numb, had to rescue Eddy.

'There'll be enough of that later, in private, Vi,' Pop laughed.

'Ay-thang-yaw!' Eddy said breathlessly, laughing and apologising to Vi, while all the time he was being slapped on the back. A bottle of brown ale was put into his hand and in no time, he and Jack Callaghan were swapping heroic war stories until dawn. The old-timers, like Pop and Cyril Arden, joined in with their tales of the last war, and all had a jolly good time.

Except Violet.

'Well,' she said, 'you don't see your own husband for months on end and then he goes and gets himself side-tracked by a bottle of brown ale!'

'Never mind, Vi,' Rita laughed. Suddenly the night had become much more enjoyable now that Eddy was here – and Jack, of course.

'I'll just open some of those tins that accidentally threw themselves into my kitchen cupboard when the warehouse blew up,' Dolly said, and everybody in the shelter roared with laughter.

'Let's hope it's not dog food, Doll,' Pop laughed when he saw the tins without a label.

*   *   *

'Oh, Stan, you musn't – someone might see us . . . Oh!'

A throaty giggle told Sarah she should not have stopped in the bus shelter to get out of the rain. She had walked the three and a half mile journey from the infirmary to Sandhills Station when the heavens opened and the deluge forced her to take shelter by the bus stop, only to discover she had stumbled upon a courting couple. At least she hoped they were a courting couple and she had not interrupted one of those ladies of the night with one of those foreign sailors off the dock. However, as she crept towards the exit furthest from the couple, the next thing Sarah heard made the hairs on the back of her neck stand on end.

Obviously thinking they were alone, owing to Sarah's rubber-soled shoes, the woman said in a drunken, giggling slur, 'Here! Be careful where you're putting those hands, Stanley.'

Sarah knew that voice. *Oh my word!* Her heart beat faster and she felt sick.

'Come on, Nance, don't be a tease . . . You know I love you . . . And who'd miss a slice off a cut loaf . . . ?' The man gave a low rumbling laugh as the woman gasped indignantly.

'You cheeky devil!' There was a pause and Sarah felt she was intruding even though the other two could not see her.

'Come on Nancy, you can't put me off for ever.'

'Well, I can see you're the persistent type,' Nancy said teasingly.

'Why don't you come back to Gran's? She'll be asleep now and she won't hear anything.'

'My mother would have your guts for violin strings if she heard you talking like that!'

'Go on, Nancy – just come in for five minutes.'

'Maybe . . .'

Sarah couldn't quite credit what she had heard. How could Nancy even contemplate going back to Stan's grandma's house? Poor Sid, getting Nancy for a wife, she thought as she slipped unnoticed from the blacked-out bus shelter into the teeming rain.

When she got back to Empire Street she was still not allowed into her own street and was directed by the warden back to the church hall.

How was she going to face Mam and Pop? What would she say?

Cold, tired, hungry and soaked to the skin, Sarah entered the church hall to find it was bouncing with Christmas cheer. Pop was playing his accordion and Mam was plink-plonking on the piano while Gloria's mother was doing a pale imitation of her daughter. She wasn't holding the crowd as well as Gloria did. Gloria would have had the entire gathering up on their feet and raising the roof by now.

However, it looked jolly enough and everybody seemed to be having a good time, which made Sarah feel even worse. What a blooming night! 'Sarah! Over here.' Sarah looked over and was thrilled to see Danny Callaghan, who had been allowed out of hospital to join in the Christmas celebrations. He was sitting on a pile of bean bags the scouts used for throwing practice. 'Come and sit over here. You look done in!'

'I am, Dan. When did you come home?' Sarah yawned.

'They let me out this afternoon. Fancy that: Christmas Day in me own home; it was great! Then this happens. I was just getting stuck into the comics you brought me and had the wireless on – it was lovely.'

'It's great to just kick your shoes off and put your feet up.'

'I've had me feet up long enough,' Danny laughed, 'and anyway, my big toe pokes through the hole in me sock, so I don't think I'll bother.'

Sarah's eyes twinkled. There were no sides to Danny; what you saw was what you got: down to earth, with no fancy ideas. She liked that.

Sarah yawned again and covered her mouth with her hand.

'You look beat, Sar,' Danny said, and she nodded, folding her feet under her on the bean bags.

'Wouldn't you be after a fourteen-hour non-stop shift?' Sarah looked embarrassed. 'Sorry, Dan. I seem to have mislaid my sense of humour.'

'What's the matter? Come on, Sar, I can always tell when something is up,' he coaxed. 'Tell Uncle Danny all about it.'

Sarah leaned her head to one side and her tired eyes narrowed. She shouldn't say anything to anybody – not before she'd spoken to Nancy. But where would she start?

She could not approach Nancy about her infidelity! They would never be able to look each other in the face again. But Sarah hoped she didn't have to. She would try and stay out of her sister's way for a few days, which wasn't hard as she was working nights and sleeping days.

'It's obviously bothering you, Sar,' Danny said, 'and you know what they say about a trouble shared.'

'Yeah,' Sarah laughed, 'it usually means shared all around the street.' Danny looked hurt and she quickly backtracked. 'Not that you would say anything, I'm sure.' She had to make amends. 'Well, it's like this . . .'

Sarah wondered if she dare tell Danny all she had seen. Could she trust him to say nothing?

'Has something happened, Sarah?' Danny was suddenly solemn. 'Has someone done something to you?' He sat up straight now. 'You just tell me and I'll—'

'No, Dan, it's nothing like that.' Sarah shook her head, remembering the time when his sister, Kitty, was accosted on the dock road and, luckily, her brother Frank was able to help her.

Sarah hesitated, knowing she and Danny had always told each other everything and it went no further.

'I do trust you, Dan,' she said, 'just like you trusted me with your secret – before you nearly did yourself a mischief saving the docks.'

She had to tell someone or she would burst. And Mam had enough to cope with.

'It's a friend of mine – well, not really a friend, more an acquaintance really . . .' Sarah didn't go into detail because she would not be able to find the words to tell a man, not even Danny.

'Well, if this friend of yours is heading for trouble it might be better if you have a word – steer her in the right direction.'

'Oh, I couldn't!' Sarah gasped. 'It's not my place. She would never listen to me.'

'Well, what about a trusted friend, then?' Danny suggested. 'Or maybe her mam?'

'Oh, her mam is far too busy. She'd have a pink fit!' Sarah gnawed her lower lip, trying to think of the right words. She really should tell Mam, for Nancy's own good. No, she couldn't! It wouldn't be right. This was Nancy's business and nobody else's.

But what if Danny was right and somebody saw her hanging around bus shelters or shop doorways? That was no way for a respectable married woman – and a mother – to behave! It was outrageous.

'Do I know this woman?' Danny leaned over, so as not to shout over the merrymaking and wondered where these people found the energy to carry on singing and dancing until the early hours of the morning.

'You might do, but I'd best not mention any names – loose lips and all that!' After all, thought Sarah, her sister might be a trollop, but she was their trollop and she would not betray her – not even to Danny Callaghan!

'Well, if this woman is prowling the bus stops and air raid shelters maybe Pop should have a word. After all, it's not safe.'

Sarah thought about that one. Pop had always been the more easy-going out of her parents. He mulled things over and then did the right thing, whereas Mam worked on instinct, attack first and think later. Mam's approach didn't always work, though.

'Dad, can I tell you something?' It was the next day and Sarah did not want to get Nancy into trouble but she had to tell someone before Nancy got herself into worse trouble. Sarah was a nurse now and knew about the sort of things that can happen to girls who weren't careful. 'I saw someone at the bus stop canoodling with a serviceman . . .'

'Sarah,' Pop's voice held a gentle note, 'these are different times we're living in now. Women have much more freedom. They live their lives the way they see fit. Anyway, why does it matter?'

'Well . . .' Sarah hesitated.

Pop knew all of his children well and he could see that Sarah was having trouble saying what she meant. 'Come on, love, you can tell me.'

'I didn't get a good look, but I thought from her voice that it sounded like Nancy and that Stan Hathaway.'

Pop looked at her sternly. 'This is a serious thing to accuse someone of, Sarah. Are you quite sure?'

Sarah hesitated. 'Not completely sure. I didn't get a good look.'

Pop's curling grey eyebrows gathered in confusion between his good eye and his eye-patch.

'This woman looked like our Nancy, and I wouldn't want people mistaken, and telling Sid – and him thinking his wife is playing fast and loose with a Brylcreem boy!'

'Now, Sarah,' Dolly said, bringing a brown box into the kitchen and placing it squarely on the table, 'loose lips not only sink ships but happy marriages, so don't let your active imagination run away with you.'

'No, Mam.' Sarah knew she had said enough to cause second thoughts. She would shut up about it now and leave it in the lap of her parents. They would know what to do.

Once Sarah had headed upstairs for a bath Dolly and Pop looked at each other.

'Well, Dolly, what do you think? It would be better to think first before leaping into this one.'

'Bert, Nancy has been sailing close to the wind for a while now. I've left it too long already.' Dolly knew what her own daughter was capable of, even if Pop went around with his head in the clouds. She would have a word with her erring daughter as soon as she got a private moment with her. That madam was getting away with far too much these days and it didn't matter what Pop said about women having more freedom – not in this house they didn't! But for now she would cogitate and ponder. And build up her strength for one of Nancy's tantrums that would most certainly follow their mother–daughter talk. There was much work to do in readiness for the belated Christmas dinner – and she had a chicken to stuff.

'A chicken!' Sarah had forgotten about her wayward sister's behaviour for the time being. 'Where did you manage to get a chicken?'

340

'I know a woman from back home in Ireland . . . I happened to tell her I used to live in the exact same place as those chickens and she promised to save me one . . . And true to her word she did!' Dolly did not tell them that Danny had put her in touch with the woman.

'You must have been up early, Mam,' Sarah said, her mouth already watering in anticipation of the feast to come. It had been late when they finally crawled into bed and Sarah was far too tired to worry that the hot-water bottle had not slipped beneath the sheets before she did. She just pulled her knees up to her chin and she was asleep in seconds.

'I was up and out before the crack of dawn.' Dolly, who didn't take to drink in the same way as her family, looked pleased with herself – but for only a moment. 'Do you think it will stretch?' Her brows were creasing now. 'There's going to be seven of us with baby George.'

'I know,' Sarah winked at Vi, unbeknown to Dolly, 'he's such a big eater, that George, I don't know where the little fella puts it all.' They all laughed and Dolly, laughing too, threw the tea towel at her daughter.

'You know what I mean, there's Pop and me, then there's Nancy and baby George, and Violet and Eddy, and you.' She counted each person on her fingers, 'Rita's on duty at the hospital.'

'I bag the parson's nose,' Sarah said, 'and the crispy skin.' She licked her lips in anticipation. 'Remember when I used to fight our Eddy for the skin?'

'He loved it, too,' Dolly sighed.

Eddy sauntered down to the Sailor's Rest for a swift half while Vi helped with the dinner.

'Wouldn't it be lovely if Frank could be here, too?'

'Mam, sometimes I think you just love to worry – anyway, they said they'd be home for the New Year. The married men with kids get the Christmas leave and then the ones with no kids get the New Year.'

'I suppose we're lucky they'll get any leave at all,' Pop said. 'They don't give any leave to prisoners of war and I doubt poor Sid will get roast chicken for his Christmas dinner, that's for sure.'

'I wonder if Nancy will even give him a second thought . . .' Sarah said as Violet peeled more carrots and Nancy, dressed in the new cardigan her mother had lovingly knitted after unravelling an old pullover of Pop's, ran upstairs.

'Oh, now look what I've done,' Sarah said. 'I'm sorry, Mum.'

'It doesn't take much to kick her off lately!' said Dolly.

'You know they fight like cat and dog, but as sisters go they do love each other,' said Pop.

'I know,' Dolly said with one of her incomparable shrugs, believing Nancy had ulterior motives for rushing upstairs in tears – it got her out of helping with the dinner.

'Oh, by the way, Doll, while I remember, Freddy Pinkerton's missus said to tell you that she got some brown sugar on the Q.T. So if you want to pop along with a spare paper bag she'll fill it for you.'

'Spare sugar!' Dolly's eyes were wide, as she rummaged

in the sideboard drawer for a paper bag. Tea and sugar rations had increased in the weeks leading up to Christmas but that cut no ice with Dolly, who had been scrimping and saving. Ham and bacon allowances, butter, suet and margarine were particularly valued. As her family would gather here for dinner and tea, whatever food they could muster for the celebrations would be a blessing.

'I won't put me nose up to a bit of extra sugar.' Thank the Lord for Mrs Pinkerton, and for Danny Callaghan, too, who, although he had been in hospital, had become very popular with everybody, including Mrs Kennedy, as he 'knew' people who also 'knew' people who could get a nice bottle of something alcoholic for the merriments.

For, thought Dolly, we need something to take our minds off the war, even if it is only for a couple of hours. And seeing as Danny was laid up after coming out of hospital he needed all the coppers he could get his hands on for the future.

CHAPTER TWENTY

Hugging the wall after a blacked-out car nearly ran her over, Nancy knew it wasn't very far to the Sun Hall picture house now. She was meeting Stan again, but in an effort to stay out of harm's way she had turned her ankle and was sure it was sprained.

Stan was on leave until New Year, which only meant another couple of days. What harm could seeing him do, she wondered. It was just a bit of a giggle.

Gloria had gone to stay in London and did not know when she would be back. Nancy suspected she had gone to see that impresario chap, whom she missed meeting for obvious reasons on the night of the raid, as Gloria had not come home for Christmas and it was unlikely she would be home for New Year either, given the transport situation. You couldn't get a train for love nor money with troops going back and forth across the country.

Watching her limp towards him in the foyer of the picture house, Stan promised to rub her leg better when they got inside.

'Cheeky!' Nancy giggled deliciously. It was nice to have a man's attention again. However, he was seriously amorous tonight, encouraging her to think of nothing much except his ardent kisses as she crossed her long legs and aimed to settle down to watch *The Shop Around the Corner*, starring her heart-throb, James Stewart.

'Did you know you have a look of James Stewart?' Gloria said as Stan bent to caress her ankle and his wandering hands stroked her shapely calf before travelling up her skirt, which made Nancy giggle, encouraging a chorus of shushes from the people nearby.

'Stop that, you fool,' Nancy giggled, not really wanting him to stop at all, snuggling into his arms, rapturously aware of his probing fingers. She should stop but the urge to continue was strong. After all, she had been without male attention for a long time now.

It was a good thing they were in the back row, Nancy thought, where prying eyes could not see. For, as much as she wanted to see the film, she found concentration difficult as Stan nuzzled her neck and her earlobe.

'It must have been terrible for Gloria to see her fiancé have the life sucked right out of him, like that,' Nancy said, trying to cool Stan's ardour.

'It's a quick way to go, I should imagine,' Stan said distractedly, his lips searching for hers. Nancy noticed other girls, accompanied by their uniformed sweethearts, were not so shy in being forward as she was, and were having a fine old time – they weren't watching the film either.

However, for as much as she enjoyed Stan's passionate

kisses she hoped that she didn't encounter anybody who knew her. Normally she would go to a picture house nearer home, but as she was with Stan, Nancy felt it was safer to go further afield.

Suddenly she found she was no longer interested in what people thought or what James Stewart and Margaret Sullavan were up to. She was enjoying Stan's loving attention far too much.

She knew that she would have to be very careful as tongues would wag. Word may get back to Mrs Kerrigan, who would waste no time telling Sid.

Nancy's mother-in-law had been urging her to go back to her parlour because of her fear of the bombs. However, Nancy could think of nothing worse than going back to Sid's mother. She had managed to get her own way when Violet appeared and was sharing with Sarah, and she intended it should stay that way – whatever Sarah's view on the arrangement.

On her first day off after Christmas, Rita knew that if she could get through to Southport on the train she would see her children.

'Are you sure you want to go on your own? Pop can take you,' Dolly said, 'or I could always ask our Eddy.'

'Pop's busy, Mam, and Eddy's with Violet. I'll be fine, Mam, honest.' Rita was so full of determination she would get to Southport even if she had to walk the twenty-odd miles to get there. Much to her disappointment, she was still standing on the platform of Oriel Road Station an hour later.

'Trains can't get through, love,' a workman in a flat cap, using his shovel like a walking stick, informed her. 'The line's gone down at Bank Hall courtesy of a landmine. There is a bus to Southport but it runs only every couple of hours and I think you missed it by five minutes.'

Rita fought the urge to swear. Another hour-long wait would have her turn into a block of ice. She decided to go back home and see if Pop or Eddy would take her – doubting that if she started walking now she would ever get there before dark.

'Rita! Rita!'

Turning as she walked along the main road towards Strand Road, Rita stopped when someone called her name.

'Rita!' Jack called, pulling up alongside her; he was sitting on Pop's cart. 'Your mam said you'd already left. I thought I'd missed you. Pop said there might be problems on the railway so he said I could take the cart.'

'Hello, Jack,' Rita said, surprised but overjoyed to see him.

'She told me where you were going. Mind if I come along for the ride?' he asked. 'And give you a bit of moral support?'

'But, Jack, you have to rest. You've been injured!'

'That's nothing,' Jack said, looking into her eyes. Though they both knew that is wasn't 'nothing', he shrugged and said bravely, 'I hardly even feel it any more.'

Rita settled beside Jack, ignoring the pithy look of

disgust from Vera Delaney, who was walking along Stanley Road, and would surely go tittle-tattling to Mrs Kennedy. Let her! Rita thought defiantly, she was not doing anything wrong accepting a lift from an old friend on her father's cart.

'Our Tommy really enjoyed the party,' Jack said as they headed through Litherland and on to Netherton, through open countryside towards Southport. Their journey would take a long time and Rita was keenly aware of the nearness of Jack Callaghan. Even though he still showed signs of his injury, he would not let her take the reins.

'You've been working long hours; have a rest while you can.'

The clip-clop plod of the horse's hoofs lulled her and it wasn't long before her eyes grew too heavy to stay open and even the biting cold weather could not keep her awake.

She did not know how long she had been asleep when the rough rickety shaking of the cart woke her and she realised her head had been resting on Jack's shoulder.

'Oh, Jack, I'm so sorry!' Rita could feel the warm glow of embarrassment fill her neck and face! 'Did I hurt your arm?'

'You could never hurt me, Rita,' Jack laughed. But, there was something so intimate in his gaze when he looked at her then, Rita knew he was not talking of his injuries.

Pulling the reins now, Jack slowed the horse. Rita wondered what was wrong.

'Your mam made this,' Jack said as he took a Thermos flask of tea from his knapsack. He also took out a parcel of sandwiches. 'She said you might be hungry.'

'Good old Mam,' Rita laughed. She had been so excited about going to see the children she had completely forgotten to eat, which was nothing new lately. 'I'm famished.' She tucked into the sandwiches.

After a few moments she realised Jack wasn't eating.

'What?' Rita asked as Jack sat watching her. 'What? Have I got something on my face?' She wiped her face and Jack smiled, shaking his head.

'No, you don't have anything on your face. It is a beautiful face.'

'Jack!' Rita felt her colour rise. She was a married woman and yet he could still reduce her to a blushing young girl. Jack continued to look intently at her and Rita could feel something in the air change between them, like a moment had arrived that they had both been waiting for.

'I love you so much, Rita. You know that, don't you?' For a moment he looked unsure and she nodded, unable to speak, a half-eaten sandwich still resting between her fingers and suddenly she wasn't hungry any more.

He reached for her and all resistance to him seemed to slip away. She leaned forward easily into his embrace. Rita was in a daze. Could this finally be happening? All her dreams were coming true at last. There was no need for words. Just the feel of Jack's arms around her was enough, she was in the place where she should always have been and his tender touch told her what she had to do. She needed to be honest with Jack now, but most of all she needed to be honest with herself.

She no longer cared if she was doing the right thing, no matter what the cost to herself. Tomorrow they might not be here. Tomorrow they might not be alive – any of them.

The realisation brought home to Rita, not for the first time, that she must tell Jack the truth, no matter who got hurt and no matter how it changed her life. She could not even begin to show Jack the loving adoration and high esteem she held him in unless he knew the truth.

As he drew her close Rita hesitated, and the hurt expression in his eyes told her that she was about to do something that would either make him stay for ever or make him run for the hills.

'I'm sorry Jack,' Rita said, 'but there is something I need to tell you . . . it's about Michael.'

Jack's steady gaze met her own. 'He's mine,' Jack said simply. 'Michael is mine.'

Rita nodded, and suddenly the weight of the guilt she had carried around with her all these years seeped from her shoulders as the tender look in Jack's eyes told her all she needed to know. She didn't have to confess. Jack had spared her that much at least. When she looked through the dimming light she could see a glimmer of a tear in his eyes.

'I have waited so long for you to tell me – at one point I thought I would die not knowing for sure.'

'It wasn't long after you left for Belfast that I found out for sure. I wrote you a letter, Jack, but when weeks became months I thought that you'd abandoned me.'

'I would never have done that.' Jack held her to him and tears fell freely down both of their cheeks. 'I never saw that letter, Rita. You know now that I couldn't read or write and any post that I did get Bob or his wife read out for me. Either the letter didn't arrive or maybe Bob didn't want me to see it. It was wrong of him but he was a good man and he probably felt he was doing it for my own good.'

'And he wasn't wrong, Jack.' Rita looked up at the strong features of the man she had always loved. 'He didn't want you to throw your life away on some silly young girl, who should have known better.'

'It would have meant everything to me to be your husband, and Michael is a boy a father can be proud of.'

'Oh, Jack, I love you so much – I was scared you would hate me.'

'Hate you, Rita? My darling girl – never! I am glad I have a son, somebody to put my hopes in.'

'Oh Jack, what are we going to do?'

'Let's not worry about that now, let's just be together.' As the all-encompassing darkness of the night closed in, Jack wrapped Rita in his arms and, after so many years apart they were closer than they had ever been.

* * *

Frank Feeny threw the last of his kit into a Navy regulation canvas holdall. He had a meeting in the office of the Commodore at 2100 hours and as the Commodore was punctual to the point of obsessiveness, Frank knew he had better get a move on.

Looking into the mirror attached to the wall above the chest of drawers, Frank checked his appearance. He was not a vain man but he was about to meet somebody of immense importance. He did not know who it was; the details had not been at his disposal. However, his own meticulous eye for detail would not allow a single speck of dust to remain upon his impeccable uniform.

He gently stamped his leg a couple of times on the linoleum floor, a habit he had got into when he first had the tin leg fitted, and one he was loath to discontinue as it ensured the bottom half was secure.

He had also learned through many hours of practice over different levels of ground, to walk without the hated sticks and, apart from an almost imperceptible stiffness in his walk, it was difficult to tell he had a false leg. However, his fierce sense of independence still rendered him unable to accept help of any kind.

His thoughts turned to Kitty now, one of life's gentler people, who would help anybody, which was the reason he could not make the commitment she so wanted.

All her life Kitty had looked after people – and looked out for them too. First she was a mainstay to her mother, who was married to a feckless man; she then became mother to little Tommy when their mam died giving birth to him, and now she cooked and cleaned and ran around clearing up after the military. Frank fixed his cap securely on his head, refusing to be a burden to Kitty too.

It was Tommy's first night home from hospital and he was as pleased as punch to finally have been allowed to go home. Tommy thought that the nurses were glad to see the back of him but the truth was that his cheerful attitude and energy had won everyone over. Danny too was now on the mend and the hospital had discharged him although medication and regular check-ups were something he would have to get used to. He was in the mood to celebrate.

'D'you fancy going to the pictures, Spud?' Danny asked Tommy, whose eyes lit up. It did not matter what was on as long as he and Danny had a night out together.

Maybe it would be better if he were away from the docklands, Kitty thought. It would certainly be safer.

'I'll go an' get washed,' Tommy said, feeling really grown up. Going to the pictures in the blackout was a big thing for him. He didn't know he was being buttered up before his older brother and sister brought up the thorny subject of evacuation again.

'Christmas under fire!' The American voice boomed out of the screen to the watching audience. Tommy, out of hospital only that day, wriggled in his seat, impatiently waiting for Charlie Chaplin in the film *The*

Great Dictator to start. He could do with a good laugh. Sighing, he sat back and watched. Why did soppy Americans think England looked like the lid of a chocolate box, with little thatched cottages and roaring fires? And why were they still showing this after Christmas? Tommy shivered. Most people he knew would think it nice to have a roaring fire anytime, not just Christmas, he thought.

'America is happy to promote Great Britain's cause,' said the voiceover.

'Not so happy to join us, though,' Danny whispered, and Tommy nodded.

'British Christmas, history and traditions are ideals worth fighting for . . . There is no need to feel sorry for England this Christmas . . .'

'So that's their consciences salved.' Danny was getting impatient now.

'Because England doesn't feel sorry for herself . . .'

'Just as well!' Tommy decided he would join his brother, who shushed him.

'. . . Today England stands unbeaten, unconquered and unafraid!'

'Aye, and alone, thanks to you lot!' A male voice shouted from the back of the picture house as a small ripple of laughter swept the darkened cinema.

Tommy's eyes were bright when they came out of the picture house into the black street. Instinctively they looked up to the sky but it was eerily quiet tonight.

'I hear Manchester's copping it tonight,' said a voice in the darkness as the crowd dispersed.

It was right what the Yanks said on that film, Danny thought. They were standing unconquered but for how long when they were standing alone?

However, he did not want Tommy's night ruined with thoughts of more raids – they'd seen enough before Christmas – and the maudlin mood was broken when he encouraged his younger brother to recall bits of the film he liked. Soon the streets were filled with howls of laughter as they discussed Charlie Chaplin's antics.

As they neared their own front door, Tommy dreaded the cold kitchen they were about to enter. Kitty was at work so to save the expense the boys hadn't banked the fire up so the room would be nice and warm when they got home. Tommy hoped it would not take Danny long to get it going again and the place would be warm for Kitty coming home. Perhaps there would be something good on the wireless that they could all listen to when she got back.

When Rita knocked on the door of the house in Sandy Avenue she was aware of the silence inside. The place was in darkness and Rita wondered if everyone was in bed. It was now quite late. Her heart was racing. 'Perhaps we should wait until morning when everyone will be awake.'

'You can't stay here all night,' Jack reasoned. 'We'll freeze to death.' A cutting wind was blowing straight off the coast and there were still over twenty miles to travel back to Empire Street. Jack could feel the gnawing ache in his shoulder now, brought on most likely by the cold.

'You're right, Jack. I'm being selfish and you've been so good bringing me out here.'

As Rita hopped onto the cart and Jack flipped the reins and headed down the long avenue, a low bee-like buzz of an aeroplane made them look up into the black cloudless sky.

'Is it one of ours, Jack?' Rita could not prevent the quiver in her voice. The enemy did not often come this far up the west coast. There was nothing here worth bombing. No docks. No factories, but that wouldn't necessarily stop the Germans. It was a quiet coastal resort with Punch and Judy booths on the promenade and, when there was spare sugar, stripy sticks of rock. This is as far removed from the docks as it's possible to be, thought Rita, and then automatically ducked as the enemy plane soared overhead. Jack cocooned her body with his own, wrapping his arms around her. There had not even been an air-raid warning.

'It's all right, Reet. Shh, it's all right!' Moments later a huge explosion ripped through the avenue and Rita could not stem the scream that escaped her lips.

'My babies!' Quickly she turned and what she saw filled her with horror. The front door they had knocked on not half an hour ago no longer existed – nor did the front half of the house! Without thinking she jumped down from the cart but Jack was already ahead of her.

She followed him as fast as her legs would carry

her, and as they got to the mound of rubble that had once been number thirteen Sandy Avenue she could see Megan's coat draped over a straight-backed chair.

'Megan!'

'Here, was that Elsie Lowe's house?' Vera Delaney's cousin Tilly asked, hurrying from round the corner where she lived, and down the avenue in her carpet slippers. 'I was just settling down to Charlie Chester!' She stopped at the gate of number thirteen, where there was a gaping hole in the garden and in the garden of the house next door.

'I'm the fire warden,' Tilly offered without being asked. However, Rita was not listening; she was tearing at the gate bolt that had buckled in the blast, trying to get closer to the house.

'Here, you don't want to get too close – it's not safe!' An air raid warden in a tin hat, a boiler suit and Wellington boots came equipped with a pickaxe and a roll of rope hanging from his arm.

'My children are here!' Did these people not understand the urgency of rescue? Rita had seen this kind of thing before and she had helped drag people from demolished premises.

Rita eventually managed to push the gate bolt to one side and she began to frantically drag bricks from the rubble.

'Rita, don't do that!' Jack stilled her hand. 'It's dangerous. The whole lot might go.'

'But I've got to find them, Jack,' Rita whimpered. 'They're my babies.' Her eyes were pleading now and suddenly he took her in his arms and held her close as her sobs rocked both their bodies in the darkness of the night.

'Oh, Jack, I will die if I've got this far and they are . . . they are . . .' Another sob racked her body and she could not say the words. She did not care what Charlie Kennedy thought any more – there was nothing in the world that could hurt her as much as he had hurt her. If she saw him here now she would kill him – so help her! It was only Jack's loving arms around her that stopped her from collapsing altogether.

'Mam! Mam, we're over here!' Suddenly her little girl's voice could be heard from the other side of the street. Rita was thrilled to see Megan hurrying towards her, while Michael was holding an older woman's hand as they crossed the road.

'Oh, thank God you are safe!' Rita felt her knees buckle with relief.

All of a sudden there were people everywhere. Southport had seen few explosions and its people were making the most of the excitement.

'There's a designated rest centre in the church hall,' the middle-aged man in Wellingtons said in his official capacity of air raid warden. 'Everybody, get around to the designated rest centre. We don't know if there are any more bombers to come, but the ack-acks said the sky is clear.' The crowd moved to the church hall – eager now to be off the street. Later they discovered that the German bombers had dropped their load on their way home after a bombing mission in Manchester.

'Where's your father?' Rita asked her children as a super-efficient WVS woman offered tea and a sympathetic ear. All news went through her via the air raid warden and it was obvious that tonight's excitement would be a talking point for weeks to come.

'He went for a breath of fresh air with Aunty Elsie,' Michael said. 'They go every night.'

'Do they now?' Rita fumed. It was bad enough her husband had deserted her and taken their children with him – but to add insult to injury he was out every night with his fancy woman! Went for a walk indeed! She'd give him walking and no mistake.

'We were staying with Mrs Finch because Ruby's not feeling well.'

'Ruby!' Rita could feel the acid bile rise in her throat as the children moved out of the way to introduce a fair-haired female, who had enormous baby-blue eyes and an air of childlike innocence. Even with all the hubbub and confusion, Rita could see the clear resemblance to Winnie Kennedy in Ruby's face.

'Hello, Ruby,' Rita said in a softer voice, sensing Ruby was too old to be a child, yet not worldly wise enough to be called a woman. 'My name is Rita, I am—'

'Michael and Megan's mummy.' Ruby seemed delighted and her innocence shone through. Rita nodded.

'And who are you?' Rita asked as gently as she could, remembering the birth certificate.

'I'm Ruby.' The girl-woman said. 'I like Michael and Megan, they're my friends.'

'Do you know where their daddy is?' Rita asked, feeling strangely calm now. It didn't matter where Charlie was or who he was with, her children were leaving here tonight.

'He gone to walk and come back later – he stinks!' Ruby said, wrinkling her nose.

'We think he goes to the pub with Mrs Lowe,' Michael said belligerently.

'Does he now?' Rita offered. All the more reason for taking her children home. Anything could have happened tonight.

Rita and Jack took the children out to Pop's cart and wrapped them in warm blankets, ready to go home to Empire Street. Ruby came along too, and Rita had a vague idea that she'd deliver her back to the care of Charlie and Elsie. Then they settled down to wait on the corner of Sandy Avenue for Charlie's appearance.

When Charlie turned into the avenue shortly afterwards with a brassy blonde on his arm, Rita saw she was exactly like Vera had described, clinging to his arm and scraping her high heels on the pavement, obviously worse for drink. Charlie seemed more perturbed that Rita had been brought here by Jack Callaghan than that his children had almost been blown sky-high.

'Who told you where we were – my mother?' Charlie was obviously angry. Too angry to listen to reason.

'Did you think you could keep them away from

360

me for ever, Charlie?' Rita asked, just as the peroxide blonde in the leopard-skin coat stepped forward. However, Rita's angry expression silently warned her not to get much closer.

'Come along, Charlie,' said Elsie imperiously, reminding Rita very much of his mother, 'collect the children and we will be off.'

'And where exactly would you be "off" to, may I ask?' Rita knew they didn't stand a chance of keeping the children now. 'The front half of your house – or rather, the front half of his mother's house – is no longer there! Have you not noticed, lady?'

Charlie viewed the wreckage of the boarding house with dismay. 'We'll find something,' he offered limply. 'There are loads of boarding houses here.'

'Not since Jerry started leaving his calling card in Liverpool there aren't!' Rita said, hands on hips. 'They've all moved out here! Or in Crosby, perhaps?' Rita watched him squirm now. Oh, how she longed to slap that stupid expression off his face! But she would not lower herself in front of her children.

'I need to be near my place of work.'

'I wouldn't worry too much about your work, Charlie,' Rita said. 'Since you have been busy with . . . other things,' her disgusted eyes ran the length of Elsie Lowe, 'there has been a war on.' Rita leaned towards him and he retreated a little. 'You may not have heard, this far out in the green belt, but our houses are being blown up on a nightly basis.'

'Ignore her, Charles; the woman obviously has little idea—' Her words were cut short.

'The woman is his wife!' Rita felt Jack's hand on her arm and she was reminded there were children present. She did not care if Charlie left her for this woman.

'Do you know you bear more than a passing resemblance to his mother? In deed if not in looks.' Rita heard an audible gasp as she turned to Charlie.

'If only I had known you liked to be dominated by women, I'd have smacked you up and down Empire Street every day, Charlie – and I could have.' She turned back now to Elsie Lowe. 'Well, good luck to you, love, because you are welcome to him!' She turned away and then stopped and turned back.

'Oh yes,' she rummaged in her bag, 'I forgot to give you these – I think you'll find they're your call-up papers.' With a final smile of satisfaction Rita breathed a sigh of relief. She climbed onto the cart beside Jack and said, 'Come on, children, we're going home.'

As the cart rumbled away she heard Charlie crumple the papers she had just given him.

'You bitch! Just you wait – you won't get away with this.'

As his vicious words reached her, Jack pulled the cart up short and jumped out. Jack made a beeline for Charlie, who shied away from him and made to dart behind Elsie, but there was no escape from the wrath of Jack Callaghan, who grabbed Charlie by the lapel of his coat, pulled back his fist and threw an almighty punch which hit him squarely on the jaw. Charlie reeled and lost his footing, falling to one knee while massaging his already swelling jaw.

362

'You filthy guttersnipe.' Jack whispered quietly so that the children wouldn't hear. 'That's just a taste of what you can expect if I ever hear one more foul word spoken to Rita, do you hear me?'

Charlie looked up at Jack with surly, hooded eyes but dared say nothing.

'And I don't expect to see you back in Empire Street any time soon, right?' Jack left Charlie where he was, while Elsie hopped from one foot to another, clearly uncertain what to do next. Rita heard her say, 'You never told me you were married!'

'Goodbye, Charlie,' Rita shouted from the cart. 'And if Jack hasn't knocked some sense into you, then I hope the army will.'

However, Rita's victory was fleeting when, halfway down the Southport-to-Liverpool road Rita and Jack could see that the docklands were being attacked once more.

'We can't take them back to Empire Street,' Jack said. 'It's too dangerous.'

'We have to take them to Joan,' Rita said, hoping the farmer's wife would have room. The kids had been happy there. When she asked them if they would like to go and see Aunty Joan the children were thrilled.

Thankfully, Joan and Seth were delighted to see the children, too – and Ruby, who somehow had got caught up in all the commotion and had simply stowed away on the cart with her 'friends'.

'Ruby is our friend!' Michael and Megan chorused, and although Rita knew she was much more to her children than just their friend, she had no intentions of sorting out the whys and the wherefores until she got back to Empire Street. And when she did she had some very strong words to share with Mrs Kennedy.

Frank, in his usual unassuming way, wondered if Britain had not been involved in this awful, sickening war whether he would have been able to secure the post he now enjoyed in the Royal Navy he loved. Given his injury, he doubted it.

Luckily, he was able to convince the medical people who mattered, and they in turn informed the navy that Frank was of sound mind and apart from having half a leg missing, sound in body too. He would be very much of an asset to the King's naval base at HMS *Collingwood*, they said and Frank had proved them right.

Here, he was able to pass on the knowledge he had garnered from his front-line naval service to the ratings in the branch known as Weapon and Radio.

As Frank proudly walked the long corridor to the Commodore's office ratings smartly saluted and Frank did likewise, knowing it was his treasured cap badge, not the man, that they honoured with this respect.

'Enter!'

Frank smartly removed his cap and stepped into the small room furnished with little more than a telephone on a desk, a few chairs and a filing cabinet.

A middle-aged man with swept-back hair, whom Frank immediately recognised as the First Lord of the Admiralty, was sitting near the blacked-out window.

'First of all I want to say congratulations!' the commanding officer said.

Frank's eyebrows pleated in confusion.

'Congratulations, sir?' he asked.

'Yes, Warrant Officer Feeny.' The commander smiled and the penny dropped when he warmly shook Frank's hand. He had been promoted. He knew Mam and Pop would be so proud – Kitty would be, too. For it was Kitty he wanted to tell most of all.

He went on to tell Frank that now that Combined Operations had made the decision to relocate to Liverpool, he was to be based there with immediate effect, preparing for the commanding officer's arrival.

The headquarters set up beneath Derby House looked nothing special, which was deliberate. However, under the seemingly inconsequential block of offices, deep below street level in a bombproof subterranean vault, was a large operations network linked to the Admiralty.

Frank had learned that the Royal Navy, Royal Air Force, and Royal Marines would work jointly in the underground bunker on what was to be known as Combined Operations. They were responsible for the safety of naval vessels in the Western Approaches, and Derby House was the vital nerve centre of the entire war in the Atlantic.

As he walked down the concrete steps to the level below, Frank breathed the cool, still air. The electric light was the only means of illumination as there were no windows down here, and he felt a surge of pride shoot through him. He was home and he knew this building was to become as familiar as his own room back in Empire Street.

Kitty sighed. She loved her job here in the NAAFI but wished she saw something else except the kitchen and the serving hatch.

'I tell you what, Kitty,' said one of the Wrens who came in every day for their meals, 'if we had a cook like you I wouldn't chance this foul weather to come and get some grub.'

'I've been thinking about joining something,' Kitty answered cheerfully, 'although I don't fancy being stuck on one of those ships, trying to balance a pan of hot stew on a rolling wave.'

'You wouldn't get anywhere near a wave,' the Wren laughed. 'Our role is to support the naval officers, so as to free our men for the fighting.'

'That sounds right up my street,' said Kitty. She would love to serve her country in its hour of need instead of being stuck here on the dock road serving bangers and mash every day. The WRNS sounded so exciting, and the girls in their navy-blue uniforms always looked so smart and sophisticated.

But if she was honest, the biggest reason she wanted to join up was because quite simply, she wanted to get away. She didn't know who Kitty Callaghan was any more, especially when she saw, day in day out, independent women who had lives of their own. They could travel the world and see wonderful places, while every day Kitty looked out at a sea of grey – be it battleships, river or sky. Her horizons never changed.

She had been at her family's beck and call all her life.

If anybody asked her who she was she would reply Jack, Danny, or Tommy's sister. The manager of a NAAFI canteen. She needed to feel more useful; tea and sympathy just wasn't enough any more.

CHAPTER TWENTY-ONE

Danny had been told he could not do the heavy work on the docks any longer, which meant that he would always be here to look after Tommy, who had refused point blank to be sent to Ireland, but might yet be persuaded to go to the farm out Freshfield way where Rita had taken her children. She vouched for Aunty Joan personally and told Kitty that her kids could not be better looked after. Kitty was still trying to persuade Tommy to go, but without success.

'I'm joining the scouts!' Tommy told her, as if that was an argument against being safely evacuated from the city.

'The scouts?' Kitty asked, looking at his mud-stained face. Being in the scouts was better than hanging around the streets, that was for sure.

'But what about a nice holiday in the countryside?'

'No!' Tommy was adamant. He folded his arms and knew he was in danger of a clout around the lug, but he was not going to leave home ever again.

'Pop said he would vouch for me,' Tommy said

determinedly. 'He knows I'd make a good scout.' Kitty did not have the heart to tell them she was thinking of joining the WRNS.

'Here you go, Kit!' Danny said as he plonked the brown box onto the table. 'I'm sorry it's late, call it a New Year present.'

'A chicken!' Kitty and Tommy chorused.

'You can keep your gold watches, Dan,' Kitty beamed. 'I can do a lot with this.'

'Make sure you don't open the window while it's in the oven, or you'll have a riot on your hands,' Danny laughed.

'Danny, you did get this legitimately, didn't you?' Kitty asked as she took the chicken out of the box. 'I don't want the bobbies knocking on the door while we are in the middle of our New Year dinner tomorrow.'

'Of course,' Danny said. 'It could not be more legit if it jumped into the box itself.' It had been a good day when he met up with the chicken woman. He did not know her name nor did he want to – that way he could not tell lies if asked. He used the money he had saved since working on the docks to buy a box of chickens to share around the neighbourhood at cost price, just as a little thank-you to everyone for looking after their Kitty while he was in hospital.

'You should have seen Mrs Delaney's face when I asked her if she wanted a chicken,' Danny laughed. 'She nearly bit my hand off! "I won't ask where you got them from, Danny," she said, as if she was doing me a favour taking one off my hands.'

'Oh, take no notice,' Kitty said, putting the chicken onto a large plate. 'She wouldn't pay you the compliment of gratitude, that one.'

'I'm expecting their Alfie over any time to see why he wasn't included in the deal.'

'Tell him they were a present from your family in Ireland,' Kitty laughed.

'Hey, Kit, that's not a bad idea!' Danny gave her a huge hug, almost taking her breath away. 'He can't say anything about that, can he?' Danny gleefully rubbed his hands together. 'And I dare say he's hardly likely to turn his nose up at a chicken dinner tomorrow,' he murmured.

'Me neither,' Tommy said, causing Kitty and Danny to turn quickly in the direction of the sofa where he was sitting swaddled in a blanket.

'When did your hearing come back so good?' Kitty asked, thrilled but knowing she and Danny would not have spoken so freely had they known he could hear them.

'What was that Kit?' Tommy's hand cupped the back of his ear.

'Don't you come the old soldier with us, Tommy, lad,' Danny laughed, glad his brother was not permanently deaf. Grinning now, Tommy informed them his hearing had been improving enormously over the last day or so, causing Kitty and Danny to review any incriminating conversations they may have had.

'Oh, you are a tinker, Tommy Callaghan,' Kitty said

hugging him. 'You had me really worried that time.'
She was so happy for him. Being deaf had been so
hard for her little brother, who always liked to know
what was going on and it meant he had been cut off
from them in a way that Kitty could never imagine.
Tommy wriggled out of her loving grip and leaned
back on his pillow, perched against the arm of the
sofa. He had not intended to let them know he could
hear again so soon, because while he was poorly he
could get away with anything.

'Kitty, you know when you were making goo-goo
eyes at that young doctor?'

'I was not!' Kitty spluttered indignantly. 'I was just
talking to him, that's all!'

'Well,' Tommy dismissed her explanation, 'you
know when you told me he asked you if you fancied
going to the town hall dance?'

Kitty nodded, guessing what was coming next. He
was going to use emotional blackmail to get his own
way.

'You went bright pink!' Tommy threw his head
back and laughed and, moments later, seeing Kitty
defensively shrug, Danny laughed, too.

'Woo, Kitty's got a sweetheart,' Danny cooed. 'Are
you going to the dance with him, Kit?'

'No I am not!' Kitty said, annoyed that her little
twerp of a brother had been eavesdropping all the
time and ruined her moment of joy.

'Oh, go on, Kit,' Tommy coaxed, knowing there
was a good police drama on the wireless that Kitty
wouldn't let him listen to if she stayed in. 'It's been

ages since you went for a night out. Our Danny will mind me, won't you, Dan?'

'I've got too much to do,' Kitty began. 'I've got to make the stuffing for that chicken and I've got to peel the veg and then I've got to—'

'We will do it, won't we, Tom?' Danny answered, sitting down at the table and unfolding his meagre newspaper. 'I was only going to go down to the Sailor's for a few jars, anyway.'

'I'm not well,' Tommy whined unconvincingly, and when he saw Danny's warning glance he relented, 'but you do need to enjoy yourself, Kit. It'll do you good.'

Kitty was in two minds. She would love to go dancing. She could not remember the last time. She did not count that dance with Frank Feeny at his sister's wedding last year. Thinking of Frank now, her heart skipped a beat. No, it would not be right going to a dance with another man when she still had feelings for Frank.

'It's only a town hall dance, Kit, not a declaration of lifelong commitment,' Danny said, reading her hesitation, and Kitty sighed, already warming to the idea of her first New Year dance. 'Anyway, if you don't like him you don't have to see him again.'

Kitty was quiet for a moment. That was what she was afraid of. She did like him, this Dr Fitzgerald, who was handsome in a clean-cut kind of way with his short dark hair and bright blue eyes. He was not as tall as Frank but he carried himself with an assured air. She did not like him the way she liked Frank, but then she didn't like anybody the way she liked Frank. It would not be fair to accept his hospitality knowing she could not commit to the kind of relationship he might want.

'I can't go out with a doctor!' Kitty said. What was she thinking of? 'I wouldn't have a clue what to talk to him about. I don't know a thing about medicine.'

'I imagine medicine will be the last thing he wants to talk about.' Danny rolled his eyes to the ceiling. 'Do you want to talk about making big pans of scouse in the NAAFI canteen? Or baking cakes for afternoon tab nabs?'

Kitty shook her head. 'I do more than just cook, you know – I have got brains in my head.'

'Then he won't want to talk about lancing boils and fixing broken bones, will he?'

Kitty nodded to her brother, whose eyes were still on the newspaper, and she felt strangely relieved. Their Danny could be quite clever when he put his mind to it.

Then another thought struck her. 'I've got nothing to wear.'

'I'm sure that Nancy will have something you can borrow,' Danny said.

If she went over and asked nicely, Kitty was sure that Nancy wouldn't mind . . . Suddenly she felt little explosions of delight and her heart began to beat quickly. She was not going to get a better offer, and Danny was right, it was about time she went out and enjoyed herself. It would take her mind off the worry of Tommy, always getting himself into scrapes.

*   *   *

Dolly was bouncing George on her knee while waiting for Nancy to come back from another visit to one of her so called 'friends'. It was high time that she had that chat with Nancy. Everyone was either out at work or engaged elsewhere and this was the best moment that they were likely to get. Even though she knew that Pop didn't like to think that it was their Nancy that Sarah had heard at the bus stop with another fella, Dolly had strong suspicions that Sarah was right. She'd seen it all and she knew her daughter like the back of her hand. Dolly felt sure that Nancy had got herself tangled up in something silly and she just hoped that it wasn't too late to nip it in the bud.

The front door went and Dolly could hear Nancy's clip-clop heels coming up the hallway.

'Georgie, come to your mammy!' Nancy swooped in on George in an exaggerated show of motherly love. Dolly could see that Nancy was a bit flushed and as she took George from Dolly's arms she even thought that she could smell drink on her breath.

'Had a nice evening?' Dolly asked. 'Where did you go?'

'Oh, I went out with a couple of the girls from George Henry Lee,' Nancy replied, airily. 'We had tea and a slice of carrot cake at the Lyons Tea House.'

'And would that be tea laced with brandy, Nance?'

'What do you mean?' Nancy looked indignant.

'Well, Nancy, you looked mighty dolled up for just a cuppa and to be honest, my girl, I'm not sure I believe a word you're saying.'

Nancy bristled defensively. 'I don't know what you're talking about.' She busied herself with George, but the brandy that she'd had with Stan in The Eagle on the other side of Bootle was making her feel a bit lightheaded.

'I think you do know what I'm talking about. You've been seen.'

This brought Nancy up short. 'By who?'

Dolly's heart sank. Nancy asking who it was, rather than what or why was enough to tell her that Nancy really did have something to hide.

'Never mind who by, it's enough that you were seen gallivanting with a man who isn't your husband.'

Nancy tried a different tack. She needed to think clearly and could always get round her mam. One of the local busybodies must have spotted her out with Stan and word had obviously got back to her mother. Damn and blast. Why did everyone have to stick their noses in around here?

'Listen, Mam, it isn't anything to worry about, I've just been visiting Stan's Hathaway's granny as he asked me to while he was away on duty. Once, he turned up there while he was on leave and he walked me home. I promise, Mam, that's all it is.'

Dolly wasn't in the mood to to be soft-soaped. 'Now you listen to me, I'm proud of my kids and I intend to stay that way. Don't you dare give me any reason to be ashamed of you, Nancy. You've got a husband who is holed up in some prisoner of war camp and you'll do the decent thing by him – do you hear me?'

Nancy blushed. Sid's predicament was something she chose not to think about but mention of it now made her very uncomfortable.

'And while I'm at it, it is high time you and George went back to Mrs Kerrigan's. Perhaps you'll be less likely to get into trouble over there.'

Mention of going back to Sid's mother forced any feelings of guilt into the background. Living there was like bloody purgatory!

'Mam!'

'No arguing. I've made my mind up.' Nancy could see from the set of Dolly's firm lips that she meant business.

'Well, then, me and Goerge had better go and start packing.'

Nancy flounced off up the stairs, taking George with her. She had no intention of going back to Mrs Kerrignan's if she could help it, or of giving up Stan Hathaway. No, Mam had her dander up but Nancy could win her round. She'd get her rollers out and do Mam's hair tomorrow; she'd been asking for Nancy to set it and she'd been so caught up with Stan that she hadn't time. Yes, that would do the trick. And as regards Stan, well she'd just have to be more careful from now on, wouldn't she . . .

Kitty's hair tumbled in wide S-shaped waves, lifted back off her heart-shaped face and secured with the tortoiseshell combs that had once belonged to her mam. The peacock-blue taffeta dress had once belonged to Gloria, but Nancy hadn't worn it since before she was pregnant and it fitted perfectly after Kitty had tacked the sides in. She wore it with a little puff-sleeved bolero jacket she had made herself last summer, surprised when it perfectly matched the dress.

She recalled how her brothers whistled their admiration when she did a twirl in the kitchen, but now she was here at the town hall among the rich and confident, she was not so certain. The men, including Dr Fitzgerald, were dressed in 'black tie', and their shoes shone like glass in the bright lights of the town hall, while their glamorous female guests looked assured in their sparkling, low-backed evening dresses and high-heeled shoes. Kitty's were small-heeled black leather: the only pair she owned and the ones she wore for work. Feeling dowdy in comparison she wished the lights were not so bright . . .

'I'll go and fetch us both a drink,' Dr Fitzgerald said.

The other women looked relaxed, holding their wine glasses by the long stems and conversing and laughing easily together. Kitty felt so out of place. She had more in common with the waitresses than she did with the guests. All the practised conversations in her head disappeared. Who was she trying to fool, coming to a smart dance? She was no more sophisticated than the blackout blinds. What did she know about the world apart from the fact that after this war it would never be the same again?

Each minute was like an eternity, and when Dr Fitzgerald still had not returned with the drinks a short while later, Kitty wished she were invisible, imagining she stood out like a weed in a flower patch. Her toes were curling with embarrassment. She looked a fright and she knew it. It was all well and good making do and mending but there were certain functions a girl must make an effort for, and this was one of them.

Her toenails scraped the innersole of her shoes, she was so tense. And she desperately looked around for something interesting, something that would enable her to look relaxed. Kitty willed herself to look bright-eyed and interested, as if she came to these do's all the time. However, when Dr Fitzgerald still had not returned, she did not even know where to put her hands. There were only so many times she could swap her handbag from one arm to another so that people did not mistake her for a rather inelegant statue, while all around her, people chatted excitedly.

Kitty tried not to eavesdrop on conversations but it was impossible, and when she involuntarily happened to glance at the animated conversationalists, they moved away – but not so discreetly that she did not notice.

She did not belong here. She would have been better off staying at home.

'Sorry I took so long,' Dr Fitzgerald said, offering her a glass of wine. 'Professor Wetherby always catches me, and wants to tell me all about the old days.'

'The old days?' Kitty asked, taking a sip and wrinkling her nose. She never cared for alcohol. Maybe it was seeing Dad rolling home blind drunk and unable to stand that put her off. But she would just sip it and hope he didn't bring her any more.

'Thank you, Doctor, I . . . I . . .' Kitty said, and to her surprise he started to laugh.

When his mirthful moment was over, he said soberly, 'I'm sorry, Kitty, but you don't have to call me "Doctor" here. If you do, you will have a whole roomful of men answering you.'

Kitty could feel a warm flush creep up to her cheeks and when she thought about it she too started laughing.

'Sorry! I still can't get used to it. You'll always be Dr Fitzgerald to me.'

Kitty never thought of him as Elliott. When she told him that, his raised eyebrows did relax her somewhat.

Moments later, they were shown to their table and Kitty was glad she could now rest her aching legs. The band struck up and, humming along to songs she recognised, she tapped her fingers on the table.

Elliott took hold of her hand and nodded to the dance floor, and something in the way he smiled encouraged her to forget her awful dress and take to the floor.

With his hands around her waist, Elliot proved to be a great dance partner as he gracefully and expertly manoeuvred her around the polished floor.

'You dance very well,' Kitty said, smiling as she was swept from the floor and back to her seat.

'Bart's Ballroom Dance Champion 1935,' Elliott said with some pride. 'We took the Hospital Cup.'

'We?' Kitty asked and she saw a small cloud cover his face.

'My fiancée. She had just passed her finals – with honours – and after our spectacular win we went off to Switzerland with her parents. We loved to ski.'

Kitty thought it all sounded very romantic and extremely exotic. Ski-ing! She had never been further than a day trip to North Wales. And the most exotic thing she had ever seen was a new-born lamb.

'Where is she now?' Kitty asked, wondering why he had asked her to come to the dance when he had a fiancée. He really was sending out all the wrong messages. Maybe they did that kind of thing where he came from but there was a name for people like that in their street. It wasn't very pleasant and she did not want to acquire it.

'She died,' Elliott said quietly and then he was silent for a moment. Kitty didn't know what to say except, 'I'm so sorry to hear that.' She and her big mouth. She always did ask too many questions. It was nerves. When Kitty could not think of anything worthwhile to say she asked questions. She tried to show interest, but sometimes – like now – she suspected she just sounded downright nosy!

'It's fine,' Elliot said, looking a little wistful. 'You weren't to know . . . It's my fault; I should have mentioned it earlier, when I told you about Professor Wetherby.'

'He's . . . ?'

'Her father. Oh, don't look so worried, he thinks it is a wonderful idea I have finally crawled out of my shell and brought somebody to the annual shindig.'

'But won't he think—'

'He won't think anything. Anyway, life is for living. I realise that now.'

After that, Kitty couldn't remember the last time she had enjoyed herself so much. Elliott was the perfect gentleman and they danced the night away together. Despite her shyness, Kitty felt completely comfortable with him and he barely left her side all night. He told her all about his family and his training to be a doctor. Some of the stories he told her about the things he had seen on the ward would make your hair curl, but he did it with such humour and humanity, Kitty thought.

'I'm having such a great evening, Kitty,' he said, as they had a rest between dances.

'Me too.' Kitty was unaware of it but she was positively glowing.

At that moment, a young Wren passed by their table and stopped to chat to Kitty.

'Hello, you're that manager from the NAAFI canteen, aren't you?' she asked Kitty. The woman looked so handsome and exuded authority in her tailored uniform. How Kitty longed to be doing something useful.

'Yes, that's right. I'm Kitty Callaghan.'

'My name is Carrie Buchanan. I've watched you at that canteen. You're very good, you know, managing all those servicemen. You seem to be able to keep an awful lot of balls in the air. That's something we need in the Wrens.'

'Oh, I couldn't possibly. I'm just good at dishing up six hundred meals a day and making sure no one drops any plates.' Kitty blushed at the idea she'd ever be good enough to be a Wren.

'You'd be surprised how handy a skill like that can be in wartime. Organisation and keeping a cool head are everything.'

'Really?' asked Kitty, incredulous that such things as she took for granted were taken seriously by the WRNS.

'Why don't you come in and have a chat to us? I'm at the recruitment office in town. We'd love to see you. Follow your heart, Kitty,' Carrie Buchanan told her. 'Faint heart and all that . . . This is the most exciting time women have ever known!'

And with that Carrie headed off to join her friends in the WRNS, who looked to be having a great time. Kitty felt something stir inside her that she had never felt before. Ambition, she thought they called it. Kitty did not know where this determination would lead her, but it had to be as far from Empire Street as she could get!

Her eyes were shining as she turned to Elliott. He smiled and his eyes were full of encouragement.

'I hope you'll have time to see a lowly doctor like me when you're directing the war, Kitty?'

Kitty laughed as the bandmaster started counting down to midnight. Elliott pulled her up to the dance floor, they swayed to the strains of 'Auld Lang Syne' and wished each other Happy New Year.

'They do say, Kitty, whoever you're with on New

Year's Eve will be the person you'll spend the rest of the year with,' said Elliott.

'I don't know about that,' said Kitty. 'But this next year is definitely going to be different. I can feel it.'

CHAPTER TWENTY-TWO

'D'you like this wallpaper, Eddy?'

Hark at me! Violet thought as she snuggled up to her man on the parlour sofa. They had finished their dinner made with the finest ingredients that Dolly could find and they were enjoying their precious time alone. Vi could not be happier. This was everything she ever dared dream of. A comfortable house. A supportive family and a husband who loved her. All she wanted was a home of her own – like most young people in these parts, of late.

'Change the wallpaper?' Eddy asked in mock horror. 'Mam would faint clean away if you suggested redecorating. The wallpaper has got to be up for at least five years before anybody even thinks of changing it. By that time it is so yellow with soot we can never remember the original colour. Anyway, you can't get wallpapcr – there's a war on, if you haven't noticed.'

'But, Eddy, it's making me bilious! I can't live with all those green stems. It's bad luck!'

'Bad luck?' Eddy laughed. 'You are so superstitious,

Vi. You're as bad as Mrs Kennedy – she went on a mile a minute at our Nancy's wedding . . . How can a colour be bad luck?'

'It is, I tell you. I'm only in here now because it's the only place we can be on our own.' Violet loved the way Eddy would do anything she asked; he was so easy-going. Not a bit like that brute her mother married.

'Right,' Eddy said, sitting up and looking into her lovely hazel eyes, 'I'll go straight down the town hall when they open and I'll say my wife wants a house – with a garden.'

Vi laughed and nodded. She had never been happier.

'Right – and a garden with no greenery!'

'No, I don't mind grass!' She squealed with happiness.

'But it's green, Vi!' Eddy shook his head. 'Women! I'll never understand them.'

'Oh, Eddy, I'm that glad,' she said and kissed the top of his nose. 'Do you think they will give us a house?'

'Not a chance!' Eddy gave her a hug. 'You can't get a house for a big clock, so you can stay put and let Mam spoil you – after all you've been through losing your own mam and dad!'

Violet felt a little black cloud float over her head. It looked like it was now or never. She had to tell Eddy the truth. But what if he never forgave her? What if he stopped loving her, saw her as a fraud? Oh, this was going to be so difficult.

'Come here and give us a kiss.' Eddy pulled her

towards him and so cut off the words she was just about to say. Tomorrow – she would definitely tell him tomorrow.

'You are a daft ha'p'orth!' Vi laughed, and the firm set of her aquiline features was softened, showing the girl Eddy had fallen in love with. 'I s'pose we'll have to wait until we're old and grey before we can get a house of our own. It were bad enough before the war so it'll be nigh on impossible now that Jerry has come and wiped a lot of property out.'

'Never mind, Vi,' Eddy said, taking her in his arms, 'when the war's over we'll get our own place. I'm handy with a hammer, I'll build you one.'

It were all right fer him, thought Vi, but what about when he had to go back? He didn't have to put up with their Nancy day in and day out. Lordy lord, that one could moan for England.

'I'll make you a nice house with a garden and a little replica one in the garden for the children to play in,' Eddy said, loving being here with her in the cosy parlour, no matter what colour the walls were.

'Will you, Ed?' Vi's voice was soft and dreamy. All she ever wanted was a home of her own and a man who loved her – but fifty per cent of that wasn't bad right now. The children could come along later. She and Eddy had their whole lives ahead of them . . .

It wasn't long, however, before their peace was shattered when Sarah came into the parlour asking if she could play the piano. Jack, Danny and Tommy had come over and everybody wanted a little singsong.

'Go on, Vi,' Eddy coaxed, 'you'll enjoy one of our little get-togethers! We'll have a great time.' Violet reluctantly agreed to share her beloved husband with the rest of his family and in no time she was in the back kitchen helping Dolly and Nancy make ham sandwiches.

'Go easy with that butter, Nancy,' Dolly said. 'You've put half a week's ration on that bread!'

Nancy rolled her eyes to the ceiling that had been badly cracked after the last air raid, wondering if there was any pleasing some people.

'How long's our Eddy home for?' Nancy asked eventually and Vi told her he had to be back on board at eight the next morning. He'd had a good long holiday because the ship was being refitted.

'You'll miss him,' Nancy said, wondering what Stan was doing now. She swallowed hard. Dolly's words had made some impact, but she really wished she didn't like Stan as much as she did, but she couldn't help herself. It had been impossible to resist his advances and Nancy didn't really want to. What had started out as a bit of fun had turned into something more. But she was more careful now – she had to be.

'Shall I put mustard on this ham?' Violet said, waving the yellow concoction she had just made under Nancy's nose.

Instantly she felt her stomach heave and excused herself as she rushed to the privy.

Must have been all that chicken she scoffed. Violet did not voice her thoughts.

'That rum Eddy brought home will be the culprit,' Dolly said, unperturbed, as she cut the bread into thin slices – but leaving the crusts on to fill everybody up a bit.

Nancy rested the flat of her hand against the cold, whitewashed lavatory wall and watched the contents of her dinner disappear down the pan. She and Stan had been seeing each other whenever they could. If she was honest, Nancy thought when Stan took her in his arms that this was a true romance and not just a wartime fling. Stan understood her like no man had ever done before, including her husband.

'Are you doing your voluntary work tonight as usual?' Violet asked when Nancy came back into the kitchen.

Nancy turned towards her sister-in-law. 'What's that supposed to mean?' Her face glowed a guilty pink as she watched Violet quickly scrape the margarine on to thin slices of brown bread, and her stomach lurched again as Violet filled the bread with paper-thin slivers of ham.

Did Vi suspect something? Were they all talking about her?

'It's not supposed to mean anything,' Vi said, efficiently cutting the column of sandwiches from corner to corner and then halving the triangles again, making dainty sandwiches. If this had been her own kitchen she'd have cut off the crusts for a bread and butter pudding; the Feenys liked to eat now and worry later – and, besides, nothing was ever wasted in this house.

*   *   *

A loud ran-tan on the front door sent Dolly scurrying down the long lobby. It was like Lime Street Station in here today, people in and out all day long. She opened the front door and to her dismay she saw the telegraph boy standing on the step.

'Pop!' Dolly called, knowing she did not have the strength for bad news today. Pop came out of the parlour where their Eddy was playing a lively tune on the old upright piano, while everybody was having a sing-song and really enjoying themselves.

'It's all right, love, you go in. I'll see to it.' Pop went to take the telegram but the boy held on to it.

'Does Mrs Violet Feeny live here?'

'Yes,' Pop said slowly, cautiously. Thank God Eddy was home, otherwise they would have to pick his Dolly up off the floor. He turned to Violet, who was already behind him, having heard her name being mentioned.

She took the telegram and tore it open. It told her that her beloved mother, her poor mam, who was forever plagued by dark clouds of depression and bad luck, had been killed when the house took a direct hit.

Violet felt her shoulders sag and then the rest of her body seemed to crumble – unable to hold her upright. Her poor, poor mam! Why couldn't it have been that horrible specimen who had never worked a full day in his life, while her mother had scrubbed her fingers to the bone keeping other people's houses clean?

'Oh, love,' Dolly cried, taking Violet in her arms,

'what is it? Who is it?' She had never seen Violet lose her cool before and it worried her.

'Mam,' Violet said, 'there's something I've got to tell you. Can I have a word in the back kitchen, please?'

'Of course, love.' Dolly turned to her concerned family. 'You lot go back into the parlour. We'll be in shortly.' She gave Eddy a little shake of the head that told him he too must wait.

Then, guiding Violet through to the back kitchen, Dolly placed her in a chair before she put the kettle on. Then she sat opposite.

'Go on, love, tell me all about it.'

Nearly half an hour later, Eddy was allowed into the kitchen to comfort his wife. The tale had been told and then imparted to Eddy, and Violet felt as if a great weight had been lifted from her shoulders. It was up to her husband what he was going to do next.

'We take as we find, love,' Eddy said, taking her in his arms as Dolly slipped quietly out of the room. 'No airs and graces in this house.'

'Oh, Eddy, I should have been honest with you. I'm not a vicar's daughter.'

'Our Vi, I'm so glad to hear it – Father Harding was beginning to ask questions. I couldn't tell him I'd married outside the faith no matter how much I loved you,' Eddy said, and he took her handkerchief from her and gently mopped away her tears. 'I'm right sorry about your mam but let's make a new start. No more secrets. I had my secrets, too, don't forget, and for a

390

while I thought I'd rather face them U-boats than tell Mam I'd married without her say-so.'

Violet gave a quiet version of her raucous laugh and then nodded and smiled through more tears. There was a bit of a rumpus in the other room and Vi quickly dried her eyes. She had been shown more compassion and – dare she say it – love, in this house than at any other time in her life.

'Look who's here!' There was an excited squeal of delight coming from the hallway as Sarah opened the door.

'It's our Frank – he's managed to get home, Mam!'

'Oh, he's a good lad getting home to his mother.'

'To say nothing of his father,' Pop said as he shook hands with his elder son. Frank laughed too, accepting the slaps on the back with good grace as he looked around the family, all gathered together in the parlour and the back kitchen where he always pictured them. But there was one face he did not see.

'Our Kitty?' said Tommy. 'She's went dancing with Dr Fitzgerald last night. She's a bit delicate today.' Tommy cupped his mouth with the palm of his hand and stage-whispered, 'They're courting, you know.'

'You can see he has not signed the Official Secrets Act, can't you, Frank?' Nancy said, and Frank laughed, although there was no humour in it and it didn't quite reach his lovely eyes.

Kitty had a sweetheart. A doctor, no less. He felt as if he was back on board ship, sure that the floor moved a little. Frank did not think he would be so disappointed. No, not disappointed. Devastated. He wanted to give her the good news that he was in Liverpool for the foreseeable, and that he'd been promoted, but that would not be of any interest to her now.

'Hey, Frank – what do you think? Kitty's thinking of joining the Women's Royal Naval Service.'

'So she'll be leaving Empire Street after all.'

Frank steadied his racing heart as he took a deep breath. It was clear already that 1941 was going to bring some big changes. A future without Kitty stretched ahead of him and for a moment he felt desolate. Then he glanced around at his family, from Pop to baby George. So much to be thankful for. Already there were more Feenys than there had been last New Year. Pray God they would all be spared to celebrate the next New Year's Day together.